Save the Date

ALSO BY MORGAN MATSON

Amy & Roger's Epic Detour

Second Chance Summer

Since You've Been Gone

The Unexpected Everything

Save the Date

MORGAN MATSON

SIMON & SCHUSTER BFYR

New York London Toronto Sydney New Delhi

SIMON & SCHUSTER BFYR

An imprint of Simon & Schuster Children's Publishing Division

1230 Avenue of the Americas, New York, New York 10020

SIMON & SCHUSTER BFYR is a trademark of Simon & Schuster, Inc.

For information about special discounts for bulk purchases, please contact Simon & Schuster Special Sales at 1-866-506-1949 or business@simonandschuster.com.

The Simon & Schuster Speakers Bureau can bring authors to your live event. For more information or to book an event, contact the Simon & Schuster Speakers Bureau at 1-866-248-3049 or visit our website at www.simonspeakers.com.

Book design by Lucy Ruth Cummins

The text for this book was set in Adobe Caslon Pro.

The illustrations for this book were rendered in ink.

Manufactured in the United States of America

First Edition

10 9 8 7 6 5 4 3 2 1

Library of Congress Cataloging-in-Publication Data

Names: Matson, Morgan, author.

Title: Save the date / Morgan Matson.

Description: First edition. | New York : Simon & Schuster Books for Young Readers, [2018] | Summary: When seventeen-year-old Charlie Grant's four older siblings reunite for a wedding, she is determined they will have a perfect weekend before the family home is sold, but last-minute disasters abound.

Identifiers: LCCN 2017047401 (print) | LCCN 2017058854 (eBook) | ISBN 9781481404570 (hardback) | ISBN 9781481404594 (eBook)

Subjects: | CYAC: Weddings—Fiction. | Brothers and sisters—Fiction. | Family life—Fiction.

Classification: LCC PZ7.M43151 (eBook) | LCC PZ7.M43151 Sav 2018 (print) | DDC [Fic]—dc23

LC record available at https://lccn.loc.gov/2017047401

ISBN 9781534431430 (B&N proprietary edition)

In memory of Amanda Mierzwa

Acknowledgments

As ever, my first and biggest thank-you is for Justin Chanda, my beyond-words brilliant editor. Justin, over five drafts and two years, your faith in this story and belief that I'd get there someday never wavered, even when it was seven hundred pages long and full of weird movie theater subplots. THANK YOU for helping me to find this story, for your amazing notes, and for being an all-around dream to work with. I'm beyond lucky to have you as editor; I'm luckier still to count you as a friend.

Thank you to Emily van Beek, agent extraordinaire, and the entire team at Folio, for always taking such good care of me and my books.

I am so incredibly grateful that I get to have my books designed by Lucy Ruth Cummins. This one might be my favorite cover *ever*, and that's a high bar. And thank you to Meredith Jenks for the incredible photos!

I'm so thankful to Eric Sailer for his amazing comic strips and for bringing *Grant Central Station* to life—it's so much better than I ever dreamed it could be.

Thank you to Alexa Pastor and Alyza Liu, who read draft after draft of this book and provided invaluable notes.

It has been a privilege to be published by Simon & Schuster for the last eight years. I get to work with the best and most talented people in the business. Thank you to Jenica Nasworthy, Chava Wolin, Chrissy

Noh, Anne Zafian, Anna Jarzab, Lisa Moraleda, KeriLee Horan, Lauren Hoffman, Michelle Leo, Anthony Parisi, Amy Beaudoin, Christina Pecorale, Emily Hutton, Victor Iannone, Karen Lahey, Jerry Jensen, Lorelei Kelly, Jon Anderson, and many more. You guys rock.

I am incredibly indebted to Siobhan Vivian, Anna Carey, and Maurene Goo, amazing writers and even better friends. Ladies, I can't thank you enough for your invaluable help with this book. Whether it was talking through a scene, being a coffee shop writing buddy, or the endless texts and FaceTimes, I couldn't have done it without you.

Thanks and love to Jane Finn and Katie Matson. And thank you to my brother, Jason Matson, for sharing (and fighting over) the comics with me all those Sunday mornings, and for your help with all things Michigan and baseball.

Thank you to Todd VanDerWerff and Myles McNutt, two writers I've so long admired. The idea for this book was sparked by a Twitter conversation we had in the summer of 2015, and looking back now, I am so grateful I took that moment to procrastinate.

And lastly, thanks to Murphy, who contributed . . . not very much at all. But he sure did look cute while doing it.

The Grant Family
Eleanor Sheridan Grant and Jeffrey Grant
Sheridan Grant (Danny), 29
Linnea Grant (Linnie), 28
Jameison Jeffrey Grant (J.J.), 25
Michael Grant (Mike), 19
Charlotte Grant (Charlie), 17

The Daniels Family
General Douglas and Rose Daniels
Ellis Daniels
Elizabeth Daniels
Rodney Daniels

The Wedding Party
Linnie Grant, Bride
Rodney Daniels, Groom
Max Duncan, Best Man and Officiant
Jennifer Kang, Maid of Honor
Danny Grant, Groomsman
Jennifer Wellerstein, Bridesmaid
J.J. Grant, Groomsman
Priya Koorse, Bridesmaid
Mike Grant, Groomsman
Elizabeth Daniels, Bridesmaid
Marcus Curtis, Groomsman
Charlie Grant, Bridesmaid

GRANT CENTRAL STATION

Christmas BREAK

I WASN'T SURE HOW IT HAD HAPPENED. BUT JESSE Foster was kissing me.

I was kissing him back, opening my eyes every few seconds to verify it was really, actually happening, to see the twinkle lights and garlands strung up around the basement, the Santa hat listing on the banister post, and sure enough, Jesse Foster above me, his hands in my hair, his brown eyes closed.

Usually, when something you've dreamed about your whole life actually happens, it's a disappointment. The reality never quite lives up to the fantasy, where everything is perfect and you never get hungry and your feet never hurt. But this was everything I had ever imagined it would be, and more.

Whenever I'd had dreams about kissing him—and there had been a *lot* of these, starting from age eleven onward—everything had built up to the kiss. The moment he saw me, the words he said, the way it all seemed to go into slow motion as he bent his head toward mine. And then there had always been kind of a fade-out into blackness, and I'd start imagining the future, the two of us walking down the halls of

Stanwich High together, his hand in mine, as he smiled happily at me.

But kissing Jesse Foster in real life was beyond anything I'd even known to dream about. He was an amazing kisser, to start with, putting to shame the four other guys I'd kissed, who'd been fumbling and hesitant. He was utterly in control, but would pause every now and then, looking down at me, like he was making sure I was okay—and I'd stretch up to kiss him back, losing myself in him once more.

The part of my brain that could still think of things beyond *lips* and *hands* and *oh my god* and *Jesse Foster* was trying to understand how I'd gotten here. I had known Jesse my entire life—when he was six and short for his age, with a mop of brown curly hair; with braces and glasses when he was twelve; and now, at nineteen, his hair cut short, his arms strong and muscular, his legs tangling over mine as he eased me underneath him. He was my brother Mike's best friend, but it wasn't like we'd ever hung out, just the two of us.

I was only here, in the Fosters' basement two days after Christmas, because Mike hadn't come home for the holiday. After what had happened in February, he hadn't been home all summer—he'd stayed at Northwestern and done a summer program, and had skipped Thanksgiving. But up until the last moment, I hadn't quite believed that he would skip Christmas, too. It was one thing to bail on Thanksgiving or the Fourth of July. Not *Christmas*. But he hadn't come home, texting on the twenty-third that his plans had changed. There was no other explanation.

My mother had channeled her anger and disappointment into cleaning, and when she got to Mike's room, she'd found a box labeled JESSE STUFF and had handed it to me to do something with.

And even though I was beyond annoyed at my brother, I'd jumped at the chance. After all, this was a completely legitimate way to see Jesse, one that didn't involve me concocting some excuse. I'd texted him, sending drafts to my best friend, Siobhan, first so he wouldn't be able to

MORGAN MATSON

see my three-dot bubbles going on too long, proof that I was hesitating and changing my mind. He'd texted back that people were hanging out tonight at his place and to swing by whenever, which I'd interpreted to mean nine thirty. When I'd gotten there, after changing my outfit five times and working for an hour on my hair to get it to look like I hadn't spent any time on it at all, he'd waved at me cheerfully from across the basement, motioned for me to put the box in the corner, then pointed at the cooler of beers bobbing in melted ice water. I took a Natty Ice, but mostly just held it as I found myself in a conversation with one of Jesse's roommate's friends about how there are multiple timelines and the one we're living in is but one example of potentially infinite parallel universes, and that if I wanted proof, I could find it on the Internet.

I'd nodded and tried to look like I wasn't finding this ridiculous as I watched Jesse out of the corner of my eye. Siobhan called it my Jesse-dar, and she wasn't wrong—I always knew where he was in any room, and how near he was. Jesse had been the center of the party, dominating the beer pong table, greeting people as they walked in the basement door, sitting in a chair backward and arguing intensely about the last season of *Game of Thrones*. Every now and then, he'd look over at me, and I'd smile and then pretend to be really interested in whatever conversation I'd found myself having, needing to prove that I could hold my own with his friends, that I wasn't just Mike's little sister.

But after two hours, I was ready to go. Jesse's friends were starting to gather up coats and hats, the rain that had been on and off all day had started up again, and Jesse appeared very occupied with a girl in a red V-neck who was sitting close to him on the couch, her long black hair spilling like a curtain in front of them, shielding them from view. The bathroom in the basement was locked, so I headed up to the main house, which was quiet and dark, except for the white lights of a Christmas tree in the corner.

When I came back to the basement, I stopped short on the bottom step. I could faintly hear doors slamming and a car starting up. But mostly, I was focused on the fact that everyone else had departed, and Jesse was sitting on the couch. Alone.

"How long was I gone?" I asked as I crossed the room for my coat, and Jesse smiled without taking his eyes from the television, which I could now hear was playing some kind of sports recap.

"Come on come on," he muttered, leaning forward. "Come—" Something sports-related and disappointing must have happened then, because he sighed and sank back against the couch. He turned off the TV, and then tossed the remote aside, leaving only the sound of the rain against the windows. Then he looked over at me and smiled, like he'd seen me there for the first time. "You don't have to leave, Charlie," he said, nodding at my coat. "Just because I'm a loser and all my other friends have deserted me."

I dropped my coat like it was on fire, but then gathered my wits and made myself walk over to join him on the couch slowly, like this wasn't a big deal at all and I really couldn't have cared less.

Jesse didn't move over from his spot on the middle cushion, so when I sat on the couch, I was closer to him than I had ever been before, except for two memorable occasions—when we'd been stuck in an elevator together at a laser tag place for Mike's fourteenth birthday, and a memorable car ride when I was twelve and we'd been coming back from playing mini golf in Hartfield, all of us crammed into the car, and somehow, I'd ended up in the way back next to Jesse, Mike on his other side. And Jesse kept turning to talk to Mike, which meant he kept leaning into me, his bare leg pressing against mine. It had been a thirty-minute ride home, and the whole time, I'd prayed for a traffic jam, a road closure, a flat tire— anything to keep it going longer. So, as I sat on the couch next to him now, it was with full awareness that this proximity to him—voluntary, as opposed to car-logistic mandated—was a brand-new thing.

His arm had been draped across the top of the couch when I had walked over, and he didn't move it when I sat down next to him. It even—and this was enough to make my palms start to sweat—seemed to inch down a little, closer to my shoulders.

"You want to watch something?" Jesse asked, leaning over to retrieve the remote from where it had ended up on my side of the couch, which meant he was leaning over me, across me, his arm brushing mine and setting off an explosion of stars in my head.

"Sure," I managed, hoping that I sounded cool and composed and not like I was somewhere between elation and throwing up. Jesse smelled like fabric softer and faintly of the beer he'd been drinking, and when he'd retrieved the remote, he was closer still, and not moving away.

"Maybe a movie?" Jesse asked, pointing the remote vaguely toward the television but not moving his eyes from mine.

It was then that the penny dropped and I finally understood what was happening. I may have only kissed four guys, and the closest thing I'd ever had to a boyfriend was a tenth-grade relationship with my chemistry partner, Eddie Castillo, that had lasted all of three weeks, but I hadn't been born yesterday. I suddenly knew exactly why Jesse had asked me to stay, why I was sitting on the couch next to him, and that it was absolutely not to watch a movie.

"Sure," I said again, making myself keep looking right at him, resisting the urge to leap up and run to my purse so that I could text Siobhan and tell her what was happening and get her advice on what, exactly, I should do. I kicked off my flats and drew my legs up underneath me. "A movie sounds great."

Jesse gave me some options, and I pretended to care about this decision, but I knew we were both just marking time. And sure enough, the movie was only a few minutes in—from what I could tell in my distracted state, it seemed to be about a by-the-book cop who switches bodies with his police dog partner—when Jesse looked away from the screen and into my eyes.

"Hey," he said, one side of his mouth kicking up in a smile.

"Hey," I said back, not able to keep the nervousness out of my voice this time. He reached over and tucked a lock of hair behind my ear, then stroked his thumb along my jaw as he tilted his head and leaned in, eyes already closing.

And then he kissed me.

From the first moment our lips touched, it was clear Jesse knew what he was doing. These were not the shy, tentative kisses I'd had before, and I felt my breath catch in my throat as he kissed me, fast and deep. I was trying to keep up, trying to understand that this really, truly was happening. I kissed him back, hoping that my inexperience wasn't showing. But if it was, Jesse didn't seem to mind. My heart was galloping even as it felt like I was turning slowly to liquid, pooling into the Fosters' worn corduroy couch. Jesse broke away for a second and looked down into my eyes, and I tried to catch my breath, tried to gather my thoughts into something beyond his name repeating over and over in my head.

"So," he said, as he slid an arm underneath my hips and emerged a second later with the remote. He gave me a smile like we were sharing a secret and raised an eyebrow. "I don't think we need this on, do you?"

I smiled back at him. "Probably not." Jesse pointed the remote at the TV again, as the straitlaced police captain exclaimed, "I've heard of a dog's life, but this is ridiculous!" The sound cut off, and it was suddenly darker and quieter in the basement, just me and Jesse and the rain against the windows.

"Well then," he said, smiling at me before bending his head to kiss down my neck, making me gasp and then shiver, while I silently thanked Siobhan for talking me out of wearing the turtleneck I'd been considering. Without even realizing it was happening, he was easing me back on the couch, so that my head was on the armrest. Jesse was above me, his legs tangled in between mine.

He started to kiss me again as he slipped his hands underneath the hem of my sweater, and I drew in a sharp breath. "What?" Jesse asked, straightening up and rubbing his hands together. "Are they cold?"

"No," I said, sitting up a tiny bit more as I looked down at my bare stomach and my sweater that was gathered around my ribs. Jesse started tracing his fingers across my stomach gently, and I could feel myself start to go melty again. But the most I had ever come close to doing before this was kissing—and even then, I'd never gotten to lying-down kissing.

"Is this okay?" Jesse asked, his eyes searching mine, his hands on either side of my rib cage, his thumbs tracing slow circles on my bare skin. I looked back at him and hesitated a second before nodding. It wasn't that I wanted him to stop—it was just that we were moving at speeds far beyond anything I'd ever experienced. It had taken Eddie a week to get up the nerve to hold my hand. I drew in a breath as his hands slipped back under my sweater, and I lost myself in what was happening, in his hands on my skin and our kisses that were growing more and more fevered, until he pulled my sweater over my head and tossed it aside and his hands went straight for the front clasp of my bra. I stiffened, and Jesse leaned back, his brow furrowed.

"You okay?"

"Just—" I glanced up the stairs. Suddenly I was all too aware that at any moment either of Jesse's parents could come down. And I wasn't sure that I could deal with the Fosters—both of whom had known me since I was five—seeing me half-naked on their couch, kissing their son. "Um . . . are your parents home?"

"They're asleep upstairs," Jesse said confidently, but I saw him look up toward the staircase as well.

I pushed myself up so that I was sitting, feeling like this—whatever it had been—was starting to slip through my fingers. Because I knew I wouldn't be able to go back to kissing Jesse now that all I could think about was his parents walking in on us.

"Tell you what," he said before I could say anything. He leaned closer to me, smiling. "I know where we can go." He nodded toward the door, and I held my breath, hoping he wasn't going to suggest his car, when he said, "Guesthouse."

I'd never been in the guesthouse, but I'd heard about it—it was why Jesse had always won at elementary school games of hide-and-seek until Mike had figured it out. I nodded, and Jesse held out his hand to help me off the couch. I started to reach for my sweater, but he was already pulling his off, reaching around behind his neck to yank it over his head by the collar. He held it out to me, and I put it on, trying not to be too obvious as I breathed in the smell of him that seemed to permeate the soft gray cashmere. "Won't you be cold?" I asked as I smoothed my staticky hair down. Jesse was now just in his jeans and a white T-shirt, and it had been below freezing the last two nights.

"I'll be fine." He held out his hand to me, making the world tilt on its axis a little, and led me to the door that opened onto the Fosters' backyard. But when Jesse opened it, I took a step back. The rain was coming down harder than ever, and the temperature seemed to have dropped since I arrived; I felt myself start to shiver, and I realized a little too late that I'd left my flats over by the couch.

"Ready to make a run for it?" Jesse asked, squeezing my hand.

"Wait," I said, taking a step toward the couch. "Let me get my shoes."

"It's okay," Jesse said, and he pulled me back and then closer to him. He leaned down to kiss me and then, a second later, lifted me into his arms. "I got you."

I let out a sound that was halfway between a shriek and a laugh, and before I even had the chance to be mortified, Jesse was opening the door and carrying me outside, into the rain.

I wrapped my legs around his waist and he was kissing me as he walked. Jesse stopped for just a moment, both his arms around me tight, and we kissed as the rain poured down on us. It was like I could practically feel his heart beating against mine through his T-shirt. Then Jesse swung my legs over his arm—when had he gotten so strong? He was carrying me like I weighed nothing—and started to half run, half walk across the grass to the guesthouse.

It was a miniature version of the Fosters' house—a peaked wooden roof and glass panes that ran the length of the house, a balcony on the second story. I thought Jesse was going to go in the main door, but he continued to carry me over to the staircase that led up the side of the house to the second floor. He set me down on the bottom step, but he did it slowly, not dropping me, his hands sliding up my legs to my waist. "After you," he said, and I could hear that his teeth were chattering. Now that we were no longer kissing, I was starting to feel just how cold it was, that my feet especially were getting numb. I hurried up the stairs, Jesse behind me, and then he led the way across the balcony and opened the unlocked second-story door.

Jesse didn't turn on any of the lights, and I blinked as my eyes adjusted. It was an open loft space—maybe the kitchen and living room were downstairs—just a king-size bed in the center of the room with nightstands flanking it and a bathroom off to the side, the door slightly ajar. Before I could even get my head around the implications of this—because a bed, like an actual *bed*, seemed somehow really different from a couch—Jesse had shut the door behind us and was in front of me again. He kissed me—this was never, I decided, not going to feel miraculous—but I could feel how cold his lips were and that his teeth were full-on chattering now.

"Maybe," he said, pulling his T-shirt away from his skin—it was practically transparent with the rain—"we should get out of these wet clothes?" He raised an eyebrow at me as he said it, and even though I laughed, I couldn't help thinking that it might not be the worst idea, just from a practical standpoint, all too aware of how my clothes were soaked, heavy and dripping on the beige carpeting.

Jesse looked down at me and, not breaking eye contact, reached back and pulled his T-shirt over his head. I just blinked at him for a second—it was all I could do not to reach out and touch his bare chest, trace my fingers down the ridges of his abs. There was a question in his expression, not quite a challenge, but almost. I stood there, my hair dripping, shivering in Jesse's sweater, aware all at once of the implications of what was happening here. I was in a room that was mostly bed with the boy I'd loved practically all my life—a college sophomore, who had experience, who would never have taken weeks to try to hold somebody's hand. He'd kissed me. He'd carried me through the rain. I knew I could leave now—everything that had already happened was so far beyond what I'd ever dreamed might happen tonight—and go home happy, with enough to think about and hold on to for months.

Or I could stay.

I stood there, wishing I didn't have to decide this right now, that I could take a time-out to think about it and get back to him sometime next week. Suddenly, I thought about the guy I'd been talking to earlier and his parallel universe theory. Maybe there had been another version of tonight, where Jesse had waved good-bye to me from the couch and I'd put my coat on and had just gone home, thinking about him like always, not even daring to imagine the situation I was in could even be possible. What would that Charlie have said to me right now, somehow in the throes of indecision because the thing I'd always dreamed would happen to me was actually happening to me?

I took a breath, telling myself that I could change my mind at any time, that this didn't mean anything, while knowing full well that I wasn't going to, and that it did. I pulled Jesse's sweater over my head, and he looked at me, his eyes searching mine, and I nodded.

Jesse found the guesthouse thermostat and cranked it up and we dove under the covers together, him helping me out of my jeans and then kicking his own off, both of us cracking up at how frozen all our extremities were. I'd touch my foot to his calf and he'd yelp, and then

MORGAN MATSON

he'd place his hand just over my collarbone and I'd shriek. But soon, as we started kissing again, our legs and feet tangling together, my hands exploring his neck, his chest, his leg, suddenly we weren't so cold any longer. And it didn't seem that funny anymore.

While this was happening, while everything was just his lips and his hands and the spot I'd found on his left side that made him straight-up giggle like the Pillsbury Doughboy, a thought flashed into my mind before I could stop it—*Mike wouldn't like this.*

But a second later, I pushed this away. I didn't at all care what Mike thought. As far as I was concerned, he had given up having his opinions matter. He'd made it clear that he didn't want to be part of our family, when he hadn't come home in a year. And even though Jesse was Mike's best friend, and on some level I knew this was crossing a line, it wasn't like my other siblings hadn't done it.

Mike and I had grown up seeing Danny and Linnie and J.J. basically star in their own soap opera called *Hey, Is Your Friend Dating Anyone?* in which they all dated each other's friends, with disastrous results. So I'd kept my Jesse crush secret from Mike and had never told any of my other siblings either, not even Linnie, because I knew that at some point it would become too valuable to keep. The five of us traded secrets like baseball cards—it was the highest form of currency we had. And I knew that this—me, nearly naked with Mike's best friend—would have been a big one.

"You okay?" Jesse asked, breaking away and looking down at me.

"Yes," I said quickly, trying to focus on him—the last thing I wanted to think about right now was my *brother*. "I'm good."

And he smiled and kissed me again and then, not very much later, he was stroking my hair back from my forehead as he looked into my eyes and asked, "Ready?" and I nodded as he reached down to the floor where he'd tossed his jeans and found his wallet in the back pocket.

There was a pause, and then Jesse muttered, "Shit." I looked over, not sure what was happening, but not sure if I should ask, or if it would just highlight the depth of my inexperience.

"Are you, um . . . ?" A second too late, I realized I had no idea how to finish this sentence and just let my voice trail off.

"So here's the thing," Jesse said, swinging his legs back under the covers and looking at me, propping himself up on one elbow. "I thought I had one in my wallet—I was almost sure that I did. But . . ."

"Not there?" I asked, and Jesse shook his head. I wasn't sure if I was relieved or disappointed—I seemed to be feeling both equally and at the same time. Outside the guesthouse, I heard thunder rumble somewhere off in the distance and then the sound of the rain picking up again.

"I could get dressed, go out and buy some," Jesse said. "And—oh shit, my car would need a jump first. My battery died last night. We could take your car. . . ." But even as he was saying this, the conviction was ebbing from his voice, and it seemed like he was feeling the same thing I was—that the moment was passing right now, slipping away from us.

"Or maybe," I said, "another time would be better? Like tomorrow or something?" I was warming to this idea even as I was saying it. Tomorrow would give me enough time to talk to Siobhan, get her take on this, let me think about it in the light of day, away from Jesse and the way my brain seemed to turn to mush around him.

Jesse groaned and shook his head. "We're leaving to go skiing tomorrow," he said. "And then I'm heading straight back to school from there."

"Rutgers, right?" I asked, hoping this sounded casual and not like I'd committed this fact to memory since the day Mike had told me where Jesse was going, not like I occasionally visited the school's website, looking at the "candid" pictures of the students wearing a suspicious amount of branded school gear, laughing together in the library or the quad, searching for Jesse in the happy multicultural groups, imagining him walking past that building, those stacks of books.

"Yeah," he said, giving me a quick smile, like I'd surprised him. "Good memory." He dropped onto his back and then pulled me closer to him, so that I was lying next to him with my head on his chest. My left arm was getting totally squished against him, but I didn't know where I could put it if I moved it, and besides, it wasn't like I needed it for all that much anyway. "What about you?" he asked after a moment. "Do you know where you're going yet?"

I shook my head slightly, not wanting to move it too much from where it was resting. I hadn't applied anywhere early decision, so some of my applications weren't even in yet. "Not yet."

He laughed—and I felt it more than heard it, like a rumble in his chest. "Well, where do you want to go?"

I looked up at him as the names of the schools I was thinking about flashed through my head. But the true answer to Jesse's question was that I wanted to stay right here, right where we were. And that if I had my choice, I wouldn't be going anywhere. "I'm still figuring it out," I said, moving closer to him still.

"Nothing wrong with that," Jesse said, running his hand over the top of my head and playing with my hair.

I closed my eyes for a second, just trying to commit it all to memory, since I had a feeling, when I was back in my room, in my house, this would all seem like a faraway dream—that I'd been lying naked in bed with Jesse Foster, his arm around my shoulders, my head on his bare chest, hearing his heartbeat. I didn't want to think about when I might or might not see him again, or what would be happening next year, where I would be. I just wanted this moment, right now, to last forever.

I opened my eyes and stretched up to kiss him again, and as he kissed me back, he pulled me close and the rain started up again, harder than before.

GRANT CENTRAL STATION

FRIDAY

CHAPTER 1
Or, Never Trust Anyone
Named After a Fruit

---

*T*HE DAY BEFORE MY SISTER'S WEDDING, I WOKE UP
with a start, like an alarm had just gone off. I looked around my
room, heart hammering, trying to figure out what had woken me. I was
still half in the dream I'd just had—Jesse Foster was there, my brother
Danny, and there was something about *Schoolhouse Rock!*, that old cartoon my sister had shown me when I was in elementary school . . .

But the harder I tried to hold on to it, the faster the dream seemed to
slip away, and I shrugged and lay back down in bed, yawning and pulling my covers over my shoulders, closing my eyes and halfway to falling
asleep again before I realized that an alarm *was* going off.

There was a persistent beeping coming from downstairs, and it
sounded like the alarm that monitored the front and kitchen doors of
the house, the one we only ever turned on when we were going on vacation and sometimes not even then. It was loud up on the third floor, so
I had a feeling it was probably deafening down on the first.

I reached for my glasses from my bedside table and then stretched
over to get my phone from the floor, where I'd plugged it in to charge
last night. I pulled up my group texts, all of which were for different

combinations of my family members. There was even one that had all of us and my brother Mike, though I could see that hadn't been used in a year and a half now. I pulled up the one I'd been using the last few days, which was all the people that were currently in the house—my mom, dad, my sister, Linnie, and her fiancé, Rodney.

Me

Why is there an alarm going off?

I waited a moment, then got a series of responses, one right after the other.

Mom

There's something wrong with the panel, we think—should be off in a minute.

Dad

Why did you text? Why not come down and investigate? What if there had been a burglar?

Linnie

IS there a burglar?

Dad

No

Dad

But there COULD have been

Dad

And if the house were being ransacked, I'm not sure

MORGAN MATSON

the best course of action would be to text about it.

Rodney
Morning, Charlie!

I was about to text back when the alarm stopped suddenly, and my room seemed extra quiet now.

Mom
It's off.

Me
I hear. I mean, I don't hear.

Mom
Coming down? Your dad made coffee and Rodney's picking up donuts

Linnie
Wait, Charlie why are you even still here? Did Stanwich High change their start time?

Mom
I called her out

Me
Mom called me out

Linnie
Why?

So I can help with wedding stuff

Linnie

If that's the case, why didn't you get the donuts?

Rodney

I don't mind!

Me

I'll be right down.

I dropped my phone onto my comforter and stretched my arms over-head as I did the time math. My sister was right—on a normal Friday, I would be between classes right now, heading to AP History, but not in any real hurry. Once our college acceptances had started to roll in, all the second-semester seniors—myself included—were a lot less concerned about getting to class on time.

I'd given my mom the hard sell last night, telling her that I could be useful, helping with any last-minute things that might crop up before the rehearsal dinner tonight and assuring her that I didn't have anything big going on at school today. This wasn't entirely true—I was the editor of the student newspaper, the *Pilgrim*, and we had our weekly editorial meeting this afternoon. We were also supposed to discuss the final issue of the year. But I knew that my news editor, Ali Rosen, could handle things for me. Normally, I never would have missed a staff meeting—but all my siblings were going to be here this afternoon, and I didn't want to waste time that I could be spending with them arguing with Zach Ellison about how long his movie reviews were.

I pushed myself off the bed and made it quickly, smoothing back the covers and fluffing up the pillows, then looked around my room, trying to see if it would be considered neat enough in case relatives or bridesmaids wandered by later.

We'd moved to this house before I was born, so though my two oldest siblings could remember living somewhere else (or so they claimed), this house, for me, had always been home, and this had always been my room. It was the smallest of the bedrooms up on the third floor, where all four of the kids' rooms were. It was probably just what happens when you're the youngest, but I'd never minded. There was a slope to the ceiling that perfectly formed a nook for my bed, and it wasn't drafty like Danny and J.J.'s room always was. And best of all, my room was connected to Linnie's room via a long shared closet, which had been perfect both for stealing my sister's clothes and for hanging out with her, the two of us getting ready at the same time or sitting on the floor of the closet, our legs stretched out, talking and laughing, the clothes hanging above us.

Figuring that my room was probably as clean as it was going to be, I headed over to my dresser, bent slightly to see myself in the mirror, and ran a brush though my hair. Like all my siblings, I was tall—five nine, with long light-brown hair and a slightly crooked nose due to a trampoline mishap when I was six. I also had hazel eyes, the only one of my siblings to have them—like for the last kid, the genetic lottery had been split down the middle. I tugged the brush through the ends, wincing—my hair had reached the length where it would get tangled in a second. But I'd also gotten used to having it long, and even as I knew I *should* cut it, I also knew I probably wouldn't.

I pulled a sweatshirt on over my pajamas and was halfway to the door when I heard my phone buzz, the sound muffled. I looked around and, after a moment, realized that I'd accidentally made the bed over it. I retrieved it from under the covers and smiled when I saw it was my favorite brother calling.

"Hi, Danny." I pulled the phone away for just a second to check the time. "It's early out there."

"Well," he said, a laugh somewhere in his voice, "some of us have to fly all the way from California."

"You could have come in last night." This was what I'd been pressing for for the last few months, since having just a weekend with my siblings didn't seem like nearly enough. I'd been trying to get everyone to come on Tuesday or Wednesday, so that we'd get some Grant time before relatives and guests descended. But only Linnie and Rodney had come home early—both Danny and J.J. had to work and could only take Friday off.

"Not this again." I could hear a smile somewhere in my brother's voice.

"Wait," I said, my eyes going wide. "Why aren't you on the plane?"

"I'm calling you *from* the plane," he said, and I could suddenly picture him, on the tarmac in San Francisco, kicked back in his first-class seat, a cup of to-go coffee by his side. "You're allowed to make calls from planes, you know. We haven't taken off yet and I wanted to check in. How's it all going?"

"Great," I said immediately. "It's been awesome to have Linnie and Rodney here again."

"I mean is everything going okay with the wedding? No last-minute disasters?"

"It's all good. Clementine's taking care of everything."

"Glad I'm getting my money's worth."

"You should be sure to mention that in your speech."

Danny laughed. "Maybe I just will."

Clementine Lucas was Linnie and Rodney's wedding coordinator—Danny had offered to pay for a planner for them, calling it his engagement present, when they'd moved up the wedding date. They had gotten engaged two years ago but seemed in no real hurry to set a date or plan their wedding, and we'd had a running joke that they'd get married sometime in the next decade. The only thing they knew was that they wanted to get married at our house—it had been Linnie's dream since she was little.

Since Rodney was in his third year of law school and studying for the bar and Linnie was finishing up her master's in historic preservation, this spring was probably not the best time for them to be attending a wedding, much less planning their own. But when my parents told us they were putting the house up for sale, things on the wedding front suddenly went into hyperdrive.

I looked over at the stack of cardboard boxes that I'd pushed up against my closet door, like that might make me forget about why they were there in the first place. I was supposed to begin the process of cleaning out my room, because our house had been bought by Lily and Greg Pearson, who would be moving in, along with their three extremely loud kids, as soon as the escrow process was complete. I had secretly hoped there would be no buyers, that our house would languish on the market for months, but when it sold, and fast, I wasn't surprised. After all, who doesn't want a house that had been featured in one of America's most beloved comic strips?

So, in the midst of all this, Clementine had been incredibly helpful— Danny had found her through Pland, a start-up his venture capital firm had invested in. It had contacts with wedding planners all over the country, and matched couples with the best ones. And apparently, aside from a serious disagreement about the napkin colors, everything with Clementine had gone great.

"Well, I can't wait to see it all myself this afternoon."

"You're still getting in at two?"

"That's the plan." Danny cleared his throat. "And I'll have a surprise when I see you."

I grinned; I had a feeling I knew what this was. "Is it a Double-Double?"

Danny sighed. "I never should have taken you to In-N-Out when you came to visit."

"So that's a no?"

"That's a 'hamburgers shouldn't go for six hours without being refrigerated.'" There was a small pause, and he added, "You could have access to In-N-Out constantly if you moved out here next year."

I smiled and glanced, automatically, at the stack in the corner of my desk—the bright, shiny folders that were my college acceptances. I'd applied to eight schools and gotten into three—Northwestern, outside Chicago; College of the West, in a small town in Los Angeles; and Stanwich, the local university in town where my dad taught. I'd decided last week to go to Stanwich, and had told Danny my decision even before I'd told my parents. He'd been trying to talk me into joining him on the West Coast ever since. "Well, I really think all major life decisions should be based on fast food chains, so . . ."

"I knew you'd come around." I could hear, in the background, an announcement about buckling seat belts and making sure all overhead bins were secure. "I should go. See you soon, Chuck," he said, using the nickname for me that only he was allowed to use.

"Wait," I said, realizing he'd never told me what his surprise was. "Danny—" But he'd disconnected the call. I left my phone on the dresser and walked over to my desk, set aside the orange College of the West folder, and picked up the bright purple one from Northwestern.

I'd gotten into Medill, Northwestern's journalism school, which was the whole reason I'd applied there in the first place. My guidance counselor hadn't believed me, thinking that I wanted to be at the same school where Mike was, not understanding that this was actually a bug, not a feature. I flipped through the brochure from Medill that had been sent to me, looking at the glossy pictures of students in the newsroom, the possible internships with major media companies, the journalism study-abroad program. . . . Before I got too far, I closed the folder and picked up the Stanwich College one, running my fingers over the lamp that was part of the school's crest.

Northwestern had stopped appealing to me right around the time my parents told me they were selling the house. The idea of going away had sounded a lot better when I had a house to come home to. Suddenly, the thought of losing both my house and my town was too much, and I'd started to think more and more about Stanwich. I'd practically grown up on the campus, and I loved it—the tree-lined quad, the stained-glass windows in some of the classrooms, the truly epic frozen-yogurt topping bar. And it just began to seem like the best choice—I'd get to start something new while still holding on to the familiar. And it was a great school, and I knew it was going to be really, really great.

I hadn't officially accepted or told the other schools I wasn't coming, but I'd made my decision, and even though my parents had seemed a little surprised by my choice, I knew they were just getting used to it— and that they'd be happy when my first tuition bill came due and I got the discount for being the child of a professor.

And as soon as the wedding craziness was over, I'd figure out what the next steps were—telling Northwestern and College of the West that they hadn't made the cut, finding out about Stanwich deposits and paperwork. But I didn't want to think about any of that—not this weekend. After all, right now my sister and future brother-in-law—and possibly donuts—were downstairs waiting for me.

I was halfway to the door when my phone rang again, and I picked it up immediately, hoping it was Danny calling back—only to see the contact picture of my best friend, Siobhan Ann Hogan-Russo.

"Hey, Shove-on," I said, picking up, turning my phone onto speaker. This was the way Siobhan told people how to pronounce her name, which was most people who weren't expecting a name with a silent *b* in it.

"Oh," she said, sounding surprised. "I didn't think you'd pick up. Why aren't you in history?"

"I got my mom to call me out. I'm taking the day off so I can help with wedding stuff."

"I thought all of that was taken care of by Tangerine."

I shook my head, even though I knew she couldn't see me. "You know her name is Clementine. You just have a weird prejudice against her."

"You know my policy," Siobhan said. "Never trust anyone named after a fruit." I sighed; I'd heard this more times than I'd wanted to, and could practically feel Siobhan teeing up her punch line. "After all . . . they might be rotten."

"I know you think that's funny," I said, and sure enough, on the other end, I could hear Siobhan laughing. "But it's really not."

"My dad thought it was funny."

"Which one?"

"Ted. Steve is still trying to get us into some alumni dinner thing tonight."

Siobhan had been, with her dads, up at the University of Michigan since Wednesday. It was where she was going next year—unlike me, she'd never had any question about where she'd go. Both her fathers had gone there and had met years later at an alumni networking event. In the Hogan-Russo household, there was a prominently displayed picture of newborn Siobhan in a Michigan onesie, posed with a mini maize-and-blue football. Apparently, there had been a serious discussion about naming her Siobhan Ann Arbor Hogan-Russo to help her chances of getting in. But fortunately, she hadn't needed it—she'd found out back in December that she'd been accepted early decision.

"How's the campus?"

"It's amazing." There was a happy sigh in Siobhan's voice. "Wait," she said, sounding suddenly sharper, like she was coming out of her Michigan happiness daze. "Why are you skipping today? Don't you have your editorial meeting?"

"Yeah," I said, "but it's fine. Ali can handle things." There was silence on the other end, and I added quickly, "She wants to be editor in chief next year anyway, so she should get used to running these." Siobhan still wasn't saying anything, but I could picture her expression all too well—arms folded, one eyebrow raised. "I swear it's fine."

"You're doing the thing you always do."

"No I'm not. What thing?"

"The thing where your siblings come to town and you forget all about everything else."

I took a breath to deny this, but then decided not to—it was a fight Siobhan and I had had many times over the years, and she usually won it because, frankly, she wasn't wrong. "This is different. Linnie's getting married."

"She is?" Siobhan said, her voice sounding overly shocked. "But why didn't you *mention* something about it?"

"Sio."

"Oh no, wait—you did. Like every three minutes."

"It's going to be amazing," I said with certainty, feeling myself smile. "Linnie's dress is so beautiful, and I've seen the pictures from her hair and makeup tests—she's going to look gorgeous. You'll see." Siobhan was coming to the wedding—she'd known Linnie her whole life, after all. She was flying back from Michigan tomorrow morning, with more than enough time to get ready before the ceremony.

"Is everyone there?" she asked. "The whole circus in town?"

"Not quite. Linnie and Rodney came in Wednesday night. Danny gets in this afternoon, and J.J. . . ." I stopped and took a breath. "And we're all going to be together." As I said it, it was like I started to feel warmed up from the inside, like I'd just taken a long drink of hot chocolate.

"Not exactly."

I blinked at the phone. "What do you mean?"

"Mike," Siobhan said simply. "Mike's not going to be there."

"Who wants him here?" I muttered.

"Well—Linnie did, right?" Siobhan asked, and I crossed over to my desk again and started straightening the piles of papers, mostly just to have something to do with my hands. "Didn't she invite him?"

"Of course," I said quickly, ready to talk about something else. "But he's not coming, and it's better this way."

"Okay," Siobhan said, and even through the phone, I could tell that this was her letting the subject go, even though she still disagreed with me. "Now." There was a getting-down-to-business tone in Siobhan's voice, the same as she'd had when we were five and trying to decide who got to be Belle when we were playing *Beauty and the Beast* and who was going to be stuck being the teapot. "What are you wearing on *GMA*?"

I winced. *Good Morning America* was going to be coming to our house in two days to interview all of us, because my mom's comic strip—*Grant Central Station*—was, after twenty-five years, coming to an end. And despite the fact that this was rapidly approaching, I hadn't yet gotten as far as deciding what I would be wearing.

Grant Central Station depicted the lives of the five kids, two parents, and a dog that made up the Grant family—the *fictional* version, since those of us who lived in the real world were also the Grant family. It was syndicated in newspapers across the country and around the world. It was about a large family dealing with everyday things—work and crushes and bad teachers and siblings' fights. As the years had gone on, it had transitioned away from broad gags and more cartoonish illustrations and had slowly gotten more serious. The humor had become more poignant, and my mother would sometimes trace one story line for weeks. And unlike most strips, in which characters lived in a kind of stasis—Garfield perpetually hating Mondays and loving lasagna; Charlie Brown forever missing the football; Jason, Paige, and Peter Fox stuck in fifth, ninth, and eleventh grade, respectively—*Grant Central Station* followed real time. My siblings and I each had a strip equivalent that was a version of us, and for the last twenty-five years, the strip had charted the progress of the fictional family, moving in step with us in the real world.

The fact that it was ending had come with an onslaught of requests for publicity—my mom had been doing phone and e-mail interviews for weeks, and taking the train into New York for photo shoots and taped interviews—but it seemed the really big ones were happening closest to when the strip was actually ending, probably so she could give her take on how she was feeling, now that the moment had arrived. There had been comic retrospectives in newspapers around the country, and the Pearce, our local museum, was doing a whole show on her artwork. We were squeezing in an appearance tonight at the opening, before we'd all rush to the rehearsal dinner.

But the biggest of all these promotional appearances was *Good Morning America* on Sunday morning, a live interview with all of us that they were calling "The Family Behind *Grant Central Station*."

When Linnie and Rodney had decided on their wedding date, my mother had set the strip's end date for the same weekend, so we'd all be together. And apparently, *GMA* had gotten a lot more interested in doing the piece on us when they'd found out we would all be available. Linnie and Rodney weren't thrilled about this, and J.J. had commented that if we were expected to appear on national TV the day after a wedding, they might want to change the name of the segment to "Grant Central Hangover." But I was just happy we'd all be together, that when this thing that had defined all our lives came to an end, we'd see it through as a group.

"Um," I said to Siobhan now, stalling for time. "Clothes?"

"Charlie." The disapproval in my best friend's voice was palpable. "Jackson Goodman is coming to your house on Sunday."

"I'm aware of this."

"*Jackson Goodman.* And you don't know what you're *wearing?*" Siobhan's voice rose sharply at the end of this. She and her dads watched

Good Morning America together every morning until she had to leave for school, and Jackson Goodman—the laid-back anchor with the wide grin—was by far her favorite. When she'd found out that he was going to be at our house, she'd pretty much lost her mind, then promptly invited herself over for the taping.

"You can help me pick an outfit, how about that?"

"Deal. And you'll introduce me to Jackson, right?"

"Sure," I said, even though I had no idea how things were going to run on Sunday.

I could hear muffled voices on Siobhan's end. "I should probably go. This accepted students thing is starting soon."

"Have fun. Hail to the victorious."

"Hail to the *victors*," Siobhan corrected, sounding scandalized. "Have I taught you nothing?"

"Clearly not. Um, go Wolverine."

"*Wolverines*," Siobhan said, her voice rising. "It's not like Hugh Jackman is our mascot."

"See, but if he was, maybe I would have applied."

"Steve and Ted are still mad you didn't, you know."

"Just tell them to be glad I didn't apply to Ohio State."

I heard the sharp intake of breath that followed whenever I mentioned Michigan's rival school, which I found ways to bring up as often as possible. "I'm going to pretend you didn't say that."

"That's probably wise."

"I gotta go. Tell Linnie congrats for me?"

"Of course. See you tomorrow." I hung up, then after a moment opened my photos and started looking through them. I scrolled past my photos, stopping at the ones with my siblings, trying to find one of us all together.

There I was with Linnie and Rodney last night, picking up pies at Captain Pizza. And then me and Danny and J.J. in front of the Christmas tree, both Danny and me giving J.J. bunny ears—Linnie and Rodney had spent the holiday with Rodney's parents in Hawaii. And then me and J.J. and Linnie at Thanksgiving—Danny had had to work, jetting last-minute to Shanghai, trying to save a deal that had started falling apart. There I was with Danny in September, sitting outside at a Coffee Bean—he'd sent me a surprise "Come and visit me for the weekend!" plane ticket, and I'd flown out to California and back again in less than forty-eight hours. And then there was one from last summer, me and J.J. trying—and failing—to play Cards Against Humanity with only two people.

But there were none of all of us together, and looking at the pictures was evidence that we hadn't all been together in a while. But at long last, this weekend, we would be. For three days, my siblings were going to be home and it was going to be *us* again—playing games and standing around the kitchen laughing and making bagel runs and just *being* together.

I'd spent so much time thinking about it, and now it was so close. I was so near to the way it felt when we were all together, like finally things had been put right again. Not to mention that this weekend was the last time that we'd all be together in this house, so it was going to be perfect. It *had* to be perfect. I would make sure of it.

I headed for the door and was halfway down the stairs to the kitchen when the alarm went off again.

CHAPTER 2
Or, Everything Is Fine!!

"IYA, KID," MY DAD SAID, SMILING AT ME AS I CAME into the kitchen. He was sitting on one of the stools at the kitchen island, a mug of coffee in his hand, and he raised it to me in greeting. "Morning."

"The alarm went off again?" I said, peering at the panel mounted by the door. But it was silent, all the lights on the console dark. The alarm had stopped as abruptly as it had started, and by the time I'd made it to the main floor, it was quiet again.

"Your sister's checking it out," my mother said, looking up from where she was sitting at the long wooden kitchen table, mug of tea on the table next to her. "She thinks maybe one of the window sensors is setting it off."

I nodded, then pushed myself up to sit on the kitchen counter and looked around. The kitchen had always been the center of the house. It was where everyone seemed to congregate and the first place I looked when I was trying to track down either siblings or parents. And even though it was a big room—the island and stools on one end, the kitchen table at the other, with an area by the door that was kind of like an ad hoc mudroom, hooks on the wall for coats and a bench to remove snowy boots that inevitably ended up kicked underneath it—the kitchen always felt cozy. I thought briefly about one of Lily or Greg Pearson's horrible kids running around in here when this place would no longer be ours and felt my stomach drop.

"You okay, kid?" my dad asked as he crossed toward me and opened the kitchen cabinet. Even a month ago, it had been stocked full to bursting, with a collection of mismatched mugs and dishes we'd accumulated over twenty-five years of living here. But now there were only a handful left inside, the only ones that had survived my parents' *we're-selling-the-house* purge and subsequent massive tag sale on the front lawn, the one I'd refused, full stop, to participate in. And when my parents had realized that I was planning to make loud comments to potential buyers about bedbugs and fake antiques, they'd sent me to spend the weekend with Linnie and Rodney in Boston.

"I'm fine," I said quickly, giving him a smile. I nodded at the mug he was pulling down. "That for me?"

"Obviously," he said, pouring me a cup of coffee and adding just the amount of milk I liked, then handing it to me with a wink.

My dad, as ever, looked a little rumpled, even though he couldn't have been up for very long. Despite the fact he wasn't teaching today— he was a botany professor and the head of the physical sciences department, which meant he had enough pull at Stanwich College that he hadn't had Friday classes in more than a decade—he was wearing what he always wore during the week, corduroy pants and a button-down shirt with an elbow-patched cardigan over it. His glasses were pushed up into his hair, which was mostly just salt now, with a sprinkling of pepper.

"Hungry?" my mom asked. There was a pencil holding up her curly blond hair and she was wearing her drawing clothes, an oversize sweater and black pants, even though she hadn't had to draw new strips for six weeks now—there was a lag time so that the strips could get inked and colored. So while she'd known for weeks how *Grant Central Station* ended, none of the rest of us had any idea. Linnie really wanted to know, but I wanted to read it in the paper and find out the end of the story along with the rest of the world. "Rodney should be back any minute now."

"Well, it's not the window sensor," my sister said as she came into the kitchen from the dining room. She smiled at me. "Nice of you to join us."

I grinned back at her. "I thought I might as well make an appearance." My sister laughed as she pulled down a mug and slid it across the counter to my dad, who caught it, then poured her a cup of coffee.

"Happy wedding eve," I said, clapping my hands together. When I was six and Linnie was seventeen, I used to think she was the most beautiful girl in the world. And now that I was seventeen and she was twenty-eight, I still pretty much thought that. She took the most after our dad—his dark wavy hair and blue eyes and, to her eternal disappointment, his sticking-out ears. At five seven, she was just two inches shorter than me, but the fact that she'd inherited our mother's curvy figure, and I decidedly had not, meant that while I stole Linnie's clothes whenever I could, most of her dresses were off-limits to me.

"I don't think that's a thing," Linnie said, taking a sip from her mug and then nodding at my dad. "That's good coffee, Daddy."

"I do my best."

The doorbell rang—on the front door, the one that was only used by deliveries and company, since we all used the kitchen door almost exclusively. "Who's that?" my mom asked, squinting at the kitchen clock. "I didn't think any guests were coming until this afternoon."

"It's probably a delivery," Linnie said, starting to move toward the door, but I shook my head and hopped off the counter.

"I'll get it," I said, taking my mug with me as I pushed through the kitchen door and headed to the front hall. "I should make myself useful!"

I could hear my dad laugh as the door swung closed again behind me and I crossed the front hall, taking a sip of coffee as I walked. The front door was half glass, and I could see someone standing on the step outside, their back to me. I unlocked the door and pulled it open, and the guy standing there turned around.

"Hi there," he said with a smile, and I immediately took a step back. I don't know who I'd been expecting, but not this—a guy who was very cute and who looked around my age.

He was tall and lanky, an inch of wrist showing below the dark-green fleece jacket he was wearing with jeans and rubber-soled duck boots. He was holding a matching green binder in one hand and a cup of to-go coffee in the other, the name on the cup an illegible scrawl. He had thick, dark-brown hair that swept down long and straight across his forehead, reminding me for a second of an actor in a movie my siblings had shown me when I was little, about a werewolf who plays basketball. When he turned his head slightly, I couldn't help staring at his profile—he had a snub nose, almost squared off at the end, like Matt Damon or Dick Tracy. I'd never seen it before on anyone who wasn't a movie star or a cartoon character.

"Hi," I said, glancing down at myself briefly and wishing that the sweatshirt I'd pulled on over my pajamas had not been this one—an ancient one of J.J.'s that read GO BIG OR GO GNOME on the front. (A fierce-looking gnome was printed on the back.) "Can I help you?"

"Yes," the guy said, smiling even wider. "Where There's A Will."

"Ah," I said, nodding as I took a step back and started to ease the door closed, wondering what kind of weird cult person I'd just opened the door to. He didn't look like a weird cult person—but then again, he probably wouldn't have been very successful if he had. "Good point. Thanks for stopping by—"

"Wait," he said quickly, his face falling as he stuck a foot out, keeping the door open. "Sorry—I mean I'm from Where There's A Will. The event planners?"

"We already have an event planner," I said firmly, knocking the door against his boot, trying to get him to move it. "Thanks though."

"Yeah, Clementine Lucas," the guy said, raising his voice, and I paused and opened the door a little wider.

"How did you know that?"

"Pland sent us to take over," he said. "I guess my uncle hasn't arrived yet? I was kind of hoping he'd be here to explain."

I opened the door all the way. "Come in." Normally I might have been embarrassed about the way I'd just treated him, but right now I needed to figure out what was happening, because it really didn't sound good. The guy carefully wiped his feet on the mat and stepped inside, and I noticed now that "Where There's A Will" was written in script on his fleece, just over his heart, sewn in gold thread.

"Charlie?" Linnie called from the kitchen. "Who is it?"

"It's, um . . ." I looked at the guy.

"Bill," he supplied. "Bill Barnes." I nodded, trying not to look surprised. There were a ton of Wills and Williams at my school, and even a Willem who got really annoyed if you didn't pronounce his name correctly, but I wasn't sure I'd ever met a Bill my age before.

"I'm Charlie."

Bill nodded. "Bridesmaid, right?"

"Um," I said, wondering exactly how he'd known that and what, precisely, was going on. "Yeah. But—"

"Charlie?" Linnie called again.

"It's Bill," I yelled back, even though I knew this wouldn't mean anything to her. I headed toward the kitchen and gestured for him to follow me.

"Who?" Linnie asked, as we walked through the swinging door.

"You're new," my dad said, frowning at Bill and then taking his glasses off his head, putting them on, and squinting at him. He turned to my mom for reassurance. "Eleanor? Not one of ours, is he?"

"I'm Bill Barnes," Bill said. "Um—I work with my uncle Will Barnes at his event planning business, Where There's A Will. Pland contacted us last night and asked us to step in because they'd had some . . . um . . . issues with Clementine Lucas?"

"What?" Linnie asked, and it looked like she'd gone about three shades paler. "What do you mean *issues?*"

Bill cleared his throat and looked around, like he was waiting for someone else to take charge, and I remembered what he'd said about expecting his uncle to be here already. "Um. So apparently she has been mixing up clients' events, not responding to e-mails, embezzlement . . . not booking venues . . ."

"I'm sorry?" Linnie asked, staring at him. "Did you say *embezzlement?*"

"Has she been arrested or something?" my mother asked, standing up from the table and walking over to my sister, who looked like she was about to fall over.

"Um. Well," Bill said, clearing his throat. "Pland didn't tell me that, but apparently she's stopped making contact with them or with any of her clients, so their working assumption is that she has skipped town."

"No," Linnie said, pulling out her phone. "There must be some mis-understanding, because she just e-mailed me last night. . . ." She scrolled through it, then held it to me. "See?" I squinted down at the screen. The e-mail was one sentence long, with no subject line. It just read *EVERY-THING IS FINE!!!*

"I don't know," I said, looking at my sister. "This actually seems like kind of a bad sign."

"Huh," Linnie said, staring at her phone. "I guess I just thought she was being reassuring."

"So what happens now?" my dad asked, crossing his arms over his chest. His voice, I noticed, had dropped into his *frighten the underclassmen* timbre. "You do realize my daughter is getting married tomorrow?"

Linnie, who'd started typing frantically on her phone, let out a sound that was halfway between a sob and a slightly hysterical laugh.

"We're aware," Bill said quickly. "Pland is deeply upset about this and has hired us to take over on Clementine's behalf. You'll have your fee completely refunded."

"I don't care about that," Linnie said, her voice going high and panicky. "I realize this isn't your fault, but my wedding is *tomorrow*. And that's pretty late to be getting a new wedding coordinator."

"I completely understand," Bill said. He took a step farther into the room, set down his coffee on the kitchen island, and flipped open his binder. "And my uncle can certainly speak to this in more detail than me—he should be along at any moment. But he drew up a plan last night, and I think—"

EEEEEEEEEEEEEEEEEE. The alarm went off again, much louder down here than it had been up in my room.

"Aaaagh!" My future brother-in-law had just entered, jumped at the sound, and fumbled the pink bakery box he'd been holding, sending it crashing to the floor.

"My bear claw!" my dad cried, running over to the donut box.

"Why is this happening again?" Linnie yelled, covering her ears.

"It's fine," I yelled as I hurried to the panel. "What's the code?"

"Twelve thirty-four," my mom yelled, and I punched it in. It took a second, but then the alarm shut off, and Linnie cautiously moved her hands away from her head.

"It's off," I assured her.

"The donuts are okay," my dad said, sounding incredibly relieved as he stood up with the box.

"What," Rodney asked, looking at the alarm panel, "is going on with that? Twice in one morning?"

"Three times," I said, taking a step back from the panel slowly, like I might set it off again. I turned to Rodney. "Did you get me a strawberry glazed?"

Rodney adjusted his glasses, which had gone a little askew. "Of course I did. I didn't just get here." Linnie had met Rodney Daniels on their first day of Dartmouth. He was one of the very first people she'd encountered in the school—he'd been wandering the halls alone, clutching his laundry hamper and shower caddy, trying to find his room. They'd met again that night at a new-student mixer, and they'd been together ever since—except for the five months they'd broken up when they were twenty-three. But even at twelve, I'd known that their split wasn't going to last long. Linnie and Rodney just belonged together. They were incredibly similar, well matched from the very beginning, even though Linnie was white and had lived in the same house in Connecticut practically her whole life and Rodney was black and an army brat, and had grown up on bases all over the world.

Rodney's dad, an air force general, and his mom, an army nurse, had eventually settled on a base in Hawaii, where he'd spent high school. Because getting from New Hampshire to Honolulu and back again was time-consuming and *really* expensive, Rodney had spent Thanksgiving and Christmas with us all four years of college. When I'd had a meeting with my guidance counselor last week, she'd asked me how I felt about adding a new member to the family. And it had honestly taken me a minute to work out what she was asking me, because Rodney had already *been* a member of my family, for the last ten years.

"I got your text," Rodney said as he crossed over to my sister, slinging an arm around her shoulders and kissing the top of her head—at six two, he was nearly a head taller than Linnie. He tended to keep his head shaved and had been dressing pretty much the same way since he was eighteen—in jeans and a crisply pressed button-down. My parents frequently pointed to Rodney as an example when they were trying to get my brothers to dress more like adults and less like middle schoolers with credit cards. "I didn't—quite understand it."

"What do you mean?"

Rodney pulled out his phone and squinted down at it. "Where are you? You need to get here. Ducking Clementine is gone and I'm about to ducking lose it. DUCK."

"Stupid autocorrect," Linnie muttered, shaking her head.

"Clementine *quit*?"

"She didn't even have the decency to quit! She just embezzled a bunch of money and disappeared!"

"What?"

"Hi, I'm Bill," Bill said cheerfully, not reading the room very well as he smiled and held out a hand to Rodney. "Where There's A Will."

"Uh . . . sure, man," Rodney said, shaking his hand. "Good attitude."

"Bill and his uncle are taking over for Clementine," I explained. "So they're going to handle everything." I said this with more confidence than I felt as I crossed over to the donut box, nudged my father out of the way, and picked up my strawberry glazed.

"Where's your suit?" Linnie asked Rodney. "Weren't you going to get it along with the donuts?"

Rodney winced. "It wasn't ready yet. They said I can pick it up first thing tomorrow."

"But tomorrow's the *wedding*," Linnie said, her voice going wobbly, like she was on the verge of bursting into tears. Everyone in the kitchen who wasn't Linnie exchanged a quick, panicked glance. It was like we all were thinking the same thing—*don't let the bride cry*.

"I can go get it," I said immediately. I grabbed Linnie's favorite donut—chocolate with sprinkles—and put it on a plate for her. It seemed like she could maybe use some carbs right about now. "I'll go out and get it tomorrow morning. You don't need to worry about it. Consider it taken care of."

"But . . . ," Linnie said, looking around.

"And I'll go call the alarm company, how about that?" my dad asked, his voice soothing. "So we can make sure it doesn't go off again."

"And I'm sure Bill and his uncle are going to have everything handled," my mom said while looking right at Bill.

"Yes," Bill said, giving Linnie a smile. "And he should be along at any moment."

"How does that sound?" Rodney asked, widening his eyes at me in thanks as he took the donut plate. Linnie nodded, looking like she was starting to pull herself together, but before she could answer, the landline rang.

The handset was closest to me, and I tossed it to my mother, who caught it with one hand. "Honestly," she said, shaking her head. "What is with you kids and not answering the phone?" She pressed the button to speak, her annoyed tone immediately turning into something more polite. "Eleanor Grant." She listened for a moment, and when she spoke again, her voice was warm, like she was thrilled to be talking to whoever was calling. "Yes, hello. If you'll just hold on a moment, I'll take this in my office." She pressed the button to put the call on hold, then grabbed her donut and headed across the kitchen. "That's the *Times*," she said to us as she headed toward the door Rodney had left slightly ajar. "So if you could not get on the line for the next twenty minutes or so, I won't have to disown any of you." She pushed her way out through the door, heading across the backyard toward her office, the one she'd built when the strip really took off and she could no longer work from the kitchen table.

"The *Times*?" Bill echoed, looking after my mom, his brow furrowed. "Like—the *New York Times*?"

"Yeah," Rodney said, gesturing toward the donut box. "Did you want a donut?"

"Thanks," Bill said, taking a step closer to the box, still looking confused.

"I'm going to try to see what's happening with this alarm," my dad said, taking his mug with him as he headed upstairs, ruffling my hair as he passed me and giving Linnie's arm a squeeze.

I took a restorative bite of my donut and a long drink of coffee, though I wasn't sure I needed it—the last few minutes had been more than enough to wake me up.

"Okay," Bill said. He set his glazed donut down and picked up the binder he'd been carrying. It was green like his fleece and had the Where There's A Will logo printed across the front. Underneath it was written GRANT-DANIELS, and just the sight of it—proof that someone was organized and was going to be keeping this wedding on track—was making me feel better. When I'd pictured this weekend—all of us together, everything going perfectly—it had not allowed for things like an embezzling wedding planner disappearing on us. "So it looks like everything is pretty much on—"

The kitchen door flew open with a bang, and everyone in the kitchen jumped, including Bill.

"Well, well, well," J.J. said from the doorway, glaring at each of us. Then, maybe feeling like this hadn't been enough, he added, "*Well.*" My middle brother had arrived.

CHAPTER 3
Or, Acronyms Are Not Always a Good Idea
Or, AANAAGI

"Hey, man!" Rodney said, smiling at J.J. "Welcome home. Want a donut?"

"Oh, you'd like that, wouldn't you?" J.J. spat.

"Um . . . sure?"

J.J. scoffed. But just as he'd done ever since he'd read this phrase when he was twelve, he said the word "scoff" instead of just making the sound, and none of us had been able to convince him this actually wasn't correct. He strode into the kitchen, dropping things—his jacket, a garment bag, a suitcase—as he went. "Like a donut is going to make up for being abandoned." He looked around and, maybe seeing he was out of things to drop, took off his Pirates cap and flung it to the ground. "All of you have disappointed me. Linnie, Rodney, Charlie—" He was glowering at all of us in turn, but he faltered when he got to Bill. "Who are you?"

"Hi there," Bill said, taking a step closer to him. "I'm—"

"Do you know how *long* I was waiting at the airport? Assuming *someone* in my family would come and get me? Looking at all the cars driving past, and none of them for me?"

"Uh . . . ," Rodney said. "Did you *tell* anyone to pick you up at the airport?"

"Of course I did!" J.J. exploded. "Do you think I would have just . . . just . . ." He trailed off, his expression changing from angry to thoughtful. "Actually, let me check one thing," he said, pulling his phone out of his pocket and scrolling through it. "Huh," he said after a moment. "You know, looks like that e-mail never made it out of drafts. Whoopsie." He put his phone back in his pocket. "So hi!" He strode over to us, now smiling. "How's it going, family?" He and Rodney did one of their back-pounding hugs, then he gave me a quick one-armed shoulder squeeze.

"Hey," I said, squeezing him back. "Glad you're here."

"Good to be here," he said, then headed to Linnie, giving her a bear hug that picked her up off her feet. "Happy almost wedding!" He spun her around once and then set her back on the ground and smiled down at her. "How are you feeling? Happy? Excited?" He glanced back at Rodney and lowered his voice theatrically. "Second thoughts? Cold feet?"

"Stop it," Linnie said, shaking her head even though she was smiling. "Welcome home."

"Thanks," J.J. said, stepping over the bag he'd dropped and pushing himself up on the counter. He reached for my coffee and took a sip of it before making a face and pushing it away. "God, how can you drink that, Charlie? It's like drinking warm milk."

"Hey," I said, trying to sound mad and knowing I was failing. The kitchen with my siblings in it was my favorite place to be, and it was finally starting to feel like home again. "Get your own coffee."

"But I just got here," he protested, and I rolled my eyes. Jameison Jeffrey Grant was eight years older and six inches taller than me, with unruly light-brown curly hair that he'd only really learned to deal with a few years ago, thanks to some Swedish grooming paste Linnie found for him in Boston. He had brown eyes like Mike and our mom, and eyebrows that Linnie had once described as "Bert chic."

"So what's happening?" he asked, peering into the donut box. "Is Danny here yet, or can I take both maple frosteds?"

"He's on the six a.m. out of San Francisco," I said, hurrying over to the donut box. "So he'll be here at two. And you're *not* taking both donuts." I pulled a maple frosted out of the box, put it on a plate, and then grabbed the plastic wrap out of the cabinet to cover it.

"Oh, so *Danny's* schedule you know," J.J. said, shaking his head. "Scoff."

"You didn't actually tell anyone," Rodney pointed out. "How did you even get here?"

"Took a cab," J.J. said, grabbing a donut, then pausing. "Oh! He's actually still out there. I just came in to get cash to pay him."

"The cab is out there with the meter running?" I asked.

"Yep," J.J. said, taking a bite of his donut. "Who's got cash? I've only got nine dollars, and half of that's in change, and half of *that's* Canadian."

"Why Canadian?" Rodney asked, sounding genuinely curious.

"From the last time we played the Blue Jays."

"How are you a functioning adult?" Linnie asked, throwing up her hands. "How on earth did MIT let you graduate?"

"You have to bribe the right people," J.J., his mouth full of donut as he gave her a wink. The fact that J.J. had held a fairly important job for years now, apparently successfully, had been a bit of a shock to me as well. But the fact was, out of all my siblings, he'd had the most consistent success. He was a quantitative analyst for the Pittsburgh Pirates, using sabermetrics data to help build the strongest team possible and, therefore, get the most wins. At least, that's how he explained it to me—I still didn't really understand it, even after he helpfully gifted me a copy of *Moneyball* one Christmas. All I really knew was that J.J. had found a way to get paid for combining his two loves, math and baseball.

"You didn't come in from New York, did you?" Linnie asked.

He shook his head. "Hartfield-Putnam." Hartfield-Putnam Airport was a tiny airport twenty minutes from us, but if J.J. hadn't flown in there, he would have landed at one of the big New York airports, all an hour and change away, leading to a much more expensive taxi fare.

Linnie nodded, then immediately grabbed her right earlobe, and J.J. and Rodney followed suit—this was our *not it* gesture, one we'd all been doing so long I didn't know the origin of it.

"Seriously?" I asked, sounding more annoyed than I really was. This was one of the thousands of tiny things that only happened when we were together, one of the things you didn't know you'd miss until it was gone.

"Can't be slow on the uptake," J.J. said, taking another sip of my coffee, then making the same disgusted face and setting it aside.

I didn't have any cash on me—in fairness, I was still in my pajamas—so I grabbed two twenties out of the mason jar that had always held the cash for things *like pay the pizza guy* and *tip the delivery person* and *buy up all the Thin Mints*. It had always sat on a teetering stack of cookbooks, but there were only two left there now. I spun the lid shut on the jar, then pushed my way out of the kitchen door. The sun was shining weakly, and it was a bit overcast. I crossed my fingers that everything would clear up by tomorrow as I hurried across the wooden deck that wrapped around the back of the house. Beyond the deck, the backyard was a huge expanse of green, almost a perfect rectangle that backed up into the woods bordering our house. My dad's garden ringed the front and the sides of the yard, but there was a big, open empty space in the center that was free from plantings. It's where the tent would be set up and where the wedding would take place tomorrow, the spot that we'd always campaigned for a pool to go, without any success. The closest we'd gotten was a trampoline that split the space between my dad's greenhouse and my mom's office.

I crossed the deck, went down the stone steps, past the side entrance to the garage, and out onto the driveway. Sure enough, there was a black Stanwich Taxi idling there.

The driver inside was staring down at his phone, so I knocked on the glass. He jumped, and looked over at me, then rolled down the passenger-side window. "Hey," I said, leaning in slightly. "Sorry about that. I have your money." I glanced at the meter and saw that it was thirty-five dollars, and handed him the twenties, hoping the change was somewhere in the realm of the right tip amount.

"Thanks," he said, taking the money from me and hitting a button on his meter, then looking back at the house. "Have you guys called me before? I keep thinking I know this house from somewhere."

I glanced at where he was looking. Our house was from the turn of the century and had started out as a Victorian, but over the course of years and owners, it had Frankensteined (*Frankenstein's monstered*, Danny always corrected) with extra additions and wings, into something that no longer belonged to any one architectural style. But it was still striking—three stories, white with black trim and green shutters, a widow's walk at the top of the house and a wide front porch that got festooned with pumpkins in autumn and twinkle lights from Thanksgiving until approximately Valentine's Day.

It would have been familiar to the millions of readers of *Grant Central Station*, since the fictional Grants lived in an identical house, down to the color of the shutters. And I had a feeling this was why the taxi driver recognized it. "My mom draws a comic strip," I said proudly. "Maybe that's where you know it from?" The second after I'd asked this, I felt my smile falter as I realized I'd just used the present tense, and that it was no longer technically correct.

The guy's face cleared, and he nodded. "I think so . . . the comic strip about the beagle, right? The one that's always eating everything?"

I nodded. Waffles the beagle was unquestionably the breakout star of *Grant Central Station*. He'd been introduced when I was five, and for a while there, the Waffles merchandise was selling like hotcakes. He was the only character without a real-life counterpart. We'd never had a pet—Linnie was allergic to cats, and my mom always claimed that five kids was chaos enough without bringing a dog into the mix. "That's the one."

"Cool." He nodded and backed out onto the road, the only car on our always-quiet cul-de-sac.

I was just starting to walk up to the house when a flash of something pink caught my eye, and I whipped back around to face the street. Sure enough, Sarah Stephens was riding her bike slowly up the road, zigzagging back and forth. She may have been a twelve-year-old seventh grader, but that didn't mean she didn't have the ability to inspire a slow-burning fury in me whenever I saw her.

For most of this past year, Sarah had just been our papergirl, and if I happened to be leaving the house early and she was delivering copies of the *Stanwich Sentinel*, I might wave at her as I passed, but that was basically the extent of our interactions. But in the last few months, something had changed. For whatever reason, she'd stopped delivering our paper altogether. We hadn't gotten a paper since February. My dad kept calling to complain, but Sarah kept insisting that we were mistaken and that she *was* delivering it, that she hadn't missed a day yet. This had led to a standoff, both of us insisting to the subscription office at the *Sentinel* that the other one was lying. My dad tried to cancel our subscription, only to be reminded that he'd prepaid for the entire year. So now, not only did we not get our local paper, but we also had fraught interactions with the middle schooler who lived down the street.

This had, of course, all made it into the final months of *Grant Central Station*. The appearance of Sophie Silver, rogue papergirl, had not made things any more pleasant with Sarah, and I had a feeling that this bike-by she was doing now was just to harass me.

"Hey." Sarah was biking in circles in front of the house that somehow felt threatening, her eyes narrowed underneath her pink bike helmet.

"Why aren't you in school?"

"Stanwich Academy is on spring break. Tell your mom to stop putting me in her stupid comic strip."

"You're not in the strip," I said automatically. This was the Grant family mantra. Never tell anyone they're represented in the comic. Even if you think they are. Even if it's *obvious* that they are. Before I even knew what litigation was, I was aware that it was a thing you shouldn't ever give anyone the chance to do, and I knew the words "plausible deniability" before I started preschool. "Plus, it's ending on Sunday."

"Oh." Sarah braked and dropped a foot to the ground. "Well—tell your dad to stop complaining about me."

"Start delivering our paper," I said, crossing my arms over my chest, "and we will."

"I delivered your paper," Sarah said, her voice rising.

"Uh-huh," I said, looking a little dramatically around the empty driveway. "Wow, how could I have missed it?"

"I'm required to deliver all the weekday papers no later than six a.m., and the weekend editions by eight. So I *did* deliver it this morning. Like, three hours ago."

"Well, we never got it."

"That's not my problem," she said, starting to ride off again. "I did my job."

"Give us our newspaper!" I yelled at her retreating back, but she just lifted one hand off her handlebars to make a very rude gesture at me. Cassie, my *Grant Central Station* character, would have had the perfect snappy retort to this, but I just turned and headed back to the house.

"So tell me," J.J. was saying to Bill as I walked into the kitchen. "Is

Bill a nickname for something? It's not short for Billiam, is it?"

I could practically feel Rodney's reaction to this; it was like he was doing a mental double take. *"Billiam?"*

"It's a name," J.J. said, taking a sip of coffee—it looked like he'd finally gotten his own.

"I really don't think it is."

"It is," J.J. insisted. "It's a thing. I got my master's with a guy named Billiam."

"No, you didn't," Linnie said.

"Oh yes, I did," J.J. said, and I exchanged a look with Rodney. J.J. always did this—he would dig himself into increasingly deep holes, always steadfastly refusing to back down. "You want me to prove it to you?"

"I do," Rodney said.

"Me too," I added.

"Fine!" J.J. yelled as he got down from his stool. "In that case, I will!" He stormed out of the kitchen in what I knew my dad would have described as "high dudgeon" before returning a second later, retrieving his coffee cup, and then storming off again.

"Uh . . . it's short for William," Bill said a moment later, clearly not sure if he should answer the question, now that the person who'd asked it had left. "But I was named after my uncle, and he goes by William, so . . ." His voice trailed off, and he cleared his throat. "Okay. So I heard from my uncle. He wanted me to just go over some stuff with you two so when he gets here, he can jump right in."

"Sounds good," Linnie said, as J.J. wandered back in, like I had a feeling he might—he'd left his donut on the counter.

"So," Bill said, "your guest list is capped at one twenty, right?"

Rodney nodded, and Linnie started to, then stopped, mid-nod, and whirled around to face J.J. "Who are you bringing?"

J.J. choked a little on his donut. "Bringing?"

"As your date," Linnie said, raising an eyebrow. "Because you RSVP'd for two. And apparently you're both having the steak."

"Ah," J.J. said, blinking a little more than usual. "Right. About that. So when I RSVP'd—which was *months* ago, by the way—I was certain that I would have a serious girlfriend by now. There were many promising ladies who were in consideration. But then . . . uh . . ."

"Pay up," Linnie said, turning to Rodney.

"Thanks a lot, J.J.," Rodney said as he reached for his wallet.

"For what?" J.J. asked, frowning.

"Yeah," I said, slightly hurt that I hadn't been a part of this.

"I didn't really think you'd be bringing a date, when you hadn't mentioned anyone in months," Linnie said, as Rodney handed her a twenty.

"I believed in you, though," Rodney said, then sighed. "For all the good it did me."

"You guys had a bet?" J.J. asked, sounding scandalized. "About my future potential love-slash-possible heartbreak?"

"And you didn't even involve me?" I added.

"I just can't believe the lack of *faith*," J.J. said, his voice rising. "From my own sister no less."

"It's fine," Rodney said, looking at Bill, clearly trying to get things back on track. "So, you mentioned the guest list?"

"Yes," Bill said, flipping open the binder. "The list is capped—"

"Wait a second," J.J. said, smacking his palm down on the kitchen counter like he'd just thought of something. "I don't think it said anywhere that this was going to be a binding thing, if I was going to bring a date or not. It didn't say anything about that on the STD."

We all just stared at him for a moment, and I noticed that Bill was looking fixedly at his shoes. "*What?*" Linnie finally asked.

"When you and Rodney gave me the STD," J.J. said, shaking his head, clearly impatient that we weren't keeping up. "There wasn't any disclaimer that—"

"You mean the save the date?" Rodney asked, and J.J. nodded. "Dude. Acronyms aren't always a good idea."

"I'm just saying, if you'd put anywhere on any of the invitations that I would be held accountable for what I wrote—"

"J.J., just admit you couldn't get a date," Linnie said, shaking her head. "It's not a big deal."

"Well, I don't think you should say for sure I can't get a date," J.J. said. "I mean, I don't want your guest count to be off, after all."

"Don't worry about the number of guests," I said quickly, since I had a feeling I knew where this was going.

"Linnie, give Rodney his money back," J.J. said grandly. "I'll get a date yet."

"By tomorrow?" Linnie asked. "To a *wedding*? No way."

"Do you not think I can do it?"

"No," Linnie said, shaking her head. "That's literally what I just said, Jameison."

"Well, then, another challenge accepted, Linnea," J.J. said, pulling his phone out of his pocket with a flourish. "I *will* bring a date to your wedding. See if I don't!"

"Guys," I said, trying to head this off. J.J. showing up with whatever rando he could get to come to a wedding with him on one day's notice really didn't seem like the best idea, and certainly didn't fit in with my plan for the weekend. "Let's not—"

"Fine," Linnie said, talking over me. "And if you can't, which you won't—"

"Which I *will*—"

"You have to publicly admit that you were wrong. And pay me twenty dollars."

"Oh, it is on." J.J. stuck out his hand, and Linnie shook it. "Witness?"

"Witness," Rodney and I replied in unison. "But I don't think you're going to pull this off," he added.

"You don't, eh?" J.J. asked, arching an eyebrow. "You want to make this interesting?"

"Things are interesting enough," I said.

"Side bet? Fifty bucks says I can."

"I'm already out twenty," Rodney pointed out.

"Fine, I'm in," I said, relenting. There was no conceivable way that my brother was going to be able to find a date, so I might as well get fifty dollars out of it.

"Say good-bye to your shekels," J.J. said, raising his eyebrows at me. He turned to Bill. "Billiam? Want a piece of this action?"

"No," I answered for him. "What were you saying, Bill?"

"Right," Bill said, flipping open his binder, looking relieved to be back on track. "My uncle wanted confirmation that the rest of the wedding party would all be here by six for the rehearsal."

Linnie nodded. "There's an exhibit at the Pearce Museum for my mom. And it starts at four, but we should be back in time."

"Got it," Bill said. "But everyone else in the wedding party is confirmed for six?" He squinted down at a piece of paper. "Max, Jennifer, Jennifer, Priya, J.J., Danny, Charlie, Elizabeth, Marcus, and Michael?"

I rolled my eyes. "You can take Michael off the list."

Linnie sighed. "Charlie."

I just looked at her as I picked up my donut. "He's not going to come." Mike had been invited to the wedding, of course—Linnie and Mike had always been close, just like me and Danny. But he wasn't coming—I'd just assumed that Linnie had invited him so that he would feel included, but without any expectation he'd show up, same as Rodney asking him to be a groomsman. They were both just gestures.

My siblings had all seen Mike in the year and a half he hadn't been home—when Danny had business in Chicago, or when J.J. was in town when the Pirates were playing the Cubs. And Linnie and Rodney had gone to see him last summer. But I hadn't, and neither had my parents, and I didn't think a wedding would be the best time to have what was sure to be an incredibly awkward reunion—and I had a feeling Mike probably felt the same way.

"I don't know. I mean—he did RSVP yes," Linnie said, and even though she shrugged as she said it, I could hear the hope in her voice. "I don't think he would have done that if he wasn't going to show."

"*And* he said he was bringing a plus-one," Rodney added. Then he looked at J.J. and sighed. "Although I guess that doesn't necessarily mean anything."

"I'm going to get a date," J.J. insisted, brandishing his phone at us. "You'll see. You'll *all* see—"

"He's not going to come," I said, pushing the very thought away. In all the times I'd pictured this weekend, Mike had never, not once, been a part of it. If Mike showed up, there would be drama—and not fun, gossipy drama, like when we were all speculating that J.J.'s former girlfriend was secretly a Scientologist. It would wreck everything I'd imagined for this weekend, one perfect last Grant adventure with my siblings in our house—the ones who wanted to be there, that is. The ones who'd never once tried to break away from our family.

"I was just surprised by the plus-one," Rodney said. "I guess Mike is dating someone at school." Then he shuddered. "Unless Corrine is back in the picture?"

Corrine had been Mike's high school girlfriend, and she'd been a nightmare. To say that none of us were fans would be an understatement.

"He's not going to show up," I said firmly. He may have told Linnie he was coming, but he'd told my dad he was coming home last Christmas, and that hadn't happened, so it wasn't like Mike's word meant anything.

"Did *you* RSVP for a plus-one?" J.J. asked, waggling his eyebrows at me.

"Me?" I asked, startled. "Um, no. Who would I even—" As soon as

I said it, Jesse flashed into my head. I was suddenly back with him in the rain, laughing with him as he carried me up to the guesthouse, his hands sliding up my waist. . . .

"Charlie?" I looked over to see everyone looking at me. "You were saying?" Linnie prompted.

"Right," I said, clearing my throat. "Um, no. No date."

"It might not be too late," J.J. said as he scrolled through his phone.

Bill's phone beeped with a text, and he looked down at it just as the front doorbell rang. "My uncle's here," he said. "And everything's going to be okay. I promise."

He smiled reassuringly. And then the alarm went off.

CHAPTER 4

*Or, Can't You Hear,
Can't You Hear the Thunder?*

WILL BARNES, THE HEAD OF WHERE THERE'S A Will, seemed nice, very efficient, and looked nothing like what I'd been expecting a wedding planner to look like. He was tall and built more like a linebacker than Rodney's brother, Ellis, who'd been an *actual* linebacker for the air force. But he'd come in with such an aura of confidence—like it wasn't going to matter that Clementine had vanished the day before the wedding—that I could feel myself start to relax in his presence, and it looked like Linnie and Rodney were doing the same.

Feeling like things were in good hands, I'd used his arrival as an opportunity to take a shower, put in my contacts, and finally change out of my pajama-and-gnome ensemble. I'd put on jeans and, even though it wasn't quite cold enough for it, the cashmere sweater I'd worn home that night from Jesse's house. I shook it out and breathed it in, trying to see if I could still detect any of him—but since I'd brought it to imPRESSive Cleaners at least twice since then, it just smelled like dry-cleaning solution. I pulled it on anyway, twisted my wet hair into a knot, and left my room, heading back down the two flights of stairs.

The third floor, also known as the kids' floor, was barely decorated—probably because nobody ever saw it except people who lived here. Our four bedrooms—J.J. and Danny had the biggest room and had always shared—branched off from a central landing, and for a while there, we'd all been involved in an indoor paintball game and had gotten very good at aiming from behind our cracked doors, sniper-style. You could still see the faint colored circles on the wall if you looked hard enough.

The second floor was at least a little more decorated—family pictures lining the walls and a decorative bench that inevitably became where bags and stuff got piled. The second floor was also four bedrooms that split off from a central landing—my parents' master bedroom, my dad's study, and the two guest rooms that we'd always called the Blue Room and the Ship Room. It seemed crazy, as I took the last flight of steps down to the front hall, that in only a few hours, all the rooms we had would be filled with wedding guests.

I was nearly to the front hall when I heard raised voices, and I stopped short. My parents had been fighting a lot earlier in the year—I'd walk into the kitchen and everything would go silent, like they were counting on the fact that I'd gone temporarily deaf before I'd opened the door. There was a crackling tension in the house, so that it felt like even the smallest exchanges, about what to get on our pizza, or who was supposed to buy the milk, had taken on a different significance. For a few months there, it was like I was trapped in a foreign film where everything was a metaphor. I hadn't told my siblings, because there wasn't really anything I could point to that was *wrong*. There was just the uneasy feeling that something wasn't right, which was much harder, somehow, to prove.

But it all changed a few months ago, right around the time they'd told me they were selling the house. The whole vibe between my parents seemed better since then, which I took to mean they'd been fighting over what to do about the house—and once the matter was resolved, the fighting had stopped, and now arguments about pizza toppings were just about pepperoni versus sausage again. But I didn't want it to be happening again—not during Linnie's wedding weekend.

"Because you're not the only one who lives on this street, Don!" I heard my dad snap, and, relieved, I took the rest of the stairs down to the front hall two at a time, now knowing exactly what I would see.

Sure enough, my dad was standing in the foyer across from Don Perkins, our two-doors-down neighbor. He was in his sixties and had lived on our street longer than we had. He was nosy, forever in our business, always calling or stopping by when he thought things were too loud. He was also in the Gardeners' Association with my dad, and over the years, a rivalry had developed, Don always trying to outdo my father's garden in the yearly competition. This rivalry was mostly one-sided, though, since he'd never once won and my dad had won three times, the last two years consecutively. This had only served to make him a worse neighbor, and his complaints increased with each one of my dad's victories. Don had, of course, become a character in the strip—though the fictional Grants' neighbor Ron was eventually revealed to have a soft side under his gruff exterior, which I really didn't foresee happening with the real-life Don.

"Morning," I said, widening my eyes at my dad as I came to stand next to him.

"Oh," Don said, giving me a curt nod by way of a greeting. "You're still here, are you?"

"Um," I said, glancing at my father.

"Thought maybe you'd gotten them all off to college, now that you're selling this place."

"Charlie's starting Stanwich in the fall," my dad said, giving me a smile that didn't quite meet his eyes.

"Why on *earth* would you go there?" Don asked, shaking his head. "Oh—were you not a very good student?"

"You know I teach there, right?" my dad asked, his voice frosty.

"My condolences."

My dad's face turned a very dark shade of red. "Listen here—"

"Like I said, Jeffrey," Don said, talking over him, his very bushy eyebrows meeting in a frown, "I don't want to be disturbed this weekend. There have already been all kinds of people coming and going, your alarm going off . . ."

"As I'm sure you remember, *Donald*, we sent out a letter to all the neighbors about this wedding months ago—letting you know it would be happening and asking for your patience and good neighborliness for just the one night."

Don snorted as he looked through the open kitchen door, toward our backyard. My dad immediately took a step to block his sight line. He always suspected that Don's coming over to complain about things were just excuses to see what my dad was doing with his garden and steal a win from him by spying.

"Well," Don said with a huffy sigh, "it had better not get too loud tomorrow night. There are noise ordinances in this town, you know."

"Yes," my dad said, his tone getting calmer and more pleasant, always a bad sign. "Just like there are zoning laws that would have prevented you from building that gazebo. But some of us don't feel the need to mention these things. Yet."

"Yeah, well," Don muttered, glaring at my father. He glanced toward the backyard one more time, then shook his head. "Just keep it down and we won't have a problem."

"Charlie," my dad said, giving me a look that clearly told me whatever would follow wouldn't exactly be a suggestion, "why don't you show Don out? Through the *front door*."

"Sure thing," I said, quickly crossing to the front door and motioning for Don to follow, as my dad stalked away. "Hey, have you been having problems getting the *Sentinel*?" I asked as I pulled the door open for him. "The papergirl hasn't been delivering to us."

Don scoffed. "I don't read the *Sentinel*," he said, heading down the front steps. "I subscribe to *actual* newspapers."

"Hey, hey, Maddie." I turned to see J.J. passing through the front hall, his phone to his ear. "Yeah, I know it's been a while. But isn't it good to hear from me? Wait, not even a *little*?"

I shut the door, then headed into the kitchen. Linnie, Rodney, Will, and Bill were clustered around the center island. I could see that Will was wearing the same green fleece as Bill, except that under WHERE THERE'S A WILL was written WILL, which seemed to me to be a few too many Wills for one piece of clothing.

"Well, if you'd *told* me it was your birthday, I wouldn't have broken up with you!" J.J. said, following me into the kitchen. "Maddie? Hello?"

"Date search going well?" Linnie asked, raising an eyebrow at him.

"This is just like the '86 Mets." J.J. had a habit of bringing everything back to baseball; as far as he was concerned, there was a baseball analogy for every situation in life.

"Is it, though?" Rodney asked.

"Everyone counted them out too. But then—"

"Okay," Will said, in a voice that wasn't particularly loud, but was authoritative enough that we all quieted down. "I've made a list of the vendors Clementine was working with, and I've gotten in contact with all of them, so they know not to reach out to her. I'm still trying to reach Party in the Stars. . . ."

"What's that?" J.J. asked.

Will shot him a look that made it clear he didn't appreciate the interruption. "Wedding band."

I could have told J.J. that. I'd heard *a lot* about Party in the Stars in the run-up to the wedding. Linnie and Rodney had seen them at one of their friends' weddings and they had been their first choice, even though my parents had told them a DJ would require a lot less equipment and wouldn't need a stage.

"Moving on," Will said. "The tent should be up later this afternoon, and once it's up, we'll get the electrical and the furniture—" There was loud buzzing sound. Will stopped and pulled his cell phone out of his belt holder. "Will Barnes." He listened for a moment, his brow furrowing. "I see. And you just found this out now?" He listened again, his expression growing more annoyed. "I'll send someone to help out. They should be there in twenty. You too."

He hung up, and I saw that during this conversation, my sister had silently been getting more and more stressed—I could see the vein in her temple, the one that I used to tease her about endlessly, starting to show. "What's wrong?"

"There's a small problem at the Inn," he said, referring to where the rehearsal dinner was taking place tonight. "Something about the decorations. I'd go myself, but I need to supervise the tent guys—"

"I knew this would happen," Linnie said, her voice getting shakier and higher with every word. "Our wedding planner disappears, and then everything starts—"

"I'll go!" I jumped in. "I can get it sorted out."

Will nodded. "Sounds good. Bill, you go as well, okay? And report back."

"Sure," Bill said, nodding. Then he looked at me. "If it's okay with you."

"Of course," I said. I gave Linnie what I hoped was a confident *I've got this* look. "I'm sure it's not anything big. But whatever it is, we'll handle it."

"Thanks, Charlie."

I grabbed my keys off the hook by the door and raised my eyebrows at Bill. "Let's go."

It was a twenty-minute drive from our house to the Inn, and for the first fifteen, either Bill or I had been on the phone. Bill was fielding texts and calls pretty much nonstop—apparently, they'd had to move some things around to take on Linnie's wedding at the last minute, so he was having to reschedule appointments. And Siobhan had called me, wanting to know what the text I'd sent her—*Your fruit name theory was right*—meant. We'd had a quick talk, but since I was driving, the call was over the car speakers, and I was all too aware that it wasn't just me listening. It wasn't until we were nearly there that Bill set down his phone, looked across the car, and smiled at me.

I smiled back, and in the quiet that fell between us for the first time this whole ride, I suddenly realized that I was in a small enclosed space with a guy I didn't know—like, at *all*.

"So," I said, figuring that I could just treat Bill like he was the subject of a profile I was writing and get the basics of his background. *The Wedding Planner's Nephew*, it could be called, even if it kind of sounded like a bad romantic comedy. I was just going to cross off the "who" of the all-important five *W*s—who, what, where, when, why—that all journalists used. These words were painted three feet high in a mural in the Stanwich High newsroom. "Do you like working in event planning?"

Bill looked over at me with a smile, and I was starting to realize that this was his default expression—it was like he had resting cheerful face. "I do," he said. "It's always something different, at any rate. I worked for Where There's A Will all through high school, and I didn't have any exciting spring break plans, so when my uncle offered to fly me out if I would help him this week, I said sure."

I nodded. This had always been my favorite part of the work at the newspaper—talking to people, putting their story together, knowing when to jump in and when to hang back and nod and hope they'd tell you more. Maybe it came from being the youngest and having to listen and observe, but for whatever reason, it had always come easily to me. "Where are you on spring break from?"

"University of Chicago. In . . . Chicago," he added, then laughed. "I guess that's pretty self-explanatory. I'm finishing up my first year."

I took a breath, about to mention my Northwestern acceptance, but stopped myself before I spoke. I wasn't going to Northwestern, and there didn't seem to be much point in talking about where you *weren't* going to college. "Did you go to Stanwich?" I asked instead, even though I was pretty sure the answer was no. Stanwich High was a huge school, but most of the people there were at least vaguely familiar. And Siobhan and I had made it our mission to know who the cute guys were. And while Bill was no Jesse Foster, he was someone we definitely would have noticed.

He shook his head. "I'm from Putnam," he said, naming the town one over from Stanwich. "And . . . sometimes Albuquerque."

I glanced over at him, surprised, but before I could ask a follow-up, I saw the sign for the Inn and signaled to turn down the long and winding driveway that led to the main building.

"I think I've been here before," Bill said, squinting as he leaned forward. "I can't remember what for, though. Maybe someone's sweet sixteen?"

I nodded. "Sounds about right." The Inn was where I had attended lots of various functions over the years—weddings, receptions, birthday parties, the bar and bat mitzvahs that seemed to take up every weekend of my seventh-grade social calendar, and even junior prom last year when a pipe burst at the school and we couldn't hold it on campus. It was an old mansion with a carriage house that had been converted to a hotel, with guest rooms upstairs and a restaurant and ballroom downstairs. I pulled into one of the empty parking spots out front and killed the engine, getting out of the car at the same time as Bill.

"Charlie?"

I turned around and saw that there was a guy standing in front of me. He was wearing a baseball cap and a long-sleeved T-shirt with STANWICH LANDSCAPING printed across the front of it, and jeans with dirt stains on the knees. He looked like he was the age of my older siblings, with blond hair and green eyes, and it took me a moment to place him—this was Olly Gillespie, Linnie's high school boyfriend.

"Hey, Olly," I said, lifting a hand in a wave.

Olly and Linnie had been pretty serious in high school—they'd dated through junior and senior year, and then the summer before college. She'd broken up with him before she went to Dartmouth. Apparently, after Linnie and Rodney had gotten together, he hadn't taken the news that Linnie had moved on very well. I wasn't clear on what had happened in real life, but Olly's strip doppelgänger drove to Dartmouth in the middle of the night to stand under her dorm window with an iPod and a portable speaker to try to win Linnie back. It obviously didn't work, and I didn't see much of Olly until Linnie moved back after her split with Rodney.

A few weeks after she'd moved home, Olly Gillespie started showing up again—he was in the driveway, picking Linnie up, standing around the kitchen with us, in the backyard talking mulch with my dad. From what I'd been able to gather, he'd never really left Stanwich, and after college he'd started working for his dad's landscaping company. Although it was clear to all the rest of us that Linnie and Rodney were going to get back together eventually, it seemed like Olly had never gotten over Linnie. I was never sure what, exactly, had happened with them when she and Rodney were broken up—but as soon as she got back together with Rodney, Olly disappeared again.

"I thought it was you," he said. "What are you doing here?" He crossed to the Stanwich Landscaping truck that was parked two cars down from mine and hoisted out a leaf blower. I turned to gesture to Bill, to introduce him, only to see that Bill was on his phone again and had walked halfway to the steps.

"Just wedding stuff. Linnie's getting married this weekend, so . . ." I immediately wondered if that had been tactless.

Olly grabbed a rake with his other hand and nodded. "I know." I was about to ask how he knew this, when I remembered that you couldn't be following any of Linnie's social media feeds and not be very aware that a wedding was in the mix. "Don't let me keep you," he said with a quick smile. "I'll see you soon." He gave me a nod after saying this, and walked with his equipment around the side of the building.

I turned away from Olly and hurried to the Inn's front steps, where Bill was waiting for me. "Sorry," I said. "That was . . ." I glanced back to where Olly had disappeared to, but there was no sign of him. "Just a family friend," I said, figuring that was true enough, and also that the wedding coordinator's nephew didn't necessarily need to know details of my sister's romantic history.

We headed up the steps to the Inn together, and as I walked in through the door Bill held open for me, I looked around. The lobby of the Inn was just like I remembered it. There were chandeliers above, dark wood furniture, and woven, patterned carpets. There was a bar in the lobby, which always became the reception area when there were events. From the beginning, it had been Linnie and Rodney's choice for the rehearsal dinner, and they'd rented out the private dining room in the restaurant. I glanced around, wondering what exactly the problem here was and who we should talk to to fix it, but Bill was already making a beeline toward the tiny check-in/concierge desk.

By the time I joined him, a woman in a pantsuit was crossing around from the desk and motioning us to follow her toward the restaurant. "I'm glad you're here," she said, her voice low and serious, the way people talked about impending disasters and grave illnesses. "I had a feeling it wasn't right when the boxes were delivered, but they had the correct name on them, so they were signed for. . . ." We followed her through the restaurant—empty except for a few yawning servers setting up for lunch—to the private dining room in the back. She opened the door and hit the light.

Immediately, a song I vaguely recognized started blasting, something about coming from a land down under. My eyes widened as I looked around, and Bill took a startled step backward.

There were life-size cutouts of kangaroos, koalas, wallabies, and crocodiles placed around the room. There was a map of Australia stretching across one wall, streamers with the Australian flag on them hanging in delicate, twisted loops from the ceiling, and a blown-up picture of two of the Hemsworths.

"I assumed these were *not* the decorations intended for the rehearsal dinner," she said, and Bill and I both shook our heads wordlessly. She sighed and crossed the room to where an iPod had been docked and shut the music off.

"There were supposed to be pictures of my sister and Rodney," I said, noticing now that there was a stack of gift bags in bright neon, lined up in neat rows. "Everything was supposed to be peach and gray? And there weren't . . . supposed to be marsupials."

"Well, this clears it up a little." I turned and saw Bill holding up a banner, the kind that was clearly meant to be stretched across a doorway. G'DAY, CLAY! HAPPY 9TH BIRTHDAY, MATE! was printed in huge letters across it.

"Okay," I said, nodding. "So there was obviously just a mix-up. And this Clay kid probably got our decorations by mistake, that's all."

"You have to admire a kid who wants an Australian-themed birthday party," Bill said as he rolled up the banner. "That's a pretty awesome move. I'm pretty sure the theme of my ninth birthday was just 'eat as much pizza as possible without puking.'"

The woman behind us cleared her throat. "I let William know this already. But my staff needs to have the proper decorations in enough time to get set up before the event begins."

"Right," I said, nodding, like that would help me come up with a plan for tracking down what had happened to Linnie and Rodney's stuff. "We'll get them to you," I promised recklessly.

"Absolutely," Bill agreed.

"Great," she said, heading toward the door. "Just let us know when you have the right materials here and my staff can get started."

When she'd left, I looked at Bill, hoping that he secretly had some plan beyond the one I had formulated, which was to google "Clay birthday location nine Australia."

"Okay," Bill said, "so I'm guessing this is a Clementine issue? Pland said that she was getting events mixed up."

"You're probably right," I said, silently cursing Clementine in my head.

"I'll get in touch with Pland," Bill said, already typing on his phone. "Find out where this birthday party is taking place. And—"

My phone buzzed in my back pocket, and I pulled it out, expecting that maybe it was Linnie, wanting an update on the decorations. But it wasn't Linnie. My screen read MIKE CALLING.

I hesitated; then right before voice mail would have picked up, I answered. I couldn't remember the last time I'd even spoken to Mike. "Hello?"

"Hey, Charlie."

I turned away and took a few steps toward the door. It felt too surreal to talk to my brother while a kangaroo cutout looked back at me. "Um. Hi."

"Sorry to bother you," he said, speaking, as usual, more quietly than most people, so that you had to lean in to hear him. Linnie always claimed that Mike being soft-spoken was just a normal reaction to following J.J. in the birth order, but I knew it was a low-key power move.

"What's going on?" I asked, not in the *let's catch up* way, but in the *what do you want* way.

"Can you come get me?"

"Come *get* you?" I asked, turning the volume up all the way on my phone and pressing it closer to my ear.

"Yeah. I'm at the airport," Mike said, and I felt my breath catch somewhere in my throat. "I came for the wedding. I'm here."

CHAPTER 5
Or, The Prodigal Son Is Waiting at Baggage Claim

WENTY MINUTES LATER, I DROVE THROUGH THE entrance of the Hartfield-Putnam Airport. Bill had assured me that he could handle things at the Inn—he'd texted another of the Where There's A Will employees to come over to the Inn and help get to the bottom of the decoration mistake. "But if we can't," he'd said, eyeing another banner, this one reading HAPPY PERTH DAY!, "how do Rodney and Linnie feel about Australia? Are they fans?" My expression must have given away how I felt, because Bill immediately looked stricken. "I was just kidding," he said quickly. "Total joke. It'll be fine, I promise. Here." He grabbed what looked like a wrapped salami and held it out to me. "Want a Great Barrier Beef?"

Feeling like things were being handled, I'd left, after exchanging numbers with Bill so that he could call me as soon as there was news. I'd texted Linnie that Mike was coming after all and that I was going to the airport to pick him up. She'd texted me back a series of emojis—startled, confused, then turning into a stream of happy faces. I'd texted her back a thumbs-up, then headed to the airport, not exactly hurrying. I even stopped at Stubbs Coffee on the way and picked up an iced latte. I knew Mike was at baggage claim—but there was a piece of me that, frankly, didn't mind that he was waiting. He shouldn't expect the world to revolve around him and that I'd drop whatever was going on to come get him. If he'd wanted to have someone there to meet him at the airport, he should have let us know he was coming.

The taxi in front of me slammed on its brakes, even though it was going only about four miles an hour, and I slammed on mine as well. Shaking my head, I drove around it, pulled forward toward baggage claim, and put the car in park.

I got out and looked around, but there was no sign of Mike. Which was so typically my brother—call for a ride but then not be there when you came to pick him up.

I took a drink of my latte, then pulled out my phone to call him just as it buzzed with an incoming text from Siobhan.

Siobhan
Want anything from Zingerman's?

Me
YES
One of the brownies PLEASE
Also

Siobhan
What?

Me
Mike's here

Siobhan
WHAT?

Apparently he's coming for the wedding

Can you ducking believe it?

I'm at the airport now

UGH

Siobhan

Whoa

Linnie must be happy though, right?

Me

Yeah

But still

I looked down at my phone, feeling like if anyone was going to understand this, it was my best friend. I took a deep breath and started typing faster.

Me

He's going to wreck things. He's going to make it about HIM

He's going to derail this whole weekend

He wasn't supposed to be here!

It's bullshirt

Bullshirt

SHIRT

I give up

Siobhan

But Lin wanted him there

And it's her wedding

MORGAN MATSON

And I'm sure he's not going to ruin anything
He wants Linnie to be happy

Me

Right, that's Mike. Mr. Selfless.

Siobhan

Anyway, guess what!
My roommate next year is here too
So I get to meet her!

Me

The one who never used exclamation points?

Siobhan

Yes. Correct. That's the one.

Me

Lol
Let me know how it goes!

Siobhan

Be nice to Mike.

Me

I'm always nice.

"Charlie?"

I glanced up from my phone, and there my brother was, standing in front of me, for the first time in eighteen months.

We just looked at each other. I was sure it was only a few seconds, but it seemed to stretch on longer as I tried to replace the version of him in my head with this one. Mike was the shortest of all the boys, just an inch taller than me, with curly light-brown hair and brown eyes. His hair had been cut short since the last time I'd seen him—and unlike the baggy shirts and cargo shorts he'd seemed to live in then, he was wearing a fitted button-down shirt and dark jeans. It was still Mike—but this seemed like a different version of him, older and more polished somehow.

"Hey," I said, and then we were in motion at the same time, giving each other the kind of hug we always did—fast, a pat on the back, barely touching.

"I didn't know you were here," Mike said, gesturing toward baggage claim. "I was waiting inside."

"Yeah, I just got here."

Mike looked down at the iced latte in my hand and raised his eyebrows but didn't say anything. Mike was the only person I knew who could be somehow passive-aggressive even while remaining silent.

"So, I guess we should go," I said, heading around to the driver's seat.

"No, it's okay. I can get my own bags," Mike muttered under his breath.

"Did you want help?"

"I'm fine." This was classic Mike—he'd mutter something that he wanted you to hear, but if you called him on it, he'd back away.

I rolled my eyes as I got into the driver's seat, slamming the door probably harder than I needed to. A second later, Mike got into the passenger seat, and I put the car in gear and headed toward the exit.

We drove in silence, Mike hunched over his phone, his eyes fixed on the screen. As I concentrated on getting out of the tangle of streets that led from the airport, I pledged to myself that even though Mike was here, it didn't mean I was going to let him derail this weekend. I would just have to work harder to make sure that everything went off perfectly, that was all. But he wouldn't wreck it. I wouldn't let him.

"What?"

I looked across the car. "I didn't say anything."

"Oh." Mike shook his head, then looked back at his phone, and I rolled my eyes. I'd been around my brother for five minutes, max, and I could already feel my Mike-specific slow-burning anger begin to bubble. I decided that I wasn't going to speak unless he did. The conversational burden shouldn't be on me—after all, he hadn't seen me in eighteen months, not to mention the fact I was currently doing him a favor. But as I drove on, the silence in the car seemed to expand, like it was taking on physical properties.

Mike apparently had no desire to catch up, ask me anything about myself, or even exchange basic pleasantries. And this had always been Mike—even before everything that had gone down last February with our mom. For as long as I could remember, he'd been keeping himself separate, standing slightly outside our family, like he was just visiting for a while and not really part of us. Mike not participating, Mike not playing along, Mike always putting a damper on things when the rest of us were all in, the one person rolling his eyes while we played running charades. I knew my older siblings noticed it, but it had never bothered them like it did me. When everyone else had moved out and it was just me and Mike in the house, I sometimes felt like I was the one holding up the kids' end of things myself while Mike would be hunched over his phone, headphones on, like he was trying to pretend he was somewhere else entirely.

When we were halfway home, Mike finally looked up from his phone. "Actually," he said, peering out the windshield, "if you could just take the next turn, that would be great."

"What?" I asked, even as I took a right into the first street I saw. "Why?"

"Not this one," Mike said with a sigh. "It's the next left. Juniper Hill."

"Well, why didn't you say that?" I asked as I looked around for a driveway to turn around in. As I did, I realized where we were—Grant Avenue.

It was just a small side street that bordered Stanwich Woods, the gated community that had an actual guard in a gatehouse out front. I'd never been, but I knew Grant Avenue well, entirely because of my older siblings and their reign of terror on the street—specifically, the street sign.

"Why did you need me to take Juniper Hill?" I asked as I pulled into a driveway, then started to turn around.

"Because that's where I'm staying."

"What do you mean that's where you're staying? You're not staying at home?"

"No, I'm not."

"But . . ." I just looked at him. Mike not staying at the house frankly sounded great to me, but I had a feeling my parents wouldn't see it that way. "What's Mom going to say?"

"Not being a psychic, I really have no idea."

"Mike."

"Can you just drive, Charlie? I'm already running late because you took an hour to come to the airport."

Just like that, I was suddenly, instantly furious, in the way that only Mike was able to make me. "Well, maybe if you'd let anyone know you were coming, someone would have been there to meet you."

"Oh, do I get a Charlie Grant lecture? *Goody.* It's been way too long."

"Listen—"

There was a knock on my window, and we both jumped. I turned and saw a police officer motioning for me to unroll the window. I did, immediately, trying to figure out what I'd done wrong. "Hi," I said as the officer—his name tag read RAMIREZ—leaned down to look into the car. He looked like he was in his midforties, in a dark-blue Stanwich Police uniform.

"You need to move your vehicle," he said.

"Sure," I said, nodding emphatically. "I'll do that."

"Why?" This was from Mike, who was leaning over the center console to talk to Officer Ramirez. "I mean, did we do something wrong?"

"You're not residents, are you?" Mike and I both shook our heads. "Then you need to move. Security is increased when the governor is at his Stanwich residence, and we're limiting all non-resident traffic."

I looked toward the entrance of Stanwich Woods and saw that in addition to a black SUV, there were two white-and-black Stanwich Police cars on either side of the gatehouse. Alexander Walker, a Stanwich resident and our former congressman, had won the governorship in November, but I'd had no idea he lived here.

"We were just turning around," I said. "We'll leave now."

"Drive safe," Officer Ramirez said, tapping the top of the car once before walking away, already speaking into the walkie-talkie clipped to his shoulder.

I pulled back out to the road and made sure to carefully come to a complete stop and to signal before merging into traffic, just in case the Stanwich Police were still watching me.

I turned onto Juniper Hill and followed the rest of the directions Mike gave me, barely paying attention to where I was going. It was like I could still feel the unfinished fight lingering around both of us in the car, making the silence somehow even more strained than it had been before.

"It's better I'm not staying at home," Mike finally said after telling me to just keep driving straight. He set his phone down in the cup holder and turned to look at me. "Seriously. I don't want to make a whole scene, or upset Linnie. I just wanted to come for her wedding." I took a breath to answer, but Mike pointed ahead. "It's just up here on the right."

I turned down the driveway, heart pounding as I suddenly realized, much too late, exactly where we were. The last time I'd been here it had been dark and rainy, but I still should have recognized it, so that I could have prepared myself.

Because we were at Jesse Foster's house.

And Jesse Foster was standing in the driveway, right in front of me.

CHAPTER 6
Or, Heart Eyes for Days

I N *GRANT CENTRAL STATION*, WHENEVER CASSIE Grant had a crush on someone—always more reciprocated than in my real life—she would float several inches off the ground, her toes trailing on the carpet or pavement, and cartoon hearts would appear in her eyes and hover around her head.

But as I stood there looking at Jesse, I felt the opposite, like I was being tethered to the earth, pulled down into it, so that the thought of moving—of doing something as simple as walking toward him—felt like an utterly impossible task.

I'd gotten out of the car when Mike had, but when he'd walked around the back to get his bags, I'd just stood there by the driver's side door, frozen, my heart hammering so hard that I was certain Jesse, twenty feet away from me, could hear it.

The last time I'd seen him, it had been nearly in this same spot on the driveway, me in my car, Jesse outside it. Jesse standing in the rain, leaning in to kiss me through my open window, both of us laughing in between kisses, as he cupped his hand under my chin, pulling me close to him, and closer still.

"Okay, bye," he'd said, even as he'd leaned in to kiss me again—a kiss we didn't break away from for quite some time.

"You're getting all wet," I'd said as I'd reached up to brush some of the droplets from his hair.

"It's just drizzling," he'd said with a smile, as the sheets of rain poured down on my car and thunder rumbled somewhere in the distance. "I'll let you go." But he stroked my cheek with his thumb and pulled me nearer.

"Okay." I'd stretched up to kiss him, still somehow amazed that I got to do this, that I got to kiss Jesse Foster in the rain.

"Okay," he'd said a few minutes later.

"Bye." I'd smiled against his mouth as we kept kissing, with a new intensity now.

"Bye." He'd kissed me back.

"Bye."

"Hi there." I blinked, startled out of these memories, and forced myself to focus on Jesse—this Jesse, present-tense Jesse, the one who was smiling and walking over to me.

I reminded myself to breathe, that I knew how to do it, that I'd been doing it all my life. "Hi," I finally managed, smoothing my hair back from my forehead, wishing I knew what to do with my hands.

I'd had a million conversations in my head with Jesse since that night over Christmas break. But now that he was here, it was like my entire brain had been wiped clean as I tried to think of something to say.

The Jesse in front of me looked pretty much the same—his hair was just a little longer now. He was wearing a dark-blue sweater with his jeans, and when he raised his hand to run his fingers through his hair, it rode up for just a moment, giving me a flash of his hip and stomach before it fell back down again.

"Charlie," Jesse said, taking a step toward me. His words were light and friendly, but he was looking right at me and not letting his gaze drop. As I met his eyes, I could feel my pulse beating places I usually wasn't aware of it—at the base of my throat, in my fingertips, thudding in my ears. "I didn't know I'd be seeing you. It's my lucky day."

"I know," I said, my voice coming out high and strangled. I cleared my throat and tried again. "I know." I gave a one-shouldered shrug, trying to appear casual and breezy, like this was the way I'd talk to anyone and not just someone who had seen me naked. At the thought of that—and of all I'd seen of Jesse—my palms started to sweat, and I wiped them quickly on my jeans before sticking them in my back pockets. I glanced back at the car but couldn't see Mike—he was presumably still getting his bags. Now that I was here, it was hitting me, a little too late, that I had no idea how to act in front of Jesse. Was I supposed to pretend that nothing had happened with us and things were the same as they'd always been?

"It's good to see you," Jesse said, taking another step closer. His tone was still easy and friendly—like if you read the transcript of our conversation, it would all seem aboveboard—but his eyes weren't leaving mine, and there was an undercurrent to everything he was saying. He glanced down at what I was wearing and smiled wider. "Nice sweater."

"Oh," I said, tugging at the hem. "Right. I probably should have given it back."

"Keep it," he said, taking a step closer to me still. "It looks way better on you."

I was getting flushed all over, like the sun had just started shining directly on me alone. "Thanks," I said. "When did—"

"There he is!" Jesse smiled wide as Mike came around the side of the car, carrying his suitcase and garment bag and shooting me an irritated look.

"Thanks for the help," he said as he and Jesse clasped hands and bumped shoulders.

"Sorry," I said, even though I wasn't, not even a little bit.

"When did you get in?" Mike asked, already taking a step toward the Fosters' house, clearly indicating that he was done with me being part of this conversation.

"Drove down last night," Jesse said, not moving, his eyes still finding mine every few seconds. "I decided I really didn't need to go to any of my Friday classes." He raised an eyebrow at me. "I guess you thought the same thing?"

"Pretty much," I said with what I hoped was a casual shrug.

Mike stopped, patted his pockets, then turned and headed back to the car. "I left my phone," he said, shaking his head.

The second Mike turned his back on us, Jesse closed the distance between us, so that he was near enough to touch, and my knees went wobbly. "Hi," he said again, this time just for me, his voice low and velvety.

"Hi," I repeated back, my voice barely above a whisper.

"I've been thinking about you."

"Oh?" I was trying to hold it back, but I could feel my smile starting to break through.

"Uh-huh." He reached out and brushed my hip with trailing fingers, setting off an explosion of sparks in my brain, then slipped his hand under the hem of my—technically his—sweater, his thumbs tracing a pattern on my bare skin as my heart started beating triple time.

"That's good," I said, trying to keep my voice steady, all too aware that Mike was going to be back any second now and might have some very big questions about what, exactly, his sister and best friend were doing.

Out of the corner of my eye, I saw him coming around the side of the car. "Mike," I said to Jesse, who immediately took a step away, his hands dropping down to his sides.

"Found it?" Jesse's tone had immediately shifted, becoming more jovial—more public, unlike the voice he'd just been using, which had been meant only for me.

Mike nodded. "I'll see you at the rehearsal dinner," he said to me as he walked toward the house.

"You know about the thing at the Pearce?"

Mike stopped and turned to look at me, his expression inscrutable. "I know," he said, then turned his back on me and continued on.

"Bye, Charlie," Jesse said. His tone was easy and vague, the way he would have talked to me if we hadn't had that night together in his guesthouse—like I was just the little sister of his best friend, nothing more. "I'll see you soon."

"You—will?" I asked, but Jesse just smiled at me, reached out, and brushed my arm quickly, giving my hand a squeeze, before he turned and jogged to catch up with Mike.

I got into my car, my head spinning. I wanted to take out my phone and call Siobhan, but I didn't want Jesse or Mike to see me doing it, especially since I had a feeling I wasn't going to be able to have that conversation calmly or without outsized facial expressions.

So, trying to appear blasé and unfazed, like this was no big deal, I backed my car out of the driveway and turned down the street, concentrating on stopping at the lights and pausing at stop signs, trying to sort through the steady, pounding drumbeat of my thoughts.

It wasn't until I was nearly to the Hartfield border that I realized I'd been driving the whole time in the wrong direction.

CHAPTER 7

*Or, 98% of All Statistics
Are Made Up on the Spot*

ALF AN HOUR LATER, I PULLED INTO OUR driveway and cut the engine. I didn't get out of the car, though, just sat there for a moment as I relived every moment of the interaction with Jesse. The way he'd looked at me, the way he'd smiled at me. That he'd been thinking about me. And that he would see me soon. I wished we'd had more time, and that Mike hadn't come by when he did, before we could make a plan.

Because all those feelings from Christmas break had come roaring back, and I couldn't help thinking ahead. Like maybe after this weekend, things didn't have to end. I could drive to Rutgers, it wasn't that far from Stanwich, and next year, since I'd still be here, it would be easy to see him. . . .

I'd called Siobhan and left three rambling messages explaining the Jesse situation, but hadn't heard back yet, and I checked my phone as I got out of the car. I'd just slammed the door when someone behind me yelled, "Hey!"

I jumped and turned, heart hammering, to see Sarah Stephens standing at the edge of our driveway, the paper in her hand and a glower on her face. "What now?" I muttered, taking a step toward her. It was odd to see her without her pink bike helmet—it was like she was missing a crucial part of her head.

"I assume you've seen this?" Sarah said, brandishing the newspaper at me, turned to the comics page.

"No," I said shortly, slinging my bag over my shoulder. "You haven't been delivering the paper to us."

"Look," she said, thrusting it under my nose, and I immediately glanced at the upper-left corner—the prime real estate of the comics section, which my mother had occupied for more than two decades now. It was a comic I'd seen her drawing six weeks ago—all the fictional Grants were coming together for a family dinner, which was interrupted by the papergirl, Sophie Silver, throwing the paper through the living room window. "Are you telling me that's not based on me?"

I looked away from the drawing. Usually my mother didn't make people resemble their cartoon alter egos, exactly—she just somehow captured their essence, so even if someone looked nothing like how they were depicted in her comic, you could tell who they were. But she really had abandoned that approach with her send-up of Sarah. The cartoon version looked identical to the real-life subject, down to the oversize bobbles on the ends of her braids. "It's not based on you," I said automatically.

"You're not going to get away with this," she said darkly, shaking her head at me. "I will *not* stand for it." I just stared at her, wondering if all the people trying to build up self-esteem in middle schoolers had actually gone too far.

"Good-bye, Sarah," I said as I started to walk toward the house, lifting my phone to my ear. "Hi," I said, pretending there was someone on the other end. "How's it going?"

"I know you're not talking to anyone," Sarah called after me, sounding disgusted. "You could at least do a better job of faking it."

"Uh-huh," I said, keeping up my fake conversation. "Interesting . . ." I pushed open the kitchen door and stepped inside.

"You're back." My dad was sitting at the kitchen table, and he jumped up as I came in. "Charlie's back," he called toward the family room. "Everyone, Charlie's back!"

"Well, that's a nice welcome," I said, smiling at my dad as I crossed to the fridge. I pulled open the door, but then just stared—clearly, while I was gone, someone had gone to the store. It was like staring at a solid wall of food.

"You're back," my mother said, and I closed the door to see her hurrying into the kitchen, looking anxious. She glanced around the kitchen. "Where's your brother?"

"Oh," I said, my stomach sinking, suddenly realizing what was happening and why my parents seemed so on edge. Of course Linnie had told them about Mike after I'd texted her. "So here's the thing. . . ."

"Mike!" Linnie called as she came into the kitchen, her smile fading as she looked around. "Where's Mike?"

"Does he need help with his bags?" J.J. asked, hurrying in behind her.

"Um, no," I said, realizing I should have texted Linnie right away to tell her Mike wasn't going to be coming home with me. Normally, I would have, but it was like just seeing Jesse Foster had wiped all rational thought from my brain. I took a breath. "Mike's not staying here," I said, figuring it was best to do it fast, like ripping off a Band-Aid.

"Of course he is," J.J. said. "Linnie said he's coming to the wedding."

"He is. But he's staying at Jesse Foster's. He—um—told me to drive him there." There was silence in the kitchen, so much that I could hear the ticking of the crooked silver wall clock. "But he said he'd be at the rehearsal dinner." The second I said it, I wondered if I'd just drawn attention to the fact that he wasn't going to be at the Pearce. I wished Danny were here, helping me navigate this.

"Hey." I looked over to see Rodney standing in the doorway of the kitchen. "Everything okay?"

"Mike's not staying here," Linnie said to him quietly, and behind his glasses, Rodney's eyebrows flew up.

"Oh," he said. "Um . . ."

"Did your aunt get settled in okay?" my mother asked, with what seemed like a lot of effort to change her focus.

"She's great," Rodney said. "Just resting after her trip."

"Your aunt?" I asked.

"My aunt Liz," Rodney explained. "She's staying in the blue guest room. I picked her up at the train station."

"Did Michael explain why he didn't come home, Charlie?" my dad asked, his voice low.

"Um, not really." I glanced at J.J. and saw he looked the way I felt. We all hated it when our dad got serious and quiet like this—somehow, it was much worse than if he'd just yelled.

"Well, we'll see about that," my dad said, taking a step toward me and holding out his hand. "Give me your keys."

"What?" I asked, even as I took them out of my bag. "Why?"

"Because my car is blocked in and I need to leave."

"Where are you going?" Linnie asked, exchanging a glance with J.J.

"I'm going to get Michael," my dad said, his voice clipped. He held out his hand again, and I hesitated, looking at my mom, who shook her head at me.

"I'm not sure that's going to work, Dad," J.J. said.

"He can't—he can't just drop in for the wedding like he's an out-of-town guest," my dad said, his voice rising. "He's not an acquaintance or a third cousin. He can be a part of this family or not, but he can't—"

"Jeff," my mom said, taking a step closer to him. "He came back. I mean . . ." Her voice shook slightly. "He's here. Maybe we should let that be enough." My dad hesitated, his hand still outstretched toward me. "Please," my mom said, more quietly, and after a moment, my dad lowered his hand.

"Nobody actually thought he was going to come to the wedding," I pointed out.

"I did," Linnie said quietly, but I kept talking over her.

"So is it really *that* big a deal he's not staying at the house? We shouldn't let this affect the weekend. It's still going to be great. We have the event at the Pearce today, and Danny's coming soon. . . ." Nobody looked particularly convinced, and I tried to think fast. I was not about to let Mike ruin this weekend—especially if he wasn't even here to do it. "I mean, it's not like we even have room for him here."

"What about my room?" J.J. asked.

"Your room is also Danny's room. And I think Danny might want to stay there."

"I just meant he could put a sleeping bag on the floor or something. Who's in Mike's room?"

"Bridesmaids," Linnie and I said together. It was admittedly going to be a tight fit with three of them, but Linnie had decided that it was much better than having them wandering around the Inn. When all Linnie's friends were together, noise complaints and property destruction inevitably followed.

"Well, I just hope your brother knows," my dad said, shaking his head, "that we expect him to be a part of this family. And he can't just—"

The kitchen door swung open again, causing the alarm system to issue a single, brief *beep*, and Will stuck his head in the room. "Jeffrey," he started. He must have taken in everyone else's expressions because then he said, "Uh—is everything okay?"

"It's fine," my dad said briskly. "Did you need something?"

"Just wanted you to okay the final placement," Will said, gesturing to the backyard. "Linnie said you were particular about a few plantings. . . ."

"She's right about that," my dad said. "I'll be right out." Will nodded and went back to the yard, closing the door behind him. My dad sighed and looked at my sister. "You realize this is my last chance to win the garden competition at this house?"

"You realize this is my only time getting married?"

"Well," J.J. said, clearing his throat. "I mean, statistically, that's probably not true."

"I don't think it's a great idea to talk about marriage statistics the day before a wedding," my mother said, shooting J.J. a look.

"I don't think it's a great idea to *ever* talk about statistics," I added. For years, J.J. labored under the belief that the rest of us were just as interested in hearing about statistics as he was in telling us about them. His favorite joke when he was younger, until we declared a moratorium on it, was "Did you know ninety-eight percent of all statistics are made up on the spot?"

"The data doesn't change depending on what day it is or is not," J.J. said, sounding offended by the very notion of this. "And the fact is, half of marriages end in divorce."

"Well, what about Mom and Dad?" I asked, gesturing to them.

"I think Mom and Dad are outliers," J.J. said with a shrug.

My dad headed for the door. "I should go say good-bye to my flowers."

"I'll come too," my mom said. My dad held the door open for her, and as they stepped outside, before the door closed behind them, I heard my dad ask, "Are you okay?"

I could hear my siblings talking—J.J. was apparently exchanging texts with some girl he'd met online, who wanted to come to the wedding but might also be a felon—but it was like it was all happening underwater, or in another room. My thoughts had gone right back to Jesse, and what he was going to do, and what *I* should be doing. What if he was waiting to hear from me right now and thought it was strange I hadn't reached out yet? Should I text him? But then, what if Mike saw the text and started asking questions? Maybe I should just text him something benign, like *hey*.

"Charlie!" I looked over and saw that everyone in the kitchen was staring at me.

"Um." I blinked, trying to focus, trying to pull my thoughts away from Jesse Foster. "What was that?"

"I asked if you'd heard from Bill," Linnie said. "Is everything okay at the Inn?"

"Is Billiam not pulling his weight?" J.J. asked, *tsk*ing. "It wouldn't surprise me. I thought he looked shifty."

"His name's not Billiam," Rodney pointed out. J.J. waved this small detail away.

"Right," I said, looking down at my phone. "Um . . ." The truth was, I hadn't thought about Bill or the decorations at all. "I think he's got it under control." I hoped I sounded more confident than I felt. "I haven't heard otherwise."

"Okay," J.J. said, holding up his phone. "I got more details. She was arrested but never actually served time. It was just a Mardi Gras–related offense that I'm very interested to know more about."

"No felons," Rodney said.

"I'll check in with Bill now, and—" My phone buzzed with a text.

Danny
Hey. I'm here.

I felt my heart leap in my chest as I looked down at my message. My big brother—my favorite person—was back.

"Danny's here," I said, feeling a smile start to take over my face as I ran toward the kitchen door. I didn't wait for a response, just pushed my way through it, and ran across the deck, past the garage, and toward the driveway.

There was a luxury SUV parked behind my car, and Danny was climbing out of the driver's seat. He grinned when he saw me. "Hiya, Chuck."

"Hey!" I ran toward him, and he pulled me into a bear hug that lifted my feet off the ground. I hadn't seen my brother in two months, but he looked the same—same dark hair sweeping over his forehead, same tan, like he lived in Southern California, and not Northern, same crinkles in the corners of his blue eyes. He set me back on my feet and smiled down at me from his height of six three.

"Come on," I said, pulling him toward the house. "How was your flight? We have *so* much to catch up on—"

"Wait a sec, Charlie," Danny said, laughing. "There's actually—I should—"

"Oh, right," I said, remembering. "So, what's your surprise?" I looked around. "Did you bring me a Double-Double after all?"

Before he could answer, the passenger-side door opened and a girl got out. She looked around Linnie's age. She was tall and blond, wearing what had to be four-inch heels, and she was smiling at me.

"Charlie, I'd like you to meet Brooke Abernathy," Danny said, then took a breath. "My girlfriend."

CHAPTER 8
Or, Double-Double, Toil and Trouble

———————————

THE SECOND WE STEPPED INSIDE THE KITCHEN, the alarm went off again.

"What's the code?" Rodney yelled, running over to the panel, which was flashing with red and orange lights.

"Twelve thirty-four," I yelled, and Rodney nodded. He punched in the numbers, but nothing happened for a few seconds—and then the alarm shut off suddenly.

"Seriously?" J.J. yelled, then seemed to realize a second later than he no longer needed to yell. "That's really the alarm code?"

"Yeah," I said. "Why?"

"There's the bride," Danny said with a smile as he crossed to Linnie and gave her a hug and a kiss on the cheek. "You're radiant. Isn't that what you're supposed to say to brides? Glowing?"

"Only if it's true," she said, whacking him on his arm.

"Jameison," Danny said, continuing across the kitchen.

"Sheridan," J.J. said, as he smiled at Danny and gestured to his outfit—button-down, dark pants, blazer. "So I take it you took one of those airplanes with a dress code?"

"What?" Danny straightened his cuffs. "People used to get dressed up all the time to fly. It's a lost art." He hugged J.J., then Rodney, and as Danny made his way around the room, I glanced quickly over at Brooke, who was still standing in the doorway.

By the car, I'd only gotten a cursory impression of her, so I used this opportunity to take a closer look. She was strikingly pretty—all Danny's girlfriends were—and thin, with hair that fell over her shoulders in soft curls. She was wearing a sleeveless tight-fitting floral-print dress that ended at her knees, with a cardigan over it. But for some reason, she hadn't put her arms through her sweater—instead, it was placed over her shoulders, like she was combating some weird temperature affliction, where her shoulders were cold but her arms were hot. She was tall even without the four-inch stilettos, so she looked like she was almost close to Danny's height with them. I could see, as she looked around the kitchen, a smile on her face, that she had sharp cheekbones and bright-blue eyes with black eyeliner that winged out from each eye in a tiny, precise point. As she tucked a lock of hair behind her ear, I noticed she had on diamond studs, each one looking bigger than the stone in my sister's engagement ring.

Linnie looked from Danny to Brooke and back again, widening her eyes at him. I saw that J.J. and Rodney were also staring at Brooke, like they were waiting for some explanation as to who, exactly, this person was. "Are you going to introduce us?"

"Whoops," Danny said with a quick, crooked smile. "Sorry—we've been on an airplane for too long. This is—"

"Oh, let me do it," Brooke said, stepping forward and clapping her hands together as she smiled brightly. "I've heard so much about everyone, I bet I can. Linnie, Rodney," she said, pointing as she went around clockwise, "J.J. and Charlie."

"Nicely done," Danny said, giving her a smile as he walked over to the fridge.

"And you are . . . ?" Linnie asked, after a pause.

"I'm Brooke," she said with a laugh, like this should have been obvious.

"Are you Danny's assistant?" J.J. asked, going to join Danny by the fridge. "He promised he wasn't going to do that anymore."

"You did promise," Rodney agreed.

Two years ago, during Mike's graduation, Danny had been in the middle of some huge deal with one of the start-ups his venture capital firm had funded. Mike had told him he didn't have to come for it, but Danny had insisted—and had showed up with his assistant, a really nice guy named Vikram. My mother had put Vikram up in one of the guest rooms, but had not been happy about the fact that Danny had basically spent the whole weekend working, and had dragged his assistant across the country to do it, and before he'd left, she'd made Danny promise not to do it again.

"What?" Brooke asked. Her smile faltered as she blinked at J.J. "No—I'm Danny's girlfriend." All my siblings just stared at her, and I took a little bit of comfort in the fact that they were having the same reaction I'd had—that it wasn't like everyone had known about her except me.

It wasn't that it was unusual for Danny to have a girlfriend. Both in the world of *GCS*, and from the stories I'd heard, there had been girls interested in Danny from middle school onward. But he'd never been serious about anyone. He was usually dating someone, and he was always really excited about whoever it was—these Madisons and Katies and Jessicas and Ashleys. They were always super awesome, super smart, and he couldn't wait for us to meet them. And then the next time it would come up, he would be dating someone new, and would be equally enthusiastic about her. But he'd never once brought anyone home—which, frankly, I hadn't minded. I didn't get to see Danny as much since he moved to California, and I was happy not to have to share his time with anyone.

"Danny," Brooke said, turning to him. It looked like she was blinking a little faster than most people did. "Did you—did you not tell your family . . . ?"

The sentence just hung in the air for a moment until Linnie jumped in. "Oh, *Brooke*," she said, snapping her fingers. "Right, of course. Of course Danny mentioned you."

"Totally," Rodney agreed, a little too quickly.

"Many times," J.J. said, nodding. "Many, many times." Then after a pause, he added, "Not like a weird amount of times. Just the normal amount."

Brooke nodded, but I noticed her smile now looked a little forced. "Well—it's so nice to meet you all."

"So, I was thinking we would take the blue guest room," Danny said, pulling a veggie tray out of the fridge, along with a can of Coke. "I didn't think Brooke would appreciate sharing a room with J.J."

I blinked at my brother for a second. Why had I not put this together the second Brooke had shown up? Danny wouldn't have brought his girlfriend all the way from California to say hi and then leave again. But it was like I was watching what I'd hoped this weekend would be—me, my siblings, hanging-out time in between wedding stuff—get farther and farther away, like a mirage in the desert.

"So you're staying the weekend," Linnie said, giving Brooke a very fixed smile, in between staring daggers at Danny. "You're . . . coming to the wedding?"

Brooke's head whipped over to Danny. "You didn't—"

"I told you I was bringing a date," Danny said, as Linnie and Rodney both shook their heads.

"Wait, this is perfect," J.J. said. "She can take the spot my date was going to have. I hope you like steak, Brooke."

"What date?" Danny asked.

"Exactly," I said.

"So now that your guest count isn't going to be off," J.J. said, "maybe we, um, just end the bet?"

"Great idea," I said quickly, really not wanting my brother to invite a felon to the wedding. "Forfeit?"

"Forfeit agreed," J.J. said. He pointed to me and Rodney. "Forfeit accepted?"

"Accepted," we said in unison.

"Not that I *couldn't* have gotten a date," J.J. said, and I noticed that under his usual bravado, he looked very relieved. "But this way, I can concentrate on enjoying your wedding."

"So!" Danny said, leaning back against the counter and cracking open his can of soda. I noticed Brooke was still standing in the spot where she'd first come into the room, shifting her weight on her high heels back and forth from foot to foot. "Tell me things! What's been going on?"

"Well," I said, raising an eyebrow at Danny. "You might need to get a refund on your wedding planner."

"What happened to Clementine?"

"She skipped town," Linnie said.

"Embezzlement," J.J. added.

"*What?*" Danny asked, looking around at all of us. "Is this a joke?"

"Nope," I said, pushing myself up to sit on the counter. "We found out this morning, and—"

"Who's Clementine?" I looked back to see Brooke still standing in the doorway, smiling as she asked this. I glanced over at her, annoyed. Because this—us—all of us together, joking around and talking, it was what I'd been looking forward to for months. And it was getting derailed by this girl in our kitchen, the one who shouldn't have been there and was only getting in the way.

"She's the wedding planner," I said shortly, then turned back to my siblings. "Guys, should we have a General Grant Meeting at some point this weekend?"

"I thought all five of us had to be here for a GGM," Danny said, taking another drink of his soda.

"The wedding planner quit?" Brooke asked, but J.J. was already talking over her.

"All five of us *are* here," he said. "Mike's back. He came for the wedding."

"Really." Danny glanced at Linnie, who nodded. "How's that been going?" Then he looked around, like he was just now noticing Mike wasn't in the kitchen. "Wait, where is he?"

"Staying at Jesse Foster's," Rodney responded.

Danny's eyebrows flew up. "And how'd that go over?"

"Not great," J.J. and I said in unison.

"I bet," Danny said with a short laugh. "Jeez. Remember that one time—"

"Mike's here?" Brooke asked brightly, and we all turned to look at her. "I'm glad I'm going to get to meet him. I wasn't sure, because Danny said he wasn't coming, because there was a . . ." Her voice trailed off, and her cheeks turned pink. "I mean," she said, speaking more quickly now. "Just that Mike and your mother—"

"Did I hear the alarm *again*?" my dad asked, pushing through the kitchen door that Brooke had left ajar. He stopped and smiled when he saw Danny and pulled him into a hug. "Our firstborn! When did you get here? Good trip?" He must have noticed Brooke then, because he took a step back, and his eyebrows flew up.

"Oh—hello," he said. "Are you Clementine? Did you change your mind and come back to us?"

"No," Brooke said, her voice rising slightly. "I'm—"

"This is my girlfriend," Danny said smoothly, widening his eyes slightly at my dad. "Brooke. I told you about her."

There was only a tiny beat before my dad said, a little too heartily, "Of course, of course. Welcome. I'm Jeffrey Grant. Very nice to meet you. I think Danny told us you have a business selling cookies online."

"What?" Brooke frowned, and looked at Danny. "I—no."

"She doesn't," Danny said, looking hard at my dad, clearly trying to tell him to shut up.

"No, you told me," my dad said, missing this as he wandered over to the counter and helped himself to some celery sticks from the veggie tray. "I was so impressed—it was that app? All about how people can get fresh cookies delivered whenever they want? What was it called?"

"I . . . don't know," Brooke said.

"That's not Brooke," he said. "That was . . . someone else. Brooke's a doctor."

I looked over at her, surprised. Maybe it was just that my doctor was a middle-aged woman who always wore sneakers, but I wasn't used to doctors looking quite so glamorous. But maybe things were different in California.

"Well, that's very nice," my dad said, nodding. "Good for you! You're actually making a difference, unlike my layabout children."

"Hey," Danny, J.J., and Linnie said together.

My dad shot them all a grin, then turned to Danny. "But what *was* that cookie business called? This is going to bug me now."

"Crumby Service," Danny muttered after a moment, and my dad broke into a smile.

"That's right!" he said, chuckling. "So! Brooke. How long are you in town? And where are you staying?"

"We're staying here," Danny said. "We're here for the weekend."

"But it's your sister's wedding this weekend," my dad said, frowning.

"Right," Danny said, shooting me a glance, clearly wanting me to help. Our dad was one of the leading botanists in his field, but that didn't mean he couldn't be incredibly slow on the uptake sometimes. This had migrated into his character in the strip, Geoff, an absent-minded professor who was always losing things, which Waffles the beagle would inevitably find.

"They're coming to the wedding," I said, making my voice upbeat and cheerful. "Isn't that great?"

My dad looked over at Linnie. "Did you know about this?"

"It's—fine," Linnie said, even though it sounded like she was speaking through clenched teeth. "The more the merrier, right?"

"Not for a wedding," J.J. muttered.

"Well—welcome," my dad said, giving Brooke a smile. "We're very happy to have you."

"I, um," Brooke said, turning around and reaching into a paper bag, which she'd set down by her feet. She stood up, holding a very ugly-looking plant in her arms—it mostly looked like someone had put a bunch of twigs in a decorative pot. "I brought this for you. Danny's told me so much about your garden, so I just thought . . ." She held out the plant toward my dad.

"That's not a Parrot's Beak?" he asked, patting his head, then bringing his glasses down to look at it more carefully. "Truly? How unusual. Thank you so much."

"Apparently it takes a while to bloom. But if you plant it now, by this time next year, it should be in flower."

There was a silence in the kitchen, as my dad looked down at the plant. "Well," he said, clearing his throat. "That's a nice thought."

"You can always plant it in your new garden, right?" J.J. asked, his tone more upbeat than usual.

"I'm sure that . . . wherever I end up, I'll have a garden there. And I'm sure it'll look lovely." He shot Danny a look, but it was over before I could read into it.

My parents hadn't yet bought another house—they said they were waiting until the escrow closed. But I also hadn't asked them any questions about where we'd be moving or what the house would look like, mostly because if I didn't talk about the fact that we were going to leave this house, maybe it wouldn't happen. Talking about it—about logistics and specifics—would make it real in a way I didn't yet want to deal with. There was a piece of me that knew this was elementary school logic, but I couldn't help it. And even though I knew rationally that I couldn't blame her, I found myself glaring across the kitchen at Brooke—she had brought up the one thing I really didn't want to think about this weekend.

"Anyway," my dad said, setting the plant on the counter and walking over to the alarm panel, "did this go off again?"

"Yeah," J.J. said, shaking his head. "And we *really* need to have a talk about what you picked for your alarm code."

"It's twelve thirty-four," I said. "What's the big deal?"

"Just think about it," J.J. said. I did, and realized what he was talking about a second later.

"The alarm code is one-two-three-four?" I asked my dad, who just shrugged.

"You mom and I could never figure out how to change it."

"Did I hear Danny?" my mom called as she came inside and hugged my brother. "How was your flight?"

"No complaints," Danny said, ducking out of the way as she tried to fix his hair.

"Hello," my mom said, looking at Brooke, a question in her voice. She glanced at Danny. "I thought you promised you weren't going to bring your assistant with you again."

"That's *Brooke*," Linnie, J.J., and I all said together.

"Danny's girlfriend," Linnie said.

"We've totally heard about her!" J.J. added.

"She does not," my dad jumped in, "sell cookies on the Internet."

"Danny's mentioned her," Linnie said.

"Oh, yes, of course," my mother said after a small pause. She exchanged a glance with my dad, who gave an exaggerated *I have no idea* shrug. It made me glad that my parents weren't responsible for keeping state secrets, since they weren't very good at subterfuge. "Welcome," she said with a smile that didn't quite mask her confusion.

"I brought this for you," Brooke said, reaching into her bag and pulling out a cellophane-wrapped basket of soaps. She held it out to my mom. "To thank you for your hospitality."

"My . . . hospitality?"

"I was thinking we'd stay in the Blue Room," Danny said as he crossed back to where Brooke was still standing in the doorway and picked up his rollerboard.

"Brooke is coming to the wedding," Linnie said, meeting my mother's eye, even as her tone remained upbeat. "Isn't that great?"

"I thought that you knew," Brooke said, her face flushing a dull red as she glanced at Danny, "I thought . . ."

"It's all good, right?" Danny asked. "We have rooms to spare here."

"Well, not this weekend," Rodney said. "My aunt Liz is already in the Blue Room. And my parents are going to be in the Ship Room. . . ."

"We had you in your old bedroom," my mother said. "But that was when it was just you, staying with J.J. We didn't realize . . ." She stopped herself and glanced down at the basket of soaps.

"Well, then, we can just stay in Mike's room," Danny said. "Since Mike's staying at Jesse's. Right?"

"Bridesmaids are in there," I said, shooting him a grimace.

"What, the three of them?" Danny asked, his eyebrows flying up, and Linnie nodded. "So we no longer care about the house burning down?"

"They've promised to behave," Linnie said.

"What about Dad's study? J.J. could stay in there, we could take my room—"

"Max is in there," Linnie said.

"*Max* is staying here?"

"He's the best man, and he's officiating the ceremony," Linnie said, starting to sound annoyed. "We thought the least we could do was offer him a place to stay."

"And who's in the Ship Room again?"

"My parents," Rodney reminded him.

"And your aunt can't stay at the Inn?"

"*No,*" Rodney practically yelled, and we all looked over at him. "Uh," he said more quietly. "There's . . . kind of a family feud happening with my aunt Liz and my uncle Jimmy. They can't really be around each other. So it's best if they're not in the same hotel."

"What's the feud about?" J.J. asked.

"Well, this is just great," Danny said, dropping his suitcase with a loud sigh. I could tell he was getting frustrated—which was the last thing I wanted. We were all supposed to be having fun this weekend, after all.

"You can stay in my room," I volunteered.

"Charlie," my mom said, shaking her head. "You shouldn't have to give up your room."

"It's *fine*," I said quickly. "Really. I can stay in J.J. and Danny's room."

"Great," Danny said, smiling at me, looking instantly more relaxed. "You're the best, Chuck."

"Well—okay," my mother said, nodding, sounding like she was trying to regroup. "If you're sure."

I nodded, and Danny mouthed *Thank you* to me. *You owe me,* I mouthed back to him, and he laughed. "I'll just get my room ready."

"I'll help," Danny said, following me to the kitchen stairs.

"Race you up?" I asked.

Danny shook his head. "No," he said. "We're not—"

But I took off running, and sure enough, a few seconds later, he was racing up the stairs next to me.

* * *

"So," I said as I shook out the fitted sheet and looked over at him. "I . . . didn't realize you were bringing anyone to the wedding."

"Yeah," Danny said, and he gave me the tiniest of eye rolls as I tossed his half to him and we pulled it over my mattress together.

I arched an eyebrow. "Stage-five clinger?"

He laughed, and then cleared his throat, like he was fighting to be more serious. "No. Brooke's great. She's super great." We tucked in the sheet, then the top sheet, and pulled the comforter over them, then tossed the pillows onto the bed. I straightened them out and gave them a quick fluff and decided that was probably as good as it was going to get.

"Good enough?" I asked, and Danny nodded.

"Good enough." He wandered over to my desk and sat down in my wheelie chair, spinning himself around once. "But I'm sorry for springing her on you. We're still going to hang out this weekend, just you and me. Right?"

I grinned. "Right."

"Knock-knock!" I turned and saw that Brooke was standing in the doorway, not actually knocking. "I came to see what I can do to be of assistance."

"I think we're all set here," Danny said, giving her a smile. "You should just relax."

"I'm happy to help out."

"We're good," I said. I got so little time with my older brother, I didn't necessarily need Brooke intruding on it—and in my own room, no less.

I heard a buzzing sound, and Danny pulled his phone out of his pocket. "I should get this," he said, pushing himself up to standing, already heading toward the doorway. "Be right back." He crossed the landing, and I could hear his voice getting fainter as he went downstairs. "Yeah, I'm here. Walk me through what's happening."

With Danny gone, it was just me and this girl, who I didn't know at all, looking at each other across my room. The silence between us seemed to expand and stretch out, and I was suddenly aware, in a way that I hadn't been just a few seconds earlier, that my room probably looked stupid and childish to her—the posters on my walls, the photos of me and Siobhan pinned up on my corkboard, the jewelry in a heap on my dresser.

"So!" Brooke said brightly, giving me a smile. "What can I do?"

"I really think we're all set. I just need to grab a few things." My dresses for the wedding and the rehearsal dinner were hanging in my closet, but I could get to it from Linnie's room. I just needed a few odds and ends to get through the weekend—I wasn't sure how much access I'd have to my room once Danny and Brooke settled in. I pulled a canvas bag off my doorknob and crossed over to my dresser.

"I'm happy to help if I can."

"There's nothing to help with," I said, then wondered if I'd been too sharp. "Really. This is a one-person job." I grabbed a clean pair of pajamas from my drawer and tossed in some underwear and a few T-shirts.

"I'm really sorry to put you out of your room," Brooke said, twisting her hands together. Her nails, I could see, were long and perfectly painted a dark shade of pink.

"It's fine."

"I guess I just thought—I mean, I had no idea that you wouldn't . . ." Her voice trailed off. I knew I should probably say something—lie, like Linnie and J.J. had done, pretending we'd known who she was and that she had been coming. And she clearly wanted me to tell her that I didn't mind at all being displaced out of my own room. But I wasn't about to do any of that.

An awkward silence fell as I looked around, trying to figure out what else I would need for the weekend, so that I could get out of here as quickly as possible.

"Are these from your college?" I glanced over to see Brooke standing by my desk, looking at the blue Stanwich College folder.

"Yeah," I said, not liking at all that she was going through my stuff. "But don't—" But Brooke had already picked up the stack of shiny, brightly colored folders and was flipping through them.

"Oh, College of the West is a great school," she said, stopping on the orange one. "I almost went there."

"Oh yeah?" I was trying to fight being interested, and leave it at that, but my curiosity overruled me. "Where did you go?"

"USC," she said, flipping open Northwestern's purple folder. "For med school too. You got into Northwestern?" she asked, sounding surprised.

"Yes," I said, feeling my defenses start to go up. This girl didn't even know me; why was she surprised at my college acceptances? "Why?"

"Nothing," she said quickly, setting the folder down again. "Sorry. I just . . . When Danny told me you were staying around town, going to the local college here, I guess I just assumed . . ." Her voice trailed off, but it was like I could practically see the words she wasn't saying floating in the air between us. *I assumed you didn't have any other options.*

"It's not the *local college*," I said, hearing my voice rise. "It's a hugely respected liberal arts school that just happens to be in this town."

"Right," Brooke said quickly. "I didn't mean—"

"Not everyone has to go away to school," I continued. "There's nothing wrong with staying close to home."

"Not at all," she said, nodding a little too emphatically. She looked at the folders on the desk, then back at me. "So . . . I guess you don't need these anymore, huh?"

"Just leave them," I said, not liking at all the look on her face, like she understood something about me that I didn't. "I still need to let the other schools know I'm not going, that's all."

"Right." She stacked the folders in a neat pile on my desk, then turned to me. "I've no doubt Stanwich is a great school too," she said, a note of false cheer in her voice.

"Yeah," I said shortly, pulling open my top drawer and looking around for the necklace I wanted to wear tonight. The last few minutes had confirmed beyond a shadow of a doubt that I didn't want to come back in here—or deal with Brooke in any way—unless I absolutely had to.

"Oh my gosh!" she said, and I turned to see her picking up the picture that I kept on my nightstand, the one of me and Danny that had run in the newspaper, him at eighteen, me at six, leaning back against his dented ancient Volvo, both of us in sunglasses, arms folded across our chests. "This is the greatest picture! This is when Danny won that contest, right?"

"Right," I said, fighting the urge to walk over and take the frame back from her.

"He told me all about it," she said, still looking at the picture with a smile on her face. "I couldn't believe it. Like, who does that?"

"Yeah." It wasn't like this was a secret—most articles that were written about Danny had it in there somewhere. It was a human-interest detail, a fun fact about the successful venture capitalist. But I still, somehow, didn't like this girl talking about one of my favorite memories like she'd been there.

It was the summer after Danny's senior year, and Coke was running a bottle-cap contest—find the winning cap, win up to a quarter million dollars. Danny had figured out what the winning cap would say, and also that by tilting the bottles at a certain angle, he could see just enough of one letter to tell if it was a winner. And since I was six and didn't exactly have pressing summer plans, I rode shotgun with him as we crisscrossed the tri-state area, going into every supermarket and CVS and convenience store, Danny working his way up and down the aisles, tilting the bottles and buying us candy that we would share and keep between us on the front seat. He'd found the winning cap—the one worth two hundred and fifty thousand dollars—on a Diet Coke bottle, in August, but I would have been just as happy if he'd never found it, if it had just been me and my brother, driving through New Jersey, windows down and radio on, singing along as the sun set behind us. Danny gave me twenty thousand dollars of it—much to the shock of my older siblings, who felt that a first grader didn't need that kind of money—which my parents immediately took and invested for me. Danny used his remaining money to start a fund out of his Princeton dorm room, and of course my mom put the whole thing in the comic strip. And the next year, Coke changed their rules so that all you could see under the cap was a code.

"Such a great story," Brooke said, setting the picture down and smiling fondly at it.

I finally found my necklace, and dropped it into my bag. "You should be all set," I said, already heading for the door.

"Oh, great," Brooke said. "Thanks so much, Charlie."

"Uh-huh," I said as I left my room. I could feel resentment bubbling up, even though I had volunteered my room and it wasn't like I hadn't understood what would happen. But as I looked back and saw Brooke pick up her suitcase and set it on the bench at the end of my bed, tucking her long hair behind her ears as she did so, I was annoyed anyway. I wouldn't have cared if it was just Danny in my room, but somehow this girl was upending everything.

I walked straight over to J.J. and Danny's room and knocked on the door—it was ajar, and it swung open. "I'm coming in," I called through the open door, giving my brother fair warning. When I didn't hear anything, I walked in, my eyes adjusting—I always forgot that my brothers' room didn't get as much light as mine. It was pretty close to what it had looked like when they had been in high school—cleaned out a little bit since the tag sale, but with the same decorations in place—Danny's trophies, J.J.'s plaques, the chair in the corner shaped like an oversize baseball glove, and the decade-old posters on the wall of actresses in bikinis, all of whom now had cookbooks and lifestyle websites.

And filling the entire back wall were the Grant Avenue signs. I sometimes forgot just how many of them there were—some with just the sign, some with the sign and signpost, and some with only portions. RANT AVENUE, for instance, had a place of distinction toward the top.

In my mind, it was always blurred—what had happened with the Grant Avenue saga in real life, what had happened in the comic strips, and what had become family legend. But everyone agreed on how it started. When Danny was a junior, Linnie was a sophomore, and J.J. was still in eighth grade, the Grant Avenue sign started disappearing with some regularity. By the third time it happened, people—like the residents of Grant Avenue and the police—were starting to pay attention.

Both my parents denied that they knew it was going on, but I had clear recollections—even at five—of being in my brothers' room and seeing the stolen street signs. Linnie had had one as well, propped up by her mirror. We were not the only Grants in Stanwich, so I'm sure focus wouldn't have turned to us, except for the fact that my mom started featuring it in her comic strip.

Whenever the subject of the signs came up, when we were all sitting out on the back deck, our dinner long finished but nobody going in yet, or all of us in the family room, with books and board games, my mother would ultimately be the one who was blamed for what happened. "I wasn't the one who *stole* them," she'd point out, which was a word all three of my siblings took umbrage with.

But a few weeks after the first articles appeared in the paper about the missing street signs, a similar story line started in the version of Stanwich that existed in two dimensions in the comics section. She teased it out, with Donny and Lindsay having a secret, and A.J. eventually finding out about it—and then the reveal, on a Friday, of Cassie opening the door to Donny's room and seeing the purloined street signs.

Suffice it to say that the adventures of the fictional Grant teenagers didn't go unnoticed by people in real-world Stanwich. Suddenly, the police were on the doorstep and reporters were calling—first, just from the *Sentinel*, but then it started to gain national traction. It was a ready-made human-interest story—a comic strip leading to a real-life break in a possible case over, of all things, stolen street signs. My mother defended herself to us by saying she put it in the strip to teach my siblings a lesson, but I always thought it was more than that—I think part of her must have seen what an opportunity this was for publicity.

The whole thing ended up going to court, with a judge ruling that a comic strip about a fictional family didn't provide sufficient grounds for a search warrant. My parents, alarmed that it was going this far—and by this point, I think they'd discovered just how high the penalty for stealing town property could be—got it settled quietly. My siblings never had to admit guilt, but, coincidentally, all of them spent a month doing community service that summer. My parents made a large donation to the Stanwich Public Works Department, a new Grant Avenue sign was installed, *much* higher than street signs normally were. And that seemed to be the end of it—at least for the Grants in the real world.

On the comic side of things, though, the sign strips were a kind of a turning point. Maybe it was because of the extra publicity, or, more likely, it had just been building for years, but the comic collection that featured these strips—*Give Me a Sign*—was my mother's first bestseller, and the beginning of what would end up being the height of the strip's popularity, though we didn't know that at the time.

I crossed over to the wall of signs to look closer just as the door swung open with gusto, and I jumped out of the way to avoid being hit by it as my middle brother barreled through, blinking when he saw me. "What are you doing here?"

"I'm staying here, remember?"

"Oh, right. Well, we need to go downstairs. Mom wants everyone in the family room in five."

"Why?"

"Because," he said, widening his eyes at me. "*Good Morning America*'s here."

---

*W*ELCOME TO 'THE FAMILY BEHIND GRANT *Central Station.*' I'm Jackson Goodman," said Kevin the Lighting Guy, as he sat in an armchair facing the two couches in the family room.

I sat up straight and looked at Kevin, who was standing in for Jackson during this rehearsal. Danny was perched on the arm of the couch next to me, J.J. was on the other end, and the pillow representing Mike was in the middle. Linnie and Rodney were sitting on the other couch with our parents, and everyone had slightly fixed smiles on their faces. I glanced toward the back of the family room, where the *GMA* crew was, then looked away quickly. I'd already been admonished once for looking at the tape marks on the ground where the cameras would be and not at the fake Jackson who was preparing us for this interview.

Because even though this wasn't real—even though it was Kevin the Lighting Guy reading off cue cards, and there were no cameras rolling—I was having to work hard not to stare at everything that was happening around us and fight to contain the excitement I was feeling. Even though I wasn't a devoted watcher like Siobhan was, this was still *Good Morning*

America. In our house, coming to talk to us about our family and our mom's strip. If it hadn't been Linnie's wedding this weekend—and if Jesse Foster hadn't unexpectedly reappeared in my life—it would have easily been the most exciting thing that had happened in a long, long time.

It was still a little surreal to see them there at all. There were five crew members—Kevin, Jill the segment producer, her assistant Lauren, and two guys who hadn't been introduced but who kept holding up light meters and looking into viewfinders and shaking their heads at each other.

They'd swept in, decided the interview would take place here, and commenced marking down where the cameras would go, moving plants and tables around, and arranging us on the couches. They'd even carefully moved the model Linnie and Rodney had been fussing with for weeks—the one of the guests' tables and chairs, the way they would be set up tomorrow, with little pieces of paper tied to each chair, indicating who was supposed to sit where. Apparently, nothing in planning the wedding had taken as much time and energy as figuring out the seating arrangements.

The crew from *GMA* was here so that we could go through the questions Jackson would be asking and make sure everything was in place so that the full crew could come in on Sunday morning with minimal setup time. Jill had told us, with a great deal of confidence, that it wouldn't take more than twenty minutes, but that had been forty minutes ago.

Kevin cleared his throat and then read from an index card, "I'm here in the Connecticut home of the cartoonist Eleanor Grant, where she and her family have lived for more than two decades. We're here to talk about her wildly popular comic strip *Grant Central Station*, which came to an end this morning—and to meet the people behind your favorite cartoon family."

We all turned to look at my mother, who realized this after a moment, and jumped. "Oh, right, me." She cleared her throat. "Welcome to our home," she said, sounding incredibly stilted. "We're so happy to have you here."

"Eleanor, you've been drawing a version of your family for twenty-five years," Kevin-as-Jackson read from his card. "What has been your favorite part of this journey?"

My mother took a breath to answer, then turned to Jill. "I'm sorry," she said, as the rest of the crew audibly groaned. "I don't mean to keep going over this, but can't this be more organic? Not so scripted like this?"

"Eleanor," Jill said with a tight smile as she crossed over to us. We'd been through this at least twice already—my mother hadn't realized that any of the questions would be set in advance, but it hadn't surprised me that Jackson Goodman wasn't the best at improvising. While very handsome, he'd never seemed to me like the sharpest tool in the drawer. "This isn't a hard-hitting interview. It's three minutes with Jackson Goodman in your home to mark the end of the strip. I'm sure you can . . . Jeff, where are you going?"

I turned around to see my dad was halfway across the family room, heading for the back door. The tent guys were working, and my father seemed convinced that rather than just hammering in pegs and putting up the wedding tent, they were secretly out to damage all his plantings. He'd been trying to escape the family room and supervise them ever since we'd all gathered here. "Me?" he asked, looking around. "Um . . . I just thought I'd check to make sure those maniacs aren't damaging my flowers. You know, since we've stopped."

"We *haven't* stopped," Jill said, her voice rising slightly.

"Actually," one of the other guys said as they stepped forward, "we do need to stop. We're getting some shadow at the end of that couch." He nodded toward the couch Linnie was sitting on. "I think we're going to have to move it."

"While you do that, I'll just take a look outside," my dad said, making a beeline for the backyard.

"Jeff, let them do their work," my mother called after him. When she didn't get a response, she shook her head and followed behind him.

The rest of us were shooed in the direction of the doorway as the crew members started moving our furniture around yet again.

"Can we switch seats?" J.J. asked me. "I think they're getting my bad side."

"You have a good side?" Rodney asked.

"My left side," J.J. said, like it should have been obvious. He turned his face one way and then the other. "Can't you see it?"

I exchanged a look with Danny and took a breath to respond just as I heard heels clicking on our hardwood floors and turned to see Brooke walking through the doorway, an apologetic smile on her face.

"Sorry about that!" She came over to stand next to Danny, who gave her a quick smile. "Work. I reassigned my patients and told my office I needed to be off the grid this weekend, but . . ." She looked around at the crew arguing over couch placement. "Are you guys still rehearsing? I thought you would have been done by now."

"Us too," J.J. muttered.

"So, Linnea," Brooke said, smiling at my sister, "is there anything I can do to help get things ready for tomorrow?"

"Call me Linnie," she said. "And that's so nice of you! But seriously, you should just enjoy yourself."

"I'm happy to help, though," Brooke said, taking a step closer. "I've been a bridesmaid, like, eight times by now, so I've pretty much seen it all."

"Eight times?" Linnie laughed.

"That's what happens when you're in a sorority," Brooke said, laughing too.

"Linnie!" My dad was yelling from the other end of the family room. "I had a thought. Why put the tent in the *middle* of the yard? What if we pushed it way to the back of the yard and spared my nasturtiums? Doesn't that sound like a great solution?"

"No," Linnie said, shaking her head at him. "We talked about this—" But my dad had disappeared through the door again. *"Dad!"* she yelled, but he didn't reappear. "Be right back," she said to me, already heading in his direction, deftly stepping around the *GMA* crew, who had moved the couches to nearly the center of the room and were currently pacing around them, light meters in hand.

"Weddings are always crazy." I looked over to see Brooke smiling at me, like we were in this together, like we were friends. "I remember when my brother got married, it was two days of chaos leading up to the big day. I swear, everything that could have gone wrong did. But it all worked out in the end."

I nodded. I knew I should respond to this, hold up my end of the conversation. I didn't know anything about this girl, after all—I should ask her how many siblings she had, or where this nearly chaotic wedding took place, or even what kind of medicine she practiced. I could have treated this like a profile for the *Pilgrim. Babbling Brooke! The Girlfriend Nobody Knew Existed Tells All.* But I didn't. I just stared down at my feet and crossed my arms over my chest. And as the silence between us stretched on, I became increasingly aware that I was behaving badly, but also that I wasn't about to do anything to change this.

The doorbell rang, and I jumped at the opportunity to get out of there. "I'll get that," I said quickly, already heading for the front hall. As I reached it, I looked back for just a second to see Brooke standing alone where I'd left her, a fixed smile on her face, looking a little bit lost. I pulled open the door and smiled when I saw who was standing on the other side—Max Duncan, Rodney's best friend, best man, and wedding officiant. "Hey, Max."

Max looked the same as when I'd seen him last, at Rodney and

Linnie's engagement party. He'd been Rodney's roommate freshman year and had been the one to officially introduce Rodney and Linnie at the first-night-of-school mixer. He was short and stocky, with an incredibly bushy beard, which he'd had since college—I honestly wasn't sure if I'd ever seen the lower half of his face. He'd gotten ordained online to perform the ceremony, and had, in my opinion, gotten a little too into this, signing e-mails on the bridesmaids-and-groomsmen e-mail chains as Reverend Duncan. There was a suitcase at his feet, and he was holding a large duffel bag tightly with both arms.

"Hey, Charlie. Is everything okay?"

"Sure," I said immediately, then wondered if Rodney had told him about our embezzling wedding planner. "Why?"

"I saw news vans in the driveway," he said as he stepped inside and I shut the door behind him.

"That's just *Good Morning America*," I said. "They're interviewing us on Sunday, so they're here to prep."

"Whoa," he said, craning his neck toward the family room. "That's pretty cool."

"How was the drive?"

"Not bad," Max said with a slow smile. Max didn't seem to ever move too quickly or get too upset about anything—and he always, frankly, seemed fairly stoned, which Rodney had assured me was not an incorrect observation.

"I thought I heard the best man," Rodney said as he came into the front hall from the kitchen. He reached out to hug Max, but Max just tightened his arms around his bag and took a step away.

"Hey, man," he said, adjusting his bag and then smiling at Rodney. "How are you?"

"Fine," Rodney said, glancing at the bag Max was clutching to his chest. "Uh—can I help you with your bag?"

"No!" Max yelled, then cleared his throat. "I mean . . . I'm fine. I'll just . . . handle this one myself."

Rodney exchanged a look with me. *Stash?* I mouthed to him, and Rodney rolled his eyes but then nodded. "Everyone's in there," he said, tipping his head toward the family room. "Want to come say hi?"

"Um," Max said, shifting his weight between his feet. "I'd actually like to put my stuff down if that's okay? Get settled in?"

"Sure," Rodney said, giving him a knowing nod. "Just open the window this time, okay?"

"No," Max sputtered. "That's . . . that's not . . ."

"He's staying in Dad's study," I said, and Rodney nodded as he picked up the suitcase resting at Max's feet.

"I'll get you situated," Rodney said, heading up the front stairs, Max following behind, still gripping his bag tight.

They had just disappeared up the stairs when there was a loud *crash* from the family room, followed by silence. I hurried into the room and felt my eyes widen as I saw what had happened. The model of the seating arrangements was lying on the ground, the tiny chairs and tables scattered around it, most of them smashed. J.J. and Kevin the Lighting Guy were each holding one end of our couch, and both of them were looking very guilty.

"Uh," J.J. said as he dropped his end of the couch, causing Kevin to stumble forward. "It's okay, right? No big deal . . ."

The back door slammed, and a moment later, Linnie was walking fast into the family room, followed by our parents. "Is everything okay?" she asked. "I heard—" She stopped short as she saw the model on the ground. "What *happened?*"

"So," Jill said, sounding more and more tightly wound. "Can we just get this cleaned up and reset? If we could be ready to go in the next five, we should be okay."

"We won't be *okay*," Linnie said as she looked up from the pieces of the model, "because the seating arrangements have just been wrecked!" He voice was high and trembling, the way it always was before she was about to burst into tears.

"It'll be okay," my mom said as she bent down next to Linnie and helped her gather up the pieces of the tiny chairs. "Surely you had the table numbers on the place cards?"

"No," Linnie said, and I could tell that she was now meltdown-adjacent. "Because *Clementine* was supposed to do the place cards. So that model was all we had to tell us the seating arrangements!"

"Maybe Clementine did the place cards and Will has them," I said, jumping in, even though I doubted it. If you're neglecting your clients and fleeing with their money, I'm not sure you're taking the time to fill out place cards. "I'll call him, and—" I pulled out my phone and saw I'd missed a call and text from Siobhan.

Siobhan

OMG JESSE! We must discuss.

Also call me ASAP I need to talk to you!

I made a mental note to call her back later as I scrolled through my phone, looking for Bill's number.

"We need to figure out what to do," Linnie said. "Because if Clementine didn't do the place cards, all the work we did figuring out where everyone would sit is just gone."

"I actually took a picture of the model." This was Brooke, of all people, holding out her phone to Linnie as she took a step forward. "So maybe you can use that to see the seating arrangements?"

"You took a picture?" J.J. asked.

"Yeah," Brooke said, her cheeks going slightly pink. "Sorry if that's weird. My sister is getting married, and I thought it was such a neat idea. . . ."

"She is?" Danny asked. "Since when?"

"Since four months ago. We talked about this."

"Oh, right. Sure."

"I hope it's helpful," Brooke said, handing her phone to Linnie.

"Thank you," my sister said, sounding grateful, and much calmer. "I really appreciate it. Mom, can you help?"

Feeling like this crisis had been resolved for the moment, I started to put my phone in my pocket just when it buzzed with a text—from Jesse.

Jesse

Hey. So great to see you today.

Thinking about you.

I stared at the words he'd written, trying to keep a smile off my face, my heart pounding. I quickly walked over to the front hall, feeling like I needed some privacy as I wrote back.

Me

Me too

Maybe I can see you soon?

A second later, Jesse replied.

Jesse

You know it.

I smiled and continued walking, wondering if I should reply to this—like ask him for specifics—but stopped short when I realized I was walking in on a conversation between Rodney and his aunt Liz. I'd met her just before we'd all been hustled into the family room. She really resembled Rodney's mom, and had seemed very sweet, chatting with Linnie about wedding plans.

"What do you *mean* your uncle is coming?" Aunt Liz snapped, and I realized the nice older lady that I'd met was gone. This Aunt Liz was glowering and steely-eyed and looked *pissed*.

"Well," Rodney said, glancing around nervously, like he was hoping someone would come and help him. "We invited both of you to the wedding, of course. But you're sitting far away from each other, and . . ."

Sorry, I mouthed to Rodney as I started to back away, realizing this must have been the family feud he'd mentioned earlier. I pulled open the front door, thinking that if I needed privacy, outside might be one of the few places I could get it—only to see Rodney's parents, General and Mrs. Daniels, heading up the walk.

"Um. Rodney?" I smiled at the Danielses and waved to them. "Your parents are here."

Mrs. Daniels waved back at me, and the General nodded as they reached the front door. I'd only met Rodney's family a few times—his older brother and sister had both followed their parents into the military. His sister was in the JAG Corps, and his brother was in the air force, stationed in Japan, which meant he had to miss the wedding. Even if you didn't know Rodney's dad was a three-star general, you'd get it from just a few minutes in his presence. I somehow always found myself standing up much straighter when I was around him.

"Charlotte," he said, crossing the threshold into the house and giving me a quick, firm handshake. The General shook everyone's hand—if he was feeling particularly emotional, he might give you a pat on the shoulder as well.

"Hello, dear," Mrs. Daniels said, giving me a quick cheek kiss and then patting my hair and straightening the sleeves of my sweater.

I smiled at her automatically. "Can I help with your bags? How was your flight?"

"I'm perfectly capable of handling the luggage, though I appreciate the offer to assist," the General said. "And we had a bit of turbulence as we crossed the Great Plains. It lasted, what, twenty minutes, Rose?"

"About that," she replied, nodding. I shut the door behind them as they greeted their son with a handshake and a hug, respectively.

"Liz!" Rodney's mother said, smiling at her sister and going to hug her, but Liz just pointed at Rodney.

"Did you know about this?" she asked. "About *Jimmy* being welcomed to this wedding?"

"Well, here's the thing," Mrs. Daniels started.

"If everyone could please reset," Jill yelled from the family room. "We need to get this wrapped up."

"What's going on?" the General asked.

"*Good Morning America,*" I said. "It's just a rehearsal." Mrs. Daniels looked more confused than ever, and I took a breath to explain just as my phone rang.

I pulled it out of my pocket and saw that it was Bill. I slid my finger over to answer immediately, realizing a bit too late that I never had checked in on him and asked how things were going at the Inn. But maybe he was just calling to tell me that everything was fine, that everything had been sorted out, and that there were no problems whatsoever. "Hi, Bill," I said, taking a few steps away from the Danielses.

"Hey, Charlie," Bill said, sounding slightly out of breath and stressed enough that my hopes that things were okay were immediately dashed. "Um . . . can you come help? There's . . . a little bit of a situation."

CHAPTER 10
*Or, You Better Run,
You Better Take Cover*

———————————

*Y*ou're wrong," I said to Bill.

"I don't think I am."

"It shouldn't go there."

"Says who?"

"Says me. That's absolutely the wrong place for a koala." I said this with a great deal of confidence, like I was somehow an expert in marsupial placement. But honestly, in the last twenty minutes, I felt like I'd become one.

We were in the party room of Indoor Xtreme, the extreme sports place that had opened when I was in middle school. For a while in sixth grade, it was *the* place to have your birthday party—there was a paintball course and a skate ramp and rock climbing. The party room was where the pizza-and-cake portion of all the birthdays I'd attended here had been held, and apparently in the last few years, this hadn't changed—because this, Bill had found out, was the spot where Clay was going to be having his ninth birthday.

As soon as we'd wrapped up with *GMA*, I'd driven over to Indoor Xtreme. And even though Bill had prepared me, I didn't quite get it until I stepped into the party room and saw just how fully Clementine had messed up. In the neon orange and green room, with phrases like "Xtreme Attitude" spray-painted on the walls, were Linnie and Rodney's decorations. There were blown-up photos of the two of them through the years, delicate peach and gray streamers, and an oversize card where people could write well-wishes to the couple. The decorations could not have looked more out of place with their setting, and we'd taken them down as quickly as possible. We'd been about to leave when the girl who seemed to be in charge of things told us, without looking up once from her phone, that we were welcome to leave Clay's decorations behind, but that Indoor Xtreme had a one-setup-per-party policy, so decorations for the birthday party Bill had brought from the Inn were just going to remain in the pile where he had left them.

And even though this was entirely Clementine's fault, it felt wrong to leave this Clay kid with his birthday decorations in a heap. So Bill and I had started decorating the party room for him and hadn't gotten very far before we'd had a serious disagreement about antipodean animal placement.

"I think he looks good," Bill said, straightening the cardboard koala cutout that he'd placed near the door. "He's welcoming everyone inside."

I shook my head. "He's going to get crushed. There's going to be a stampede for the pizza and soda and he'll be the first casualty. Trust me."

Bill smiled at me and took a step back. "Are you sure this isn't just the wallaby fight all over again?"

"I was right about that," I said as I picked up the koala and moved him so that he was presiding over the gift bags, which we'd arranged in neat rows. "Nobody's going to get that but you." Bill had insisted on taping the wallabies over the door so that people would see them as they left. "It's a walla-*bye*," he kept repeating. "Get it?"

"Didn't you ever go to a birthday party here?" I asked, changing the angle of the koala. "I would have thought you'd be familiar with the pizza stampede."

Bill smiled but shook his head. "There's was a place kind of like this in Putnam when I was a kid, so we kept it local."

"And you said you lived in Albuquerque too, right?"

Bill raised an eyebrow at me. "Good memory."

I shrugged. "I work on the school paper—it means you get really used to remembering details."

"Journalism? Is that your major?"

"Well, I'm just finishing up my senior year now," I said, angling the koala once again. "But next year . . ." Unbidden, an image of the state-of-the-art newsroom at Northwestern flashed into my mind, but I pushed it away. "I'm going to Stanwich."

"Oh." His eyebrows flew up. A second later, though, he smiled at me and went back to twisting the streamers with the Australian flag on them, but it was like he'd been about to say something, then stopped himself. It was amazing how quickly you could learn these kinds of things about another person when you're trapped together in a small room filled with Australian paraphernalia.

"What?"

"Nothing," he said quickly, climbing down from the ladder and moving it forward a few feet. "Just—J.J. told me you were going to North-western."

I rolled my eyes, wishing J.J. would stay out of my business. "Well, I'm not. I got accepted there, but I'm going here."

"Got it." Bill nodded, then reached up and gave the streamers another twist. "Well, it's too bad. If you were in Chicago too, we could hang out and you could lecture me some more about koalas." I smiled at that as Bill descended the ladder. "Think we're good?"

I looked around the room. Basically, it looked like Australia had thrown up on it. There were animal pictures and photos of Australian landmarks everywhere you looked. Who knew why this Clay kid loved Australia so much, but clearly he did, and would not be disappointed when he saw his birthday decorations. "I think we're good."

Bill folded up his ladder and we started gathering Linnie and Rodney's decorations, carefully loading them into a giant Where There's A Will canvas bag—it seemed like Bill's uncle sure was into his monogramming. "Thanks so much for helping out, Charlie," Bill said as he slung the bag over his shoulder. "I couldn't have done this without you."

"And if you had," I said, picking up the two largest blown-up pictures, the ones that hadn't fit in the bag, "you would have put *all* the marsupials in the wrong place."

I heard Bill laugh as he followed me out the door. As we crossed the main Indoor Xtreme floor, I saw how much things had changed since we'd gotten there. It was practically deserted when I arrived, but now the techno music was thumping, there were kids on the skate ramp and bike jumps, and there was a long line for the paintball course. My hands were full and I couldn't reach into my pocket to check my phone, but I realized school must have let out for the day—which meant I needed to hurry if I was going to make it home and get ready for the Pearce in time.

"I'm going to have to get home before going to the museum—will you be able to get these set up at the Inn?"

Bill nodded. "Not a problem." And even though he was carrying much more than I was, he somehow managed to pull the door open for me. I'd just stepped outside when my phone rang. I suddenly remembered I hadn't gotten back to Siobhan when she said she needed to talk to me, and felt a wave of guilt hit me. But it wasn't Siobhan—my sister's contact picture was flashing across the screen as I answered the call.

"Hey, Lin."

"Where are you?" she asked, her voice high-pitched and stressed out.

"Um, I'm heading back now," I said, exchanging a glance with Bill, hoping something else hadn't gone wrong with the seating arrangements. "Everything's fine with the rehearsal dinner decorations!"

"Forget the decorations," Linnie snapped, and I didn't respond, even though I had a feeling she would *not* have been happy if her rehearsal dinner had been Australia-themed. "Did you know about this?"

"About what?"

Through the phone, I could hear Linnie take a breath, like she was trying to calm herself down. "About the *dog*."

CHAPTER 11
Or, Bankruptcy

I STARED AT THE BEAGLE, WHO WAS SITTING IN the center of the front hall, staring steadily back at me. Then I looked from Danny, who was next to me, to my sister, who was pacing in front of the door, her arms folded across her chest. "This isn't good."

The dog looked like he was just a little older than a puppy—his face still had that soft roundness to it, and his paws seemed a little oversize. He was brown, with black and white spots and long, swinging ears that seemed too big for his head. He had a wet, black nose that was twitching as he looked around, like he was trying to figure out where, exactly, he had landed.

"You *think*?" Linnie asked, then sneezed. She'd gotten me up to speed on the dog situation while I drove home. He'd been dropped off by a volunteer from a shelter two towns over. Apparently, it was *GMA*'s idea to have a beagle standing in for Waffles during our interview. He was a rescue, and up for adoption—there would be information on the *GMA* website and across the bottom of the screen about how he could be adopted. They'd even named him Waffles to appeal to die-hard *GCS* fans. Jill had apparently cleared this with my mother months ago, who had forgotten to mention any of it to us. I was fine with a beagle at the interview, and happy that it might help a dog find a home. What I didn't understand was why he was here on Friday when the interview wasn't until Sunday.

"But why is he here now?"

"That's what I asked," Linnie said. "But the shelter's not open on Sundays, and Saturdays are their busiest days, so they decided to drop him off early."

"But . . ." I looked at the dog—Waffles, apparently. He didn't seem to be acting like a typical dog. He wasn't running around, or wagging his tail, or begging for treats. He was just sitting there, staring at me. This wasn't normal dog behavior, was it? "We have a dog now?"

"It seems that we do."

"Maybe he can count as your something borrowed," I said, and I saw my brother start to smile before he cleared his throat and put on a more serious expression.

"At least it seems like he's housebroken," Danny said, bending down to ruffle the top of Waffles's head. The dog just stared at Danny, looking a little affronted, like his personal space had just been invaded.

"I didn't need this on top of the tent thing." Linnie ran her hands through her hair.

"What tent thing?"

"Apparently Clementine ordered the wrong kind," Danny said, shooting me a look. "But Will's taking care of it, and there's a new one coming tomorrow."

"So that sounds good," I said, trying to put a good spin on this for my sister as I silently cursed Clementine. "Will can handle everything tomorrow. And this way, there's less of an opportunity for dad to sabotage it."

Linnie gave me a tiny smile just as the alarm let out a single, long *beeeeeeep*. It wasn't as loud as it had been this morning, but it was still loud enough to make me cover my ears instinctively. The dog leaped to his feet and ran in the direction of the kitchen, squeezing in through the gap in the swinging door.

"Oh god, the stupid alarm," Linnie said, stalking toward the kitchen.

"How's everything else going?" I asked, turning to my brother.

"Except for the dog and the tent?" Danny asked with a laugh. "It's good."

My phone started to buzz in my back pocket, and I pulled it out—and saw that it was the paper's news editor. "Hey, Ali."

"Where are you?" she hissed, keeping her voice low.

"I told you I couldn't make the editorial meeting," I said, but a second later I felt my stomach drop. I *had* texted Ali to tell her that. Hadn't I?

"No, you didn't," she said, her voice getting a little louder. "We've been waiting for you for half an hour!"

"Look, I'm sorry," I said, very aware that Danny was standing a few feet away from me and could hear every word of this conversation. "But you can run the meeting, can't you? I mean, if you're going to be editor in chief next year . . ."

"But . . . did you just forget?" She sounded more baffled than mad now. "I mean—"

"My sister's getting married and I'm dealing with some family stuff," I said, taking a few steps away from my brother. "But I'm sure you can handle things. And we can talk through the final issue on Monday."

There was a long, loaded pause before Ali spoke again. "Sure," she said, and even though I couldn't see her, it was like I could practically hear her rolling her eyes as she hung up.

I dropped my phone in my pocket and turned to see my brother looking at me, his arms folded over his chest. "What?"

"Nothing," he said, but in a way that clearly meant *something*. "I just think—"

Beeeeeeeeeep. The sound came from the kitchen again, and this time it didn't stop. Danny headed toward the kitchen, and I followed behind him—but stopped short once I crossed the threshold.

There were just too many people in the room.

My dad and J.J. were by the door, hunched over the alarm panel, which was still making the low, loud beeping sound. Linnie was standing at the island with Max. Mrs. Daniels and Aunt Liz were sitting at one end of the kitchen table, and the General was on the other end. He had a pair of reading glasses on and was methodically filling out place cards. If the sound of the alarm was bothering him, it wasn't apparent to me, as he continued to write steadily. I didn't see my mom or Rodney, which was a good thing, since I was pretty sure we were at capacity.

"What did you do?" Linnie yelled at J.J., her hands clamped over her ears.

"Nothing," J.J. yelled back. "I'm trying to fix it." He stared at the panel for a moment, then smacked the side of it. The alarm immediately shut off, the flashing lights on the panel going dark, but a second later, I realized I could still hear the *eeeeee* sound.

I looked around and saw the dog standing under the kitchen table, his head back, howling softly, making a noise that wasn't exactly the sound of the alarm, but was more like he was harmonizing with it.

"Is that the dog?" Linnie asked, walking over to him, then promptly sneezing three times.

Maybe it was just Linnie getting closer, or maybe it was her sneezing, but at any rate, Waffles stopped howling mid-note and retreated under the kitchen table, near Mrs. Daniels's feet, turning around twice before lying down, resting his head on his paws, and looking out into the kitchen, like he wasn't quite sure about this place and wasn't about to take his eyes off us if he could help it.

"Nicely done," my dad said, clapping J.J. on the shoulder.

"It's going to be fixed, though, right?" Linnie asked. "We're not just going to rely on J.J. hitting this thing in the middle of the wedding?"

"The alarm company promised they'd send someone first thing in the morning," my dad assured her. "It'll be fixed way before the wedding." Linnie nodded, then sneezed three more times.

"I thought you were only allergic to cats," Danny said, crossing to the fridge and pulling out a can of Coke. "Is it dogs now too?"

"You're allergic to cats?" Max asked, and Linnie nodded.

"But I've never had an issue with dogs. We were dog sitting for a friend last month, and I was fine."

"Maybe you're getting sick," J.J. volunteered, and my dad shot him a look.

"I'm *not* getting sick," Linnie said, glaring at him.

"Of course not," Danny said, whacking J.J. on the back of the head as he came over to the fridge. "I'm sure it's just . . . seasonal allergies."

"Right!" I jumped in. "It's probably just the . . . pollen."

"You'll be fine by tomorrow."

The kitchen door swung open and Brooke stepped into the kitchen. "Danny?" she called, looking around. She had changed out of the outfit she'd been in when she arrived this morning and was now wearing a cream-colored dress with lace sleeves, her hair pulled up into a knot, and another pair of four-inch heels, this time in pale pink. My brother gave her a wave, and she started across the kitchen toward him, but stopped when she spotted the dog.

"Look at this *puppy*!" she said, her voice rising in pitch and her face lighting up. "He's so precious! Hello, buddy," Brooke said, bending down to meet him at his level. "Aren't you just the cutest?" The dog looked at Brooke solemnly for a moment, like he was considering this, but then his tail started wagging very slightly. I wasn't sure I'd ever seen a dog with a poker face, but this one seemed to be coming close.

"Whose dog is this?" she asked, scratching his ears as she looked around.

"He's a loaner for the weekend," J.J. said.

"Wait, what?"

"Okay!" I looked over and saw my mother coming down the kitchen stairs, dressed in the black pantsuit she always wore when she was doing events or presentations. "We need to leave for the Pearce in ten minutes, so . . ." She stopped and looked around. "Why isn't anyone ready?" she asked, throwing up her hands.

"I'm ready," J.J. said, brushing some crumbs off his T-shirt.

My mother just looked at him. "No. Go up and change. You too, Charlie."

"I was going to," I protested.

"Then do it, please," she said, shaking her head. I glanced at the kitchen clock and realized that I did have to get moving. I hurried out of the kitchen and was halfway across the front hall when there was a loud, insistent knocking on the door.

I pulled it open and saw Don standing there, his arms folded across his chest and his face redder than normal.

"I need to talk to your mother or father," Don sputtered. "Because this is just *unacceptable*."

"Um, what is? *Dad!*" I yelled toward the kitchen. "Could you come here?"

"I am retired," Don said, shaking his head. "And I need a certain amount of peace and quiet. And—"

"Twice in one day," my dad said as he joined me. "How nice for us. Did you need something, Don?"

"Yes," Don said, pushing his way inside. "I need you all to keep it down over here or I'm going to call the police with a noise complaint. There are trucks coming and going, a dog barking, your alarm going off—"

I backed away slowly, more than happy to leave this conversation— when my dad and Don were left alone together, things very quickly devolved into trading insults about begonias. I turned and hurried up the stairs, taking them two at a time.

By the time I'd changed into my dress and hurriedly applied some makeup, everyone else who was going to the museum—Linnie, Rodney, my parents, Danny, Brooke (apparently), and J.J.—was waiting for me on the driveway. My mother had extended the offer to come to the Pearce with us to the rest of the people staying in the house, but everyone else had decided to stay behind—to rest after their travels (The Danielses) or greet the other people who'd be coming in (Aunt Liz), or get into a slightly altered mental state (Max).

"Finally," my mother said as I hurried to meet the group, barefoot and carrying my heels.

"Sorry," I said, smoothing back my hair and hoping it looked more or less presentable. I was terrible at doing my own hair, and not much better at my makeup, so I was very relieved there would be professionals coming tomorrow who would take care of both of those things for me.

"I think we can do this in two cars," my mother said. "Danny, why don't you take Brooke, Charlie, and J.J., and Linnie and Rodney can ride with me and your father?"

We'd just started to head to our separate cars when a taxi pulled into the driveway. I figured it was just one of the bridesmaids arriving early, until the taxi door opened and my uncle Stu—my dad's younger brother, who was generally agreed to be the Cheapest Man Alive—got out.

"Hello, Grants!" Stu called, waving. "This is a nice welcoming committee."

I glanced at my parents, who seemed just as baffled by this as I was. Stu wasn't in the wedding party and wasn't coming to the rehearsal dinner. My mom had invited out-of-town guests to come by the house tonight for pizza while we'd be at the rehearsal dinner, but we were still a good few hours away from that.

Stu hoisted his suitcase out of the cab, then walked toward us, smiling broadly. Stu looked like a slightly scrunched-down version of my dad—shorter and rounder, with less hair. Their relationship was somewhat strained by the fact that Stu had gone bankrupt twice in the last decade and my father had been the one to bail him out. "Nice to see everyone!" he said, pulling my dad into a hug and kissing my mom on the cheek, then ruffling J.J.'s hair. He noticed Brooke and held out his hand. "Hey there. I'm Stuart Grant. Uncle of this lovely bride-to-be. You here for the wedding too?"

"Um." The cabdriver got out of his car, and I saw it was the same guy from before, the one who'd recognized the house. "Sir? You didn't pay the fare."

"Ah," Stu said, nodding as he patted his pockets. He turned to my dad. "I don't suppose you could handle that, could you, Jeff? I'm fresh out of cash."

"We take cards, sir," the driver called, but my uncle seemed not to hear him.

"Thanks, brother," he said, giving my dad a punch on the shoulder. "I appreciate it."

"Wait a second," my dad said, shaking his head.

"I guess we thought you'd go to the Inn first," my mother said, glancing down at his suitcase, a strained smile on her face. My mother had never been a huge fan of my uncle Stu, not since he'd invited the random strangers he'd been playing golf with the day of their wedding to attend the reception, all without telling my parents.

"I just need thirty-five fifty," the driver said, a sigh somewhere in his voice.

"My brother's handling it," Stu said, clapping my dad on the back. "So I'll just get settled in inside, how 'bout that?"

"Settled in?" my dad asked, his voice a bit strangled. "Why . . . ? I mean, what do you mean?"

"I take cash," the driver said, raising his voice to talk over us. "All major credit cards . . . One guy even gave me a check once. . . ."

"I mean settled in!" Stu said heartily. "What do you think? I've come for my niece's wedding."

"I didn't *want* to take the check," the taxi driver went on, shaking his head. "But what was I going to do? And it worked out in the end, like, it didn't bounce or anything, so I guess I take checks now too. . . ."

"But . . ." Linnie glanced at my mother. "We thought you were staying at the Inn."

"The Inn?" My uncle made a *forget about it* gesture. "Why waste good money so that they can charge you for bathrobes?"

"They only charge you for the bathrobes if you take them," J.J. pointed out, but my uncle kept going.

"I just figured I'd bunk with you. You know I'm not picky—just put me anywhere."

"I can take a combination of cash and charge," the driver continued, sounding more and more exasperated.

"I've got it," Danny said, reaching into his pocket for his wallet and peeling off some bills, then handing them to the driver. As soon as the driver got the money, he started backing down the driveway, like he didn't want to spend any more time with us than he had to.

"We have to get going to a function," my mother said, looking at her watch again. "But—"

"I'll get Stu settled in," Rodney said. "And then I'll meet you at the Pearce. How about that?"

"Thanks, son," my dad said, giving Rodney a smile. "We appreciate it."

"What's this function?" my uncle asked, raising an eyebrow. "The kind with an open bar?"

"No," my mother, father, and Linnie said simultaneously.

"It's at an art museum," I explained, and my uncle immediately looked less interested.

"I'll leave you to that, then," he said, clapping Rodney on the back. "Lead on!"

We watched Rodney and Stu heading up to the house, and when they'd disappeared inside, my mother turned to us. "Okay," she said, taking a deep breath. "Let's do this."

CHAPTER 12

Or, The Family You Never Had

O KAY, IF YOU COULD ALL JUST SMILE . . . AND
hold it . . ." I held my smile even though my cheeks were
starting to ache, as the photographer from the *Stanwich Sentinel*
snapped away. It was all of us and Rodney, my mother in the center,
holding the plaque that had been presented to her when the governor
had named her, during the ceremony, a Connecticut citizen deserving
of exemplary recognition. We were standing in the central lobby of the
Pearce Museum, in front of the marble fountain, and I tried not to blink
too much as the camera clicked.

I'd been coming to the Pearce my whole life—for school trips and
special exhibits and kids' art classes. It consisted mostly of the collection
of Mary Anne Pearce, and it reflected her very eclectic tastes. I'd always
loved how varied it was—how there would be a unicorn tapestry next to
a Warhol, next to a Kara Walker. The museum had continued collect-
ing after she'd passed away, but was more focused now on exhibits. I'd
seen the banners for them when I'd driven past, but it had been exciting to walk up the white marble steps today and see the one hanging
above me, huge and blowing back and forth in the wind—ELEANOR

The ceremony had been lovely. Governor Walker had introduced my mother, thanking her for putting Stanwich on the map—or at least the funny pages—which was a joke that sounded like some speech-writer had written it for him, but nonetheless got a round of polite laughter. Then my mother had stood up and given her speech, thanking her syndicate and her team, and all the readers who'd been following the adventures of the fictional Grants over the years. And then she'd thanked us, her family, for being her inspiration, and also for letting her take liberties with our lives. She'd said how much it had meant for her to have her family with her today, but as she did, my eyes fell on the empty seat next to me.

A row of chairs had been reserved for us, but there was one extra, and I knew my mother had kept it aside in the hopes that Mike would show up. I hadn't had any expectations that he would, but somehow, seeing the empty seat was bothering me more than I'd known it would, and finally I turned my back on it, angling myself slightly so it wouldn't be in my peripheral vision.

There was a large crowd—every seat had been filled during the speeches, and while we smiled our way through the pictures, people were milling about on the other side of the lobby, where there was a bar and coffee station and waiters circled with trays of pastries and lemon squares. The exhibition would officially open after the reception was over. From where I was standing, I could see the gallery where the exhibit was, a ribbon stretched across the entrance.

"And last one, over here . . . ," the photographer said, and I brought my attention back to him. "I think we're good." He pulled the camera away and squinted at the viewfinder. "If I could now get just Eleanor and Governor Walker?"

We all took a few steps away as the governor stepped forward, already smiling at my mother. I noticed his security detail, who'd been doing a very good job of blending into the background, now came a little bit closer.

Danny walked over to join Brooke, who'd been standing alone by the coffee station, and J.J., Linnie, Rodney, and I wandered away from the fountain. "Have you see the girl with the lemon squares?" J.J. asked. "I saw her like twenty times when we were getting our pictures taken and now she's vanished."

I looked over and saw my mother and the governor shaking hands while the camera clicked. "I think it went well, don't you?"

"I guess I thought Mike might show up," Linnie said, lowering her voice as though she was worried about being overheard. "I mean, I wasn't expecting it, but . . ."

"Why should Mike do anything for someone else?" I asked, my voice coming out with a bitter edge. "Why should he think about anyone other than himself?"

"Charlie." Rodney shook his head.

"He did come for the wedding," J.J. pointed out. I looked around for Danny, to see if he would back me up, but he was still talking to Brooke. I glanced over and saw the photographer rearranging my mom and the governor, this time bringing my dad in—and I noticed that Andie Walker, the governor's daughter, was starting to head in our direction.

I didn't know Andie super well—I'd been a sophomore at Stanwich High when she was a senior. But after her father won in November, I'd reached out, to see if she'd be willing to do an interview with the *Pilgrim*. She'd agreed, and the feature I'd written on her for the paper—*Walker Hits Her Stride*—about her relationship with her dad, her life at Yale, her boyfriend who was a fantasy novelist, had been picked up by some national outlets, which had pretty much been the highlight of my year.

Now, I gave her a quick smile and a nod as she passed, and she returned it automatically, then stopped, tilting her head to the side. "Hey," she said, looking at me. "It's Charlotte, right? From the paper?"

"That's right," I said, trying not to be too pleased that she remembered me. Politicians' kids were probably taught to do that kind of stuff automatically.

"Well, it's nice to see you again," she said, then seemed to notice the three other people who were watching this exchange. "Hi, I'm Andie Walker," she said to the collective group. She gestured to the cute, glasses-wearing guy next to her. "And this is my boyfriend, Clark McCallister."

Both Rodney and J.J. made a weird strangled sound, like they'd simultaneously gotten something stuck in their throats. I looked at them, wondering what was going on. "You guys okay?"

"You're . . . ," Rodney started, his eyes wide. "You're C. B. McCallister, right? The novelist?"

Clark smiled. "Uh, yeah," he said. "That's me."

"Okay," J.J. said, walking up to him and tugging him a few steps away, not seeming to notice—or care—that Clark was still holding Andie's hand. "So, I have to know about the ending of *Realm*. There's going to be another one, right? You're not going to leave us hanging like that?"

"The new book comes out in a month," he said, and I saw Andie shoot him a small, proud smile. "It's probably a five-book cycle now, not a trilogy. And I promise all your questions will be answered."

"But tell me," Rodney said, joining them a few steps away from the rest of us, "because I never quite understood Ward's backstory. Was he supposed to be evil from the beginning?"

Andie turned back to me, shaking her head. "This could go on for a while."

"I'm really sorry about that," Linnie said, glancing over to where their three-person group had moved even farther away, and it looked like J.J. and Rodney had Clark cornered, both of them asking him questions simultaneously, J.J. gesturing wide as he did so.

Andie waved this away. "It happens a lot. His book tour was insane."

She turned to me with the practiced ease of someone who's gotten very good at small talk with people she didn't really know that well. "So where are you going to school next year?"

"Here," I said, then shook my head a second later. "I mean Stanwich, not the Pearce."

"Oh, cool," Andie said, nodding. "That's where Clark went. He was there for a year before he transferred to Yale. I know he really liked it."

I nodded, and before the silence that fell got too awkward, I gestured to my sister. "So, Linnie's getting married tomorrow."

"Congratulations," Andie said, then paused. "Wait, I think that's for the groom. Best wishes?"

"Either one," Linnie said with a smile, but then it faded as she looked down at her watch. "There's a ton to do, so I'm hoping we can sneak out of here soon."

"You're not going to stay and see the exhibit?" I was well aware of the schedule we were on, but I'd imagined all of us looking at the comics and the art that depicted our family, walking through the rooms of the exhibit together.

"I can come back another time," Linnie said, raising an eyebrow at me, "you know, when it's *not* the day before my wedding."

"I actually don't think we can stay either," Andie said. She looked over at her father and I could see the governor shaking hands with both my parents—it appeared that the photo taking had finally come to an end. "I know my dad has a fundraiser to get to." She walked a few steps away and tugged on Clark's hand. "Sorry to interrupt," she said, "but we need to get going."

Clark just looked at her. "You just want to see Duke, don't you?"

"I haven't seen my dog in two months!" she said. "And video chatting just isn't the same."

"She loves that dog more than me," Clark said to J.J. and Rodney, shaking his head.

"Were you waiting for me to disagree with that?" Andie asked, and Clark laughed as the governor approached us.

"Hello," he said with a wide smile that I recognized from the cover of *Newsweek* when he won his election. "You must be the rest of the Grants."

We all just stood there looking at him for a moment, and it was Linnie who remembered her manners and stopped being impressed the fastest. "Thank you so much for coming, sir," she said.

"It was my pleasure," Governor Walker said easily. Then he dropped his voice a little lower, leaning closer to us. "I'm actually a *big* fan. I read it every morning, right after the political news."

"This is true," Andie said. She raised her eyebrows at her father. "We good to go?"

"She misses her dog," the governor said with a smile. "And unfortunately, I've got a schedule to keep. It was nice to meet you all. Take care!" He gave us a politician's smile and he, Andie, and Clark headed for the exit, the governor laughing at something his daughter said and his security team following behind them at a discreet distance.

"Hey." I turned to see Danny at my elbow. He nodded toward the gallery where the exhibit was. "Want to get a private showing?"

I looked over at it, at the official-looking ribbon still stretched across the entrance. "Are we allowed?"

Danny just gave me a smile. "Follow me." He started across the marble lobby toward the exhibit. "Now," he said, lowering his voice as we passed a guard in a museum blazer who seemed more interested in his phone than in paying attention to what was happening to the priceless art around him. "What did I always tell you about sneaking into places?"

"Frown and walk fast," I said automatically.

"Exactly." We picked up our pace, and with a great deal of authority, Danny walked right up to the rope and lifted it for me to duck under, then followed behind.

I took a few steps into the gallery, letting my eyes adjust—it was a little darker in here than in the sun-filled lobby, lights positioned at intervals and shining on the artwork. Danny had walked ahead to where the exhibit started, and I hurried to catch up with him.

"Look," he said quietly to me, and I turned to face the wall in front of me, feeling my breath catch in my throat. Covering the whole wall, much more than life-size, was a picture of the Grants. It was the most famous picture of the fictional family, the one that still ran as the strip's header, from when my oldest siblings were teenagers and I was six. It was a family portrait gone wrong—my character tipping nearly upside down over Donny's arm while Lindsay shoved A.J., and Mark secretly fed cookies to Waffles. Geoff, the character based on my dad, was the only one who didn't seem to notice the chaos around him and was smiling broadly at the camera.

MEET THE GRANTS, read the sign on the wall, THE FAMILY YOU NEVER HAD.

"Wow," I said, looking around. There was text on the wall—going through the history of the strip, how my mom had started it when she was still working as a librarian, drawing pictures to entertain toddlers Danny and Linnie. How it had grown in popularity over the years, finding a global readership.

I walked farther into the gallery, looking around, trying to take it all in, even though I knew it wasn't possible on a first viewing. The whole thing was overwhelming. Because on every wall, there we all were. The exhibit looked like it was presented in chronological order, starting with my mom's early sketches, the first comics, and then the strip throughout the years, interspersed with other exhibits showing the rise of *GCS*—the magazine profiles and mentions in pop culture, pictures from late-night hosts' monologues, the T-shirts and lunch boxes and stuffed Waffles toys, the stills from the very short-lived *Grant Central Station* cartoon, which had only ever aired in Canada.

As I looked around, at the finished art next to my mom's concept sketches, at the characters that never quite took off, at the cover of *Time* with the fictional Grants on it, I felt myself start to breathe easier for the first time all day.

Because looking at these strips, I was home. This was the very best of us, up on the walls of this gallery. The strip, with its four panels and the versions of us my mother had conjured, was the most familiar sight in the world to me. I was back—back in our kitchen, all of us still at home, in the chaos and laughter and busyness that had always been part of our lives when we were all together.

Siobhan had asked me once if it was weird, seeing things that had happened to me in my life translated and fictionalized and presented to strangers for entertainment while they ate their cereal. But Cassie Grant was a character millions of readers had known about before I could even talk, much less understand what a newspaper comic was. Maybe because I'd never known a world without it, it had never seemed strange to me.

We turned the corner and saw a group of comics practically taking over a whole wall, with the reproduced image of Donny, Lindsay, and A.J. climbing a street sign, Donny with a screwdriver clenched between his teeth and A.J. doing a very poor job of being a lookout. SIGN OF CHANGE was printed on the wall above a description of the comics.

"Whoa," Danny said, looking at the wall of strips depicting highlights of the story that had gone on for nearly two months. "I . . . didn't realize they'd be featuring these," he said, sounding a little nervous.

I smiled. "I'm pretty sure the statute of limitations has run out by now."

Hanging next to the comics were the newspaper articles from the *Sentinel* that covered the hearings and court proceedings with breathless intensity, next to write-ups from *Time*, *Newsweek*, and the *Times*. I turned to Danny to tell him that I'd actually been on Grant Avenue that afternoon, but he'd already wandered away, and I hurried to catch up with him.

"That's when she was having trouble with Dad's nose," Danny said as I joined him, pointing to a comic from when I was in middle school and Cassie Grant had much better hair than I'd had in real life. I looked closer at it and laughed—sure enough, my dad's nose was completely out of proportion to the rest of him. Danny shrugged as he moved down the gallery, passing a picture of the Eisner Awards, my mother smiling as Mort Walker handed it to her and Bill Amend looked on. "I think she was mad at him for some reason and that's why she did it."

"She wouldn't do that."

Danny raised an eyebrow as I fell into step next to him. "Why do you think she gave Donny that bad perm when I was in college?"

"What did you do to deserve that?"

"I'll tell you when you're older."

"Danny!"

"Shh. We're in a museum."

We both stopped in front of a wall that seemed to be representing the period when I was finishing elementary school and Danny and Linnie were finishing college. "Oh man," I said, pointing to five framed strips grouped together. "Remember that? The lake house?" These strips were out of a month's worth my mother had done about our vacation in the Catskills, part of her collection *Go Jump in a Lake*, which had been one of her bestsellers. There were four dailies and a Sunday, and just looking at them, it was like I could practically hear the cicadas, see the fireflies and the orangey pink of the sunsets. "That was such a great trip."

"Are you kidding?" Danny shook his head. "It was the worst trip *ever*."

"No," I said, looking back at the strips. Cassie and Mark were catching fireflies at dusk, Donny and A.J. were racing their kayaks around the lake, and everyone was sitting on a beach, watching Fourth of July fireworks. "It was really fun."

"*They* had fun," Danny said, gesturing toward the two-dimensional Grants. "We were miserable. It rained the whole time. Like the *whole* time. And the ceiling of my room leaked. And that was the month J.J. decided to be a vegan, and Linnie was furious Rodney couldn't be there and spent the whole time calling him in Hawaii from the landline—because there was no reception—and ran up a nine-hundred-dollar phone bill."

Suddenly, memories were starting to come back to me, crowding out the ones I would have sworn, only minutes before, had been actual and true. The room I'd been sharing with Linnie had been small and smelled musty. Our dad had insisted that a little rain wasn't going to keep him from enjoying the outdoors, and he'd caught a terrible cold and had to stay in bed most of the trip. Mike had been allergic to something—we'd never been able to figure out what—and sneezed for two weeks straight.

"There was only one movie," I said slowly, remembering. The other memories of the trip were starting to fade out. These memories, I was now realizing, had never been mine. They'd never been real, just ink and paper that I'd somehow folded into my real life, a revisionist history that I'd bought without a second thought. "Right?" I asked, looking up at Danny.

He laughed. "That's right! The DVD player was jammed, and we couldn't watch anything we'd brought with us. We were stuck watching *Police Academy 4* all week."

I laughed too, then clapped my hand over my mouth—the sound was louder than I'd expected in the quiet gallery. How could I have forgotten? Since it was all we'd had to watch, and we were stuck inside all day due to the rain, we watched it more times than anyone should reasonably watch any Police Academy movie, let alone the fourth one in the franchise. And how it was so bad that, with enough viewings, it came around to being good again, and then to somehow being deeply profound.

Danny led the way though the gallery, and I was still smiling as I caught up with him. But when I saw what was in front of me, I felt the

MORGAN MATSON

smile slide off my face. I glanced at my brother and saw that he'd also realized what this was.

Anyone else here would have just thought it was a sampling of my mother's art. You wouldn't have known that this handful of strips was anything more than another misadventure in the Grant family. You wouldn't have known that these were the strips that had wrecked so much and were the reason Mike hadn't been home in eighteen months.

As I read these comics I knew by heart, I couldn't help but feel the distance between what my mother was writing about and what had actually happened. Because it hadn't started this way, the way she'd written in her version of things, where she got to make the decisions.

It had all started at midnight, with cookies.

"Are they done?"

I leaned over to peer into the oven, then straightened up and turned to Siobhan. "Almost."

"Excellent." Siobhan grinned as she pushed herself up to sit on the kitchen counter. It was after midnight, very early on a Sunday morning in January. Siobhan had slept over, and we'd been up watching movies and talking, and about the time we were starting to think about going to sleep, right on schedule, we both decided we wanted a snack.

We'd crept downstairs, trying not to wake either my parents or J.J., who'd come home for the weekend. Mike was still home too, since he was still on winter break from Northwestern, which seemed incredibly unfair, since I'd been back at school since the second of January. But I was pretty sure we didn't have to worry about waking Mike up—he'd gone out earlier and I hadn't heard him come back in.

"They smell like they're ready," Siobhan said, pushing herself up to sit on the counter.

She wasn't wrong—the whole room was starting to smell like fresh-baked cookies—and I checked the timer just as the kitchen door swung open with gusto and J.J. strode in, wearing his monogrammed pajamas. "I smelled cookies," he announced, looking around. His eyes lit up when he saw the oven. *"Yes,"* he said, starting over toward it.

"No," I said, taking a step in front of him, blocking his view. "They're not ready yet."

"They smell ready," he insisted.

"That's what I just said." Siobhan gave me an *I told you so* look.

"Charlie?" I looked over to see my dad standing in the doorway, squinting at me, then patting his head and pulling down his glasses. "What's going on?"

"We're baking cookies," I said, glancing at the clock and starting to feel guilty. "Did we wake you?"

"Not the cooking," he said with a yawn as he knotted the tie on his plaid robe, the one he'd had forever. "It was someone running down the stairs outside our room." I pointed at J.J., and my dad sighed.

"How is it that you are *still* waking me up at night?"

"I think you should be happy," J.J. said. "I mean, other people's children leave and never come back again. Aren't you happy we stick around?"

"Not right now," my dad muttered, rubbing his eyes.

"What is happening?" I turned to the kitchen doorway and saw my mom, in her pink fluffy robe, the one Danny had bought her for Christmas last year. "Jeff?"

"J.J. woke me up," my dad said, pointing at my brother.

"Charlie was baking cookies, and the smell woke *me* up," he insisted, pointing at me.

My mother just shook her head, then paused. "I think they're ready," she said, just as the kitchen timer went off.

"That was very cool," Siobhan said, her eyes wide. "How did you do that?" My mom just winked at her, and I headed over to the oven.

Which was how, ten minutes later, we were all sitting around the kitchen table in our pajamas, with still-warm cookies in front of us. "I feel like I'm living in your comic strip," Siobhan said as she broke off a piece of her cookie. "Like, this is something that would totally happen."

My mother smiled. "We'd need to get the dog involved, though."

I took a breath to agree just as the kitchen door slammed open. I jumped and looked over—and froze. Mike was standing in the doorway, totally naked except for a car floor mat pressed in front of his crotch.

"Uh . . . ," Mike said, his eyes wider than I'd ever seen them as he looked around and clutched the floor mat with both hands. "What—what are you guys all doing up?"

"Hey, Mike," Siobhan said, waving cheerfully, not even trying to hide the fact that she was checking him out.

Mike saw her and turned even redder. "Hi, Siobhan," he muttered. He edged over to the staircase, apparently trying to move as fast as possible without showing us anything.

"What are you—" J.J. said, then started laughing so hard he had to stop and take a breath. "What are you *doing?*"

"Nothing!" Mike yelled as he made a run for the stairs and we all started laughing.

"Son," my dad yelled after him. "Put some clothes on and then come down and give us an explanation, hm?"

"We have cookies," I yelled after him, then turned to Siobhan, who was giggling. "Oh my god."

"Of all the times to not have my phone to take pictures," J.J. said, shaking his head. "Do you *know* what kind of blackmail shots I could have gotten?"

"Think he'll come back?" my mom asked. "Or is he going to sneak out the front door and never return?"

"I'd call it even odds," my dad said as I picked up my phone and pressed the button to FaceTime Linnie.

"What?" she asked as she answered, squinting at me blearily. "It's after midnight."

"Yeah," J.J. said, leaning over to look at the screen. "And you guys are still youngish! Why aren't you out clubbing?"

"What?" Rodney appeared next to Linnie, looking just as sleepy and confused—and somehow unfinished, without his glasses on. "Why is J.J. talking about clubbing?"

"I have no idea," Linnie said. "Charlie, why did you call?"

"Because Mike just streaked across the kitchen wearing nothing but a floor mat," I said gleefully.

"What?"

"Did your sister really need to know about this?" my mother asked.

"Is *everyone* awake?" Linnie asked, and I turned the camera around.

"Pretty much," my dad said. "Nice pj's, Rodney."

"Thanks," Rodney muttered, putting on his glasses.

"Ah!" J.J. said, smiling, and I looked over to see Mike standing by the kitchen stairs, now wearing sweatpants and a sweatshirt, his face still bright red. "He returns."

"I have so many questions," my mother said, shaking her head. "You *were* wearing clothing when you left earlier tonight, weren't you?"

"Do we really need to go into this?" Mike asked, shooting my dad a desperate look.

"Yes," we all said—even Linnie, over the phone.

"What's going on?" she asked.

"Why are we talking to Linnie?"

"I FaceTimed them," I explained, and Mike closed his eyes for a second.

"You didn't want to call Danny? Get the whole family involved?"

"There's an idea." I looked around. "Anyone else have a phone?"

"That's okay," my dad said, leaning back in his chair. "I'm sure we'll fill him in later. Michael, do you want to . . . uh . . . enlighten us?"

Mike looked like he would have rather done almost anything else at the moment, but he took a step toward us anyway. "Okay. So, um . . . I was over at Corrine's. . . ."

J.J. and I groaned, and over the phone, I heard Linnie do the same. "Can we not do this now?" Mike asked.

"Well, I think it's nice when people stay together from high school into college," my mother said, even though I knew for a fact she felt the exact opposite. "It shows an impressive level of commitment."

"So you were at Corrine's," J.J. prompted, taking a bite of his cookie. "Proceed."

"Well. Um. So we were . . . hanging out . . ." There was a long pause, and then we all seemed to realize what he meant at the same moment.

"God," I said, shaking my head.

"I really didn't need to hear this," my dad said.

"Anyway," Mike said, his face going a duller and duller red, like he was slowly morphing into a brick, "Corrine's parents are really strict, so when they came home early, I kind of . . . climbed out the window."

"Naked," Siobhan clarified helpfully, and Mike looked down at the floor like he was hoping it might swallow him up.

"So Corrine tossed my phone and keys and clothes out after me," Mike said, speaking very fast now, like he was just hoping to get to the end of this. "And I got the keys and the phone. But my clothes ended up . . . stuck in a tree?"

My mother made a kind of snorting sound, and I looked over and saw that her chin was trembling, like she was trying very hard not to laugh. "Well. Michael. You are an adult now and can make your own choices. But we still don't approve." She looked at my dad, who nodded, even though I could see he was fighting a smile.

"Yes," he said, then cleared his throat. "You shouldn't . . . shouldn't . . ."

"Shouldn't jump out of windows without your clothes on?" Linnie finished, then started giggling.

"It's not funny," Mike said, shaking his head, and that was enough to set me off.

"Oh my god," I said, laughing, "what—what did you do on the drive home? Were you just driving around naked? What if you'd gotten pulled over?"

"Have a cookie," Siobhan said, pushing the plate over to him.

"Yeah," J.J. said. "You deserve it."

"Thanks," Mike said, coming over to sit next to J.J. "If we could never mention this again, ever, I'd be really happy." He reached for a cookie.

"So . . . are your clothes still up in the tree?" Linnie asked, still chuckling.

Mike nodded. "My shoes, too. I guess . . . Corrine will try to get them down in the morning?"

I started giggling again as I reached for a cookie, broke it in half, and held out the other half to Siobhan, who took it.

"But seriously," Mike said, turning to our mom. "This doesn't go in the strip." My mother hesitated, and it was like I could see it playing out on her face—she was already lining up the panels and the punch lines in her mind. "Really," Mike said, not a trace of a smile on his face any longer. "Corrine's parents are super strict."

"That must be nice," my dad said under his breath.

"They'd freak out if they knew I was over there when they were gone," he said. "Mom? Promise?"

"Mom won't put it in," Linnie said around a yawn. "Well, this has been fun, but I think we'll say good night now."

"Night," we all chorused, and a second later, my screen went dark.

"And if we could also not tell Danny?" Mike asked hopefully.

"Scoff," said J.J.

"I think it's going to be hard to keep this one under wraps," my dad said, shaking his head. "But it'll stay just in the family." Siobhan cleared her throat. "And Siobhan."

"Well," Mike said, getting up and edging toward the stairs. "I'm going to bed and to try and forget this ever happened. Night."

"Don't forget to put the floor mat back in the car," my dad called after him.

"And maybe clean it first?" J.J. called, which started me laughing again.

I had thought that would be it—Mike went to Evanston to begin his winter term, J.J. went back to Pittsburgh, and I returned to being the only kid left in the house. It was about seven weeks later, in February, that Mike called when I leaving school, juggling three separate canvas bags and a stack of books, cursing the fact that the junior parking lot was so much farther away than the senior lot.

"Hey," I said, tucking the phone under my chin after I answered it. "What's up?"

"Have you seen today's strip?" Mike asked, his voice tight.

"No." I stopped walking. "What about it?" My mom had just wrapped up a storyline about Lindsay and Lawrence (the name of Rodney's doppelgänger) in a fight with their neighbors, so I had no idea who she was focusing on next—she tended to rotate the storylines between characters.

"Read it." Mike's voice was serious enough that I set my bags down, put him on speaker, and pulled up the *Sentinel* website on my phone. Feeling my eyes start to get blurry from the cold, I read it. The panels intercut between me spending the night at home watching TV, with Waffles and a bowl of popcorn, and Mark, home from college, carefully getting ready and then finally showing up on the doorstep of his girl-friend, Alice. Alice had long been a fan favorite, and my mother had put her in the strip right around the time Mike started dating Corrine. But even though Alice physically looked like Corrine, she was the complete opposite personality-wise. Alice was sweet, nicer, and got along great with the family, like my mom was trying to will into being the girlfriend she wished Mike had.

"Okay," I said, reading it once again, and then a third time, wondering if I'd missed something. "What about it?" I asked, picking up my bags and walking to my car—it was really getting too cold outside to keep standing around.

"She's writing about what happened."

"You mean the car mat thing?" I looked at my phone again. "This could be about anything."

"Bet you twenty bucks," Mike said, his voice clipped and angry. "After she promised—"

"Let's not jump to conclusions," I said, getting into the car. "At least see where she's going with it."

"Wow, you're taking her side. I'm utterly, utterly shocked."

"Mike—" But I didn't get to say anything else, because he'd already hung up.

I wanted Mike to be wrong. I wanted this to be something my mother wouldn't have done. But Mike had sensed it from the beginning, and the story started unfolding, nearly exactly as Mike had described it to us, culminating in his—or rather, Mark's—near-naked run through the kitchen. (In the *GCS* version, he interrupted book club night.)

The night the story line ended, Mike called as I was emptying the dishwasher. My dad answered and put him on speaker—what he always did whenever any of my siblings called home, so that we could all talk. "It's Mike," he called, and my mom looked up from where she was reading the paper at the kitchen table. "Hey, son," my dad said. "How's—"

"Is she there?" Mike asked, his voice shaky, the way it got when he was really angry but trying not to show it. "Is Mom there?"

"I'm here," my mother said, getting up from the table. "Are you okay?"

Mike let out a short laugh. "Um, no, *mother*, I am not okay. How could you do that to me?"

"Do what?" my dad asked.

"The strip," I said quietly.

"Yeah, the strip," Mike said through the phone, his voice getting louder and shakier. "Mom, I asked you not to put it in. I specifically asked you—"

"Put what in?" my dad asked, frowning as he put on his glasses and started flipping through the paper.

"Floor mat," I muttered. "And . . . nudity."

"Honey, I promise it's not a big deal," my mom said, leaning closer to the speaker. "When I mentioned it to my syndicate, they loved it. And I was just thinking about how funny we all found it—I mean, even you were laughing . . ."

"At something *private*," Mike snapped. "At something that I didn't want to go beyond our family. Why is that so hard for you to understand? Do you even get that this is my life? And that it's not just there for you to get material from?"

"Mike, I think you should calm down," my mother said, exchanging a look with my dad.

"Calm down? You've just wrecked my life with your comic strip!"

"I've hardly done that."

"Oh, really? Well, guess what. Corrine's parents read your stupid strip. And they figured out what happened. And she's in trouble with them and just broke up with me over it." Mike's voice cracked on the last word.

I exchanged a glance with my dad. I didn't like Corrine—none of us did—but that didn't mean I'd wanted this to happen. Not like this.

"Oh, honey." My mom had gone pale, and she put her hand over her mouth. "I didn't . . ." She took a breath. "What if I called the Nelsons? Maybe explained things?" She shot me a look, and I could see genuine regret on her face, like she hadn't realized until right this moment what the consequences might be.

"Yeah," Mike said, his tone dripping with sarcasm. "That's what I really want here. You making things better when you're the one who caused this in the first place."

"Michael," my dad said, putting down the paper. "I know you're upset, but you can't speak to your mother that way."

"Fine," Mike said. "Then I won't." And a second later, the phone went dead.

I stared at the strips in front of me, still rooted to the same spot even though Danny had wandered into the next gallery. You would have thought the resolution in the fictional world of *Grant Central Station* was the end of it. But it wasn't—nothing had been resolved as tidily as it had in four black-and-white panels.

Mike had stopped talking to our mother, but she was sure it was just a phase and would blow over. This was around the time that her newest collection was gearing up for publication, and a reporter from *USA Today* was reaching out to all of us for a human-interest piece on "Growing Up Grant." I'd e-mailed my few sentences to the reporter after clearing them with my mom and hadn't thought anything about it until I saw the interview, printed below the fold on the cover of the *USA Today* arts section.

Mike had apparently taken his opportunity to speak to a national reporter and ran with it—unloading everything he was currently feeling. He told the reporter that he loathed how our mother cannibalized our lives for strangers' enjoyment. How he always felt like he was being pushed into the mold of a perfect son in a perfect family, when the reality was much messier than that. How much he'd hated being a Grant.

I'd heard the fight he'd had with my parents the night the article came out—I'd been sitting on the kitchen stairs, hidden from view but able to hear the conversation. My dad had tried to give him a way out, suggesting that maybe he'd been misquoted. But when it became clear that Mike had meant what he'd said in the national media, every word of it, the fight really started in earnest. And even though I couldn't hear what Mike was saying, judging by my dad's yelling and my mom's crying, it was clear he wasn't doing much of anything to fix the situation, and was in fact, doubling down.

We were all mad at Mike—me more than the rest of my siblings. Even though we could all understand why he was upset, talking to *USA Today* about how much you hated your family was too much for all of us.

But I had just assumed that, eventually, it would blow over. Soon we'd all be past it, or pretend to be past it, and then it would be like it never happened. But even though Linnie mediated, my mother refused to apologize and Mike refused to apologize, and so they'd stopped talking. And then Mike stayed on campus for the summer. He claimed he was going to be taking summer courses, had already registered for his dorm, and just wanted to stay. And when the fall rolled around, he told my dad in a terse e-mail that he'd be paying his own way in college from now on, signed up for work study and took out loans. When Danny tried to tell him, over group text, just how punishing student loan debt could be, he replied that he didn't want anything that had come from *Grant Central Station*. It was like he was in a cold war with my parents, one that only escalated when he didn't come home for Thanksgiving or Christmas.

And the longer he stayed away, the harder it became to see how this would ever resolve. It was like the distance between him and my parents—especially between him and my mother—seemed to get wider and wider, so that it was like a chasm that couldn't be breached, so far apart that you couldn't even see the other side any longer, and eventually, you even forgot that it was ever there.

I looked around and saw that Danny had made his way to the end of the exhibit, and I hurried to catch up with him. As I did, I caught a glimpse of the lobby once again and saw Brooke standing on the other side of the ribbon, craning her neck, clearly trying to find out where Danny had gotten to.

And I knew I could have called out to her, or waved her in, or just pointed across the exhibit to where my brother was. But I just turned and walked over to join Danny, not letting myself look back. It wasn't asking too much to have just a little time with my brother, in an exhibit filled with our mother's art. Brooke would be fine for another minute or two. Danny gave me an easy, untroubled smile as I came to join him at the end of the exhibit. There was an empty space on the wall, reserved for where the final strip would go—it would be placed there after it ran on Sunday.

He nodded to the wall, where there was an updated portrait of all of us—a reference to the strip's header, and the portrait that was at the beginning of the exhibit. This one showed us as we were now, but in the same spots as before, and not behaving a whole lot better. Danny slung an arm around my shoulders and gestured around at the exhibit. "Look at it all," he said softly. He shook his head. "It's really something, isn't it?"

I leaned against him, resting my head against his arm as I looked at everything that was there—everything our mother had done, for good and bad, this whole world she'd brought into existence with some paper and ink. "Yeah," I said. "It really is."

CHAPTER 13
Or, Plus-One

———————————

"So, what do you think?" J.J. asked, as he rocked back on his heels. "Do you feel rehearsed?"

"Um." I glanced around the lobby of the Inn to make sure that Linnie and Rodney weren't in earshot. "Not really."

To put it mildly, the rehearsal part of the rehearsal dinner had not gone according to plan. When we'd all returned home from the Pearce, it was to find that the house had gotten a lot more crowded since we'd been gone. All the out-of-town guests, and people who would be at the wedding but weren't in the wedding party, had begun to gather in our house, taking over the kitchen and the family room, with people spilling out onto the deck. My mother had ordered a huge number of pizzas and stacked them on the counter, telling everyone to help themselves. Waffles had *not* seemed very happy about all the new people who had arrived and had escaped to the upstairs landing, his ears pressed back. I'd almost tripped over him when heading up the stairs, and he gave me a look that was incredibly put-upon, like he was despairing of his lot in life—which seemed a bit extreme to me, since only a few hours ago, he'd been in a shelter.

Because we didn't have a tent up yet, Will had tried to take us through the rehearsal in the middle of the backyard, which was empty except for the tent pegs that had already been hammered into the ground and which we were explicitly told to avoid, so we wouldn't trip over them.

But it became clear after a few minutes that the rehearsal wasn't going great. Max kept trying to run through the ceremony, but Linnie and Rodney had written their own vows and wanted to say them for the first time on their wedding day. And any rehearsal was going to have to be repeated tomorrow, since we were missing half the wedding party. Three of the bridesmaids were delayed—one on a late plane, one stuck in traffic, and one lost, driving around in circles in the back of the "world's worst Uber." Finally, it was just easier to tell them to meet us at the Inn for the rehearsal dinner. But more importantly than the bridesmaids—Mike wasn't there.

He'd texted me as I was changing into my rehearsal dinner dress—deep midnight blue, with a low neck, and a twirly, swingy skirt.

Mike

Hey can't make rehearsal see you at the dinner

As I read it, a wave of annoyance crested over me—because not only was Mike bailing, but he was expecting me to be the one to tell everyone about it. I'd sent it to the group text with the rest of my siblings and found that when I came downstairs, Linnie seemed more resigned than angry. "The bridesmaids are MIA," she said with a shrug. "And Rodney's cousin Marcus can't come until later. So it's not *that* big a deal."

But I felt it was, and even though Mike wasn't the reason the rehearsal wasn't going well, if he'd been here, there would have at least been one less unknown for tomorrow. After a few attempts, Will gave up on the rehearsal and suggested we just head over for the dinner. My mother had made sure that all the guests remaining behind were fed—Aunt Liz had promised to help keep things humming, and reorder pizza as needed—and we'd all caravanned over to the Inn.

Since we were pretty early, the private room in the restaurant was still being set up for us—but I'd texted with Bill and he'd assured me that everything was on track with the decorations. So while we waited, we were hanging out in the lobby.

I saw Linnie and Rodney standing over by the bar, with both sets of parents and Rodney's older sister, Elizabeth, and her husband, and once I'd verified they were not in earshot, I turned back to J.J. "I just hope everything goes okay tomorrow," I said, shaking my head.

"It's going to go great," someone said as they bumped me with their hip. I turned around, startled, and the next thing I knew, I was being hugged from both sides, enveloped in a cloud of perfume and spearmint gum by two of the bridesmaids—Jenny K. and Priya. When they stepped back, I saw Jenny W. standing slightly apart, and she gave me a smile.

There were five bridesmaids altogether, including me and Elizabeth, but it had never been a question that the Jennys and Priya would be in Linnie's wedding party—they'd been best friends since Dartmouth.

"Hey, guys," I said, but that was all I managed before they started talking over me.

"You look so great!" Priya said, running her hands through my hair, pulling it forward over my shoulders, then pushing it back. "Jen, doesn't she look so great?"

"She does," Jenny K. agreed, smiling at me. I'd never understood it, but the three of them always seemed to know who was talking to whom, despite the fact that two of them had the same name. People got the Jennys confused occasionally, which made no sense to me, since Jenny Kang was taller and curvy and Jenny Wellerstein was tiny and whip-thin. Priya Koorse fell somewhere in between the two of them, both in height and in temperament.

I'd gotten to know them all over the last ten years—they'd sometimes join Rodney in coming to our house for holidays, or would just show up with Linnie on a random weekend, the four of them driving down from Hanover, all of them saying they couldn't stand to be in New Hampshire for a moment longer.

"Did you get a haircut?" Jenny W. asked. "I love it!"

"No—"

"I liked it better longer," Jenny K. said, which was pretty much par for the course—the two of them could argue about anything, with Priya and Linnie playing peacemaker.

"Did you guys come from the house?" I asked, looking around and not seeing any suitcases. "You get settled in okay?"

"Yes," Priya said, then rolled her eyes. "But Jenny is worried that having roommates is going to crimp her pickup prospects." I was about to ask which one when Jenny W. smiled at that and smoothed down her sweater.

"What can I say?" she said, giving me a wink. "I've always had good luck at weddings. If you know what I mean."

"We always know what you mean," Jenny K. said, rolling her eyes. "And like I told you, you're not going to find anyone dateable at this wedding."

"I beg to differ," J.J. said, smiling widely at them.

"Oh, hey, J.J.," Jenny K. said. "I didn't see you there."

"I bet you ladies might enjoy the attentions of a younger man. Well, not you, Priya," he said to Priya, who'd gotten engaged last year. "But these ladies, perhaps?" His voice was getting lower with every syllable, to the point where he now sounded like a baritone. Jenny K. just laughed, but I couldn't help noticing that Jenny W. looked intrigued. "Anyone want a ride on the J train?"

"Okay, stop it," I said, giving J.J. a shove, which he returned.

"Who needs a drink?" Priya asked, already taking a step toward the bar. I was about to ask for a Diet Coke when my phone buzzed in my pocket.

Hey! Two simultaneous situations going on.

Need to talk to you about tomorrow

And also

MY FUTURE ROOMMATE IS THE WORST CALL ME

I had just started to text her back as Danny came to join us, a drink in each hand.

"Hello," Danny said, leaning over to kiss the bridesmaids' cheeks. "I thought it suddenly seemed more exciting in here. How are the Jennys tonight?" He held one of the drinks out to me. "Here."

"Is that my drink?" I asked. I locked my phone and dropped it in my bag. I'd text Siobhan later. I took a sip and smiled. I didn't like real Cherry Coke, but whenever I was somewhere with an actual bartender, I ordered a Diet Coke with grenadine and extra maraschino cherries.

"Of course," Danny said. "I know what you drink. I didn't just get here."

"Thank you."

"Why didn't you bring *me* anything to drink?" J.J. asked petulantly.

"So, Sheridan," Jenny K. said, folding her arms, "I hear you sprung a surprise girlfriend on Linnie."

"I thought I RSVP'd," Danny said, giving her a bashful smile. "My memory's going and I'm not even thirty."

"So, where is she?" Jenny W. asked, looking around.

"She's around somewhere," Danny said, gesturing vaguely as he took a sip of his beer, not seeming all that bothered. "I'm sure she's mingling. Has Mike arrived yet?"

"No," I said, shaking my head. "Not as far as I can see." I had angled myself so that I had a clear view of the front door of the Inn, and I'd been keeping my eye on it—which meant I wasn't paying attention when Jenny W. swiped my drink. "Hey!"

She took a sip of it, then made a face and handed it back to me. "Ugh, what *is* this?"

"Diet Coke with cherries," I said, trying not to laugh at the look on her face. "Get your own drink if you don't like it."

"Oh, I intend to," she promised just as Priya came back, holding a glass of champagne.

"So, I got pulled into a conversation with your uncle?" she said, sounding uneasy as she glanced toward the bar. "I think he was trying to get me to invest in some kind of pyramid scheme?"

"Our uncle?" I looked over at the bar to see Stu sitting on one of the stools, gesturing wide as Rodney's sister slowly backed away from him. "What is Uncle Stu doing here?"

"Uncle Stu came?" J.J. asked, craning his neck to look. "Awesome."

"Not awesome," I said. "It's just supposed to be the wedding party." I pulled out my phone and texted Bill that we'd be one more at dinner, and he responded immediately with a smiley face and a thumbs-up.

"You know he can't resist a free dinner," Danny said, shaking his head.

"It looks like you could use a drink," J.J. said to Jenny W. in what he probably thought was his suave voice.

She arched an eyebrow at him. "I can get my own drink, J.J."

"Well, want to buy *me* one?" Jenny just laughed at that and headed over to the bar, Jenny K. and Priya joining her, and when they were out of earshot, J.J. turned to us. "Think I have a shot there?"

"No," Danny and I said simultaneously, and he smiled at me. "You owe me a Coke."

"I think I've got a shot," J.J. insisted, smoothing down his hair and dodging out of the way of Danny, who tried to muss it up again.

"Hey, babe!" I looked up to see my brother waving to Brooke, who crossed over to us, a small, tight smile on her face. "There you are."

"I've been looking for you."

"I've been here," Danny said, taking her hand and giving it a kiss.

"Just hanging out—" Danny stopped talking abruptly, his eyes on the door, and I turned to see what he was looking at.

I pulled in a sharp breath and felt my hand tighten on my sweating glass. Mike was standing in the doorway in a suit and tie, but that wasn't what I was staring at.

I was looking at Jesse Foster, who was standing next to him.

I swallowed hard, trying to keep my composure as I watched Mike make his way across the lobby, Jesse by his side. Jesse was wearing a dark-blue blazer and a collared shirt, slightly open at the throat. I'd seen him dressed up before—he and Mike had taken prom pictures with their dates at our house Mike's senior year—but that had seemed like more of a costume, something rented for the night. Right now, Jesse looked so handsome it was like I couldn't quite take it all in.

"Did you see that Uncle Stu is crashing our rehearsal dinner?" Linnie asked, rolling her eyes as she and Rodney came to join us. "What is everyone staring at?"

"Mike's here," J.J. said, nodding toward the door.

Linnie took a sip from her glass of wine and squinted across the room. "Wait, why is Jesse Foster here?"

"I didn't know he was going to be here," I said, too loudly and defensively. "Why would I have known that? It's not like we talk or anything."

"I wasn't asking you," Linnie said, looking a little taken aback.

"I'm just saying, this is news to me too. That's all." Everyone was now staring at me, and I took a quick sip of my drink, then coughed as I accidentally choked on it, causing J.J. to whack me hard on the back.

"Mike *did* RSVP for a plus-one," Rodney pointed out as he took a sip of his drink. We were all just blatantly staring at them, standing across the room, not even pretending to be doing anything else. "Maybe . . ." He glanced at Linnie. "Are Mike and Jesse like *together* together?"

"Maybe Corrine ruined all women for him," J.J. said. "It wouldn't surprise me."

"Mike's gay?" Brooke asked, her brow furrowing. "Wait, who's Cor-rine?"

"Jesse's definitely straight," I said, realizing a second later that I'd said this with a little too much authority. "I mean, probably. I don't know. Maybe he's not. Who can say? Sexuality is a, um, spectrum." I took another sip of my drink, but when I looked up, I could see Linnie star-ing at me like she'd just noticed more than I wanted her to.

"Here it comes," J.J. said, his voice low, and I saw what he was talking about. My parents were walking over to Mike and Jesse, my mother hold-ing on tight to my father's arm, both of them looking visibly nervous.

I didn't know what I was expecting—raised voices, maybe, or Mike refusing to talk to my parents. But none of that happened. Mike shook my dad's hand, leaned over and kissed my mother's cheek, gave them both a smile, and then practically shoved Jesse at them as he turned and headed over toward us. It was the interaction my parents might have had with one of my second cousins—*not* their son who they hadn't seen in a year and a half. It looked like my parents were making small talk with Jesse, but they kept glancing to where Mike had gone, like they were trying to figure out what had just happened.

"You guys are *not* subtle," Mike said as he approached us, his hands in his pockets.

"Hey!" Linnie said, smiling wide at Mike and pulling him into a hug, Danny following suit. "You're here! It's so good to see you!"

"You too," Mike said, smiling at Linnie. "Congratulations. You look beautiful."

"Michael!" J.J. gave Mike a hug that picked him up off the ground. "What do you think?" he asked, looking at Danny and Rodney, Mike still hovering a few inches off the ground. "Mike Drop?"

"No!" I said quickly. Mike Drops were something that J.J. and Danny had done a lot when Mike was in elementary school and they were much, much bigger than he was. It was true to its name—Danny would pick up Mike, yell "Mike Drop!" and toss him in the air and J.J. would dash in and catch him just before he hit the floor. All of which had worked out great when Mike was six. But as they'd all gotten older, J.J. sometimes forgot to catch him, and they had a way of getting people injured, sometimes all three of them in the same Mike Drop.

"Good to see you," Rodney said, giving him a hug after J.J. finally set him back down. "We're both so happy you're here."

"I wouldn't have missed it," Mike said to Rodney. I was on the verge of saying something snarky about how he'd somehow been able to miss Christmas and Thanksgiving, but held it back. "Charlie," Mike said to me.

I nodded. "Hey."

"Hi, everyone." I jumped and turned around—Jesse Foster was standing right behind me, leaning slightly over my shoulder. He touched the small of my back, so quickly it was over before I could register it, as he walked over to stand next to Mike.

"Hey, Jesse," Linnie said, giving him a quick hug as he shook hands with all my brothers and Rodney. "It's been a while."

"I know," he said, giving her a polite smile. Then he looked at me, gave me a smile, and mouthed *Hey*.

Hi, I mouthed back. My pulse was hammering, and I couldn't stop staring at Jesse, at his hair, which was combed back, at the tiny pocket square folded into his blazer pocket, at his hands. . . .

"And this is Brooke Abernathy," Danny said, and I snapped back to reality to see Danny making introductions. "My girlfriend."

"Oh," Mike said, looking from Brooke to Danny, surprise clearly written on his face. "Nice to meet you."

"You too," Brooke said, with another tight smile.

"And this is my friend Jesse Foster," Mike said, gesturing to Jesse, who gave Brooke a smile and shook her hand.

"So *Jesse* is your plus-one?" Rodney asked, looking from Mike to Jesse. "Not that you're not welcome, of course . . ."

"I thought I could use some moral support this weekend," Mike said, glancing back to the side of the room where my parents were standing, now with the Danielses.

"Plus, I always like seeing the Grants," Jesse said. His tone was easy and light, but his eyes kept finding mine, and I found myself unable to look away. Now that he was here, it was of course making sense why he'd said he'd see me soon—he must have assumed Mike told me basic facts about his life. "It's been too long."

"Definitely too long," I said, giving him what I hoped was just a normal welcoming smile. I noticed Linnie, though, glancing between me and Jesse.

"What do you think?" Danny asked, slinging an arm around Mike's neck and another around Jesse's. "Quick stop at the bar?"

"Coming with you," J.J. said, following them across the room.

"Lin?" Rodney asked.

"I'm good," Linnie said. "I just need to talk to my sister a second."

"What—" I started, but Linnie was already grabbing me by the hand and pulling me across the lobby. I looked back to see that Brooke was now standing alone, where, a moment before, she'd been part of our group. I felt a flash of sympathy for her, but a moment later this turned into annoyance. Why was she standing by herself? Surely she could join Danny and everyone at the bar—it's not like she needed an invitation or anything.

Linnie pulled me across the lobby and then down the hallway. I could still see the rest of the room—Danny was at the bar, taking two drinks from the bartender, then walking a few steps away and handing one of the glasses to Mike, who immediately took a long sip.

"So." Linnie looked at me expectantly.

"What?"

She shot me a look. "*Jesse*. What's going on with you two?"

I thought about pretending I didn't know what she meant, but I was pretty sure that would raise her suspicions even more. "Nothing's going on," I said, shaking my head. "I mean, right this minute. We . . . um . . . hooked up over Christmas break." Linnie's jaw dropped open and I hastened to add, "We didn't sleep together." I figured that right this instant, Linnie didn't need to know just how close we'd come to it.

"So, was this a drunken hookup? Like a one-time thing?"

"Not for me." I took a breath, suddenly wishing I'd told Linnie all this years ago—that I'd talked to her the very first moment I'd looked at Jesse and felt my face get hot, suddenly not sure how to work my hands and feet when I was around him. She should have known about this from the beginning. "I don't know," I said, not sure how to explain it. It seemed like the second you tried to tell someone why you loved someone else, it took the luster off it, like pinning a butterfly down in a case—it never quite captured it. But it also occurred to me that this would not be a helpful metaphor for someone who would be speaking vows about why she loved someone in front of a hundred-person crowd tomorrow. "He's Jesse."

"I know he's Jesse," she said. "I just want to know when he became *Jesse*."

I shrugged with one shoulder, looking at the wallpaper, dotted with black-and-white pictures from when the Inn wasn't an inn at all, when it was just a family home, people who lived in these rooms and called them their own. "It started as a crush," I said, my voice hesitant as I tried to find the right words, realizing that I'd never had to explain this before. "Like, just the kind of crush you have when you're a kid. Nothing's ever going to happen. But then . . ." I flashed back to the night of his party, how dreamlike and fated it had all seemed, like a line of dominoes being nudged just the right amount, then falling perfectly. "At Christmas, it was like he *saw* me for the first time."

"Uh-huh." I could practically feel all that my sister wanted to say but was holding back, like air pressure outside a car window.

"He's just . . . ," I started, then let out a breath as I realized that even if I could articulate this, Linnie wouldn't understand what I meant, not really. She'd almost always had a boyfriend in high school, and she'd found her soul mate three months after graduating. She didn't know what it was like to look and wish and want, always two steps behind the person, always on the edges of their life. What it was like to stand next to someone and know you weren't registering with them, not in any meaningful way. That you thought about someone a thousand times more than they'd ever thought about you. To know that you were just a face in the crowd scenes while they were center stage. And then, all at once, to have the spotlight finally swing over to you. To suddenly be visible, to be seen, no longer one of the people in the background who never get any lines. To suddenly be in the midst of something you'd only ever looked at from the sidelines. What that *felt* like when it finally happened, dropped in your lap when you were least expecting it, like a gift you were half-afraid to open.

I looked up to see Linnie still looking at me, patient, and I knew she'd wait until I found the words. "It was like my best dream coming true," I finally said. "I just wanted to be able to travel back in time and tell my twelve-year-old self that this was actually happening. That there was a world in which it *could* happen."

"So, kissing Jesse. How was it?" The second after she'd asked this, she shuddered. "First of all, ew. I can't believe I'm even talking to you about this. Jesse is like two."

"He's older than me," I pointed out.

"*You're* like two."

"Thanks, Lin."

"But," she said, looking steadily at me. "How was it?"

I had a flashback to the night, to the heart-pounding sensation of it, the knee-weakening kisses I couldn't even remember without getting flushed and losing my train of thought entirely. "Amazing."

"And now?"

I glanced back at the lobby and saw Jesse standing next to Mike by the bar, laughing at something J.J. was saying. "I don't know," I said, even though I did know, a little, as I thought about the way he'd looked at me when I'd dropped Mike off, the way that he'd slipped his hands under my shirt to touch my bare skin, the way he'd just touched the small of my back. "He texted me that he would see me soon, but that was before I knew he would . . . you know, be here."

"But what do you want to happen?"

I just stared at her for a moment—the answer to that question was so obvious. I thought of Jesse, that night up in his guesthouse. And I thought of the years before that, of all the years that he'd been *Jesse Foster*, always just out of reach.

Linnie must have been able to read what I was thinking, because she nodded. "Well, it's too bad. I think Bill likes you."

"Bill?" I blinked at her, then shook my head. "No."

"You don't think he's cute?"

"Sure he's cute," I said, since he was. "But he's not *Jesse*."

Linnie looked at me for a long moment, then gave me a smile. "Go have your fun. Be *safe*," she added sternly, as I made a face.

"Linnie, ew."

"Did you shave your legs?"

"Lin."

"Is that a no?"

"That's a 'it's none of your business.'"

"Listen, I'm the one who taught you how, so show some respect."

She started to head back across the lobby, and I grabbed her arm before she could go too far out of reach and get swept up by wedding well-wishers. "Don't tell Mike."

"Of course I'm not going to tell him. But do you think you should?"

"Me?"

"If this is going to be something real," she said, raising an eyebrow at me.

I took a breath to answer her just as Will came out of the restaurant and stood in the doorway.

"If I could have your attention," he said, in a loud voice. "If you wouldn't mind following me, the rehearsal dinner is about to begin."

CHAPTER 14
Or, To the Happy Couple
Or, What's in a Name?

AND WE JUST WANT TO SAY THAT WE WISH YOU all the happiness in the world," Priya said as she lifted her glass. She was standing with the Jennys at their end of the table as they gave their shared toast.

"Yes," Jenny W. said, raising her glass as well. "We love you both and want nothing but a wonderful future for you guys."

"But," Jenny K. said, her brows drawing together. "Rodney. If you do *anything* to hurt Linnie . . ."

"Anything *at all*," Priya added, her voice growing low and serious.

"We will find you and it will not be pretty." All the bridesmaids glowered at Rodney for a second. He shifted uncomfortably in his chair, keeping a faltering smile on his face, like he wasn't entirely sure if they were joking or not.

But then Priya smiled and raised her glass again, and the Jennys followed suit. "To the happy couple!"

I smiled and raised my own glass, then set it down and speared another forkful of chocolate cake. So far, the dinner had been going great, the bridesmaids' speech notwithstanding. All twenty-one of us were around one long table—Linnie and Rodney, Rodney's parents and mine, Max, Brooke, my brothers, Jesse, Rodney's sister and brother-in-law, me, his cousin Marcus and his wife, the bridesmaids, and Uncle Stu. Bill had done a great job with the decorations—everything was arranged beautifully, and there wasn't a koala to be seen.

As the food was being served, Rodney and Linnie had welcomed everyone, thanked them for coming to share this occasion with them, and talked about how much the assembled guests meant to them. Linnie had only gotten teary once during this. For the most part, she had held it together, which I thought was a pretty good sign for tomorrow.

Rodney and Linnie had divided the toasts up so that some people would give them at the rehearsal dinner and some people would give them at the wedding. My mother had given one about how she felt like she'd watched Rodney growing up alongside Linnie, and how he'd felt like her son for long before it would become official tomorrow. Rodney had sniffled when she'd said this and then had had to clear his throat loudly before he could thank her once she was finished.

Things had started to go off the rails when my uncle Stu decided to give his own speech, which was basically a pitch to join him in selling supplements. Rodney's dad had redeemed things somewhat with his speech, talking about how proud he was of Rodney and how big transitions like this are always a challenge—but necessary to have the kind of life you can be proud of. When the General finished his speech, most people were blinking very intently down at their place settings.

The bridesmaids' speech had started out sentimental, with Jenny K., as the maid of honor, kicking things off with an anecdote about when she first became friends with Linnie. But when the other bridesmaids joined in, the toast basically turned into a litany of stories about Linnie from college that I was fairly certain a roomful of relatives didn't necessarily need to hear and now was finishing up with a not-so-subtle threat of bodily harm.

I set my fork down and glanced toward the other end of the table, where Jesse was sitting. He was looking down at his place setting, though, and I glanced away before it became obvious that I was staring. We hadn't had a chance to talk yet, just the two of us, although occasionally I would glance in his direction to find that he was looking at me and I'd hold his gaze for as long as I felt I could without drawing suspicion. It was, I had found, a unique kind of torture to be this close to Jesse, in the same room as him, and still not be able to talk. Because there was so much I needed to know: When he'd said he would see me tonight, was this *it*? Or were we actually going to have time alone together? I'd thought about texting Jesse, but the last thing I wanted was for Mike to see my number on his screen and start asking questions.

Not that I was entirely sure Mike would have noticed—even as I was mostly looking at Jesse, I couldn't help but see that Mike would smile and clap when everyone was smiling and clapping, but mostly he was hunched over the drink Danny had gotten him, not looking like he was making much of a dent in it.

Our waitress was walking around with coffee, and I nodded for a refill, pushing my cup forward and taking another bite of cake. I looked around and saw, to my surprise, Bill standing by the back doors. I'd seen him rushing around with his uncle before the dinner began, but I'd just assumed that once things had gotten going, he would have left. He met my eye, and I gave him a smile, starting to raise my hand in a wave before I realized I was still holding my fork. I quickly set it down, then checked to make sure I hadn't gotten chocolate on my dress.

"Okay, my turn." J.J. was standing up a few seats down the table from me, clearing his throat and holding up his phone. "I hope you don't mind—I wrote down my notes for my toast on this. I'm not, like, texting someone." There was scattered laughter, and he smiled broadly at the assembled guests before taking a deep breath. "So. I'd like to start by sharing a story about my dear older sister, Linnea. I think she knows the one I'm going to say." Linnie groaned and buried her head in her hands, and J.J. nodded. "Oh, she knows. So. When she was ten and I was seven, she had me convinced, I mean absolutely *convinced*—" The low, thumping beat of electronica music suddenly filled the room, and J.J. frowned at his phone. "Whoops, that's me." He squinted at the screen, and then his face brightened. "Oh, awesome," he said as he answered the call and pressed the button to put it on speaker. "Hello?"

I glanced over to see both Linnie and Rodney exchange a glance and my mother staring daggers at J.J., clearly trying to get him back on track, apparently forgetting who she was dealing with.

"Um, hello?" the voice on the other end of the phone said. It was a guy, and he sounded unsure. "J.J.?"

"Yes, it's me," J.J. said. "Thanks so much for getting back to me."

"Sure," the voice said, not sounding all that enthusiastic to be speaking to my brother. "What's up, man? Is everything okay?"

"Yep. I just had a question for you. Your name is what, again?"

"J.J., you know my name," the guy said, now speaking more slowly. "You called me, remember?"

"I know, I just needed to check something. If you could just tell me your name. Your *full* name."

I met Danny's eye two seats down from me. He shook his head and then gave me a half shrug and eye roll combo, a series of tiny, quick gestures that I could nonetheless understand perfectly: *No, I have no idea what he's doing. But really, what did we expect?*

"Uh," the guy on the other end said. "It's Billiam. Billiam Kirby."

"Billiam!" J.J. said triumphantly, raising the phone above his head. "See? Did I *tell* you? Did I tell you?" Most of the guests just stared blankly back at him while my dad gave him the hand-across-the-throat gesture that in our family had always meant *shut it down.*

"No way," Rodney muttered, reaching for his wallet.

"Dammit." Danny sighed, tossing his napkin onto the table. "I owe him twenty-five bucks."

"He got me for fifty," Rodney said, shaking his head.

I turned around to look at Bill, still standing at the back of the room. He caught my eye and shook his head, but I saw he was smiling.

"A little louder, if you don't mind," J.J. said, raising the microphone to his phone again. "Nice and loud so that everyone can hear you. You're on speaker."

"I . . . am?" Billiam asked, sounding taken aback. "Uh—where?"

"My sister's rehearsal dinner."

"Wait, *what?*"

"Here, I'll show you." J.J. held his phone out toward the table, moving it back and forth. "Say hi, everyone."

"Hi," a few people murmured, distinctly unenthusiastically.

"Wait," Billiam said on the other end of the phone. "I don't understand any of this. What's going on?"

"I just needed you to verify your name, that's all. And it worked out great, because now there's a ton of witnesses."

"J.J.," Billiam said, incredulity creeping into his voice, "was this seriously what you called me about? You said it was an emergency."

"This *was* the emergency," J.J. said. "I mean, come on, like you were doing something more pressing?"

"You know I work for the Pentagon now, right?" Billiam asked, his tone getting very cold.

"Hey, good for you!" J.J. said. "Well, it was nice to catch up. Let me know if you ever need Pirates tickets."

"What—" Billiam started from the other end, just as J.J. hung up on him. He set down his phone and picked up his glass. "To the happy couple!"

* * *

An hour later, the rehearsal dinner had technically passed the end point specified on the invitation, but nobody seemed in a huge hurry to leave and the party had just moved into the lobby, much to the apparent dismay of the guy behind the check-in counter, who was sending unhappy looks our way. Rodney's cousin Marcus had left, and his sister and brother-in-law—and Uncle Stu had disappeared around the time the server showed up with the bill—but aside from that, everyone was hanging out.

Right after the dinner, I'd noticed my mother and Mike standing together in the back of the lobby, talking, my mom's face turning red, the way it did when she was upset, and Mike folding his arms tightly and looking at the floor. I'd gotten pulled into a conversation with Mrs. Daniels, and after that I hadn't seen Mike again—or Jesse, for that matter. I wasn't sure if Mike had left, but the thought that Jesse might have left without saying anything was making my stomach knot, and I was checking my phone far more than I knew I should be.

"Okay, where's the bride?" This was Priya, flanked by the Jennys. "Are we ready to do this?"

"Do what?" I asked as I looked up from my phone.

"We're taking you out," Priya said, tugging Linnie up from her barstool.

Jenny K. slung her arm around my sister's shoulders. "We voted. We need to have our last single-girl night."

"Just a second," Rodney said.

"Nope," Jenny K. crossed in front of my sister, blocking Rodney's path. "You get to be married to her for the rest of your life. She gets one more girls' night with us."

"Guys, it's not like we're going to not hang out after I'm married," Linnie pointed out.

"But it won't be the *same*," Priya said, her voice going wobbly.

"Okay," Rodney said, clearly knowing when he was beaten. He took

Linnie's hand and gave her a quick kiss, then stepped back. "Have fun. But not too much fun." He was clearly trying for stern but not really pulling it off. "See you at home?"

"See you then," Linnie called as she was swept out the door, laughing, pulled along by her friends.

"Rodney!" J.J. yelled at a volume that was far too loud for the lobby. "Brother-to-be! Come join us. Belly up to the bar." Rodney smiled and walked over to join them.

"Hey." I looked over and saw that Bill had appeared next to me. He was wearing a white button-down and a gray tie, the shirt only slightly wrinkled and the sleeves rolled up. His tie was loosened, and his hair was as eighties-movie impressive as ever. You might have mistaken him for one of the guests, except that he had a tablet and a phone in one hand and a pen tucked behind his ear.

"Hey," I said, smiling at him—I was happier to see him than I realized I'd be. "I thought you'd left."

"Before an event is over?" He shook his head and lowered his voice to speak gravely. "Never."

"Well, then, thank you," I said.

"You guys certainly have entertaining speeches. I liked the Billiam one."

I laughed. "I thought you might. The decorations looked great."

"Thanks," he said, tugging at the knot on his tie. "I mean, it was a little easier without people telling me that my decoration placement was wrong. . . ." I laughed. "But it would have been a lot more fun if you were here. You, um . . ." He cleared his throat. "You look really nice."

"Oh," I said, glancing down at myself and smoothing out my dress. "Thank you."

"Sure," he said easily, giving me a smile.

Our eyes met, and it was a beat too long before I realized I'd just been staring at him without saying anything. "Um, you do too."

"Yeah?" Bill asked, sounding pleased as he looked down at himself.

"Thanks. I kind of had to get ready in my car. The shirt's not too wrinkled?"

"It's fine," I assured him. "Why were you getting ready in your car?"

"Well, my mom moved out of Putnam when I went to school. I've been staying at my uncle's and he lives over an hour away. So I have all my clothes with me, since I knew I wouldn't have time to go back and change before the event."

"I didn't know being an assistant wedding coordinator was so intense."

"You have no idea," he said, his voice low and faux serious, making me laugh.

"Charlie!" I looked over to see J.J. motioning me over to where he, Danny, and Rodney were all sitting at the bar. It currently looked deserted, and I wasn't sure if this was because the bartender's shift was over, or if he'd just gotten sick of my brothers—both seemed equally plausible. "And young Billiam! Come join us."

I glanced over at Bill, but he was already smiling his usual wide smile—apparently he had not had enough of my family already today. As we walked over, I felt my shoes pinch for the first time—I would have to get out of them soon if I didn't want to have blisters tomorrow.

"Here," Danny said, taking his suit jacket off the stool next to him, clearing it for me, and I sat down.

"Thanks." I smoothed my skirt under me and crossed my legs, letting my shoe hang off my heel and immediately feeling better about things. "Where's Brooke?" I asked, finally noticing she wasn't with them.

"Calling her sister," Danny replied.

Rodney frowned down at his watch. "It's getting kind of late, isn't it?"

"She's in California," Danny explained, and Rodney nodded.

"Not so late then."

"And Mike?" I asked as I looked around the lobby, which was empty-ing fast, people gathering up jackets and purses and heading toward the doors. *And Jesse,* I added silently.

Danny shrugged, but I could see that he looked a little worried about this. "I haven't seen him in a bit. He probably just left early."

I nodded, trying not to let the disappointment I was feeling show on my face.

"Did everyone have a good rehearsal dinner?" Bill asked, looking around at the group.

"No thanks to J.J.," Rodney said.

"What's that supposed to mean?"

"What are you still doing here?" Danny asked Bill. "Aren't your official duties over? Considering that the event is?"

"Just making sure everything got cleaned up okay," he replied. "Do any of you need rides back to the house?"

J.J. shook his head. "Your job sounds exhausting, young Billiam."

"It's okay," Bill said with another smile. "And, uh, it's really not Billiam. Just Bill is good. Bill Barnes."

"That's a good name," J.J. said, pointing at Bill. "That's a superhero name."

Rodney raised an eyebrow. "How is it a superhero name?"

"The double letter thing."

"Alliteration," I supplied.

Danny smiled at me. "Charlie knows what's what." Then he turned to J.J. "I still don't get how it's a superhero name."

"They all have them," J.J. said, gesturing expansively.

"I'm waiting to hear specifics."

"It's true," Rodney agreed. "You can't make a claim like that without evidence."

"Rodney's a lawyer," J.J. explained to Bill.

"Not yet," Rodney said, shaking his head. "Not until I pass the bar."

"That's a *total* lawyerly qualification to make," J.J. sighed.

"Still waiting to hear examples," Danny said as he took a sip from his nearly empty glass.

"Fine!" J.J. said, slapping his hand down on the bar. "Okay. How about . . . ?" He paused for a moment, furrowing his brow. "Peter Parker? Or Sue Storm? Or Bruce Banner?"

"Whoa," Bill said, his eyebrows going up. "I guess I never realized that before. There are two superheroes named Bruce?"

"Who else?" I asked.

"Bruce Wayne," Danny, J.J., Bill, and Rodney said at the same time.

"Oh, right, him."

"Bruce Wayne is the exception," J.J. said, shaking his head. "All the rest of them have the double letters."

"Alliteration," I supplied again, and Danny smiled.

"Reed Richards," J.J. continued, starting to tick them off on his fingers. "Wade Wilson, Stephen Strange, Bucky Barnes, Lex Luthor, Lois Lane—"

"She's not actually a superhero," Bill pointed out.

"You're not helping, Billiam," J.J. snapped.

"What about . . . I don't know . . . ," Danny said. "Diana Prince, Tony Stark, Steve Rogers, Barbara Gordon, Clark Kent—"

"That *sounds* alliterative," I pointed out. "So it might count on a technicality."

"Archie Andrews," Rodney supplied, apparently joining J.J.'s side on this. "Jughead Jones . . ."

"Okay, in what universe is *Archie* a superhero?" Danny asked, causing me to draw in a sharp breath.

"Hey now," I said, and Danny rolled his eyes.

"Oh, sorry," he said. "I forgot about your thing for those comics."

"It's J.J.'s fault," I said, and Danny muttered, "Most things are." J.J. had had a huge collection of Archie books that he'd declared himself over and too old for when he started eighth grade, so he'd passed them on to me. I'd loved them, nursing an elementary school crush on Reggie that I'd told nobody except Linnie about.

"There's also Beetle Bailey—" Rodney continued, and Danny threw up his hands.

"So we've just moved arbitrarily into the newspaper comics?"

"You think Superman was never a newspaper comic?" Rodney challenged, raising his eyebrows.

"I still think the majority of superheroes have them," J.J. said stubbornly, clearly trying to get us back on track.

There was a beeping sound coming from Bill's tablet, and he glanced down at it. "I should get going," he said. "Need to go over some last-minute checks with my uncle." I nodded, giving silent thanks that Pland had sent Bill and Will to us. I didn't even want to imagine what things might have looked like without them. "I'll be at the house first thing tomorrow to help get everything ready for the big day."

"Great," Rodney said, standing up and reaching out to shake Bill's hand. "Thanks for everything. We really appreciate it." Bill nodded and lifted his hand in a wave before continuing out the front door of the Inn.

I turned to my brothers, ready to jump back into the discussion, when I felt my purse start to buzz. I immediately slid off my barstool—I was pretty sure this was Siobhan calling, reminding me that I'd meant to call her back. But this was perfect timing, because things had wound down enough that we could finally talk. "Just going to take this," I said, then hurried across the lobby. I pulled out my phone as I walked, and then nearly dropped it when I saw that it was Jesse calling me.

"Hi," I said, answering the phone as I looked around. I glanced at my brothers and brother-to-be, but they were all still at the bar, arguing about superheroes and paying no attention to me.

"Hey, you," he said easily, and just the sound of his voice was enough to make me feel like my insides were slowly turning to liquid. "Where are you?"

"I'm still at the Inn," I said. As I spoke, I realized that maybe this was the first time Jesse and I had ever talked on the phone—beyond him calling the landline for Mike when we were in elementary and early middle school, before we got our own phones. And even then, those conversations had never been more than *Sure, hold on a second. Let me get him.*

"I meant where in the building," Jesse said, a laugh in his voice, and I realized that he was still here—he hadn't left yet. And he wanted to see me.

"Oh," I said, spinning in a circle, my heart starting to beat hard, trying to figure out how best to describe where I was. "I'm kind of like off to the side of the main lobby, over by the check-in counter? And—"

A hand snaked around my waist and I jumped, then turned and saw Jesse, phone to his ear, giving me a half smile. "Hey, gorgeous."

"Hi," I said. I smiled wide, then tried to tone it down a little as I lowered my phone and pressed the button to end the call. "I didn't see you—or Mike—so I wasn't sure if you'd left."

"Without seeing you?" he asked, taking a step closer and giving me an easy smile. "Never." He glanced around. "I'm not sure where Mike went to. I saw him talking to your dad earlier, and it looked like kind of an intense conversation, so I thought I'd give him some space."

"Ah," I said, glancing around the lobby, like Mike might suddenly reappear. But this didn't sound great—if Mike had been arguing with our dad too, that meant he'd fought with both our parents in a very short time, which meant he was doing just what I'd thought he would do—bring drama into Linnie's wedding. I could feel my frustration with him start to bubble up again.

"So," Jesse said, moving a step closer to me. "Want to get out of here?" I'd taken a breath to respond, when I noticed, across the lobby, my parents and Rodney's sitting together in a cluster of armchairs, talking and laughing.

Jesse seemed to notice this as well and took a step away, tipping his head to the right. I glanced around, making sure nobody was watching—nobody seemed to be—and followed a few steps behind him, down the hallway. Jesse headed into a room I hadn't ever noticed before, and I followed him in. He shut the door behind me and I looked around.

"Wow," I said. It was a games room, with a pool table in the center, pool cues in holders all along one wall, and a series of dartboards along another. There were whiskey-colored leather sofas—the kind that had round feet and looked almost tufted—and what looked like a very stocked bar cart in the corner. "How did you know about this?"

"I went to a *lot* of bar and bat mitzvahs here."

"I did too," I said immediately. "Do you remember Ariel Franken's? She had the early-Hollywood theme?" Jesse and I hadn't gone to many social events together, but I remembered every one in blinding detail.

Jesse frowned, looking up slightly, like he was trying to bring something to mind. "I think I went to that one. . . ."

"You did," I said immediately. "You, me, and Mike ended up in the photo booth together. Don't you remember? You were—"

"Wow," Jesse said, shaking his head. "You've got a good memory."

I smiled. I didn't want to tell him that, when it came to him, I had a perfect memory. "I just remember that you—"

"Charlie." Jesse took a step closer to me. "We don't need to talk about kid stuff."

"Right," I said quickly, suddenly feeling the gap in our ages. He was in *college*, after all. Why was I trying to talk about things that happened years ago? But it was right there in my mind, so vivid I couldn't believe he hadn't remembered. He'd worn a black tie with white stripes, and during the last song, we'd danced together. It was one of the Jesse memories I had turned over and over in my mind so often that the edges had all been worn smooth, like sea glass. We'd been dancing in a group, but for one perfect moment, he'd reached out, taken my hand, and spun me around twice before letting me go, leaving me dizzy from more than the dancing.

"And after all," he said, bringing me back into the present as he came even closer. "We've got more important things to talk about." But Jesse didn't say anything else. He just he took my head in his hands, leaned in, and kissed me.

And just like that, it was as though no time had passed. It was like we were pressing play again on a song that had been paused right before the beat drop—that easily, we were back in it. In the months that had passed, I would sometimes wonder if I'd remembered it correctly, or if time and far too much going over the events of that night had clouded my memory. That maybe Jesse really hadn't been that good a kisser. That I'd let my imagination run away with me.

But all it took was one kiss for me to remember that I hadn't gotten it wrong. If anything, I hadn't remembered just how good it was. We were falling into a rhythm together right away. In a matter of seconds, I was breathless, my heart beating hard and my hands twining in Jesse's hair.

He walked me backward toward one of the leather couches, then somehow managed to ease me down onto it, all without stopping kissing me. "Did I mention," he said, in between kisses, "just how nice it is to see you again?"

I laughed at that and kissed him back as he ran his hand along the side of my silk dress. "So," he said, just as there was a loud, electronic-sounding *beep*. It wasn't my phone, and Jesse paused for a moment before leaning in again—just as it beeped four more times, in quick succession.

"I'll turn that off," he said, pulling his phone out of his pocket and then frowning down at the screen.

"Everything okay?"

"You tell me," he said, handing me the phone. "They're all from Mike."

I took it from him, feeling my eyes widen as I read through them.

Hey man. Where'd you go?

I'm hiding in the back of the lobby trying to avoid
my parents

Family drama—what's new

My mom thinks that this is a great time to like go
inot everything

Like in the middle of the rehearsal dinner

And my dad's mad at me too

He would have yelled at me if you were there too

I know

They seem to think me being g here means I want
to have a wholething about it

Annnnyyyyywayyyyyyyy

Where did you go? Text me text me

text me

I looked up from the phone and handed it back to Jesse. "It kind of sounds like he's drunk."

Jesse nodded. "That's what I thought too. I recognize a Mike drunk text. Usually there's more autocorrect mistakes, though."

"But . . ." I tried to figure out how this could even be possible. I'd seen Danny get him a drink from the bar, but then it looked like Mike had just been slowly sipping it all night. Unless . . . I suddenly realized the much more probable answer was that he'd been getting refills from the waiters, which meant he might be something like four or five drinks in. And I wasn't sure I wanted Mike, full of liquid courage, to suddenly start telling my parents what he thought about them. "I think we should go find him."

Jesse nodded and gave me a steady look. "We'll sort Mike out," he said, reaching to take my hand, sending shivers throughout my body, "and then . . ."

I had been waiting for him to finish the sentence, but a moment later I realized what he was implying. For just a second, a headline flashed across my mind—*Clueless Virgin Very Slow on Uptake.*

We headed back into the lobby, and I saw that my brothers, Rodney, and Bill were no longer at the bar—I didn't see them anywhere. "He said he was in the lobby—" I stopped short when I saw Mike was standing near the restaurant entrance, swaying on his feet like he was actually on a boat that nobody else could see. He was frowning down at his phone and jabbing at it with one finger, which I had a feeling explained the number of typos in the texts he'd sent. "There he is," I said, lowering my voice slightly as I nodded toward him.

"Oh jeez," Jesse said, shaking his head. "This is looking like senior prom all over again."

"What happened at senior prom?"

"Another time," Jesse said, flashing me a quick smile.

"Right," I said, focusing on the task at hand. "Of course." We were halfway across the lobby, walking toward Mike, when he looked up from his phone and squinted at us.

"Jesse!" he said, too loudly, throwing his arms up and sending his phone flying. "Oops! Where—did you guys see—"

"I've got it," I said quietly, bending down to pick up his phone, like if I talked more softly it would somehow balance out Mike talking too loud.

"Did you get my texts?" Mike asked. "Because I like just texted you. Look, I'll show you the time . . . thingy. . . ." He looked at his empty hands, then patted his suit pockets, then shook his head. "I don't know—I think I lost my phone?"

"Here," I said, handing it to him, and Mike brightened.

"My *phone*," he said, his volume getting loud enough that I glanced around. He frowned at me. "Why'd you take my phone, Charlie? Why are you always taking my stuff that's mine away from me?"

"Um," I said, trying to remember the last time I'd seen him like this. I got the sense that Mike didn't party as much as our older siblings— neither of us did—but I knew he had his fun.

"Dude," Jesse said, seeming to give up on trying to get Mike to sit down and just steadying him instead. "How much did you *drink*?"

"Not much," Mike insisted, jabbing at his phone again. "Just the same as the same amount as what I drink usually. Same same."

"Did you eat anything first?" Jesse asked, and Mike shook his head carefully, just once to each side. "Do you think maybe you should have?"

"Ohhhh," Mike said, trying to snap his fingers but then giving up after a few tries and just pointing at Jesse. "You know, maybe that actually does make me some sense. Didn't think about that. Didn't do the math. Didn't crunch the numbers."

"I think we should get him out of here," I said, and Jesse nodded.

"Great idea!" Mike said, again too loudly. "I'll drive." He patted his pockets again. "No, I won't."

"No," I said firmly, hoping that Jesse was keeping his keys far away from my brother. "You won't."

"I'll drive him back to my place," Jesse said to me after a slight pause, not sounding too happy about this idea. "And then . . ." He sighed. "I should probably keep an eye on him tonight."

I nodded, knowing exactly what this meant—that whatever we'd been starting in the game room was not going to continue tonight, because Mike had gotten himself sloppy drunk.

I tried to think of some way to get around this, some other plan that we could think of where this wouldn't have to be the way the night went. But I couldn't seem to see any other avenues, and finally I nodded. "That's probably a good idea."

Jesse and I looked at each other, and it was like there was a whole silent conversation between us. I could see regret and disappointment on Jesse's face, and I knew that's what I was feeling too.

"What?" Mike asked in a loud whisper, looking between us. "What's going on?"

"Nothing," I said, feeling like the sooner we got him out of here, the better. "Let's go."

We managed to get Mike out the back entrance, which was closer to where Jesse had parked his car anyway. And it turned out to be a good thing, since Mike seemed to be getting drunker with every step he took toward Jesse's hatchback. We maneuvered Mike into the passenger seat, where he went boneless, sprawling out across the seat and closing his eyes.

"Hey," Jesse said. He glanced at the car, then took my hand and pulled me a few steps away, so that we were by the next car over, one of those SUVs that's so long they really seem like at some point they should be properly called buses.

"Hey," I said, looking back quickly at his car. I could see through to the passenger seat—Jesse had parked adjacent to one of the parking lot's lights—and it looked like Mike's eyes were still closed.

"Sorry about this," Jesse said, shaking his head. "Not exactly the evening I'd imagined."

I smiled at that. "Me neither." He started to bend his head toward me, and although most of me was screaming to just kiss him back, I couldn't help glancing over at the car once again. "What about Mike?"

Jesse just shook his head. "He's three sheets to the wind," he said with confidence. "He won't see."

I nodded, even though there was a piece of me that suddenly realized I wanted him to say that it didn't matter—that he didn't mind if Mike saw, or if everyone saw, because he liked me and didn't care who knew it. He leaned in and gave me a quick kiss, but unlike the kisses in the game room, I could feel that we were under the clock—without nearly enough time to lose myself in him like before.

"Okay," he said as he broke away and took a step back, regret etched on his face. "I should get back to your brother. Who I want to murder, by the way."

"Right," I said as reality—which was so much less fun than kissing Jesse—intruded once again.

"So." He slid his arms around my waist and pulled me toward him. "I'll see you at the wedding tomorrow?"

I nodded, starting to smile. Jesse would be at the wedding tomorrow—and we'd have the whole reception, and hopefully this time we would dance together longer than just a few seconds. And then after the reception . . .

"It's a plan," I said. Jesse leaned in to kiss me once more, and when we broke apart, I glanced over at the car. It looked like Mike's eyes were still closed and he was still leaning against the window, but for just a second, I could have sworn he had been looking over at us.

CHAPTER 15

Or, Never Bet Against
Anderson General Life Insurance

B Y THE TIME I GOT BACK TO THE HOUSE, IT was after midnight. I'd returned from the parking lot to find that everyone else had left. I didn't take it personally that nobody had realized I was still at the Inn—we'd all caravanned over in a line of cars, and everyone had probably assumed I'd gotten a ride back with somebody else.

I was about to use a ride-sharing app—Danny had linked my account to his when I started high school—but there was a Stanwich Taxi idling in front of the Inn, and after making sure the driver was taking rides, and not just a nap, I got in. As I told him my address, he visibly winced, and I realized it was the same driver who'd brought both J.J. and Uncle Stu to the house. So I could get why he wasn't thrilled—between the two of them, he clearly thought we were a family full of grifters.

I'd expected the house to be quiet and dark when I got home. It was late, after all, and we had a big day ahead of us tomorrow. But as I headed up the driveway, I could see lights shining through the front windows.

I crossed around the side of the house to let myself in through the kitchen door, holding my heels by their straps, wincing as I eased the door open inch by inch, until I was sure that the alarm wasn't going to sound and wake up the whole house.

I shut the door gently and then turned to see that the kitchen was packed—J.J. and Rodney were sitting at the island, both with bottles of beer, Linnie was sitting on the counter, and Danny and Brooke were at the kitchen table, Waffles on Brooke's lap, getting his ears scratched. There was a box of pizza on the counter, with one lone slice and a bevy of crusts left. I just took in the sight for a moment, wishing I could somehow preserve this moment, freeze it in amber. Because this— minus Brooke and the dog—this was what I'd been picturing when I'd imagined this weekend.

All of us, together again. At last.

"Hey," I said as I came inside and dropped my shoes by the kitchen stairs. "I thought everyone would have gone to bed already."

"Ha," J.J. said, waving this away as he took a sip from his bottle. "The night is young."

"It's really not," Rodney said as he rolled up his sleeve to look at his watch.

"Why are you back?" I asked Linnie, crossing barefoot to the fridge. "I thought you were going out with the girls."

"I did," she said. "But then Jenny K. met someone, and we decided to clear out and give her some space. And then when we got back here, Priya realized she was exhausted. . . ."

"Priya was on the right track," Rodney said around a yawn. "We should probably turn in."

"Yeah," Linnie said, pushing herself off the counter.

"Wait," I said quickly, shutting the fridge door without taking anything and turning around to face everyone. "We can't go to bed yet!"

"It is kind of late, Chuck," Danny said.

"But—we all just got here." I knew this wasn't technically true, but it felt like it. I was finally with my siblings, in the kitchen, without alarms going off or tent crises or guests coming and going. And yes, technically there was both an unexpected girlfriend and a beagle. But just going to bed felt like I would be letting this chance slip by. How many more times would we even be in this kitchen together? I had a feeling I could probably count them on one hand, and the thought made me feel panicky. "We need to do something fun, something to mark Linnie and Rodney's last single night."

"Like what?" Linnie asked, leaning back against the counter. My thoughts were racing as I tried to think of something that would fit the criteria I had given. Playing a board game or watching a movie just wasn't going to cut it. It needed to be something more than that, something epic.

"Something we can all do together," I said, stalling for time in the hopes that something would come to mind.

"And Brooke, too," J.J. added.

"It's fine," Brooke said, glancing at Danny. "I don't have to . . . I mean, whatever it is, you guys can just . . ."

"Aw, come on," Danny said, taking her hand across the table and giving it a squeeze. "Don't be a spoilsport."

"I'm *not*," Brooke said sharply, and we all simultaneously felt the need to look at either the ceiling or the floor.

"I've got it," I said. We hadn't done it in forever, but it had once been a Grant family tradition, something we did every Fourth of July, and even Christmas, if it wasn't snowing, and sometimes even if it was. "Anyone fancy a game of CTF?"

"What is that?" Brooke asked.

"Really?" J.J. tilted his head to the side. "We haven't played CTF in years."

"I know!" I was bouncing on the balls of my feet now. "That's what makes it perfect. We can bring back an old tradition before we have to say good-bye to the house."

"Only if J.J. finally admits I am the master," Danny said, starting to smile.

"Um, I believe I beat you the last time we played."

"Wasn't that, like, five years ago?" Rodney asked.

"So?" J.J. and Danny said simultaneously.

"Linnie?" I asked. She was the bride, after all—and if she wanted to go to bed, I had a feeling the game wouldn't be happening.

"I think a midnight game of CTF the night before my wedding actually sounds like a great idea." She grinned at me. "Let's do it."

Wait," Brooke said, hurrying behind Danny as we all trooped out to the backyard, a furrow between her eyebrows. "What are we doing?"

"Capture the flag," J.J. said with a grin. "Grant-style." He looked at her and shook his head. "Don't you want to change? Charlie, lend her my gnome sweatshirt."

"Why?" Brooke asked, her voice going higher. "What is this?"

"You've never played capture the flag?" Danny asked, his eyebrows flying up. "Didn't you ever go to camp?"

"No," Brooke said, looking around at all of us. "I . . . didn't."

"You're definitely going to want to change," J.J. said as we arrived in the center of the backyard—in the spot the tent would be tomorrow. "I have extra clothes upstairs if you need them."

"Thanks," Brooke said, "but—"

"Hey!" J.J. yelled toward the house. "What's the holdup?"

"Shh," Danny and I said immediately. There were still nine people and a dog inside the house—and Uncle Stu in my mother's studio—all of whom were presumably asleep. When we'd agreed in the kitchen to play, Rodney had put on the condition that it happen quietly enough not to wake up anyone inside. The center of the backyard was far enough away from the bedrooms so that we should be okay, but there was no need to push our luck.

Capture the flag had been a Grant tradition ever since Danny spent a summer at sleepaway camp when he was eight. He'd brought the game home to us, and though we'd had others throughout the years—we'd gotten very into Manhunt for a while, despite the fact that we never seemed to have enough flashlights—CTF was the game we'd always come back to when we could play outside. Over the years, we'd devised a set of rules that had made the game uniquely ours. But a few years ago, we'd just stopped playing it, and I hadn't realized how much I'd missed it until I ran out into the backyard in the moonlight, feeling the cold night air on my face and my hair streaming behind me as I ran to catch up with my favorite people.

Once we'd agreed to play, J.J. had yelled "Break!" and we'd dashed upstairs to change out of our rehearsal-dinner clothes. I knew from past experiences that when we played CTF, things could get very messy—J.J. especially was not above pushing you into the dirt if the flag was in his reach—and the last thing I wanted to do was wreck my dress.

Since I'd left Brooke and Danny in the kitchen, I figured I had at least a few seconds to duck into my room and grab some clothes before they made it up there, since none of the clothes I'd taken out of my room in preparation for this weekend were CTF-appropriate.

I opened the door and stepped inside, taken a little aback by how, after only a few hours, it felt like I was in a room I needed permission to be in, that somehow being here without asking was like trespassing. Danny's suit for tomorrow was hanging in my closet, and there were three dresses next to it—just how many times was Brooke planning on changing during the wedding, anyway? The top of my dresser was now covered with a huge, professional-looking makeup case, a curling iron, a hair straightener, and three separate brushes. I just stared at it all for a second, a little amazed that Brooke had brought all this with her from California. When I heard footsteps coming up to the third floor, I realized I needed to get a move on. I grabbed my clothes, then hurried out the door, closing it quickly behind me.

Danny had turned on the outside lights, and then we'd all stood perfectly still in the kitchen, waiting to hear if it sounded like people were waking up, if the light coming in through windows was bothering anyone. When we didn't hear anything after a solid minute of listening, we decided it was probably okay and had headed out to the backyard to wait for Linnie and Rodney, who were getting the flags. I'd put on sneakers, sweatpants, and a T-shirt with a sweatshirt over it, and while J.J. and Danny had also both changed into jeans and long-sleeved T-shirts, Brooke was still in her rehearsal-dinner dress, though she had taken off her heels and was standing barefoot on the lawn, a look of apprehension on her face as she glanced around, her arms crossed over her chest.

"It'll be fun," Danny said, smiling at her. "It's always a good time."

"I just don't understand how this works," Brooke snapped, sounding annoyed and tired. "And if someone's not going to explain it—"

"It's easy," J.J. assured her. He pointed to one side of the lawn, then the other. "So, there are two bases. We divide into teams and the goal is to steal the other team's flag and bring it back to your base without getting tagged."

"When you get tagged," I said, looking at my middle brother in the moonlight, "someone is supposed to *lightly* tap you. They are not supposed to shove you over, or push you into a pile of dirt, or pick you up—"

"Anyway," J.J. said loudly, talking over me, "if you do get tagged, then you have to go to the other team's jail."

"Jail?" Brooke asked, looking from J.J. to Danny, her brow still furrowed—it didn't seem like this was clearing anything up for her.

I nodded. "Yeah. We use the trampoline"—I pointed to it—"and the doorway of the greenhouse. If you get tagged you have to go to jail, and you can only get out if one of your teammates tags you for a jailbreak."

"Or if they get the flag," Danny said, snapping his fingers. "Didn't we decide that was a get-out-of-jail-free card?"

"Yes," J.J. said, nodding. "But if they don't manage to get back to their base with the flag, then you have to go *back* to jail."

"But don't forget about the sixth amendment!" This was Rodney; I turned to see he was jogging toward us, wearing jeans and an ancient green Dartmouth sweatshirt.

"Rodney added this," Danny said. "It's how we should have known he would end up a lawyer."

"It's a good addition!" Rodney said, smiling wide. "So, if you're in jail, you can yell 'sixth amendment!' and then you're allowed to present your case for why you should be let out of jail. If even one person on the other team agrees, you get to go free."

"It only ever works with Rodney, though," J.J. said, shaking his head.

"What?" Rodney said with a shrug. "I believe in one's right to represent oneself at trial. It's my favorite amendment."

"You have a favorite amendment?" J.J. asked.

"You *don't?*"

"Got it?" Danny asked, smiling at Brooke.

"Um . . ." She looked around at us, then at the backyard. "I'm not sure . . ."

"Got the flags," Linnie said, jogging up to us. "They were both pretty dusty. When was the last time we played this?"

"It's been a while," I said as I watched Linnie shake them out.

One was a beautifully handmade triangular flag that read GRANT on it—my mother had drawn a strip about us playing CTF and a reader had given it to her at a Comic-Con years ago. The other flag was a small white towel that read ANDERSON GENERAL LIFE INSURANCE in blue letters that were mostly faded out. This towel was one of our house's many mysteries, since my parents didn't have Anderson General Life Insurance and were baffled as to how a promotional towel had ended up in our house. But since we'd been playing, it had always been our other flag, mostly because it had a loop at the top so you could put it on a stick.

It was one of the many things that had become completely irreplaceable simply because we'd been using it for capture the flag my whole life. I had hidden both flags in the games closet during the tag sale purge, terrified that while I was up at Linnie and Rodney's, my parents would have found them and sold them to people who wouldn't understand their importance. Because the Anderson General Life Insurance towel technically wasn't worth anything—except for the fact that it was priceless. And where would we play CTF in the future?

"Did you want to change, Brooke?" Linnie asked, looking at her white dress. "I can let you borrow something."

"I think I'll sit this one out," Brooke said, starting to back away.

"Oh, come on," Danny said. "It'll be fun, babe."

"But . . ." Brooke shifted her weight from foot to foot.

"I thought you wanted to be here," Danny said, a sigh somewhere in his voice.

"Okay," Brooke said after a pause. "Sure."

"Great," Danny said, shooting her a quick smile. "So, here's the rundown. Linnie's going to throw the flags in the air to pick for teams, and you have to run to the one you want to be on—either Grant or Anderson General Life Insurance. And then the teams take the flags to their separate corners, and when we're in place, we begin."

"But if you're in the no-man's-zone when the game starts, then whoever tags you, you have to become part of their team," I pointed out.

"Unless you get tagged back," Rodney said, shaking his head, "before you get into jail. Then you can pick which team you want to be on, but you can't change after that."

"Basically, it's easier just to make sure you're on a side when the game begins," Linnie said.

"But . . ." Brooke looked around at us like she was hoping for a more detailed explanation. "But I don't . . ."

"It's really more of a learn-as-you-go type game," I said. I was tempted to suggest that she just sit out the first round and watch, but held it back.

J.J. nodded, patting her on the back in what I'm sure he thought was a comforting manner. "You'll pick it up."

"Ready?" Linnie asked, looking around at all of us, then grinned. "Go!" She threw the flags up in the air.

I raced toward Anderson General Life Insurance, mostly because J.J. had a weakness for the Grant flag. Sure enough, I was right—J.J. and Linnie ran for the Grant flag, while Danny and Rodney headed toward Anderson's, and Brooke stayed in the same spot, looking around, increasingly unhappily.

"Yes!" Danny said, holding up his hand for high fives, which Rodney and I returned. "We got this, guys. We're going to crush it."

"I . . ." Brooke edged toward the house. "I think I'll just . . ."

"Babe, you can't bail *now*," Danny said, starting to sound annoyed. "The teams'll be uneven! You can be on Linnie's team."

"Yeah, come be on our team," Linnie said, grinning at her. "It's the best team. And this way, we have a medic if someone gets hurt!"

"Don't worry," Danny said with a wink as we started to head over to our side of the yard, "I'll take it easy on you!"

"Also, everyone watch out for the tent posts," Rodney reminded us.

Danny found a stick and we planted the flag, after some quick deliberation, just a few feet away from the greenhouse entrance that would be serving as our jail. "Think J.J.'s going to put their flag in a tree again? Remember when he did that for like a whole year?"

"Start in one minute," Linnie called across the yard in a loud whisper that nonetheless carried.

I gave her a thumbs-up, and then Team Anderson General Life Insurance turned to face each other. "I call jailer," Rodney said immediately, raising his hand. "Groom's prerogative."

"Okay," Danny said, and he was smiling widely. "We ready to do this?"

"Here we go," Linnie whisper-yelled across the yard, and I turned to see that they'd had the opposite idea we had—their flag was almost as far away from the jail (the trampoline) as possible. "Three . . . two . . . one . . . capture the flag!"

We all set off running as fast as possible. I headed straight into enemy territory, then dashed to the left to avoid J.J., who was coming right at me—it was always his strategy to try to get as many people in jail as possible to make flag stealing easier. Danny ran in the opposite direction from me, and it looked like Linnie was playing defense, not offense—she wasn't moving toward our territory; she was going to guard her own. Brooke was standing still, just looking around at the rest of us in motion, like she was still waiting for a more detailed instruction list.

"Got it!" Danny yelled as he grabbed the Grant flag out of the ground and started to turn and run back to our base with it, only to have J.J. pivot from trying to get me to run full speed at him.

"Danny," I yelled, breaking left to avoid Linnie, who was advancing toward me. "On your ten!" He turned but just a second too late, and J.J. tagged him.

"Get outta here," he said, pointing to the trampoline.

"Is the game over?" Brooke asked hopefully.

"No," Linnie said, stopping and turning to her, and I took this moment of distraction to run full out toward the trampoline.

Danny saw me coming and smiled, stretching his hand out as far as it would go while still keeping a foot touching the metal base (as had been decreed years ago by the rules). I slapped his hand and he grinned at me. "Thanks, Chuck."

"I've got your back," I called to him, but he was already running in the other direction, toward our base, trying to intercept J.J., who was barreling toward the flag. Which meant—I whirled around, ready to try to grab the Grant flag, only to see Linnie standing directly in front of me.

"You're out," she said, tapping me on the shoulder and pointing. "Trampoline. I call jailer," she added to Brooke, who had now wandered a little farther from their base but still wasn't making any move to try to grab our flag—which was woefully unguarded at the moment, as Danny chased J.J. and Rodney tried to box him in. "Doesn't she realize she could grab it?" Linnie asked, shaking her head.

"Jailbreak!" I looked over, startled, to see Rodney running full out toward me, tagging me on the shoulder, then pivoting away.

"Thanks!" I yelled, sprinting away from the jail on Rodney's heels. I decided to head back to our base for a bit, regroup, maybe play defense for a while. Just as I'd had this thought, though, J.J. started running in our direction, brandishing the Anderson General Life Insurance flag.

"No!" Rodney yelled, running after him, only to have J.J. pivot and change directions—running toward Brooke. Glancing behind her, she started running—directly into one of the tent posts. She tripped over it, her feet tangling, and she windmilled her arms for a second, trying to stay upright, before falling to the ground, hitting it hard. "God!" she yelled, trying to push herself up to standing, but then losing her footing and falling again.

J.J., not noticing any of this, sprinted to his base and threw the Anderson General Life Insurance flag to the ground, then raised his arms in victory. "Take that!" he yelled, spinning around in triumph, then frowning when he saw everyone else had stopped running. "What's going on?"

"You okay, babe?" Danny asked, jogging over to her. He reached out a hand, but Brooke pushed herself up to standing. She looked down and seemed to see what had happened at the same time the rest of us did—there was a huge dirt and grass stain all down the side of her cream-colored dress.

"No, I'm not okay!" she snapped, her voice breaking. I couldn't tell, going by just the outdoor lights and moonlight—but I was pretty sure there were tears in her eyes. "I didn't even want to play this stupid game. Why did you make me?"

"I didn't make you," Danny said, sounding taken aback. "I thought it would be fun."

"Fun for *you*!" Brooke yelled, her voice going high and a little hysterical. "Did you think about if it would be fun for me? Of course you didn't. You haven't thought about how I would feel all day, so why should you start now?"

"That's not true," Danny said, taking a step closer to her, keeping his voice low.

"Why am I even here?" she asked, folding her arms across her chest—which, I couldn't help but notice, just seemed to add more dirt to the dress. "Why did you even ask me to come if you don't want me to be here?"

"Babe," Danny said, glancing from Brooke to the rest of us. "Let's not do this now."

"I'm not doing *anything*," she said, her voice breaking. She stared at Danny for a moment longer, like she was waiting for him to say something, but then turned on her heel and stalked across the lawn and into the house. A second later, I heard the door slam—but thankfully, the alarm stayed off.

"Um," Linnie said, looking from Danny and back to the house again. "Should we . . . ?" She left the sentence dangling, a question at the end of it.

Danny looked in the direction Brooke had gone, his jaw set. And after a moment, he shook his head. "Let's keep playing."

"Really?" Rodney asked. I saw him exchange a glance with Linnie. "Because it's no problem. We can stop. . . ."

"Nah," Danny said, and it seemed like he was trying, with a great deal of effort, to sound cheerful again. He walked over to where J.J. had dropped the Anderson's flag. "But that last one doesn't count at all, J.J. I think we should start over."

"Hey!" J.J. yelped, running after him.

I looked back to the house. It wasn't that I wanted to stop playing the game—and Brooke had clearly seemed disgusted with all of us—but I couldn't shake the feeling that maybe someone should have followed her.

"Chuck!" Danny called, jogging back to our base, the Anderson's flag over his shoulder. "You playing?"

"Yes," I said immediately. Then I turned away from the house and ran to catch up with my brother.

An hour later, we all trooped inside the kitchen, most of us slightly worse for wear. We'd ended up playing best two out of three, which had led to the game getting dirtier and dirtier as it went on—both figuratively and literally. Linnie had held her arms out to Rodney for a hug, only to tag him when he got close; Danny had faked a twisted ankle to tag out J.J.; and Rodney had refused to grant a single jailhouse pardon, which we'd all agreed was a record. Once we'd restarted, we'd won the first round (Linnie and J.J. complaining that we had an unfair advantage, since they were down a player.) They won the second, but we managed to pull out a win for the third round, with Rodney running faster than I'd ever seen him to bring the Grant flag back to our base while Linnie, stuck in our jail, let out a very impressive stream of curses as she watched. After he'd made it back to base safely, Danny had whirled me around in the air as Rodney had thrown down the Grant flag in victory. "You don't mess with Anderson General Life Insurance!" he'd yelled, doing a victory dance. "You don't *mess* with us!"

Now, standing in the bright lights of the kitchen, I could see that none of us had escaped unscathed—I had grass stains all over my sweatpants, Linnie had a dirt smudge that ran the length of her forehead, and Danny's sweatshirt hood had been half ripped off, though both Linnie and J.J. were trying to blame the other for it. Linnie got us all waters, and while I watched everyone argue about the fairness of a particular jailbreak and whether J.J.'s first capture should have been counted, maybe just by half, I had to bite my lip to keep from smiling. Because this was why I'd wanted to play the game. This was what I'd been missing for so long. And it felt like, finally, things were getting back to how they should be.

"We wouldn't have lost if Mike had been here," J.J. grumbled. "I need a wartime consigliere out on the field, and he's great at strategy."

"Yeah," Linnie said, her smile fading a little as she looked around. "Mike really should be here too."

I was about to argue with this, but the truth was, for all the times he'd hung back and refused to go along with us, Mike had never done it with capture the flag. He really was great at coming up with plans, and he did a sportscaster-type play-by-play on the field that always cracked Rodney up to the point where he often had to stop running. "Yeah," I agreed, but so quietly I wasn't sure anyone else heard me.

The rest of the recap didn't last too long—Linnie and Rodney peeled off first, and J.J. started yawning and headed upstairs, with Danny following, ruffling my hair on the way out of the kitchen. I waited a little bit longer—I stayed sitting on the kitchen counter, phone in hand, waiting to see if Jesse would reach out again, even though I had a feeling he probably had his hands full with Mike.

After a few minutes, I finally decided to pack it in, and headed up to the third floor, yawning. I had just reached J.J.'s room and was about to turn the doorknob when I heard voices coming from inside. J.J. and also—I leaned a little bit closer, and my eyes went wide—Jenny W. They were talking low, but I could hear Jenny's laughter, and I backed away from the door quickly, getting the sense that they would not have appreciated me showing up just then. J.J. had clearly forgotten once again that I was supposed to be staying with him. As I headed downstairs, resigning myself to the couch, I wondered why I was even surprised. I tiptoed downstairs as quietly as possible—and practically tripped over Waffles as I made it to the front hall. He was sitting dead center in front of the bottom step, just staring at me. "Um. Hi," I said as I headed into the kitchen to make sure the door was locked, feeling like of all the rescue dogs we could have gotten this weekend, we'd ended up with the weirdest.

I heard a *click-clack*ing behind me, and I turned around to see Waffles standing in the kitchen, looking at me intently. "You okay?" I asked, even though I was all too aware that he wouldn't be able to answer me. But the dog just kept looking at me steadily, until I started to get a little uncomfortable.

I looked around, like there was someone who could help me translate. How did people who owned dogs do this? You were basically inviting an animal you couldn't communicate with to move into your house with you for years of confusion. *"What?"* I asked, but Waffles just tilted his head to the side a little, his eyes not leaving mine. He let out a soft whimper, looked over at the door, then back at me, and much too late, I understood what was happening. "Oh," I said, feeling like I should have gotten this much sooner. "Um . . . sorry about that. I'll take you for a walk."

His leash was hanging up on one of the hooks by the door, and as soon as he saw me take it, he started running around in small circles and doing these little howly yips, like there was a real howl coming and he was just warming up.

"Shh," I said, trying to calm him down. Even when I got his leash snapped on, the yips just seemed to be getting louder. "If you don't stop, I won't take you on a walk," I said, then wondered why I thought the dog, who didn't speak English, would suddenly understand blackmail.

Once Waffles realized that a walk was happening, he stopped running in circles and practically dragged me down the driveway. He seemed to go crazy for the first few minutes, running to smell as many trees and rocks as possible and then appearing to regret this and circling back to get the ones he'd missed. I hadn't brought a flashlight, but it was light enough out that I could see—the moon peeking through the clouds gave me enough light to maneuver down the street. As I watched Waffles joyfully sniffing, I really started to feel bad that he'd been cooped up all day with us.

I walked him to the end of the road, and while Waffles seemed more than happy to keep going, it appeared that he'd pretty much done what he needed to and now just seemed to be sniffing for fun. Everything that had happened today was hitting me, and I was beginning to feel just how late it was. And it was also not warm out—I hadn't noticed it as much when we'd all been running full speed across the yard, but in the last hour or so, it had gotten a lot colder, especially with the wind picking up. I crossed my fingers on both hands that this was just a fluke and I'd wake up tomorrow to perfect wedding weather. I pulled Waffles over to the other side of the road and started heading toward home.

Right away, I noticed the truck. It was parked on the road, about three houses down from ours. I don't know why I hadn't paid attention to it as I'd been walking away from the house—maybe I'd been fixated on the dog. But you couldn't help noticing it—for one thing, it was the only car parked on the street. And on our street, where there wasn't a commercial district nearby, everyone just parked in their garages or driveways.

It wasn't until I got closer to the car that I realized it looked familiar.

I could see WHERE THERE'S A WILL painted across the side of it—this was the truck that Bill had been driving.

I stopped walking and just looked at it for a moment, and Waffles stopped as well, sitting down at my feet and also seeming to regard the truck, his head tilted to the side. What was it doing here? I had assumed Bill had driven back to his uncle's house after the rehearsal dinner.

I walked toward it, glancing in through the driver's-side window and then taking a small step back when I realized that Bill was inside. He was in the backseat of the cab, curled up on his side, sleeping, his suit jacket pulled up to his neck like a blanket. Before I'd even worked out if this was a good idea, I was reaching out and knocking on the glass.

Bill shot up, sitting up straight and looking around, half-panicked, and I realized too late that I probably should have knocked more gently, or tried to get Waffles to howl again, something that would have maybe not startled him quite so much.

He looked around, blinking, and I waved as his eyes landed on me. "Hi," I said, even though I wasn't sure how much he'd be able to hear me through the glass.

Bill just stared at me for a second, like he was still trying to understand what was happening. His hair was flattened on the side he'd been sleeping on and standing practically straight up on the other.

"Charlie?" he asked, his voice muffled through the glass. He reached across and opened the door, and I leaned my head in. "Hey. Is everything all right?"

"Yeah," I said, stumbling slightly as Waffles lunged in the direction of something he felt compelled to sniff at that particular moment. "Hi. Sorry—I was walking the dog and I saw your truck. . . ."

"Yes," Bill said, rubbing his eyes briskly, like he was trying to wake himself up. "I . . . well, I stopped by the house after the dinner, just to drop off some of the decorations from the Inn, and then when I tried to leave, my car wouldn't start."

"Oh," I said, wincing. "Jeez. I'm sorry about that."

"It's probably my fault," he said, not sounding particularly concerned about this. "I have a tendency to leave the inside light on." He shook his head. "I was always having to get my battery jumped back in New Mexico. My stepdad used to say he had Triple A on speed dial."

"So . . ." I looked around, like there was going to be a tow truck coming up the street at any moment. "Um . . . do you not have them on speed dial?"

Bill's smile widened. "I know," he said. "I was about to call them, but then I did the time math. And having to wait for them to come, give it a jump, then drive all the way to my uncle's, then all the way back here in the morning when I have to be here first thing . . . It just seemed easier to stay. I have all my clothes with me anyway, since I had to change for the rehearsal dinner. I'll just get a jump tomorrow morning."

"But . . ." I bit my lip and looked around the empty street. It wasn't like Stanwich was a hotbed for crime or anything, but I still didn't think it was a good idea for Bill to be sleeping on the street like this. I knew my parents would have not been happy if they'd found out I'd slept in my car. "Aren't you cold?" In just the time I'd been standing and talking to him, I'd felt myself getting colder, reminding me that some Aprils in Connecticut, it snowed.

"It's totally f-fine," Bill said with another smile, though he undercut this somewhat when his teeth started to chatter on the last word.

"It's not fine," I said, shaking my head. There was really only one solution here that I could think of—I wasn't about to let Bill freeze sleeping in his car all night. "I think you should stay with us."

"Oh, that's okay," Bill said, giving me another smile, one that seemed to turn into a grimace, though, as he was clearly fighting his teeth chattering again. "Really. I couldn't impose."

"You're not imposing," I assured him. "We have a ton of people staying already. I promise it's fine." Bill just looked at me for another moment, his eyes searching my face, like he was trying to determine if I really meant it. He must have realized I did, because he nodded and climbed out. I could see that he was back in the jeans and long-sleeved T-shirt he'd been wearing during the day. He pulled a duffel bag out of the front seat, then carefully folded his suit jacket and laid it across the backseat.

"Are you sure?" he asked me across the hood of the truck as he lifted his duffel bag out. "I really was okay in there."

"I'm sure. We can't have the wedding coordinator's assistant freezing the day before the wedding."

"But then I could've been the something blue," he said, and I laughed. We all started to walk down the center of the empty road together, Waffles leading the way. Bill nodded toward the dog. "I didn't get to meet this guy earlier. He's really cute. What's his name?"

"Oh—that's right." While we'd been getting temporary dogs dropped off, Bill had been fixing the rehearsal dinner decorations. "His name's Waffles."

Bill stopped walking, which meant I stopped walking, which meant Waffles got yanked back by his leash. "Like in the comic strip?" he asked, his voice going high and excited. "You guys actually have a dog named *Waffles*?"

I hadn't realized Bill read the strip—or that he'd known who we were. But if you read the strip, it was pretty obvious. "I guess you're a fan?"

Bill started walking again. "Oh yeah. I didn't get it at first—I mean, that you guys were *those* Grants. But I kept feeling like I'd been in your kitchen before. It was the weirdest feeling, and then I finally put it together."

"Well, he's not really our dog," I said, then explained Waffles's temporary nature. "I don't suppose handling temporary canines is anything you've dealt with before?"

Bill laughed. "It's a first."

We rounded the curve in the road and reached the house—and as soon as it was visible, Waffles pulled me forward, straining against the leash to go in. And it hit me that this dog hadn't even been in our house a full day but already knew it and wanted to get back inside. That even if it was just temporary, he wanted to go home again.

"All set?" I asked as I came into the family room. I'd arranged one couch with blankets and pillows for myself and another for Bill. When we'd come in, I had told Bill I could get him set up in the family room before it hit me that I would also be sleeping in there. Somehow, this hadn't occurred to me until that moment, that inviting him to stay meant we'd be sleeping in the same room. Normally, there would be other options, but we were, for the first time in my memory, totally out of rooms.

Since I didn't want to interrupt whatever might be happening in J.J.'s bedroom, I had just decided I could sleep in the sweatpants and T-shirt I'd played capture the flag in—my sweatshirt was muddy and grass stained, but the T-shirt had been protected and was fine. I'd taken out my contacts and found a pair of glasses floating around in the kitchen, so I could at least see.

The couches in the family room, thanks to the *GMA* crew, had ended up at right angles to each other, and looking at them now, they suddenly seemed very close. But I really didn't think I could move them apart at all without being totally obvious.

"Yeah," Bill said, looking up from where he was lying on the couch, the blankets pulled halfway over him.

He gave me a smile, and I realized there was nothing to do except turn off the lights and start what was certainly going to be the weirdest sleepover of my life. "Um," I said, reaching for the lamp but then pulling my hand back. "Okay if I turn off the lights?"

"Fine by me," Bill said.

I snapped off the light, and the room was thrown into total darkness for a second, and then a moment later, moonlight started filtering in. I blinked, letting my eyes adjust as I looked around.

I'd always loved the family room. There was a big stone fireplace at one end, surrounded by built-in bookcases filled with books and board games, most of which were missing at least one crucial piece. Unlike the kitchen, where we all hung out by chance, while eating or passing through, the family room was where we *chose* to hang out. This room was the best of us. It was where we watched movies, passing bowls of popcorn back and forth. It was where my parents had faculty parties, where the Christmas tree was always set up, and where we all found ourselves after Thanksgiving dinner, fighting off our food comas. It was having movie marathons with my siblings on rainy afternoons, all of us wrapped up in blankets. It was playing high-stakes games of Pictionary and kids-only games of Cards Against Humanity. It was where most of my favorite memories in the house had happened.

As I looked around now in the moonlight, I felt a wave of loss hit me, even as I was still sitting right here. But ever since my parents had sold the house, a countdown clock had started ticking in my brain—how many more times would I sit in this room? How many more times would we gather here? How many times would I push through the door, hang my keys on the hook, an unthinking motion I'd performed a thousand times?

And it made me furious that I'd ever dared to complain about the fact that the family room floors were always cold and the hot water in my bathroom took too long to heat up. What did I have to complain about when this was my house, before I'd had any inkling that wouldn't always be the case?

"Charlie?"

I glanced over at Bill, who was looking at me like he was waiting for an answer. "Oh—sorry. What?"

"Nothing," he said with a shrug. "I just said that I appreciated the help today. Sorry if things were a little disorganized."

"Yeah," I said, shaking my head, thinking about Clementine, the decorations, Waffles, Mike. "It definitely was kind of crazy."

"We got that all out of the way today," Bill said confidently. "Tomorrow's going to go perfectly."

He settled onto his pillow and then adjusted his blankets, and I realized that it was strange for me to still be sitting upright on my couch. I took a breath, then lay down, staring straight up at the ceiling, trying not to think about how close our heads suddenly were. I found myself aware of every movement he was making and how loud my breathing suddenly was. Why had I never thought about how intimate it was, just sleeping in the same room with someone? Because it really was—it was how I knew that Siobhan talked in her sleep, and occasionally sang, and that Linnie stole every blanket she saw and then denied it with a straight face in the morning. When you were asleep, you were who you *were*, not who you were pretending to be, and now I was going to be doing that with Bill, with someone I'd just met that morning.

I didn't know *anything* about him, I was realizing, now that I could hear him breathing just a few feet away from me. "So . . . you said something about New Mexico?" I realized that it was a terrible segue, but I felt like if I was going to be sleeping next to someone, I should at least know where they were from.

"Yeah," Bill said, and if he thought this was weird, I couldn't tell from his tone. "My parents got divorced when I was in eighth grade, and my dad moved out there."

"I'm sorry about that."

Bill was silent for a moment, but the kind of silence that has something behind it, the kind you don't want to rush over. "It was hard," he finally said. "Especially because I was splitting the school year up for a while. I always had the wrong clothes, the wrong slang. . . ."

I rolled over so that I was on my side and could see him now. He was propped up on one elbow, his hair slightly mussed. "And then your mom moved out of Putnam?"

He nodded. "Last year. She got a new job in Mystic, so she sold our house...." There was something in Bill's tone I recognized—it sounded like the way I'd been feeling ever since Lily and Greg Pearson had first walked through the door.

"My parents sold this place," I said, bunching my pillow up a little more. "Two months ago. We're moving out when the escrow is . . ." I paused, not exactly sure what the right adjective was. But then, I wasn't exactly sure what escrow *was*, so this wasn't that surprising. "When it's done. But they haven't even found a place here yet."

"They're staying here?" I nodded. "And you're staying too," Bill said, his tone thoughtful.

"That doesn't—" I sat up a little more. "That doesn't have anything to do with this. Stanwich is a great school, that's all. And I get a discount on tuition."

"Did you always want to go there?"

I thought for a moment. When I'd visited my siblings at their various schools, I'd always tried to picture myself there—walking across that quad, eating at that dining hall. But I'd never done it at Stanwich, the school I'd been to a hundred times. "I guess not."

Bill yawned, then covered his mouth with his hand. "Thank you again for letting me stay here," he said after a moment, his voice still yawn-fogged. "It really *was* getting kind of cold in the car. And I kept thinking about bears."

"Bears?"

"Yeah," he said with a small laugh. "My dad and I went camping in Oregon once, and we had to take all these precautions against bears. Especially in your car—if they smell anything, they'll basically rip it apart to get to what they think is food."

"I don't think that's a problem here," I said, trying, and failing, to think of any instance I'd ever even heard of bears in Connecticut. "I know they have them in upstate New York and Pennsylvania." I started to yawn myself, no doubt because I'd seen Bill do it. "But I don't think they're rip-cars-apart bears. I think that might be a West Coast thing."

Bill laughed. "Probably. It'd be a heck of a way to go, though, wouldn't it?"

"I can see it on the front page of the *Sentinel*," I said, raising my arm to frame a headline. *"Bad News Bear."* Bill groaned, which only encouraged me. *"Unbearable Pain!"*

"Stop," Bill said, even though he was smiling.

"Trouble Bruin?" I asked, and Bill laughed.

"It would be worth it just to get one of those," he said, rolling onto his back and folding one hand behind his head. "You should be a writer or something."

I smiled at that. "Ha ha." Silence fell again, but it didn't feel awkward or strange—more like peaceful. Or maybe I was just getting too tired to keep analyzing what our silences were feeling like, if they were comfortable or uncomfortable.

I felt myself yawn, and realized all at once just how tired I was. A second before I had been fine, and now I was struggling to keep my eyes open. I took off my glasses and tucked them under the couch, along with my phone, in the hopes that I wouldn't accidentally step on either one when I got up. "Good night, Bill."

"Night, Charlie," Bill replied, his voice already getting slow and sleepy.

I closed my eyes, then immediately opened them again—I had forgotten to call Siobhan back. I reached under the couch for my phone, only to see that it had died. But it was okay, I figured, as I pushed it back under the couch, since it was too late to call her now anyway. I'd just call her in the morning.

I lay back down and let my eyes drift closed. I could feel sleep starting to pull me under, and across the room, I could hear Bill's breathing grow slower and more steady.

I was about to drift off when I heard feet pattering across the carpet. I opened my eyes to see Waffles sitting on the floor by my couch. I looked at him, wondering what he wanted and just praying that he didn't need another walk. But a moment later, he jumped up onto the couch, turned around twice in a circle, and then curled himself in a ball in the space behind my knees, resting his head on my leg. And a second later, he started snuffle-breathing, and I had a feeling that I was the only awake one in the room—that both the dog and Bill had fallen asleep.

Even as I told myself that I probably wouldn't sleep well—not with a dog on my legs and an assistant wedding coordinator next to me—I could feel my eyes drifting shut again and feeling my own breath start to fall into a pattern.

And the next time I opened my eyes, cool early light was streaming in through the room, and it was morning.

SATURDAY

GRANT CENTRAL STATION

CHAPTER 16
Or, Nothing Is Wrong!!!

I WOKE UP TO SOMETHING COLD AND WET PRESSING
against my cheek. My eyes flew open, and there was Waffles's
blurry outline, his nose against my face, looking at me intently. "Jeez,"
I said, wiping my face and scooting back against the couch cushions.

I put on my glasses and glanced at the couch next to mine, but it was
empty, the blankets folded neatly and the pillow stacked on top of them.
I reached for my phone to check the time and then remembered it was
still dead. I'd just swung my legs down to the ground when Waffles
looked up at the ceiling and started to growl.

I looked up as well, praying it wasn't a huge spider—but there was
nothing there. "What?" I asked him. But the dog was staring fixedly up
at it, his eyes tracking something I couldn't see, his growl getting louder.
I watched him do this, wondering if this meant that, on top of a broken
alarm, we now had a ghost.

I grabbed my sweatshirt from the floor and pulled it on as I walked
across to the front hall, Waffles following at my heels. It was colder
today than it had been yesterday—and I found myself wishing I'd
brought some slippers with me as I continued into the kitchen.

I pushed open the door and saw Bill standing by the kitchen counter. "Hey," I said, stepping inside.

"Hey," Bill said, smiling wide at me. He was wearing jeans and a navy T-shirt with the green Where There's A Will fleece I'd seen the day before.

"So," I said, wondering how long he'd been up—he was dressed, after all, and certainly looked more awake than I felt. I just hoped I hadn't kept him up, snoring or talking in my sleep. I crossed the kitchen to plug my phone in, and saw on the silver wall clock that it was just after seven. "How'd you sleep?"

"Not good." This voice came from the kitchen table, and I looked over, startled, to see Max sitting there, hunched over. He had a long scratch on his arm that looked fresh—it was bright red.

"Oh," I said, blinking at him as Waffles ran across the kitchen, ears flapping. "Um, are you okay? What happened to your hand?"

Max looked down at it, then immediately pulled his hand into his hoodie sleeve. "Nothing," he said, too quickly. "I'm just . . . clumsy."

Before I could ask for details, Waffles scratched at the door with one paw, then turned and looked at me. "You need to go out?" I asked, as though the dog were going to answer me. I opened the door and he tore into the backyard. As I closed the door, the alarm system let out three long *beep*s, then fell silent. "This is doing it when you *close* the door now?" I asked the kitchen in general. "What use is an alarm that goes off when you close the door?" I looked at the coffee maker, which was, sadly, both empty and quiet. And while I knew the basic mechanics of making coffee, I really wasn't very good at it—something that was confirmed by people's reactions whenever they drank the coffee I made. I headed to the fridge and pulled out a carton of orange juice instead.

"So, Max was just going to tell me something," Bill said, widening his eyes at me as I crossed to the kitchen island with my juice carton.

"Is everything okay?" I asked, pouring my juice into a glass, even though I had a feeling it wasn't. If everything was okay, Max wouldn't be awake looking like he was about to throw up.

Max shook his head. "I think we have a problem."

"That's okay," Bill said, giving him an I've-got-this smile. "That's my job. I can fix any wedding-related problem as long as it doesn't have to do with the weather. I have no control over the weather."

"Can you make me a clergyman with a regular practice and a con-gregation?"

Bill paled. "Um. Maybe not."

I just stared at Max. "Wait, *what?*"

"I thought it would be okay," Max said, hunching down into his hoodie, like he was trying to disappear into it. "A lot of my friends have performed weddings, and all you do is sign up with this online church and you're ready to rock and roll. My one friend Zeke did it on his phone as the bride and groom were walking down the aisle. It's, like, not a big deal. And so, when Lin and Rod were talking about the wedding, I told them I'd be happy to do it—I mean, I was honored that they wanted me to do it. I mean, I've known them both forever, I introduced them—"

"Breathe," I said. "Here." I brought my still-untouched juice over to him, since on TV, whenever people were getting faint, they always seemed to be given juice. I figured it couldn't hurt, at the very least.

"Thanks," Max said, taking a gulp. I crossed back to the island and poured myself another glass, really hoping this wasn't going where I had a feeling it was going.

"Okay," Bill said, his brow furrowed. I could see that he was worried—though it seemed crazy that I'd be able to tell this after knowing the guy for just a day. But his voice was as cheerful and as ready-to-help as ever. "So you got ordained online, right?"

"I did," Max said, rolling the juice glass between his palms. "And I thought I was good to go. But then yesterday during the rehearsal dinner, someone—maybe Rodney's cousin?—was talking about how you can't do the online-ordination thing in Connecticut. And I looked it up, and . . ." Max didn't finish the rest of the sentence, just tossed back a shot of his orange juice like it was whiskey.

"It's okay," Bill said, his voice soothing, even as he exchanged a look with me that perfectly encapsulated what I was thinking. Namely, that this was *bad*.

"So," I said, pouring myself some juice and taking a long sip, hoping all those hospital shows were onto something. "Who can perform weddings in Connecticut?"

Max pulled out his phone and looked down at it. "From what I can tell, you have to be an *actual* member of the clergy. Any type of religion, but that has to be like what you do. You can't be a one-day online minister."

"Oh," I said, my hopes dimming. We weren't religious in my family, and though Rodney didn't bring it up often, what he had said led me to believe that he wasn't a fan of organized religion. I had a feeling that neither he or Linnie would be thrilled to learn they were suddenly going to have a religious ceremony—if we could even find anyone to do it, day of. And would any sort of minister or rabbi worth his or her salt even be willing to step in and marry two heathens? Could they—did you have to be a part of that religion first? My head started to hurt, and I leaned back against the kitchen island.

"Wait," Bill said, sitting up straight. "Isn't Rodney's father in the military? Can't ship captains marry people?" He pulled out his phone and typed into it, then his face fell a moment later. "No," he said, shaking his head. "It doesn't count on dry land, apparently. I guess captains lose their power on land."

"Like Aquaman," Max said with a nod.

"Hang on a sec!" Bill was looking down at his phone, scrolling through it fast. "Judges can also marry people in Connecticut. Even retired judges. They retain the ability to marry people in the state. And it's totally legal."

"That's good," Max said, nodding emphatically. "That could be good. Um . . . do you know any judges?"

"I don't," I said, trying to think if there was a possibility either of my parents would be able to call in a favor, on a Saturday, for someone to perform a same-day wedding.

"So, should I tell them?" Max asked, meeting my eyes.

I glanced over at Bill, then looked back at Max. I really didn't want to start off my sister's wedding day—which was supposed to be the happiest day of her life—by telling her we were down an officiant. "Let's see if we can figure something out," I said slowly, wondering if it was the right decision even as I was saying it. I met Bill's eye, and he gave me a small nod.

"Morning." I looked over to see Rodney standing in the doorway, yawning.

"Everything's fine!" I said too loudly.

Rodney frowned. "What?"

"I mean . . . morning to you too. How'd you sleep? Want some juice?"

"I'm okay," Rodney said, yawning again as he headed for the coffee maker. "Did anyone make coffee?"

"Did someone say coffee?" J.J. asked, vaulting himself over the last two steps of the kitchen stairs, then stumbling slightly, managing to recover without falling over, and shooting me a big smile. I glared back at him.

"I'm making it," Rodney said as he started filling the pot with water. "Apparently."

"What's your damage?" J.J. asked, pushing himself up to sit on the counter.

"Um, remember I was supposed to stay in your room last night?" I asked, then immediately hoped Bill wouldn't think I was upset that

I'd had to stay in the same room as him. "It wasn't a big deal," I added hurriedly. "But—"

"Why couldn't Charlie stay in your room?" Rodney asked.

J.J. just looked at me, his eyes wide, and I realized this wasn't something he wanted Rodney to know about, which surprised me—usually J.J. was the first one to tell you about any sort of romantic development in his life, always convinced after the first date that he'd met the girl he was going to marry.

"He, um," I said, looking at my brother, "locked the door."

"I did," J.J. said quickly, shooting me a grateful look. "Sorry about that, Charlie." I gave him a small smile back, and then J.J. squinted at Max, who looked like he was about to fall over, or vomit, or both. "What's wrong?"

"Nothing," Bill and I said at the exact same time, which I had to admit, didn't help things seem less suspicious.

"Yeah, right," J.J. said, shaking his head. "What is it?"

"Um . . ." I tried to think of something non-wedding-related. "I think we have a ghost?"

"A ghost?" Rodney asked.

I nodded. "I think the dog saw something this morning. He kept growling at the ceiling."

J.J. rolled his eyes. "Well, that's all the proof I need." He looked around. "Is there breakfast?"

"Morning." I looked over to see my dad pushing his way through the door to the kitchen, rubbing his hands together. "It's cold today, isn't it?" Rodney shot him a look, and my dad immediately shook his head. "I meant, not cold. It's not cold at all. Perfect wedding weather. Is someone other than Charlie making coffee?"

The kitchen door swung open, and my uncle Stu stepped inside from the backyard, wearing a bathrobe with WESTIN embroidered on it. The dog trotted in after him, and I noticed that his paws looked dirty. I went to try to grab him and clean them off, but maybe sensing what I was after, he took off at a run toward the family room. My uncle slammed the door, and it let out the same three beeps that had sounded when I'd closed it.

"Huh," Stu said, peering at it. "I think there's something wrong with your alarm system, Jeff."

"Thanks for pointing that out, Stu."

"So," my uncle said, looking around. "Is breakfast on the way? I could eat a horse."

J.J. nodded. "That's what I said! Well, except for the horse part."

"What's wrong?" Rodney asked, and to my alarm, I saw that he was looking at Max like he was trying to figure something out. "Max? What's going on?"

"I'll do a bagel run," I said quickly, stepping a little in front of Rodney. "It's no big deal. I have to get your suit anyway, so . . ."

"What's wrong with your suit?" The General came into the kitchen from the front hall, and I noticed nearly everyone in the room—aside from Max—stand up a little straighter. It was just his effect on people. It may have also been because while everyone else in the kitchen was either in jeans or pajamas, the General looked like he was ready to play a round of golf, wearing khakis and a button-down, both perfectly pressed.

"Nothing," Rodney said, walking over to his dad. "It just wasn't ready yesterday."

"Well, that's unacceptable."

"I agree," I said quickly. "So I should go pick it up. Along with the bagels."

"I'll help," Bill said immediately, and I could tell just by looking at him that we were thinking the same thing—that it really wouldn't matter about the suit if we had nobody to perform the ceremony.

"In the meantime, I know we have food in here," my dad said, crossing to the fridge. "Let me see what's what. . . ."

"I'll just . . . ," I said to Bill, nodding upstairs, so hopefully he would understand I meant I just needed to get dressed. He nodded, and I dashed for the kitchen stairs, nearly crashing into Priya and Jenny W., who were coming down.

"Whoa," Priya said, her eyes widening. "What's the hurry?"

"Oh," I said, starting to edge past them toward the stairs. "Just a lot to do today. You know. Weddings."

"Is J.J. in there?" Jenny W. asked, fluffing up her hair. I looked at her and noticed she looked awfully good for someone who'd allegedly just woken up.

I just smiled at her, then took the stairs to the third floor two at a time.

I put the car in park and glanced at Bill. We had found a spot up the street from Swift Tailors, where Rodney's suit was waiting for us. The whole ride over, Bill had been trying to find a judge who would be willing to work last-minute on a Saturday, but from what I could hear on this end, it hadn't sounded like he'd made a ton of progress. "Any luck?"

He lowered his phone slightly, then shook his head. "I keep trying all these offices . . ." He paused. "Chambers? I'm not sure what a judge's office is called."

"I don't know," I said. "We can ask Rodney." A second later, though, I remembered that we couldn't ask Rodney—because as far as Rodney was concerned, Max was still going to be performing his ceremony and Bill and I were not currently on a wild-judge chase.

"Anyway, nobody's answering the phone," he said, lowering his cell and looking at it. "I guess when you think about it, court's not in session on Saturday, so maybe nobody's there."

"I guess we should tell them," I said, glancing over at him. "So we can . . ." I stopped when I realized I didn't know how to finish that sentence. So that we could *what*?

"Well," Bill said, frowning down at his phone, "I'm sure we can think of something. Right? It's not like the wedding's not going to happen."

"Right," I echoed, hoping I sounded more confident than I felt.

I killed the engine, and we headed up the street and into Swift Tailors. I'd been worried that it wouldn't be open this early, but Bill had looked it up, and since their adjoining dry-cleaning business, ImPRESSive Cleaners, opened at seven, the tailor shop was open too. But maybe not that surprisingly, since it wasn't even eight on a Saturday, we were the only people in the store.

"Hi," I said to the guy behind the counter—GERALD was stitched into his shirt—handing over Rodney's claim ticket. "Picking up for Rodney Daniels?"

"Ah," Gerald said, his face creasing into a smile. "The wedding suit, of course. Just a second." He turned around and walked through a little curtained area in the back.

I leaned my elbows on the counter and looked at the pictures hung up behind the register. The wall was filled with signed pictures of well-known local customers—the governor; Storm Raines, our TV weatherman—and the headshot of Amy Curry, who'd graduated from Stanwich High before I'd gotten there and had had a small part in *Time Ninja*, last summer's blockbuster. And above them all—which probably meant it had been there the longest—was a drawing my mother had done, all the *GCS* characters reacting in horror as a muddy Waffles stood on a pile of clothes. *Thanks for always coming to the rescue!* she'd scrawled above her signature. The cartoon version of me, at six, was half hiding behind the cartoon version of Danny while Waffles shook mud everywhere.

"Here it is!" Gerald was back, carrying a black garment bag. He smiled as he handed it over. "Tell Rodney congratulations," he said, waving us out the door. Bill and I stepped outside into the cool morning air—I kept telling myself it was going to warm up, even though it only seemed to be getting colder and windier—and exchanged a smile.

"That was easy," he said as I draped the suit carefully over my arm and we walked back to the car, falling into step together.

"I know," I said, feeling my spirits lift. "Maybe it's a sign. Maybe it'll be no problem to find a judge, too."

Bill grinned at me. "I like the optimism."

I beeped the car open, then laid the suit out lengthwise in the way back, so it wouldn't get wrinkled. I felt my phone buzz in my back pocket, pulled it out, and saw that it was Rodney calling. "Hey," I said, straightening the garment bag.

"Hey—did you get the suit yet?"

"Just picked it up."

"Oh, good. Before you leave, just make sure that my vest is in there as well, would you?"

"Sure," I said, unzipping the black garment bag and then freezing. I'd seen pictures of the suit Rodney would be wearing—and the modified version that all the groomsmen would be wearing. It was a dark-gray suit and vest, with a gray tie for Rodney and a peach tie for the groomsmen. But the suit in front of me was not that at all. The suit in front of me was what could only be described as maroon, with a faint plaid pattern woven throughout, and it also looked much too small for Rodney.

"Is it there?" Rodney's voice on the other end shook me out of my daze.

"There's a suit in front of me. I'll bring you your suit. Nothing is wrong."

"Wait, what?" But I hung up before Rodney could ask me any more questions, zipped the bag up, and shut the back door.

"What is it?" Bill asked, looking over at me.

"They gave us the wrong suit," I said, shaking my head. "I'm glad we noticed before bringing it home."

"Seriously," Bill said, his eyes wide, as we hurried back into the shop.

"I'm sorry about this," Gerald said after we'd explained the situation. He shook his head as he typed on his computer. "My son updated our computer system, and it's a bit of a mess right now. He must have mistagged it and . . ." He squinted at the screen, frowning.

"What?" Bill asked. "What is it?"

"So," Gerald said, clearing his throat. "It seems like my son, in his infinite wisdom, may have accidentally mixed up your claim tags and given Rodney's suit to the owner of that one."

I found myself gripping the counter for support, hoping against hope that he was about to tell me he was just kidding, that this was just pre-wedding hazing. "Seriously?" I managed, when it became clear after a few seconds that this was actually happening.

"I'm so very sorry about this. This almost never happens."

"So it happens *sometimes*?" Bill asked, sounding flabbergasted.

"But I will reach out to the other customer right away," he went on, "and see if he'd be willing to bring his suit in today and exchange them."

"If?" I echoed, hearing my voice get higher. "There's a wedding later today, and the groom needs a suit to wear!"

Gerald winced. "I am perfectly aware of the situation," he said, spreading his hands. "But I'm afraid that's all I can do."

"Well, who did you give the suit to?" Bill asked. "Maybe we could bring it to him, and then he wouldn't have to make a trip over here." I nodded, incredibly grateful for Bill at that moment, simply for being someone who could make plans and not just give in to the blind rage I was currently feeling.

"Ah. Well, I'm afraid I can't give out customer information."

"But you can give out customers' suits!" I sputtered, even though some part of me knew this wasn't helping matters.

"Even so—" he started, just as the phone rang. He held up his index finger to me as he answered, the universal sign for *hold on a sec*. "Swift

Tailors," he said, his voice cheery and professional. I debated yelling, loud enough for the person on the other end of the phone to hear, that they should hang up, since this establishment couldn't be trusted not to give away your possessions.

"This is bad," I said, turning to Bill, who was examining the suit, which just got worse the more you saw of its fabric. It was like it had been designed to give you a headache in seconds. "What are we going to tell Rodney? What kind of place loses someone's wedding suit?"

"Charlie," Bill said, speaking softly. I glanced over at him and saw he had unbuttoned the suit and opened it up. There, on the inside of the right breast pocked was a sewn-in tag that read TAILORED EXCLUSIVELY FOR RALPH DONNELLY.

"So we know whose suit it is," I said slowly, trying to figure out why Bill looked so excited about this.

"Why don't we do what you said?" Bill said, lowering his voice as he glanced at Gerald, who was still on the phone. "I mean, nobody's going to come back in on a Saturday to return a suit. But if we bring it to him . . ."

"Right." I wasn't sure this would work, but it seemed like a better idea than just leaving the suit here and hoping Gerald would be able to sort it out before the time the ceremony rolled around. And at least if we had Ralph Donnelly's terrible suit in our possession, we had some leverage. Bill buttoned the suit again, then zipped the garment bag up. He glanced at me and I nodded. We both started to back toward the door, Bill carrying the suit. When we pushed it open, the bell above the door chimed and Gerald looked at us, his eyes widening.

"Wait a second," he said, lowering the phone. "I can't let you take that—"

But we didn't wait to hear what else he was going to say because, like we'd discussed it ahead of time, we both bolted at the same moment and ran up the street. I unlocked my car when we were a few feet away, and then we threw ourselves inside.

"So," Bill said, as I peeled out onto the street, "we need to convince Ralph Donnelly to give up Rodney's suit."

"And find someone to marry Linnie and Rodney," I added.

"And bagels," Bill added, and despite everything that was happening, I smiled.

"Right," I agreed.

Bill shook his head. "It's certainly turning out to be an interesting morning." He looked over and smiled at me. "Let's do it."

CHAPTER 17
Or, #extortion

I HAD BEEN AFRAID THAT IT WOULD BE HARD TO find Ralph Donnelly, but he proved surprisingly—and a little worryingly—easy to track down. Ralph had a very active social media presence, which was why, never having met the man, I knew not only what he looked like and that he apparently loved pugs, but also what his morning had consisted of.

> ralphdonnelly: starting the day off right— coffee run! #coffeerun

> ralphdonnelly: why such a long line at Flasks? Everyone needing that Saturday- morning coffee? #saturdaycoffee

> ralphdonnelly: heading to swift tailor to pick up my suit for today's event! #suitrun

> ralphdonnelly: not so happy about having

to get suit day of and change at the
event!! Need faster tailor! #notsoswift
#tailornotswift #slowtailors

ralphdonnelly: just realized I got the
wrong suit from the tailor!! #wrongsuit

ralphdonnelly: Not happy about this.
Maybe I should bring . . . a suit? #lol
#legaljokes #suitsnotsuits

Things went on like this for a while, to the point where I was starting to worry about Ralph Donnelly's safety since there didn't seem
to be any way he was updating this often and not doing it while he
was driving. But it had allowed us to realize he was going to a breakfast reception at the Stanwich Country Club, and since he'd already
weighed in on the food situation—#quichefail—we knew that he was
currently there.

"Hopefully we'll be able to find him," Bill said as I swung into the
parking lot of the country club. "I don't know how big this event is."

"We should just look for the displeased person by the quiche," I
said, circling the lot once. It was pretty crowded—though whether it
was people attending the same event as Ralph or braving the chilly
weather to play golf, I couldn't be sure. I spotted an open parking spot
and zoomed into it before anyone else could.

"Uh," Bill said. We both got out of the car, and I could see him taking
in the building, which was fairly intimidating up close. "Are we allowed
to just walk in?"

"Maybe not," I said, heading toward the entrance. "But just frown
and walk fast."

Bill furrowed his brow and looked over at me. "How's this?"

I bit back a laugh, as we were getting close to the valet in front of the entrance. "Perfect."

The valet looked up at us, and Bill and I gave him simultaneous frowny nods as we headed inside. "Okay," I said, looking around. It had been about a year since I'd been in the country club—we didn't belong, but I'd been there over the years for events and especially fancy sweet sixteens—and it looked pretty much the same, like an upscale living room. "The events are usually in that ballroom." I nodded toward it just as I noticed a woman in a white polo shirt and khakis—who was very much giving off an *I work here* vibe—look at me and Bill. "Let's go," I whispered under my breath, and we hurried over before anyone could ask what, exactly, we were doing there.

"I think this is it," Bill said as we approached the ballroom. He held out his phone, and I saw a selfie of Ralph Donnelly that had been taken next to the overlarge bouquet of flowers in the corner—#bloomingreat.

"Okay," I said, looking around. The entrance to the ballroom seemed to be the mingle-and-eat area—I could see chairs lined up farther in, with a small stage and podium set up at the front. Waiters were walking around with trays, and people were talking in small groups as they drank coffee and ate what looked like the disappointing quiche. As I did, I noticed that everyone around us was *very* well dressed. All the men were in suits, and the women were either in pantsuits or dresses—whatever this event was, it clearly wasn't casual. And the fact that Bill and I were both in jeans was starting to seem more obvious by the second.

"Is that him?" Bill asked, pointing toward the corner, where a short man in an oversize suit was typing on his phone. Bill held up the selfie for me to look at, and I nodded.

We crossed the ballroom to him, and though the man was still typing on his phone, after a moment, he finally noticed me and Bill standing there. "Yes?"

"Ralph Donnelly?" I asked.

"Yes," he said, a little more warily. "Can I help you?"

"I hope so," I said, and Bill held out the garment bag. "We just came from Swift Tailors—they accidentally gave you my brother-in-law's suit, and gave us yours."

"Ah." Ralph, for some reason, was starting to turn red. "Right. They had a real mix-up, huh?"

"Yeah," Bill agreed. "And we actually really need the other suit back, so . . ."

Ralph cleared his throat. "So," he said, starting to look uncomfortable. "The thing is . . ."

"Wait a second," I said, suddenly realizing that his oversize suit looked very familiar. "Are you *wearing* Rodney's suit?"

"Who's Rodney?"

"The person whose suit you're wearing."

"Well," he said, turning even redder, "I had this event, my suit wasn't ready until this morning, and I didn't realize it was the wrong suit until I was here, putting it on. What was I supposed to do?"

"So, here's your suit," Bill said, holding the garment bag out to him. "If you wouldn't mind, um, changing? And then we can take ours back. We're a bit pressed for time."

I nodded, thinking this sounded like a good plan and that as far as Rodney was concerned, he never had to know that someone named Ralph had worn his wedding suit before him. I waited for Ralph to take the garment bag, but he didn't make a movement toward it, not even when Bill brought it a little closer and nudged the hanger against his wrist. "Uh—Ralph?" I asked, looking at Bill, who seemed as baffled by this lack of response as I was. "Mr. Donnelly?"

"So here's the thing," Ralph said all in a rush. "I've gotten a ton of compliments on this suit already. Nobody ever compliments my suits!" I could understand that—especially if all the rest of his suits were as hideous as the one Bill was holding.

"Okay," I said, looking at Bill and then back at Ralph. "Well, I'm happy people like it, but . . ."

"I mean, the suit doesn't even fit you," Bill said, a note of finality in his voice, like he wanted to get this wrapped up as soon as possible.

"But that's just it! People think I've lost weight! It's fantastic."

"I'm glad you're getting good feedback," I said, and Bill nudged Ralph with the hanger again. "But we're going to need to switch with you."

He just gave us a look, then looked down at himself. "You know," he said, folding his arms, "possession is nine-tenths of the law."

"I think I've heard that before," Bill said, his voice and expression still resolutely cheerful as he held out the garment bag to Ralph again. "I also think I saw a men's room on the way in?"

"What I'm saying is that I was given this suit in good faith that it was my property," he said, talking quickly and with the practiced legal cadence that I recognized from helping Rodney study for the bar. "So how can I be assured that the suit you want me to take in exchange is even mine?"

"Because it has your name sewn into it," I said, my voice starting to rise. I saw a few people look over at me and made myself take a deep breath. The last thing we needed was to get thrown out of here before we could get Rodney's suit back.

"Nevertheless," Ralph said, straightening his cuffs, "I think this is an issue that should be handled by Swift Tailors. And . . ."

"Are you really not going to give us our suit back?" Bill asked, sounding baffled. "Seriously?"

"You can't make me," Ralph said, raising his eyebrows at Bill. He glanced between the two of us, like he was just now noticing my sneakers and Bill's duck boots. "Are you two even supposed to be in here?"

My phone buzzed, and I saw that it was someone calling me from the house line. I held up my phone, and Bill nodded, and I could somehow tell, even though we hadn't exchanged a word, that he was telling me he'd keep working on Ralph while I took my call. "Hello?" I said, walking a few feet away, toward the entrance.

"Charlie?" It was my mother, and she sounded stressed out—which wasn't that surprising, considering there were fifteen people in our house, most of whom were probably waiting on the breakfast I hadn't brought back with me yet.

"Hi, Mom," I said, and seeing one of the waiters frown at me, I took another step toward the doorway. "What's up?"

"I'm going to need you to get your brother on the way home," my mother said. "Mike," she added after a moment. "He needs to be here to take pictures with the other groomsmen. He can't just expect to show up at the ceremony."

"Um," I said, blinking. I wondered if this was one of the things my parents had been fighting with Mike about the night before. "Okay."

"And where are you with the bagels?"

"Well," I said, looking around the room, where Ralph Donnelly was shaking his head at Bill—clearly, we hadn't made any progress yet. "Um, it might be a minute. Do we have anything else to feed them instead?"

"You would think," my mother said. "But your uncle Stu's been eating up half of the contents of the fridge—" There was the *click* that indicated someone had just picked up the extension.

"CHARLOTTE LOUISE GRANT." It was my dad, and he sounded *furious*—which my dad almost never did.

"Oh, by the way, your father's mad," my mom said, just a tad too late. I immediately felt a cold sweat break out on my upper lip. What had I done? Was he mad that I'd spent the night sleeping across from the wedding coordinator's nephew? It was truly a bad sign when my dad full-named me.

"Hi, Dad. Um, what—"

"That *dog* has *dug up* my *flower beds*." My dad's voice was rising with every word, and I held the phone a little bit away from my ear, which had started to ring.

"Oh no. You mean—"

"Yes," he snapped. "The flowers that were going to *win me the title* have been ruined. Utterly and totally wrecked."

I suddenly remembered Waffles's paws when he came back in after I'd let him out into the yard. Clearly, this explained it—he'd gotten them dirty destroying my dad's dreams.

"This was my last shot, Charlie. And now it's gone."

"I'm really sorry, Dad," I said. "Um—"

"Where did this dog even come from?" my dad asked, lowering his voice. "Are we sure Don's not behind this?"

"He's not," my mother said firmly. "Charlie, just come back soon with your brother. And the bagels."

"Right, the bagels," my dad said, sounding a bit more like himself. "What's taking so long?"

"There's just, um, a really long line," I said. "Be back soon!" I hung up before my parents could ask me any more questions.

"If you could just see where we're coming from here," Bill was saying as I joined him. His voice was wheedling and friendly, but there was a definite edge to it, like his infinite cheerfulness was finally being tested. "There's a wedding in a few hours. And we really need our suit back."

"And if you could see where *I'm* coming from," Ralph said, smoothing down the lapels. "Which is not wanting to arrive in one suit and change partway through an event! I'll be a hashtag laughingstock."

"Um," I said, looking at the people standing around, none of whom seemed to care all that much about what people were wearing.

"Look," Bill said, dropping the friendly manner altogether. "I didn't want to have to get the authorities involved. But . . ."

"Oho!" Ralph said, looking not at all scared by this threat, but weirdly delighted. "And say what, exactly?"

"Well—" I exchanged a glance with Bill. "That you stole a suit?"

"But that's where you're wrong," Ralph said, shaking his head. "I was *given* a suit. I didn't knowingly steal anything."

"But now you know," Bill pointed out, shaking the garment bag in his direction. "So don't you have some obligation to, um, rectify the situation?"

I noticed with alarm that people were starting to put down their coffee cups and napkins and make their way into the area with the chairs. What if Ralph just left, still wearing Rodney's suit? Bill and I were crashing this event, so it wasn't like we could complain to anyone about it. "Look," I started, just as two men who looked around Ralph's age passed him as they made their way to the ballroom.

"Donnelly," one of them said, with a nod.

"Your Honor," the other one said.

"I have to be going," Ralph said, starting to edge toward the ballroom. "But—"

"You're a judge?" I blurted out, feeling my heart start to beat hard. "Like . . . a real one?"

"Yes," he said, folding his arms on top of Rodney's suit. "But if you think that my role changes my position about this—"

"No, it's not that," I said quickly. I looked over at Bill and saw he was pretty much thinking the same thing that I was—that maybe we had an opportunity here. "But, like, you're a *judge* judge," I said, feeling that after Max, it couldn't hurt to make sure of these things. "You're not just a judge on TV, right? You can do all the things judges can do?"

"I'm a probate judge," Ralph said, looking increasingly confused. "But I don't know what that has to—"

"What does that mean?" Bill asked. "Like—people on probation?"

"No," Ralph said, his voice heavy with disdain. "I handle wills and estates." We must have both looked blank, because he sighed and said bluntly, "Dead people."

"Oh." I nodded, thinking this might not have been a bad choice for Ralph, if this was the way he interacted with the living. "But you can do all the things judges can, right? Like . . . you can marry people?"

Ralph's eyebrows flew up, and he looked from me to Bill. "You two seem a little young."

"No," Bill said quickly, and I could see that the tips of his ears were turning red. "Not me and Charlie. We're not . . . I mean, we're just . . ."

"It's for my sister," I said, jumping in, noticing that almost everyone else had made their way into the ballroom by now, and starting to talk faster. "She's getting married tonight, and we're down an officiant. They're not religious, so we need to find a judge. . . ."

"Let me guess," Ralph said. "Someone got ordained online, then found out you can't do that here?" Bill and I nodded, and Ralph shook his head.

"So, would you be willing to do it? You can keep the suit," I promised recklessly. "And even attend the wedding if you want. You can have dinner and everything! Um . . . do you like salmon?"

"I get to keep the suit?" Ralph asked, looking down at it again. I nodded, hoping that Rodney would care more about getting married than he would about getting married in the right clothing. I smiled hopefully at Ralph, and saw Bill doing the same.

"You'd really be helping us out," I said. "And if you don't want to stay, you wouldn't have to—you could just drop in, marry them, and head out again."

"Please?" Bill asked.

Ralph sighed. "Fine," he said, reaching into the pocket of Rodney's suit—apparently, now Ralph's suit—and pulling out a business card. "E-mail me the details, the location, and when you'll need me for the ceremony."

I let out a long, shaky breath. "Thank you so much," I said, as next to me, Bill nodded fervently. "We really, really appreciate it, and—"

"All right," Ralph said, starting to look uncomfortable. "Just send me the information, and I'll see you tonight."

"Thank you," Bill called, a little too loudly. Ralph gave us a smile that was more grimace than anything else, and hurried into the ballroom, probably trying to get there before we could ask him for anything else.

I looked over at Bill, who just shook his head. We headed back the way we came, waiting until we were out of the ballroom before either one of us spoke. "Oh my god," I said, once we were in the clear. I shook my head, feeling like I was on the verge of bursting into giddy laughter.

"So, I think we can count that as a victory," Bill said as we headed toward the car. He turned to me and held up his hand. "Go team."

I smiled as I gave him a high-five. "Well, it's kind of a victory," I said, nodding toward the garment bag Bill had been holding for so long that it now just seemed like a part of him. "We're down a suit."

"But up an officiant, which is the more important thing."

"That's what I thought too. I hope Rodney doesn't kill me."

"I think he'll be happy about it," Bill said, then paused. "Well, maybe not *happy*. But probably grateful that he's actually going to be able to get married."

"Good point." I unlocked the car, and we both got in.

"So we've gotten a judge and picked up the suit," Bill said, then looked behind him at the garment bag he'd placed in the backseat. "I mean, kind of. We *did* pick up a suit, just not the one we expected. So now we need to get bagels."

"Right," I said, starting the car, then backing out of the space and driving forward, out through the country club entrance gates. "And Mike."

"Mike?"

"Yeah, we have to get him. He's . . . at a friend's."

"Cool," Bill said, smiling across the car at me. "Onward?"

I nodded as I hit the turn signal that would take me toward the

commercial district in town. It wasn't that everything was fixed—
Rodney still didn't have anything to get married in—but we had found
a judge. And somehow, it felt like I wasn't on my own with this—it felt
like Bill and I were in this together. I gave him a smile across the car.
"Onward."

"Uhhhgggggghhhhhh." I glanced into the backseat, where Mike was
curled up, moaning softly, the way he'd been ever since we'd picked
him up.

"How you doing, Mike?" I asked, even though I had a feeling I knew
how he was doing.

"Shh," Mike said, closing his eyes and leaning his head against the
window. "Why are you talking so loud? Why are you driving so fast?"

I looked down at the speedometer—I was going thirty miles an hour,
and it felt like we were crawling.

He had been this way ever since I'd pulled into Jesse's driveway and
found Mike sitting on the front steps, his head hung between his legs.
Luckily, J.J. had texted me that he'd called Mike until he'd woken him
up, and told him to be ready to meet me. This way, I didn't have to
face ringing Jesse's doorbell and having a fight with my brother—in
front of Jesse—about coming to the house early. And while I wanted
to see Jesse, there was so much going on at the moment that I really
wasn't sure I had the bandwidth for it right now. And at any rate, I
knew I'd see him tonight—at the reception, with my hair and makeup
professionally done, with these problems long solved and the wedding
going smoothly. That's how I wanted to see Jesse—when everything
was going to be perfect.

I glanced back at Mike once more. It wasn't like I'd never seen people
with hangovers—I'd covered for J.J. when we'd all gone on a family trip
to Hyde Park the day after his senior prom, when he could barely stand
up. And I'd had a particularly rough morning myself last year, when

I'd been staying at Siobhan's when her dads were out of town and we'd experimented with mixing together most of their liquor cabinet. But I'd never seen Mike like this—his skin had a distinctly greenish tinge to it. And even though he'd showered at Jesse's—his hair was damp—he somehow still smelled like whiskey, like it was coming out through his pores or something. I was hoping that maybe the wedding photographer would be able to use some kind of filter, because I had a feeling it wouldn't look great, in pictures Rodney and Linnie were going to keep forever, to have one of the groomsmen look like he was on the verge of collapse.

"Are you drinking the water?" Bill asked, pointing to the bottle in the backseat cup holder, which we'd picked up at the bagel shop for him.

Mike turned his head to look at it, grimacing. He reached out, gave a feeble attempt to open it, then slumped back against the window again. "Too hard," he moaned.

"I'll get it," Bill said, reaching into the back and opening the cap again. "There you go."

"Thank you," I whispered to him.

"It's fine," he said, glancing into the backseat again. "Think he'll be okay for the wedding?"

"He just needs sleep," I said, hoping this was true. "And water." I looked at the two huge Upper Crust bags that were sitting at Bill's feet, containing enough bagels and cream cheese to feed an army. "You want a bagel, Mike?" Bill lifted one of the bags and held it out to him.

"Oh my god." Mike groaned, turning his head away.

My phone rang, and the car Bluetooth picked it up—and I could see it was Siobhan calling. I closed my eyes for a second as I remembered that with everything happening today, I'd never called her back. "Hi," I said, answering it, already speaking fast. "I'm so sorry I didn't get back to you yesterday—things have been so crazy here you wouldn't believe it. What's happening? Tell me what's going on with the roommate situation."

"Well, before that," Siobhan said. "I have some bad news."

"What's going on?"

"They canceled our flight last night, and the next one we could get on doesn't get in until Sunday."

"But the wedding's tonight."

"I know," Siobhan said. "I'm so sorry to miss it—do you think Linnie will be mad?"

"*I'm mad!*" I snapped.

"Charlie," Mike mumbled from the backseat. "Could you just . . . maybe not with the yelling?"

"The flight was canceled," Siobhan said, her voice getting tenser. "It's not my fault."

"Well, did you ever think maybe you shouldn't have gone to Michigan the weekend of my sister's wedding? I can't believe you're telling me this now!"

"Um, well, maybe if you had *called me back* I would have told you yesterday!" Siobhan said, sounding increasingly angry.

I glanced over at Bill, who was looking fixedly down at his phone, like he was trying to pretend he'd gone temporarily deaf. "I've been really busy. There's been a lot to deal with here—"

"I don't know why I'm even surprised. You did what you always do—the second your family shows up, it's like I don't exist."

"Are we really doing this now? Again?"

"Um, yeah, because you do this *every* time. I'm always here for you, to listen to you talk about Jesse nonstop . . . ," Siobhan said. I glanced quickly into the rearview mirror, but Mike's eyes were closed. "But the second I need you, if your family's around, you're MIA. It's like I don't even matter."

I took a breath to try and argue with this, even though I knew, deep down, she was right.

"And don't make me feel bad for going to visit my college just because *you're* not excited about going."

"Oh, now this is *my* fault?"

I heard Siobhan let out a breath, like she was trying to keep herself from yelling again. "I didn't say that. But it's like you don't even want to talk about what's going to happen next year. It's like you think you're going to keep on going to high school, staying in that same house forever."

"No, I don't," I said automatically, without even stopping to wonder if she was right.

"Oh yeah?" Siobhan's tone was suddenly biting. "So then I guess you finally told Stanwich you're going there. And you told your other schools not to hold your spot. You've picked out your classes and finished your roommate survey?" This hung in the air for just a moment, and I bit my lip, since we both knew what the answers to these questions were. "All you've been talking about for months is this weekend, and getting to be with your family again. What happens when this weekend is over?"

I drew in a sharp breath. It felt like Siobhan had just gut-punched me—that unexpected, that painful.

"I'd say call me back later," Siobhan said, "but I have a feeling you won't. Tell Linnie I'm sorry." And then she hung up.

I gripped the steering wheel hard, feeling my hands shake slightly. It was the first real fight we had ever had. A fight that wasn't just about what movie to watch or how many minutes constituted being late for something or if you were obligated to share mozzarella sticks. This was a fight that had actually meant something.

But she didn't know what she was talking about. There was nothing wrong with wanting to see your family. There was nothing wrong with wanting to have a great weekend for your sister's wedding, and I wasn't about to let her make me think that there was.

We drove the rest of the way home in silence, Bill looking down at his phone and Mike groaning softly from the back whenever I took a curve too sharply. As I got nearer to our house, I realized that there was now nowhere to park in the driveway. Crowding around the drive, and in front of the garage, were twice the vehicles that had been there when I left. There were Tent City and Where There's A Will trucks, a truck with MCARDLE'S FLOWERS printed on the side, and two white catering vans in front that had people clustered around, pulling out platters and rolling trays. I wasn't sure what the dented minivan that was half on the driveway, half spilling into the road was for. It had AWYWI! printed on the side in letters that were peeling slightly, but that didn't mean anything to me.

I pulled my car over to the side of the road and shifted it into park. "Mike," I said quietly, and my brother opened his eyes with what looked like real effort. "We're here—you're just going to have to walk from here to the house, okay?"

Mike nodded, then winced. "Don't let me do that again, okay?" he asked faintly.

"What, nod?"

Mike started to nod, then winced again. "Yes," he muttered.

I grabbed one of the bagel bags, and Bill took the other one, along with the terrible maroon suit that was apparently now ours. I opened the door for Mike, who squinted, even though the day had gotten more and more overcast. When he nearly dropped his bag twice as we all started to walk—very slowly—up the driveway together, I reached out and took it from him.

"Thanks," he muttered, stopping to rest for a moment before taking a breath and continuing on.

I turned to Bill, only to see that he was staring at the van, his brows drawn together.

"Charlie?" He looked up at me, his expression grim. "I think we have a problem."

CHAPTER 18
Or, That's the Way You Need It

I DON'T UNDERSTAND," I SAID, SHAKING MY HEAD. Bill and I were standing on the driveway with Glen, the lead singer and manager of Any Way You Want It. Glen was probably in his late forties, balding but with long hair, with leather wristbands and a tattoo sleeve on one arm. "We already have a wedding band."

I stamped my increasingly numb feet on the driveway to warm them up and looked at Bill, who was turned slightly away from me. He was still on the phone, just like he'd been ever since Glen had introduced himself. Mike had gone inside with the bags of bagels, and I'd texted J.J. to meet him by the front door and get him upstairs without too many of our relatives seeing the extent of his underage-drinking aftermath.

I'd been trying ever since to understand what Glen was doing here and why he was talking about needing to see our setup so that he could get his amps plugged in.

Glen held up his arms, one of which had DON'T STOP tattooed over his bicep. "Hey, I just go where they tell me," he said, pulling out a creased piece of paper from his back pocket. He smoothed it out and squinted at it. "We're supposed to be here to set up and be ready to play Duncan Kaufman's bar mitzvah at six p.m."

"Oh," I said, feeling myself start to breathe easier. "There's been some mix-up. I think you're at the wrong address."

"Nope," Glen said, holding out the paper to me and pointing at it. There was our address, clearly printed—and above, who the e-mail was coming from. Clementine.

"Bill," I said, just as he hung up the phone and turned back to me.

"Yeah," he said, shaking his head. "I just got off the phone with Party in the Stars. They're up in Maine getting prepped to play a bar mitzvah."

"Maine?"

"Party in the Stars?" Glen asked, looking impressed. "Whoa. They're, like, big-time." Then he blinked and added, "But, uh . . . we're really good too."

"Apparently this was another Clementine mix-up," Bill said, shaking his head. "And when my uncle confirmed the band yesterday, he just assumed they were going to the right address. . . ."

"Well," I said, trying to think fast. "It's okay. Maybe they can get back here in time?"

Bill shook his head. "It's nine hours away. Without traffic." I tried to do the math, but he was right—there was no way they could safely get back in time before the wedding. "Also, then nobody would be playing Duncan Kaufman's bar mitzvah." I didn't really care about Duncan Kaufman at the moment—I was fighting the urge to go track Clementine down, wherever she was, so that I could scream at her.

"Wait, so we're not supposed to be here?" Glen asked.

"No," Bill said. "But—since you are here—we're going to need you to sub in and play a wedding tonight. The original wedding band is playing your gig in Maine."

I looked at the van again, now understanding the acronym and trying to see the bright side. Any Way You Want It as a name seemed promising, at any rate. So maybe they would be able to roll with the music choices Linnie and Rodney had planned. "Do you guys have a list of the songs you can play?"

"Sure," Glen said, still sounding a little thrown, as he pulled out his phone. He held it out to me, and Bill and I leaned over the screen together.

"That's it?" I asked after a moment of staring at the song titles and trying to get them to make sense. When we'd seen Party in the Stars's list, it had gone on for pages and pages.

"Wait," Bill said, looking at Glen. "Why are all these Journey songs?"

Glen looked at us like he was waiting for one of us to tell him we were joking. "Seriously?" he asked. "Because we're a Journey cover band."

"What?" I asked, even though I'd heard him perfectly.

"We're called Any Way You Want It," Glen said, pointing to the van. "It's not like it's a secret."

"I thought it just meant that you were super accommodating," I said. "Like, you could have the wedding music be any way you wanted it!"

"No. That's why we were booked to play this kid's bar mitzvah. The theme is Duncan's Journey to Being a Man."

I glanced at Bill, feeling my hopes deflate. It was bad enough we didn't have the band we wanted—and now we were stuck with an eighties-era cover band?

"We're really good, though," Glen said, maybe sensing what I was feeling. "We're the tri-state area's second-best Journey cover band, according to Best of the Gold Coast. I can send you the article if you want."

"There's more than one Journey cover band?" Bill asked, sounding surprised.

"Oh man, you have no idea," Glen said darkly. "It's really stiff competition. We should have won, but the Streetlight People had some pull with the judges, so . . ." He sighed and shook his head. "Well—some will win. Some will lose."

I tilted my head to the side. "That's a Journey lyric, isn't it?"

"Steve Perry is a poet of the ordinary," Glen said reverently.

"That may be so," Bill said. "But the thing is, we didn't know you were a Journey cover band. I'm sure you're great. But . . . we were kind of expecting a regular band."

"But we're so much better than a regular band," Glen said, looking appalled by this.

"Do you play any other songs?" I asked, hoping against hope that they did.

Glen brightened at this. "We have some originals."

"No," Bill and I said at the same time.

"I'm sure they're good," I added quickly, since Glen was looking offended. "But we were really hoping for some, you know, songs by other artists."

"Why would a Journey cover band play other bands' songs? We're not a jukebox. Also, you need to respect the cover band turf. If we started playing Michael Jackson suddenly, the Men in the Mirror would *not* be happy about it."

"Oh," I said. "I had no idea."

Glen nodded. "It's a tough business. Welcome to the jungle." He paused for a second. "Which is, incidentally, the name of my brother's Guns N' Roses cover band."

"Do you think you could give it a shot?" Bill asked. "We've just . . . had a lot of things go wrong with this wedding already, and I'm not sure the bride and groom can handle anything else not going according to plan."

"I can talk to my bandmates," he said grumpily. "But I have to tell you, I don't know how good any songs are going to be if we're learning them day of."

"Okay," I said, wondering if maybe one of my siblings or one of the guests had really well-curated playlists on their phones, or something. "Just . . . try? And let us know?"

"Fine," Glen said, still not sounding happy. "We'll try."

I heard the sound of a bike coming down the street and turned to see Sarah Stephens riding right in the middle of the road. When she passed me, she took one hand off the handlebars, then pointed to her eyes, then at mine, the *I'm watching you* finger point that I'd honestly not expected to be on the receiving end of from a middle schooler.

"What is that?" Glen asked, sounding panicky, and I saw that he was also looking at Sarah. He turned to me and Bill. "Do you guys see that too?"

"That's just our papergirl," I said, as Sarah biked away.

"Oh, good," Glen said, looking hugely relieved. "I thought I was having a flashback, or that it meant I only had twenty-four hours to live or something."

"So," Bill said, turning to Glen. "You're going to talk to your bandmates . . ."

"Yeah," he said, not sounding all that enthusiastic about the idea. "But right now, I just need to know where we're going to be playing. Despite the fact you don't like our music . . ." He muttered this last part in an undertone.

"Around back," Bill said, gesturing for Glen to come with him, and I followed them around the side of the house to the backyard—which was now filled with people wearing Tent City shirts. They were in the midst of erecting a tent while Will paced around, shouting instructions, and my uncle Stu followed in his footsteps, giving advice that I had a feeling wasn't actually wanted or at all needed.

"So, I'll show you where the stage is going to be," Bill said, pointing across the lawn.

"I'll take that," I said to Bill, gesturing for the garment bag with Ralph's terrible suit inside.

I crossed the deck to the house and opened the kitchen door—only to stop short and grab on to the counter to stop myself from toppling over. There was a very large man in a bright-blue shirt kneeling in front of the door, peering at the alarm panel. PISCATELLI SECURITY SYSTEMS, it read in bright letters across his back, and then in smaller, cursive type underneath it, *Don't be alarmed!*

"Um. Hi," I said, maneuvering around him. He nodded at me but then went back to fiddling with the alarm panel. I looked around the kitchen, which had gone much the way of the backyard and the driveway—suddenly much busier and crowded than when I'd left it.

My dad was standing behind the alarm guy, leaning over his shoulder, and he shook his head at me when I walked past him, clearly letting me know that my part in wrecking his flower beds had not been forgotten. Danny was standing on the other side of the kitchen, talking on his phone and pacing around, and getting in the way of the people that I presumed were the caterers—they were wearing white shirts and black pants, at any rate—who had appeared since I'd last been there.

The kitchen island and the counters were now covered with food, and the caterers were bustling around, getting things ready for tonight. Two people were chopping veggies on the kitchen island, and two more were preparing trays of food, assembly-line style. I could see on the kitchen table the remains of the bagels I'd brought—it looked like while we'd been talking with Glen in the driveway, most of them had been devoured.

I dodged around one of the caterers, who was en route to the oven with a baking tray, gave her an apologetic smile she didn't return, then headed over to the kitchen table to see if there were still any poppy seed bagels left—narrowly missing a collision with J.J., who came storming in with wet hair, in his robe, carrying a bow tie.

"Do you have a sewing kit?" he asked the kitchen in general—though neither the caterers or the alarm guy responded.

"Me?" I asked after a moment.

"Anyone!" he said, sounding annoyed. "Mom!" he yelled, continuing through the kitchen.

"Don't yell," my dad yelled after him.

"Have you seen Rodney?" I asked.

"No," my dad said, leaning closer to the alarm panel. "But did you see we're getting the alarm fixed? Leo here is going to get this sorted before tonight."

"I'm doing my best," Leo the alarm guy muttered, shaking his head as he examined the panel once again.

"Is there any more coffee, Jeffrey?" Mrs. Daniels asked, coming into the kitchen, holding a mug.

"I've got it," I said, giving my dad a smile, hoping this would help make up for his garden dreams getting crushed. I crossed over to take her cup, dodging around Danny, who shot me an apologetic look. *Work,* he mouthed to me, and I gave him a sympathetic grimace.

"No, I don't understand," Danny said into his phone. "We were supposed to see contracts months ago. . . ." He turned and left the kitchen, heading for the front hall, just as Max came barreling in.

"Hey," he said, looking around and pulling on his beard. "You don't have any milk, do you?"

"Milk?" my dad echoed. "Sure—try the fridge."

I poured Mrs. Daniels a fresh cup of coffee, then handed it to her as Rodney came in. "Mom, do you have a sewing kit?" Rodney asked. "J.J. needs one."

"I think I should have one upstairs," she said, nodding her thanks at me. "I'll use that when you're done, Maxwell," she said to Max, who I just noticed was starting to leave the kitchen holding the carton of milk.

"Oh," Max said, looking down at it, like he was surprised to see it there. I restrained myself from rolling my eyes, but it really did seem like maybe Max should take the occasional day off, since his recreational habits were clearly starting to affect him. "Right," he said, coming back with the milk carton. He held it out to Mrs. Daniels.

"Can I get you a glass or something?" I asked Max.

"I don't need a whole glass," he said. "Maybe just like a cup . . . or a dish or something?"

I pulled a mug out of the cupboard. "Here," I said, handing it to him.

"Thanks," Max said, pouring the milk into the mug, then handing the container back to me and hustling out of the room.

I went to put the milk back in the fridge, reaching for the door just as one of the catering staff did the same. "Oh—sorry," I said. He gave me a tight smile, one that didn't meet his eyes, and I stepped away quickly from the fridge, feeling like I was very much in the way.

"What does J.J. need out of the sewing kit?" Mrs. Daniels asked, and Rodney shrugged.

"Not surprisingly, he didn't elaborate."

"Um," I said to Rodney, feeling like the sooner I did this the better. "I need to talk to you about something."

Rodney's eyebrows flew up. "Sounds serious. Did everything go okay with the suit? Is that it?"

"Wait!" I practically yelled as Rodney took a step toward the garment bag. He paused, looking at me, eyebrows raised. "Um—can we talk in the other room?"

"Hey." Priya came out of the dining room, stretching her arms over her head. "When are the hair and makeup people coming? I want to jump in the shower first."

"Um." I pulled my phone out of my pocket, since I was pretty sure I had the information somewhere. Bill would probably know, I realized—but he was still outside, presumably dealing with our unforeseen cover band. "Let me just check. . . ."

"Linnie?" my mom called as she came into the kitchen from the back stairs, then stopped short when she saw the alarm guy. "Oh good. I'm so glad you were able to come," she said as she edged past him into the kitchen. "We have a wedding here today."

"You don't say," the alarm guy muttered.

"Where's your sister?" my mom asked me.

I shook my head. "I haven't seen her this morning. Why?"

"I have her something borrowed," my mother said, crossing the kitchen. "Linnie!" she called.

"Seriously," Rodney said, taking another step closer to the suit, "what's going on?"

"Nothing. I just—"

Just then, the alarm sounded, an earsplitting electronic shriek, the loudest it had yet been. I jumped and automatically pressed my hands to my ears.

"What *is* that?" one of the caterers yelled.

"Alarm," my dad yelled back.

"Sorry," Leo yelled above the sound. "This might take a second."

I heard the sound of nails skittering on the wood floors and turned in the direction of the sound to see Waffles, ears flying, tearing into the kitchen, managing to run and howl at the same time.

"Aw, there's my cutie," Mrs. Daniels said, reaching out to pet him as he came running past, but she wasn't fast enough. Waffles clearly wanted to be wherever this sound was, and stopped just a few feet from the alarm guy, threw back his head, and started howling along, making the sound exponentially worse.

"Can you do something about your dog?" Leo yelled.

"He's not our dog," my dad yelled back. "He's a loaner."

The volume on the alarm got louder, and the dog responded in kind, matching the sound of the alarm in an unexpected harmony, like this was the world's smallest, and strangest, a cappella group.

"What's happening in here?" I turned to see General Daniels come into the kitchen. "Is there an intruder?"

Waffles stopped howling for a split second and regarded the General for just a moment, then threw his head back and started up again.

"Um." I looked over to see Mike in the doorway, still looking like

Save the Date

death slightly warmed over, wincing. "Is there any way we could . . . not? It's just a bit . . . loud."

Leo just shook his head as he punched buttons on the keypad, and a second later, the sound shut off, all at once. Waffles continued to howl alone for a few seconds before he seemed to realize the sound had stopped. Like he was embarrassed, he slunk over to the kitchen table and plopped down at the feet of Mrs. Daniels, who immediately bent down to rub his long ears.

The caterers exchanged a look and, all of them now seeming disgruntled, went back to work.

"Fixed?" my dad asked hopefully.

"You're going to need a system upgrade," Leo said, shaking his head. "Should have been looked at ages ago. Frankly, I'm surprised you've made it this long without problems."

"But the problems have been fixed for now, right?" Rodney asked. "So we're all good?"

"Son, don't say 'all good,'" Mrs. Daniels murmured.

"It's just a patch job," Leo said, looking startled to see two more people in a room that hadn't been lacking for people to begin with. I was fairly used to being in a kitchen with ten people, but his reaction was a reminder that most people weren't. "You're going to have to get the system upgraded. But once you do, it should be good here for another ten, fifteen years. You'll get your money's worth out of it."

"We've sold the house, so it's not really our issue," my dad said, then looked around and patted his pockets. "Let me just find my checkbook. . . ."

"Charlie?" I looked across the kitchen to see Priya raising her eyebrows at me. "Did you find out when the hair and makeup people are coming?"

"Right," I said, pulling out my phone again. I was scrolling through my documents when the doorbell rang. "Hold on," I said, hurrying over to the front hall—and grabbing the suit off the back of the chair as

MORGAN MATSON

I went to answer the door. It wasn't until I was halfway there that I realized I'd never actually gotten my bagel. I groaned when I saw it was Don standing on the threshold, his face red. "Hello, Don."

"This is just unacceptable!" Don yelled, like we'd been in the middle of a conversation and were just now picking it up again. "Do you have any idea how noisy your house is? Are they doing construction in your yard?"

"They're putting up a tent," I explained.

"And why does your alarm keep going off?"

"We're fixing it," I assured him, lowering my voice in the hopes that it might get him to do the same. "But—"

My mother came hurrying out of the kitchen, and I saw her shoulders slump when she realized who I was talking to. "I'm sorry, Don," she said, coming to stand behind me. "But we've got a lot going on right now and we really don't have time to talk."

"This is not a *social call*," Don said, his face getting redder than ever. "This is a *warning*. Unless the noise level decreases, I will contact the authorities."

"That's a big accusation to throw around," my mother said, her voice still pleasant but with a steely edge now. Don seemed to notice this too, and he immediately looked a little more uncomfortable.

"Well, just try to keep it down," he muttered. He gave us a disgusted look, then turned and marched down the front steps.

"Just don't tell your father he was here," my mother said, pulling the front door shut behind him. "I swear, they're about to come to blows over this stupid garden competition."

"Charlie!" Jenny W. was coming down the stairs holding a white satin garment bag in her arms.

"Is that the wedding dress?" my mother asked, her eyes widening. "Why do you have it?"

"Oh, just because I'm trying to save Linnie and Rodney's marriage,"

Jenny said, like it was the most obvious thing in the world. "Rodney keeps insisting on going into her closet, and Linnie had taken it out of the bag already, so he's almost seen it, like, three times this morning."

"In fairness, it's his closet too," I pointed out, but Jenny kept right on going.

"And it's bad luck to see the wedding dress before the wedding," she said, shaking her head. "And I don't want that on my conscience. I mean, do you? Knowing that their marriage is doomed because of you?"

"No. Obviously. Nobody wants that," I said.

"Well, then," Jenny said, holding it out to me. "Here."

"You can put it in our room," my mom said. "Unless I'm mistaken, Rodney's not going to be hanging out in there."

"Okay," I said, taking it along with the other garment bag. "I'll just drop it off, then." I started to head for the stairs, then turned back to Jenny. "Do you know when the hair and makeup people are coming? Priya was asking."

"No," Jenny said, her eyes getting wide. "Is it soon? I wanted to take a shower first. . . ." She hurried into the kitchen, and I started upstairs, moving more slowly under the weight of the dress.

"Charlie, make sure you hang it carefully," my mother called to me just as the doorbell rang again. "We don't want it to get wrinkled."

"Got it." I craned my neck to see who had arrived and got a glimpse of a girl dressed all in black with a camera bag—and figured this was probably the photographer. Since I was not even close to being camera ready, I increased my pace up the stairs to the second floor and to my parents' bedroom.

I closed the door just in case Rodney was going to be walking by, since the last thing I needed was blame for more things going wrong with this wedding. Then I unzipped the white satin garment bag and felt my breath catch as I pulled it out.

I'd seen pictures, of course, that Linnie had sent of her in the dress at various fittings. But somehow, none of the pictures had done the dress justice.

It was long, and white—not a bright-white, though, more like there was some gray mixed in with it, somehow, like a pale pebble. It had an open back, and beading on the V-neck and on the straps. I looked at it, fighting the feeling that I was about to burst into tears. I'd known Linnie was getting married—obviously, I'd known it. It was all I'd been thinking about for the last few days, and it had been one of the main topics of conversation ever since she and Rodney got engaged. But somehow, seeing her wedding dress made it all that much more real. And considering I was about to start crying just looking at the dress, I wasn't sure how I was going keep it together when I actually saw my sister in it, walking down the aisle toward Rodney.

I took a breath and tried to pull myself together. I had a lot to do—and I probably didn't have time to be getting misty over dresses. I looked around for a place to put it. My parents' room was the biggest one on this floor—with a king bed, attached master bath, my mom's closets on one side of the room, my dad's on the other. There was a daybed in the corner of their room that was mostly just decorative—but as I looked at it now, I realized that someone could have stayed there, in a pinch. Not one of the guests, of course, but I certainly could have, or J.J. . . . I'd forgotten about it, and as I looked at it now, I wondered why my mother hadn't suggested it when we were looking for room options. And it looked like it was even made up, which it almost never was, so it would have been totally ready for someone—like me—to stay there.

I shook my head at this, then heard the doorbell ring again downstairs and realized that I needed to get moving. I didn't just want to just cram the dress into my mother's closet, next to her suits in their dry-cleaner's plastic and her sensible black pressed pants. This was the most beautiful dress I'd ever seen in person, and it felt like it deserved better than that. After looking around, I carefully laid it over the daybed, arranging the skirt so that it was lying flat and hopefully wouldn't wrinkle at all. I looked at it for just one more moment, gently touching the fabric of the skirt, before leaving the room, pulling the door firmly shut behind me.

I took the suit in its garment bag with me and headed out onto the landing—nearly tripping over Waffles, who was sitting, perfectly still, outside the door of my dad's study, like he was waiting for someone on the other side of the door. As I looked at him, I wondered just what kind of dog had come to stay with us for the weekend. Was this a former police dog, or something? Could he smell what Max was undoubtedly up to inside?

"Come here," I said to him. Waffles just looked at me, but then turned back to the door, now growling low at it.

"Charlie?" Max called through the door, sounding panicked. "Is that you? Is the dog still there?"

"Yeah," I said, walking over to the dog, not sure I really wanted to pick up a growling beagle. But he stopped as I got closer, and didn't protest when I picked him up. He was lighter than I'd expected him to be, and curled up a little in my arms, leaning his head against my chest. I gave the top of his head a tentative pat. "I've got him, Max."

"Okay," Max yelled through the door. "I'll just—*ow*—I'll just stay here. Bye-bye now."

"Okay," I said. I was about to tell Max that we'd found someone to perform the ceremony, when Waffles started growling at the door again, and it seemed like the best course of action might be to separate them.

I headed downstairs, the dog now resting comfortably in the crook of my arm, apparently enjoying being along for the ride. When I arrived in the front hall, it was to see people coming through the front door, three burly guys, all of them carrying cables and what looked like black metal suitcases. "Hi," I said to one of them, a question in my voice, even though they didn't seem to need any direction.

"Hey," the one bringing up the end said matter-of-factly as they continued through to the kitchen just as Rodney came out of it.

"Who are they?" I asked.

"They're rigging the electrical in the tent," Rodney said. "Did you meet the videographer yet?"

"No," I said, starting to feel my pulse speed up. "Why is everyone here so early?"

"They're not that early," Rodney said. "Plus, they want to capture everyone getting ready, getting dressed, that kind of thing." He looked from the dog in my right arm to the suit over my left. "Can I have my suit now?"

"Right." I took a breath, then realized I really didn't want to do this alone, and that I needed more backup than just Waffles. "Um, just give me a minute."

"What is going on?" Linnie asked five minutes later. We were in the family room—Linnie and Rodney on one couch, me, Danny, and Max on the other, and Mike slumped in the armchair in the corner. I'd corralled Danny into joining us, mostly so that I could have someone on my side, and I'd dragged Mike in here because I thought that Linnie and Rodney might not yell quite as loud if they were in the presence of our very hungover brother. Waffles was also there, though he wasn't really helping things—he'd jump onto the couch, curl up in my lap, and be peaceful for a moment or two, but that was as long as it would last. Soon, he'd be up, running around the room, looking at the ceiling like he'd been doing this morning, and growling up at it.

"Okay," I said, realizing that there was nothing to do but get it over with—everyone had too much to do to sit here for very long. "So, here's the thing. We found someone to marry you."

"What do you mean?" Linnie asked, looking at Max. She sneezed three times in succession, then shot all of us a look, like she was daring us to say anything about it. "Isn't Max marrying us?"

"Wait, who's *we?*" Danny asked, raising an eyebrow at me.

"Me and Bill," I said, then felt my face get hot as Danny shot me a look.

"Well, well, well."

"No," I said. "No wells. It's his job. And I'm helping."

"Sure," Danny said, giving me a wink.

"Why isn't Max marrying us?" Rodney asked.

I took a breath to answer as Waffles launched himself off the couch and ran across the room, looking straight up at the ceiling, a low, continuous growl sounding like it was coming from the back of his throat. "Waffles," I said, a little half-heartedly, since I was pretty sure the dog didn't know this was his name.

"What's wrong with the dog?" Danny asked.

"I think it might be a ghost," I said, shaking my head. "Anyway . . ."

"Are you still talking about the ghost?" J.J. asked, appearing in the doorway of the family room, still holding his bow tie.

"Yeah," I said, pointing at Waffles. "Look at him. What else could it be?"

"If it's a ghost, why hasn't it shown up before now?" Danny asked.

J.J. thought about this for a moment. "It's a ghost that hates weddings."

"Did my mom give you the sewing kit?" Rodney asked, and J.J. nodded.

"She did." He looked around the room. "Now. Does anyone know how to sew?"

"Guys," Mike said, rubbing his temples, "do I really need to be here for this?"

"Yes," I said immediately. I looked at Linnie and Rodney. "And I think we should be aware of Mike's condition and not, you know, yell or throw anything."

"Why would we yell?" Linnie asked, her voice getting louder with every word. "*Charlie?*"

"My head," Mike whimpered.

"What's happening?" Linnie asked, looking hard at me.

I glanced at Max, who looked back at me pleadingly, like he wanted me to explain this for him, and I nodded and took a breath. "So, Max found out that you can't perform marriages in Connecticut with online ordination," I said, and across the room, I could see Linnie's face pale. "You have to be a clergy member or a judge."

"What?" Rodney asked loudly, and Mike flinched.

"If we could just . . . ," he said, shaking his head slowly, "just not . . ."

"Sorry, Mike," Rodney said, in a quieter voice. "But *what*?"

"Guys, this was totally my bad," Max muttered. "I should have checked."

"Or *I* should have," Rodney said, running his hand over his eyes. "God. I should have verified this. If I hadn't been so busy studying . . ." Linnie reached out her hand to Rodney, who took it.

"But it's okay," I said quickly. "Because we found a judge to marry you. It's all set."

"You did?" Danny asked, looking impressed. "Go, Chuck!"

"Okay," Rodney said, looking like he was having trouble keeping up. "So . . . that's good."

"Who is this judge?" asked Linnie.

"Well, his name's Ralph," I said, "and he mostly does wills and estates, but he promised me that he's able to do this. Legally, I mean."

"A *probate* judge is marrying us?" Rodney asked, sounding horrified. I nodded.

"But he seemed really . . . um . . ." I hesitated, not wanting to lie to them on their wedding day. "Really competent," I finally finished.

Linnie nodded slowly. "We're getting married by someone named Ralph," she said, like she was still trying to get her head around it.

"I'm just going to . . . check on something," Max muttered, glancing up at the ceiling and then leaving the room, Waffles in hot pursuit.

"That dog is very strange," Danny said, standing up as he pulled his phone from his pocket. "You okay?" he asked me, and I nodded as Danny headed out of the room.

"But how did you get him to agree to do it?" Rodney asked, looking at me, then shook his head. "How did you even find a judge on a Saturday?"

"It's kind of a funny story," I said. "Um . . . he sort of agreed to do it if he got to keep your suit."

"My suit?" he echoed. "My wedding suit?"

"It *is* a nice suit," J.J. said, clearly trying to be helpful.

"But . . ." Rodney looked around the room, like someone there might be able to explain to him what was going on. "This isn't a fable—you're not supposed to barter goods for services."

"I know," I said, "but the tailor gave him your suit by mistake, and then, when he put it on, he really liked it, so . . ."

"What am I supposed to wear?" Rodney asked, staring at me. "To my *wedding*, which is in a few hours?"

"Well," I said, lifting the garment bag off the back of the couch, "We still have Ralph's suit. You could always . . . um . . ." Rodney unzipped it and visibly flinched when he saw the suit. I poked J.J. hard in the side.

"Ow!" he said, glaring at me. "What . . ." I nodded toward the suit, widening my eyes at him. "Um, it's not so bad," he said, finally understanding me. "I mean, it's so . . . purple."

"Mike?" Rodney asked, holding the suit out to him. Mike leaned forward to look at it, then groaned again.

"Why would you do that to me?" he asked, rubbing his hand over his eyes. "I'm feeling sick enough already."

"I'm sorry," I said, glancing between Linnie and Rodney, neither of whom looked happy. "I just thought . . . you'd rather have a judge than a suit. That's all."

There was a knock on the family room doorframe, and I looked up to see the girl I'd seen earlier, the one with the camera bag. She was standing next to a guy with a goatee, who was carrying a professional-looking video camera. "Hi, all," the girl said, with a broad wave. "Linnie, Rodney, we wanted to get both video and stills of the bridal parties getting ready. Maybe we'll start with the groomsmen, since we're still waiting on the girls' hair and makeup?"

Linnie nodded, putting a very strained smile on her face. "We'll be right there."

"That's my cue," J.J. said, standing, then flicking Mike on the head. "Your cue too."

"Gahhhh," Mike moaned as he pushed himself up off the chair—I couldn't help but notice it seemed to take him about three times as long as normal. J.J. slung his arm around Mike's neck and pulled him from the room.

I turned to the other couch, where both Linnie and Rodney were looking shell-shocked. "You guys okay?"

"I just . . . ," Rodney said, then shook his head. "Are there any more surprises coming our way?"

"Well," I said, then cleared my throat, secretly hoping that maybe the two of them harbored a secret fandom I wasn't aware of. "How do you guys feel about Journey?"

CHAPTER 19
Or, What's the Worst That Could Happen?

"O KAY, LINNEA, IF YOU COULD LOOK IN THE
mirror . . . Great . . . And all the bridesmaids, lean in around
her . . . but don't look at me. . . . Great . . . Okay one more . . ."

I held my expression as still as possible, as Jenny W., Jenny K., Priya,
and Elizabeth all clustered around Linnie, who was pretending to do
her hair. "Great!" the photographer said, lowering the camera. "I'm just
going to move the lights. . . ." As soon as she stepped away, the hair and
makeup team—they were a guy and girl named Shawn and Cameron,
but I wasn't sure which was which—swooped in.

There had been shots of the two of them pretending to do Linnie's
hair and makeup, but in between those, they needed to actually do Linnie's hair and makeup, since they were also doing the rest of us. Luckily, the videographer hadn't been there for too long—he'd just gotten
some footage of us getting ready (or pretending to) and the hair and
makeup team starting to work on Linnie. Then he'd headed downstairs,
and I wasn't sorry to see him go, mostly because it wasn't like Linnie's
room was all that big to begin with, and five bridesmaids, a bride, and
a photographer seemed more than enough—and that was without

the giant light bouncer thing the photographer kept moving around.

"This is a disaster," Linnie said as the hair guy brushed out a strand, then clamped his curling iron around it.

"No, no," I said, trying to be as cheerful as possible. I looked to the Jennys and Priya for backup, but they were talking in a small circle up by Linnie and Rodney's bed. I widened my eyes at Elizabeth, who nodded and gave me a tiny wink. It wasn't that she and Rodney looked very much alike, but their mannerisms and cadence were exactly the same—so I figured having her say something was the closest we were going to get to Rodney being here without pulling him in.

"It'll be fine," Elizabeth said soothingly. "Weddings are always crazy. I mean, you remember mine, right?"

"But your wedding was beautiful," Linnie said, her voice getting higher and a little more hysterical. I saw the hair guy exchange a glance with the makeup artist.

"Exactly," Elizabeth said, smiling at her. "You didn't see what a disaster it was behind the scenes. And now when I think about my wedding, I don't remember that either. It's all going to be okay." She glanced at me, and I gave her a grateful smile.

"But . . . ," Linnie said, meeting my eye in the mirror. "I mean . . . Mike can barely stand up. We're being married by a death judge. Rodney's suit. *Journey?*"

I bit my lip. "But it can't get any worse."

"Okay," the photographer said, adjusting the light bounce thing and then coming back with her camera. "Just a few more getting-ready shots and then I'll actually let you get ready," she said with a quick smile. The Jennys and Priya hustled back over, and all of them put big smiles on as we posed around Linnie again. "And . . . got it," the photographer said after what felt like an eternity of listening to her camera click. "Great." She nodded. "I'll give you some time, and I'll be back for when Linnie puts her dress on, okay?" Without waiting for a reply, she headed out of the room, scrolling through the pictures on her viewfinder as she went.

"You okay?" I asked Linnie, who tried to nod but was held back by the fact her hair was attached to a curling iron.

"Tell me it'll be okay," she said, meeting my eyes in the mirror. "Because I just . . ." She took a shaky breath. "It kind of feels like this wedding is falling apart, you know?"

"No," I said, maybe a little too emphatically. "It'll all be fine. It'll be *great*."

"Totally great," Jenny K. said quickly, and Priya nodded.

"Okay," Linnie said with what seemed like a real effort. "Right! Things will be fine." She looked at me as much as she could without turning her head. "Are you going to take a shower, Charlie? You should probably do it now."

I looked down at the time on my phone and realized she was right; I had to get moving. "Are we still going to have enough time?" I asked, looking at the hair and makeup team.

The makeup artist nodded. "We'll just do you last," she said.

"It's critical," Linnie said with a smile that made me think she was shaking off her panic a bit. "Charlie's terrible at doing her own hair."

I didn't even disagree with this—it was completely true. "She's right about that," I said, heading toward the door. "Okay, I'll be back soon."

"I'll come with you!" Jenny W. said in a falsely cheerful voice, following me toward the door.

"What—to take a shower?" I asked, baffled, as she manhandled me out the door and then onto the landing, pulling the door shut behind her.

"Hi!" I jumped, whirling around to see J.J. standing there, and I had a feeling he'd been lying in wait for a while.

"What?" I asked.

"Well—" J.J. said, taking a deep breath, then noticed Jenny. "Hey," he said, his voice dropping about an octave.

"Hey yourself," Jenny W. said, smiling at him, but then turning to me. "We have a problem. I think Linnie's getting sick. She keeps sneezing, and I do *not* want her to do it during the ceremony."

"What do you want me to do about it?"

"Give her some cold medicine or something! I keep suggesting it, but she keeps saying she's fine."

"Okay," I said, nodding, adding it to my list of things I had to take care of before the wedding, the list that just seemed to get longer by the minute.

"My turn?" J.J. asked, then not waiting for an answer, kept going. "So, I understand there's a problem with the wedding band."

Jenny turned to me, eyebrows raised, and I nodded. "The wedding planner booked a Journey cover band by mistake."

"Streetlight People are going to be here?" Jenny asked, her voice rising as she grabbed my hand. *"Really?"*

"No," I said, staring at her. "The, um, other Journey cover band."

"Oh," she said, looking disappointed. "That's too bad. They played my cousin's daughter's bat mitzvah, and they were amazing." She gave me a sympathetic look. "Sorry you couldn't get them."

"We didn't try to get them. We didn't want any Journey cover band playing the wedding!"

"Well, exactly," J.J. said. "So I'm offering my services."

"Your services?" I frowned at my brother. "What are you—" I remembered, all at once. "No."

"Yes!" J.J. said, grinning widely. "DJJJ is here to help. I am a professional, after all."

"Jameison, you're a *DJ*?" Jenny asked, smiling at him, and J.J. inclined his head modestly.

"You only played one party," I reminded him. One summer when he was in college, J.J. had gone through a brief phase of wanting to be a DJ. It had not turned out well, either for him or for Eloise Robert's sweet sixteen. "And they kicked you out halfway through."

"I'll have you know that I frequently pick the Pirate bus music," J.J. said, drawing himself up to his full height. "And you know I make a mean playlist." I was aware of this; J.J. usually made us personalized mixes for Christmas and claimed that the gift of music was the most precious present of all.

I glanced down at the phone in my hand and realized I didn't have time to keep arguing this point, and that, frankly, someone volunteering to take over the music sounded pretty good to me. "Fine," I said, and J.J. threw a celebratory fist in the air.

"You've never made *me* a playlist, Jameison," Jenny said, her voice flirtatious.

J.J. took a step closer to her, a smile on his face, which I took as my cue to leave. I knew I needed to get in the shower, but I'd also never gotten my bagel this morning and was feeling seriously hungry. I hurried down to the kitchen and saw only a lone blueberry left. I sighed and picked it up, and had just turned to head back upstairs when someone called me.

"Charlotte?" I turned around to see Rodney's Aunt Liz standing in the doorway of the family room. "Could I have a moment?" Aunt Liz was beautifully dressed, as usual, in a pale orange suit, complete with brooch and scarf, but I wasn't sure if this was what she was going to be wearing to the wedding, or if this was just her pre-wedding breakfast outfit. "You look very nice."

"Oh, this?" Liz asked, casting a dismissive eye down at her outfit, which pretty much answered my question. "Well—thank you, dear. And you're . . ." She looked at me, and a small, worried frown appeared on her face as she took in my sneakers and jeans.

"I haven't gotten ready yet," I said quickly, and Liz nodded, looking relieved.

"I'm sorry to bother you about this. But I didn't want to hassle Linnea or Rodney, not on their wedding day. . . ."

"I'm sure that whatever it is, I can handle it."

"Good," she said with a nod. "Because I need you to change the seating plan. I'm far, *far* too close to Jimmy." She practically spat out the name, like it pained her to even say it.

"Um . . . I'm pretty sure Linnie took that into consideration when she was making it. . . ."

"It needs to be fixed," she said, and the sweet older lady was now totally gone, replaced with someone who was steely and all business. "Otherwise, I know Jimmy. There will be a scene, and that's the last thing I want at my nephew's wedding."

"Okay," I said quickly, since Liz was looking scarier by the minute. "I'll get it taken care of."

"Oh, good," she said with a sweet smile.

I gave her a nod and left the family room, realizing that I now really needed to hurry and get in the shower ASAP. I also didn't know how I was going to fix the seating plan—especially after the General had redone all the place cards for us. I pulled out my phone to text Bill as I walked toward the stairs.

Me

Hey—having an issue with two of the relatives on the groom's side. Can you make sure Jimmy and Liz are seated as FAR away from each other as possible??

Before I'd even reached the second-floor landing, Bill had texted me back.

I smiled as I looked down at it, incredibly relieved in that moment that he was here, that he was on my side and helping out with this.

A second after I'd sent it, I realized what I'd done and looked in horror as the little DELIVERED appeared under it, letting me know that there was no taking this back. But hopefully it was fine and Bill wouldn't read too much into it. Because I didn't mean anything, really—just that I was happy he was helping all of us. With the wedding. That he was the best wedding coordinator's assistant, that was all I had meant.

Deciding I didn't have time to be overanalyzing my text message mistakes, I hurried up to the second floor, which now was bustling and busy—I could hear a hair dryer going and the sound of water running in the bathroom. General Daniels, wearing a sharp dark-gray suit, was crossing the landing toward the guest room, his tie undone but looped around his neck. He gave me a nod, then headed into his guest room, pulling the door closed behind him.

I hurried up to the third floor, where things were about the same—I could hear hair dryers and music coming from behind the door of Linnie's room and J.J. and Mike talking behind their door. Priya was standing in the doorway of Mike's room, wearing her bridesmaids' dress with a hoodie over it, laughing with Jenny K., who was still in sweatpants.

"Hey, Charlie," Jenny said, smiling at me. "Did you get champagne? They just opened a bottle in Linnie's room."

"She's underage," Priya reminded her, giving me a wink.

"Um, so were we for most of college," Jenny said. "And that certainly didn't stop us. In fact, remember the night after homecoming when—"

"I'm not sure Charlie needs to hear about that stuff," Priya said quickly. She frowned at me. "I thought you were going to get ready?"

"I'm working on it," I assured her. I headed for the shower, then realized I'd left my brush in my room. I hurried over and knocked on the door.

"Come in," Danny said cheerfully, and I pushed the door open. Danny was sitting on my desk chair, already in his suit, tying his shoes. Brooke was standing in front of my mirror in a robe, leaning forward to put on eyeliner. She stopped as I came inside and gave me a tight smile, but not a particularly friendly one.

I realized I hadn't seen her since the night before, when she'd stormed out of the capture the flag game. "Sorry," I said, wondering if she was going to say anything about it, but Brooke just raised her eyebrows at me as I edged into my room. "I . . . just needed to get something out of my drawer."

Brooke let out a short breath. "Of course you do," she said, tossing her eyeliner down onto my dresser and taking a step back.

I blinked at her. "Sorry," I said again, wondering if I'd done something.

"But if you could just take everything with you now, that would be great," Brooke snapped. "So we're not doing this over and over. Okay?"

I glanced at Danny. Now that she was taking this tone with me, it was like I was realizing just how friendly and accommodating Brooke had been up until now—it was like seeing a whole other person. "Um . . ."

"Whoa. It's Charlie's room, babe—she's just going to get her stuff and then get out of our hair."

"I'm aware it's Charlie's room," Brooke said shortly, her voice getting higher. "And I'm aware that we're only in here because nobody knew I was coming. . . ."

Danny ran his hand over his eyes. "Brooke," he said, sounding tired.

"I'll just . . ." I edged past her, grabbed my brush, and backed out of the room. Danny shot me an apologetic look as I left, and I gave him a look back, trying to let him know that I was fine.

I closed the door behind me, looking at it for just a second and hearing Danny's and Brooke's voices rising and falling behind it. Knowing I didn't have time to worry about what was going on with them, I hurried across the landing to the bathroom, figuring that I should take advantage of it while it was still free.

After I took one of the quickest showers of my life and changed into sweatpants and a T-shirt—the makeup artist had lectured us all on not changing into our bridesmaids dresses until our hair and makeup were finished—I hurried across the landing to Linnie's room. I'd towel dried my hair, but I could feel it dripping down my back—the hair guy was going to blow it out before doing whatever he was going to do with the curling iron.

"Charlie?" I looked over to see J.J. in the doorway of his room, wearing something white that covered his whole face. "Is that you?"

"What is that?" I asked, getting closer—there were eye and mouth holes, and the whole affect was like he was trying to dress up as a ghost, but was doing a very bad job of it.

"Rejuvenating sheet mask," he said, adjusting it carefully. "Want one?"

"I'm okay," I said. "How's Mike?"

"He's doing better," J.J. said, and I breathed out a sigh of relief. "He's resting now, and I made him drink, like, a gallon of water." An alarm beeped, and J.J. pressed a button on his watch, then carefully removed the mask. "How do I look?"

"Rejuvenated," I said, reaching for Linnie's doorknob. I knocked once, then opened the door without waiting for a reply. The photographer and the other bridesmaids were gone—there was just my sister, still in her robe, looking more beautiful than I had ever seen her.

"Linnie," I said, smiling at her. Her hair was down, spilling over her

shoulders in soft curls. And her makeup was perfect, making her simultaneously look utterly gorgeous and also like she wasn't wearing any
makeup at all and just happened to look this way.

"You the last bridesmaid?" the hair guy asked, and I nodded.

"Finally," the makeup artist said, shaking her head. She glanced down
at her phone, which was on Linnie's dresser. "Because we're almost at
the end of our window."

"You have enough time for me, though, right?" I asked as I sat in the
chair that was next to Linnie's in front of the mirror.

"Just about," the hair guy said, then picked up a comb and started
combing out my damp hair.

"You look beautiful," I said to my sister.

"Thanks," she said, giving me a smile. She picked up a champagne
flute that was on her dresser and took a sip, then held it out to me.
I nodded and took a gulp of it, feeling that, at the least, it certainly
couldn't hurt. "Is everything okay out there?"

"Sure," I said, a little too quickly. "Um, Liz thought she was too close to
Jimmy, but it's okay! We're switching them." I turned my head to look at
my sister and was horrified to see her bottom lip start to tremble. "Lin?"

"I just don't think I can take anything else happening," she said, and
I noticed both the makeup girl and the hair guy had stopped and were
staring at my sister fearfully, like they were terrified all their hard work
was about to get wrecked. "I mean, too many things are going wrong!
And now Rodney's relatives and their feud ..."

"Are you going to cry?" the makeup artist asked, darting forward,
tissue in hand. "Because if you do, I'm going to need time to retouch."

This did not seem to be the thing to say to my sister, whose lip started
trembling even more violently. "Linnie," I said, turning her shoulders so
that she was facing me. "Listen. It's all going to be fine. Okay?"

"But ... ," Linnie said, and I could see tears in her eyes threatening to
spill over. "So much has gone wrong. . . ."

"Yes," I said, grabbing both her hands in mine, not wanting to dispute this, mostly because I couldn't. "But you love Rodney. And he loves you, and that's all that matters." I searched my sister's expression, and it was like I could see these words sinking in. "Right?"

Linnie nodded, and I noticed with relief that I could no longer see tears in her eyes. "You're right," she said, her voice a bit shaky. "Sorry about that."

"It's your wedding day," I said, smiling as the hair guy started brushing my hair again with one hand, while the other reached for the hair dryer, which was plugged into Linnie's wall socket, along with two curling irons and a flatiron. "You're allowed to be emotional. In fact, I think it's expected."

"Everything is going to be fine," Linnie said, like she was trying to convince herself, and I nodded.

"Nothing else," I promised, "is going to go wrong." Just as I said this, there was a faint *pop* and then the room was thrown into darkness.

CHAPTER 20
Or, Just Roll with It

"OKAY, IF EVERYONE COULD JUST STAY CALM!" Bill yelled from where he was standing on one of the kitchen chairs, in the dark.

It was still the afternoon, but the fact that it had gotten so dark out meant that I'd had to make my way downstairs using my phone flashlight, trying to reassure people I met on the way—Aunt Liz, Max, the Jennys—that I would try to find out what was going on. Linnie had come down with me, and I'd found a huge group gathered in the kitchen, most of whom were trying to figure out what was happening. There was a little more light in the kitchen, thanks to the picture windows, but it was still fairly dark, and my mother was lighting the candles, long tapers that we normally only used for fancy dinners, and placing them on the table and countertops.

"How are we supposed to cook?" one of the caterers said, her voice rising. "We have a fridge full of perishables—"

"Who cares about the food?" This was Glen, who'd come into the kitchen, along with the tent guys. "If we don't have power, we're going to have to do an acoustic set, and that's *not* the Journey way."

My dad frowned at him. "Who are you again?"

"He's with the band," I explained.

"We need to be taking pictures in ten minutes," the photographer said, looking at her watch. "And if I don't have power—"

"You think I don't have the same problem?" the videographer interrupted. "Everyone cares more about the video than the pictures anyway."

"Oh, *do* they, Fred?" she snapped.

"Yes, they do!"

"I was in the middle of taking a shower!" my uncle Stu sputtered. He was in his Westin robe, soap bubbles gently popping on his bald head. "And the lights go out, just like that." He snapped his fingers, apparently to illustrate this. "I should have gone to a hotel." I saw my mother take a deep breath, like she was physically trying to restrain herself from killing my uncle.

"What does this mean?" Linnie asked, twisting her hands together. I saw her look around for Rodney, but he wasn't there—as soon as he'd started to come into the kitchen, his sister Elizabeth had screamed that it was beyond bad luck for the bride and groom to see each other and had marched Rodney back upstairs. Both he and Linnie had tried to point out that they'd been seeing each other all morning so far, but she was clearly not hearing this.

"It'll be fine," I said automatically, even though I wasn't sure how, exactly. We needed power to put on a wedding—of this I was sure.

"This is just like when the Royals played the Mets, game one of the World Series," J.J. said.

"It's really not," I said, shaking my head.

"It is!" J.J. insisted. "The game was delayed because of a power issue, but—"

"My uncle is on the way over with a generator," Bill said, speaking loudly to talk over everyone else. "It looks like we just overloaded the power in the house, trying to plug in too many things."

"It was the band," one of the tent guys said. "Did you see how many amps they had?"

"Oh, sure, blame the rock stars," Glen said, shaking his head.

"So!" Bill said, speaking up again. "The power outside will be restored as soon as he arrives with a generator. But as for the power in the house . . ." Bill hesitated, his voice trailing off.

"We need power," the caterer said again, her voice rising. "Otherwise, this food is going to spoil *and* we're not going to be able to cook anything."

"It's probably just the fuse box that got overloaded," my dad said, taking his own phone out and turning on the flashlight on it. "I'm going to go down to the basement and see what I can do." He turned to Danny, who'd been standing next to me, and raised his eyebrows. "You helped me do this before once, didn't you, son?"

"Absolutely. Not sure I remember anything, but I'm happy to take a look."

"I'll help," the General added, and my dad nodded his thanks.

"Me too," said J.J., falling into step behind them. I had a feeling things might actually go better if J.J. weren't there, but he left with them before I could say anything.

"Linnie?" My sister turned around, and I did as well, to see Shawn and Cameron—whichever one was which—standing in the kitchen doorway.

"Hey, you guys," she said, crossing over to them. "Sorry about that. We should have this fixed soon."

"That's the thing," the hair guy said, grimacing. "We're only booked for ten more minutes. And if we go over that, we're going to have to charge you our day rate again."

Even in the kitchen that was practically dark, and lit only by flickering candles, I could see my sister's face go pale. Which told me that these people had been *really* expensive. Though seeing how lovely

Linnie looked, they were clearly worth every penny. "But . . . ," Linnie said, looking over at me like she was taking in my still-wet hair and my face, which was completely bare. "You didn't get to Charlie."

"And we could stay," the makeup artist said, pulling out her phone and looking at the time. "But we just would need to charge you again. That's all."

"It's fine," I said quickly, taking a step closer to them. Linnie shook her head, like she was going to argue, and I kept going before she could. "I can do my hair and makeup on my own. I promise it'll be fine."

"But . . ." Linnie looked at me, biting her lip. "You're so bad at it, Charlie."

I was feeling a little too panicky to be insulted by this. And I also didn't want to stress my sister out any further—*or* have her pay some exorbitant rate just because I was incompetent at doing my own hair and makeup. "I promise it's fine," I said, even as a piece of me was wondering what I was saying, since I had no idea how it was going to be fine, exactly. "I'll just . . . go upstairs and get ready, then. Okay." Linnie was still looking at me, her expression worried, and I gave her a big smile and a thumbs-up before turning on my phone flashlight again and heading up the stairs, leaning on the banister for support. I tried to tell myself that it would be okay. That somehow I could figure out something to do with my hair, even though I couldn't use a blow-dryer or a curling iron and I would have to basically put my makeup on in the dark. If Siobhan was here, I realized, she could have helped me. She was good with hair, but she was great with makeup, which was the main reason I'd never gotten skilled at doing it myself. But this just made me remember the fight we'd had all over again, and I increased my pace up the stairs, like I was trying to outrun these thoughts.

I crossed to my bedroom door and pulled it open, and it wasn't until I stepped over the threshold that reality hit me once again—this room wasn't mine. Brooke was sitting on my bed with Waffles, who was lying on his back in front of her, getting a belly scratch, his left leg twitching.

"Oh," I said, taking a step back immediately. Brooke had been so unhappy to see me here before, I didn't want to think what she was going to say about me showing up now. "Sorry. It's habit. I—forgot."

"Charlie?" she asked, squinting at me slightly. There was a little bit of light coming in through my window, and she'd lit two of the half-melted candles that were on my dresser—as a result, there was both a little bit more light in the room and it smelled like vanilla and pine trees. I could see that Brooke was now ready for the wedding—she was in a gorgeous purple one-shouldered dress, and there were black patent stilettos lined up on the floor by the foot of my bed. Her hair was pulled up in a twist and her makeup looked perfect—she was doing the smoky-eyeliner thing I'd seen in tutorial videos but that always made me look like I either had a black eye or some kind of vein disorder. "What's going on?" she asked. "Is the power coming back?"

"Hopefully soon," I said, trying to sound cheerful and positive about this, even though this was getting harder by the second. "I just . . . I'm sorry to do this to you *again*, but I have to get my makeup because the hair and makeup people are leaving and I didn't . . . I didn't . . ."

I tried to fight it, to keep the emotions at bay, but it was like everything was starting to pile up—everything going wrong with the wedding, my failed attempts to make it perfect, my fight with Siobhan—it was all hitting me at once.

I was horrified to realize that my lip had started to tremble and my face was getting the hot, tight feeling that meant I was about to start crying any second now. I closed my eyes hard, trying to keep the tears back, but to my horror, they leaked out anyway. "Sorry," I said, pressing the heels of my hands into my eyes. "Sorry! I'm not—I just . . ." I couldn't believe I was crying in front of *Brooke*, of all people. "I'll go," I said, taking another step back. Then, when I realized I had nowhere *to* go, I started crying harder. "God," I said angrily, swiping my hand in front of my eyes. "I don't mean to do this. I just . . ."

"Um," Brooke said, taking a step closer to me, then one away, twisting her hands together, clearly as thrown by my tears as I was. "Are you . . . ? I mean . . ." She bit her lip, and the fact that I was making her so clearly uncomfortable wasn't helping me pull myself together.

"I'm just supposed to have my hair done," I said, raking my hands through it. "And my makeup, but they can't wait until the power comes back on, and I'm going to ruin all of Linnie's pictures, and I don't know what to do. . . ." Saying this out loud made me feel worse than ever, because there was the situation, laid out, with no solution in sight.

"It's okay," Brooke said, sounding much less uncomfortable than she had a moment ago. I just looked at her. "It'll *be* okay. Go wash your face, all right? Then come back here."

I stared at her for a moment, wondering what she was even talking about, but she just nodded toward the bathroom across the landing. "Go on," she said, her voice totally assured, like there was not even a question in there anywhere, like this was the only thing to do in this situation.

And so, feeling like I was glad to have someone telling me what to do, I crossed the landing to the bathroom. I washed my face twice, splashing it with cold water, and when I dried it and looked in the mirror, it seemed like maybe the puffiness around my eyes had subsided somewhat.

I walked back to my room, and Brooke was pulling out my desk chair. "Close the door," she said, and I did, feeling more confused than ever. "Sit." It was only when I crossed over to my chair that I saw she had laid out a set of rollers, along with a comb and a series of brushes.

"We don't have any power," I pointed out, even as I sat down. I was facing the door, and Brooke was behind me, which was making this situation that much stranger. "So I'm not sure what . . ." I tried to look at her, but she turned it so that I was looking straight forward, and I felt a

MORGAN MATSON

mist on the back of my head as she sprayed something on my hair, then started combing it through. "But . . ."

"I always like to have rollers on hand," she said, and as I turned my head as much as I could to look at the dresser, I saw that they were foam rollers, the kind my mom had sometimes used when I was little. "They don't need any kind of power, and with your hair type"—I could feel her picking up sections of it with her hands, like she was assessing it—"I think it'll look great."

"And you don't need any kind of heat?"

"Well," she said, and I felt the mist and then the comb again, "ideally, you'd hit them with some heat from a blow-dryer, just to set the curls, but they're fine without it. I promise."

I opened my mouth to protest, or say that she didn't really need to do this, but then closed it again when I realized I didn't have any other solutions. She set her comb on my dresser, then picked up her brush and started combing through my hair with quick, efficient strokes. "Thank you," I finally said quietly, looking straight ahead at my door.

"Sure," Brooke said a moment later, going back to work with the brush again, her voice also quiet. "It's the least I can do."

"I don't know," I said, glancing at my flickering reflection in the mirror.

"I do," Brooke said, wielding her tiny gold can of hair spray. "These are air-drying, but we have to do everything we can to hold the curl for when we take them out. And that means hair spray."

I hesitated, then nodded and closed my eyes as Brooke started spraying my head, which was now totally covered in foam rollers. When she seemed to have stopped, I opened my eyes again and tried not to cough, then ran my hand over Waffles's head. At some point during this makeover, he'd clambered up onto my lap, where he'd stayed ever since, dozing off occasionally, his twitching paws letting me know that he was dreaming.

Brooke and I hadn't talked much as she'd twisted my hair around the rollers, then pinned them with bobby pins, beyond her telling me to keep my head still, or turn it this way or that. And I was glad about that, since the silence—and the comfort of a sleeping beagle on my lap—had let me pull myself together a little bit more, and I no longer felt like I was on the verge of panicking or bursting into tears, or both simultaneously.

"I think you got the dog," I said, realizing that I could turn the hair on the top of Waffles's head into tiny spikes and they stayed that way.

"It's not a bad look on him," she said, and I smiled.

"He sure likes you," I said as Brooke crossed back to the dresser and started going through a gigantic makeup bag.

"I love dogs," she said as she crossed in front of me. "And this guy . . . I feel like he knows he's not really wanted this weekend. That he's a little in the way. So I wanted to give him some extra attention." I looked down at Waffles and felt a pang of guilt—after all, it wasn't the dog's fault that he'd been dropped off here. He'd had no say in the matter. She bent down so that she was almost level with me, studying my face, eyes narrowed in concentration. "Now," she said. "What did Linnea want for makeup?"

"Oh," I said, blinking at her. "Um . . . you don't have to . . ."

Brooke just shook her head. "No offense, Charlie, but I've seen the way you've done your makeup this weekend. What did she want?"

"She didn't say. She looks great, though—really natural but still somehow made-up?" I hesitated, wishing I was better at describing this.

Brooke continued to study my face. "We can do that." She nodded like she'd decided something, then crossed back to the dresser and brought over her makeup bag, standing in front of me again. "Close your eyes."

I tried to sit as still as possible as Brooke smoothed primer, then foundation, on my face, neither of which I'd worn since the prom. Even though she'd never done my makeup before, Brooke wasn't hesitating or needing to try out lots of colors before applying anything. She was working with remarkable efficiency, like in addition to being a doctor, she also dabbled as a makeup artist.

"Okay," Brooke said after a moment, and I opened my eyes. "We can do a more natural look since it seems like that's what Linnie wants." She sounded almost resigned. "But just so you know, for the future, you should lean more toward blue eye shadow. It'll make your eyes pop."

"Blue?" I'd usually gravitated toward greens and purples, but I was realizing now that was just because that's what Linnie always wore, and I'd just copied her.

"Blue," she confirmed. "A cool blue. Trust me." She leaned toward me, and I closed my eyes automatically, feeling the featherlight brush as it passed over my eyelids. "This is going to look good," she said, but softly enough that I wasn't sure if she was talking to me or to herself. "Just try and sit still."

"Okay," I said, concentrating on not moving as I felt slight pressure on my eyelid—probably eyeliner being applied. The longer I sat there, trying not to even breathe too much, the worse I started to feel. Brooke did not need to be doing this for me. It wasn't like I'd been particularly nice to her since she arrived. It wasn't that I'd been mean—at least, I hoped not—but I hadn't welcomed her in. I'd resented that she was here—messing up my plans and taking away Danny's attention. She had been nothing but sweet and kind to me, and in return, I had treated her shabbily.

"Open," Brooke said, and I opened my eyes to see she was leaning forward, uncapped mascara wand in hand. "Now look over my left shoulder and try not to blink." I stared ahead at the wallpaper by my door as Brooke leaned closer to me, carefully applying mascara to my eyelashes.

"Um," I started, running my fingers through Waffles's fur. I wasn't sure what I even wanted to tell her, but I knew I had to at least try. The longer I sat here, with Brooke helping me when I didn't deserve to be helped, I was feeling like I had to say something, even if it didn't come out right.

"Look up," she murmured.

"I just," I started, then tried again. "I wanted to say—"

"Right shoulder," she said, switching to my other side.

"I'm sorry," I blurted, and Brooke lowered the mascara wand and straightened up, taking a step back. "I'm sorry if I've been—if I wasn't—" I realized I wasn't making any sense, so I took a breath and started over. "Thank you for doing this for me. I'm sorry if I haven't made you feel welcome."

"Oh," she said, blinking. She looked down at the black tube in her hands and turned it between her fingers for just a moment, then took a slightly shaky breath, the mascara spinning faster. "I should have known, I guess. But I just thought . . ."

She uncapped the mascara and leaned forward again, and I looked over Brooke's right shoulder, trying to stay still, knowing somehow that there was more she wanted to say and that it would be easier for her if she didn't have to look right at me. "Danny and I had been dating for a few months, and we talked about me coming to the wedding. But then we broke up . . ."

I felt my eyebrows rise even as I tried to keep looking in the same direction and not get stabbed in the eye by a mascara wand.

"And then we got back together, and he said that I should come. I might have pushed him on it—I really wanted to meet all of you, and I thought it meant something that he asked me. . . ." I blinked but tried to keep looking ahead, at the height lines that crawled up my doorframe, marking every year of my life until I'd declared myself over it at eleven. "But I think it's just hard," she said, taking a step back and capping the mascara. "I don't . . . think it's what he thought it would be."

"Well," I said, taking a breath, getting my automatic defense of Danny ready. But I hesitated, Brooke's words hitting me, and letting myself see, for the first time, just how she might have felt about this weekend. I suddenly saw all the times we had made it clear we hadn't known she was coming, all the times Danny had wandered off, not making sure she felt comfortable or happy. But he probably hadn't meant anything by it. He probably just hadn't realized how she felt. I tried to tell myself this—and I believed it—but it didn't necessarily make me feel any better.

I opened my mouth to respond to this when Brooke nodded and spun my desk chair around so that I was facing my dresser mirror, causing Waffles to raise his head and look around, like he was confused as to why we were moving. "You're done," she said, stepping back with a smile.

I blinked at my reflection. My hair was in rollers all over my head, but my makeup looked amazing. I was wearing more than I normally ever did, but it didn't look like it was garish or too much—I still looked like me, but with all my features subtly enhanced.

"What do you think?" Brooke asked, giving me a hopeful, nervous smile.

"It's great," I said, returning her smile in the mirror. "Thank you." I took a deep breath. I knew I needed to try to make this better, even though something inside me knew that it was probably Danny who should be saying this, not me. "Brooke," I started slowly, picking up the dog's ears, then dropping them. "I'm really—"

She waved this off. "It's okay."

"But—"

"Really," she said firmly, then smiled at me. "But thank you. Now," she said, her voice suddenly businesslike. "I need you to leave the rollers in for as long as possible, okay? And I'm going to need to touch up your lipstick in about an hour."

I glanced down at the time on my phone and jumped, sending Waffles tumbling to the ground. He shot me a look of betrayal, then hopped up on the bed and rolled onto his belly. I pushed myself up from my chair—it was later than I'd realized and I still hadn't put on my dress. "I should go," I said, already halfway to the door. I opened it, but then turned back to Brooke, who was giving Waffles's belly a scratch. "Um . . . thank you."

Brooke nodded, then pointed out the door. "Go," she said, and I hurried out of the room. I ran out to the landing, where J.J. was standing in his suit, fastening his cuff links.

He took one look at me and immediately burst into laughter. "Oh my god," he said, doubling over slightly. "What is on your *head*? Oh my god."

"Shut up, Jameison," I snapped at him as I headed to Linnie's room, which thankfully looked empty. "They're just rollers!"

"No, wait, come back," J.J. said, sounding out of breath, still laughing in between every word. "I didn't mean it. You look, um . . ."

I slammed the door to Linnie's room, then tried to hit the lights, not remembering until I flipped the switch twice that the power was still out. J.J. being upstairs, in his suit, either meant that the group that had gone into the basement to try to fix things had either failed, or they'd just told J.J. to go away and stop trying to help. Figuring that the second option was more likely—frankly, hoping it was—I looked around in the dark. The power outage looked like it had stopped the getting-ready party that had been going on in here not that long ago, though I could still see the evidence of it—half-empty champagne glasses on Linnie's dresser and makeup and Q-tips scattered across it. I walked to the closet, opening the door wide, since there were no windows in the long, narrow space and it was totally dark in there.

I made my way to the end of the closet and, with the little light that was left, pulled my bridesmaid dress off the rack. I changed quickly, then walked back through to Linnie and Rodney's room. I looked at the mirror over the dresser, in which I could kind of see myself, but not really. My bridesmaid dress was peach silk, with spaghetti straps and a little V cutout on the bodice. We'd all had to wear the same color, but could pick our own options in straps, length, and fit. I smoothed down the skirt, which flared out slightly and which I'd felt would be more fun during the dancing portion of the evening. Peach wasn't my favorite color, and on my own, I never would have chosen this dress—but it had been Linnie's pick, and I had to admit, as I looked at it now, that I kind of liked it.

I peered out into the hallway before leaving, to make sure J.J. wasn't still lurking around, waiting to make fun of me. When the coast was clear, I hurried down to the first floor, hoping that while I'd been getting my makeup done things hadn't gone too far off track downstairs.

"No," I heard a voice say as I stepped off the last stair and into the front hall. "Still a negative on power in the house. I have the number of an electrician . . . okay. Sounds good." Then there was a sound of feedback, and Bill came around the corner, holding a walkie-talkie and wearing a tux.

I took an instinctive step back, remembering a second too late that I was right in front of the stairwell, and I stumbled slightly, reaching out to the banister post and holding on to steady myself, trying to look like I'd done all of this on purpose. But the fact was that Bill was wearing a tuxedo.

The tux fit him well, somehow transforming the lanky guy I'd been running errands with this morning. His black bow tie was perfectly tied, and his hair had been combed back. It wasn't like I hadn't seen him dressed up—just last night, he'd been wearing a suit. So I wasn't sure why I was suddenly having trouble focusing as I looked at him.

"Hey," he said, lowering his walkie-talkie and smiling at me. "You look great."

"Oh," I said, just blinking at him, then looking down at my bare feet, trying to pull myself together. "Thank you. So do you. Um, with the whole tuxedo thing."

"Thanks," Bill said, sounding pleased as he adjusted his shirt cuffs. "It's a thing of my uncle's. He thinks if we're dressed up, we blend in more with the event. You don't notice the people running around the scenes as much if they look like maybe they could be guests."

I nodded. "That makes sense." I reached up to tuck my hair behind my ears, but met only the foam of the rollers. I felt my stomach drop as I remembered, all at once, what my head looked like. "Oh my god."

"I think your hair looks nice," Bill said, his smile widening as he clearly realized what I was thinking. "It's very . . . sci-fi."

"They're just . . . for my hair," I managed to say. It was like I could practically feel the heat coming from my cheeks. "Because there's no power."

"Yeah," Bill said, holding up his walkie-talkie as he shook his head. "We're working on it. The caterers are about to kill me. We got the generator working outside, so everything in the tent is up and running, but . . ." He grimaced.

"Do you think it's going to be able to be fixed?" I asked, my humiliating hair situation forgotten as I started to walk toward the basement door. "Don't we really, really need power?"

Bill nodded. "We really do." He pulled his phone out of his pocket. "I have an electrician I can call and see if they can get here fast. I was waiting to see if your dad was able to get the fuses working again."

"But if they can't?"

Bill just looked at me, and I realized I'd been waiting for something optimistic from him, for him to say that we'd be fine, that there was some kind of solution he'd thought of. "Then we need to hope an electrician can get here and get things fixed in . . ." He glanced down at his watch. "Twenty minutes."

I swallowed as I walked over to the open basement door. It was pitch-black inside, except I could see a few flashlights bobbing around. "Hey," I called down into the basement. "Uh—how's it looking?" Nobody responded, and after a moment, I added, "It's Charlie."

"I know it's Charlie." This was my dad, sounding annoyed. "I do have the ability to distinguish between my children. I didn't just get here."

"So, how's it going?"

"We're working on it." This was Danny, and I could hear that he sounded stressed.

"Just . . . give us a second, okay?" my dad called, and I nodded, before realizing that he couldn't see me.

"Okay," I called. I glanced at Bill, and we walked toward the front hall together. "It doesn't sound great."

"I know," he said, shaking his head. "I'm giving it just one more minute before I get the electrician. I don't want to step on your dad's toes, but . . ."

I nodded. "It's the right call."

"Because we don't have that long to wait." Just as he'd finished saying this, the lights snapped back on, and the entire front hall was suddenly very bright. Machines whirred to life in the kitchen, followed by the startled yelps of the caterers, who had apparently not been prepared for this. I could hear the sound of three separate television sets blaring, all turned to different channels, and a low persistent beeping that was coming from somewhere I couldn't identify. I looked at Bill and blinked, trying to get my eyes to adjust.

It was that feeling like when the lights come up after a movie—how it takes a minute to let go of the world you'd been immersed in. Bill smiled happily at me, and now that I could see his features clearly, I was reminded all over again that, Jesse Foster or no Jesse Foster, he really was cute.

"Let's see what else has to be done," Bill said, picking up the walkie. "All of which will be *much* easier now that we have power."

"Thank god," I said. I gave him a quick smile, then headed upstairs, feeling like, judging from how unhappy the caterers had seemed, it might be a good thing to avoid the kitchen at the moment.

Save the Date

As I was coming up the stairs, Rodney was making his way down them, but with difficulty, and when he got closer I understood why. He was wearing Ralph's terrible suit—which was as purple, and checked, as ever. But even though I'd known Ralph was shorter and smaller than Rodney, I didn't quite understand just how much until Rodney was in front of me, wearing his suit. It was far too tight, and the pants stopped somewhere around Rodney's mid-calf. It was a terrible look on anyone, but especially for a groom on his wedding day.

"I can't wear this," Rodney said, shaking his head as he looked down at himself, and I had to agree.

I winced. I knew it was my fault that he was wearing it—but at the time, it had seemed like the only thing to do. Now, though, looking at the reality in front of me, I wasn't quite sure. Maybe Rodney could have worn his suit and gotten a fake marriage from Max, and then he and Linnie could have just gone to a courthouse afterward and not told anyone.

The door to the other guest room opened, and the General came out, looked at his son, and frowned. "What's the meaning of this?"

"It's a long story," I said quickly, hoping we could skip over the parts of it that I had been directly responsible for. "But . . . um . . . Rodney kind of doesn't have his wedding suit."

Rodney shot me a dark look and then nodded. "Unfortunately, it's true."

"And you thought this was a good substitute?" The General shook his head. "Son."

"I didn't!" Rodney spluttered. "I was hoping this was all a big joke, but apparently, it's what I'm expected to wear on my wedding day." Rodney's voice rose at the end of it, and I could hear just how upset about this he was. I took a breath, about to suggest that J.J. wear this and Rodney wear his groomsman suit—they were roughly the same size— when the General stepped forward and clapped his hand on Rodney's shoulder. "It'll be okay, son," he said, steering him into the guest room. "Let's get you sorted out."

"Charlie?" My mother came out onto the landing, adjusting the wrap around her shoulders. Her mother-of-the-bride dress was a pale lilac that I'd hated on the hanger (and had not been afraid to tell her this) but looked absolutely stunning on.

"You look so nice, Mom."

"Really?" She smiled, pleased, and I could see that her cheeks had gone slightly pink. "Thank you, hon. So do you. Though I'm not sure about the hairstyle . . ."

My hand flew up to my rollers. "I'm going to take them out," I assured her, figuring that maybe now that the power was back on, I could use a hair dryer on them, maybe speed up the process a little.

"I think that might be wise," my mother said with a smile. "But have you seen your sister? They need to get set up for pictures."

"No," I said, trying to think of the last place I'd seen Linnie. "Um, do the bridesmaids know where she is?" My mom gave me a look that clearly indicated she didn't trust the bridesmaids to know much of anything. "I'll check her room," I said, already heading upstairs.

I saw that the door to J.J.'s room was open, and I crossed over to it, knocking once before pushing the door open all the way. Mike was sitting on the oversize baseball-glove chair. "Hey," I said, more quietly than I normally would have.

"Hey," he said, and I was happy to see that he no longer looked like he was going to fall over in a strong wind. "The bridesmaids are in my room," he said faintly. "They're . . . loud."

"How are you doing?" I asked, not entirely sure if I meant with his hangover, or with being back in the house again.

Mike made a *so-so* gesture with his hand, which I realized might have covered either of these things.

"Seen Linnie?"

"No," Mike said, looking alarmed. "Have we lost the bride?"

"No," I said, lowering my voice. "Don't—"

"We lost the bride?" This was J.J., standing behind me in the doorway. He stepped into the room and grinned when he saw me. "Oh good, your hair still looks crazy," he said happily. "Now I just need to get a photo. . . ."

"No," I said, taking a step out of their room.

"It's not for blackmail!" he called after me unconvincingly.

"Leave me alone," I said, backing out of the room before J.J. could find his phone and take a blackmail picture of me. I checked the bathroom, but Linnie wasn't there, either. Though I did use the opportunity of having a mirror I could actually see into to finish getting ready. I went over the rollers quickly with my hair dryer, then took them out one by one and shook out my hair. I piled them carefully on the bathroom counter, giving silent thanks for Brooke. My curls were falling softly around my shoulders, and this, coupled with the makeup she'd put on me, made me feel like maybe I was ready for this wedding after all. I looked at my reflection, thinking how in just a few hours, Jesse would be seeing me, and for once, I'd be prepared to see him too.

I gave myself a last look in the mirror before I headed to Linnie's room to see if she was there, but the room was dark and quiet. I was about to go, to try and see if maybe Linnie and the bridesmaids were all somewhere together, when I noticed a strip of light extending from the closet onto the floor.

I pulled open the closet door. My sister was sitting on the carpet, underneath the hanging racks of my clothes. She'd put on her wedding dress, and she looked absolutely beautiful.

"Hi," I said, trying to fight down the lump in my throat as I looked at my sister on her wedding day.

"Don't," Linnie said, smiling up at me. "You're going to get me started and we haven't even done the rest of the pictures yet."

I dropped my heels in the doorway and walked into the closet, sitting across from her after carefully smoothing my dress underneath me. "You look so pretty."

Normally Linnie would have brushed off a compliment like this, or made a joke. But maybe you weren't supposed to do that when you were a bride, or maybe she understood just how lovely she actually looked. Because she just smiled at me and inclined her head slightly. "Thank you."

"What are you doing in here?" I leaned back against the wall, hanging clothes just inches from my head. I couldn't help but flash back to all the times Linnie and I had sat here like this, legs extended, talking about everything and nothing, or laughing until my cheeks hurt. We were in our usual spots, though we'd never been quite this formally dressed before.

"I don't know," she said, leaning back against her own wall. "I just wanted a minute of quiet before everything got started." She gave me a smile. "Your hair looks great."

"Brooke."

"Really?"

"Really. She did my makeup, too."

"Well, thank god for that."

I smiled at that, even as I wondered how long I should wait before telling her she was wanted downstairs and people were waiting for her. She looked so peaceful that I was hoping it could actually be a few minutes from now. "Oh—Siobhan can't come," I said, trying to just toss this off. "She got stuck in Michigan. I'll pay you back whatever her meal would have cost."

"It's okay," Linnie said. She leaned forward, looking at me closely. "What?"

I shook my head, not wanting to put this on her when she was getting married so soon. "It's nothing."

"It's not nothing."

I waved it off. "We kind of had a fight," I said with a shrug, like this really didn't matter to me at all. "But it's not a big deal. I mean, I don't really need her. I have you guys. And she's leaving next year for school anyway, so . . ."

Linnie nodded, but in a way that I could somehow tell meant she wasn't agreeing with me. She reached out and smoothed one of my curls down, then took a breath before speaking. "It can't always be about us, Charlie," she said, her voice a little tentative, like she was carefully choosing each word as she spoke it. "You have to have people outside the family too."

"I do," I said automatically, before wondering if this was actually true any longer.

Linnie gave me a look that clearly said she didn't believe me. "What happened with Jesse?"

"Nothing," I said, and gave her a quick recap of Mike getting drunk and ruining the mood. "But maybe tonight . . ." Even as I spoke the words, I could feel my heart start to beat faster at the thought of it—I would be seeing Jesse soon. Like, in a few hours.

"Well, have your fun. Just be careful," she said, raising an eyebrow at me.

"Girls?" I heard my dad's voice—from the sound of it, he was on the landing.

"Yeah?" we both called back in unison.

"Uh—there's someone named Ralph downstairs who claims he's here to marry Linnie."

Linnie shot me an exasperated look, and I clapped my hand over my mouth, trying not to burst out laughing. "He's going to marry her *to* Rodney," I called. "He's a judge."

"Ah," my dad said. "Well, that makes more sense. I was worried there was going to have to be a duel or something."

"Do we need to go down?" Linnie called.

"Pretty soon," my dad said, and his voice was getting fainter, like he'd already headed down the stairs. "Almost picture time!"

"So," I said, looking across at her and feeling myself smile. "Should we get you married?"

Linnie looked around the closet, then took a breath and nodded. I held out my hand to her and she clasped it, and we pulled ourselves up to standing together, the way we'd been doing ever since I was little. "Yes," she said, straightening out her train and giving my hand a squeeze. "Let's do it."

CHAPTER 21
Or, The Boy I'm Gonna Marry

---

*I*S EVERYONE HERE?" WILL ASKED AS HE WALKED past us all—the bridesmaids and groomsmen, all lined up in the kitchen in our proper order, with Linnie and my parents waiting at the end of the line, in the dining room. "Are we all ready?"

"Is this a rhetorical question?" J.J. asked, sounding not sarcastic, but genuinely interested. "Because I think we've been ready for, what, twenty minutes?"

Jenny W. nodded, and I saw Elizabeth roll her eyes. But the truth was, J.J. was right for once. We'd all been ushered into the kitchen so that we could walk across the lawn in formation to the back of the tent. It seemed that getting the bridal party in place was not such an easy thing when there was nowhere to stand hidden before processing down the aisle. Since we'd be visible the second we entered the tent, we weren't going to do it until the wedding was actually a go. According to Will, there was nothing worse than the guests seeing a bride in her wedding dress before the event had begun.

But every time it looked like we were ready to go, another guest would come in late, and we'd go into our holding pattern all over again.

I couldn't help but think about Rodney, waiting up at the front of the tent with his parents, and hoped that someone had told him we were waiting because people kept showing up late, not because Linnie had changed her mind.

The last two hours had been a frenzied blur, as it seemed like time was speeding up the closer it got to the start of the wedding. The pictures had taken far longer than I would have ever imagined pictures could take, and by the end of it my cheeks hurt from smiling—but now they were done, which was the important thing. Linnie and Rodney had wanted to do them before the ceremony, as opposed to after (which really made the insistence that Rodney and Linnie not see each other before the wedding seem that much sillier). They figured that this way, there wouldn't be a long pause while everyone waited for the bride and groom to get their pictures taken. It was a good idea in theory, even though J.J. kept pointing out that if either Linnie or Rodney changed their minds mid-ceremony and didn't say "I do," we'd be left with a lot of awkward photos.

As we'd gotten closer to the start time, Will and Bill had kicked into high gear, and it seemed like they were both in ten places at once as they ran around, both in their tuxes, communicating by walkie-talkie, looking more like they were in the midst of pulling off a heist than planning a wedding.

I had been waiting for more stuff to go wrong, but as the wedding had gotten closer to its start time, things had seemed to calm down somewhat. Brooke had taken Waffles for a walk and then closed him upstairs in my room, where he seemed happy enough to nap on the blanket that she'd folded at the foot of the bed for him, so he wouldn't start howling during the ceremony.

"So how are you feeling, Lin?" Danny asked, turning around to look at her, standing next to my dad. They'd kept their arms linked for a while, until it became clear that we were not walking down the aisle imminently, and had stepped apart, my dad sitting on one of the dining room chairs and Linnie leaning against the doorframe. "Excited?"

Linnie batted away her veil, then rolled her eyes. It was still hanging down her back—she wouldn't put it on over her face until we started the procession, whenever that was going to be—and it was clearly irritating her. "Mostly just ready to stop hanging out in the dining room."

"Same," Jenny K. said as she shifted her weight from foot to foot. "What's the holdup again?"

"People coming in late," Bill said as he passed us, shooting me a quick smile as he did. "But I think we're going to be ready to go momentarily, okay?"

I nodded and turned to Rodney's cousin Marcus, who I would be walking down the aisle with, but he was laughing about something with Elizabeth.

"Okay!" This was Will, and as he approached us, people stopped talking and joking around—he had that kind of presence. "I think we're all set. Linnea," he said, turning to my sister with a smile, "ready to do this?"

We all turned to look at my sister, who nodded. "I'm ready." The Jennys and Priya broke from their spots in line to help pull the veil over her face, and then the four of them had a quick group hug, their arms around each other. "Actually, could I have a moment?" Linnie asked just as Will had raised his walkie-talkie again. "Could I just get the Grants for a second?"

I walked back toward Linnie and my parents, and the seven of us formed a loose circle in the dining room. I was standing next to Danny, who looped his arm over my shoulders, Linnie was between my mom and dad, and Mike and J.J. were standing together next to Danny. "You okay?" Mike asked, and Linnie nodded.

"I just wanted to take a minute," she said, and I could hear that her voice was getting dangerously wobbly, which didn't seem like a great sign before she was about to walk down the aisle. Though it did now seem like a good idea we'd done pictures before Linnie's eyes had a chance to get totally puffy. "And just be here with my family." She smiled at all of us, and I felt my own eyes prickle with tears as I looked around the circle—at my brothers, all of them handsome in their matching suits, and my parents, and my sister in her wedding dress. It was a scene I could imagine my mother drawing—but it was that much better, because it was real, and happening now, right this minute. "And to just thank you guys . . . I mean, for everything . . ." Linnie's voice broke, and I saw my mom reach out and rub her back. "I wanted to let you know how much it means to me that we're all here, together." She glanced at Mike as she said this, and he gave her a small smile in return. Danny squeezed my shoulders and I saw my parents clasp hands behind Linnie's back.

"I—" I started, my voice shaky as I looked around at everyone, trying to find a way to express what I was feeling. This—all of us, right here, together, this was what I'd been waiting for and missing for so long now. But it was more than that, so much so that I wasn't sure I could put it into words—wasn't sure if twenty-six letters could capture it. "I'm so happy to be here with you." My eye met Mike's and I realized that I meant him, too. That he was a part of this family, and we would have been incomplete and off-balance without him. "I just wanted to say . . ." I pulled in a breath as I looked at everyone, about to tell them what I always felt and almost never said. "I love you guys." My tears were threatening to spill over, and I noticed my dad clearing his throat and J.J. rolling his eyes, the way he did when he was trying not to get emotional. Danny squeezed my shoulders and kissed the top of my head. It was a moment better than all the ones I'd been picturing, and I found myself wishing it never had to end.

"Hey, Grants!" This was Jenny W., calling from the kitchen. "Come on!"

Linnie laughed, and we all broke apart and headed back into the kitchen and returned to our places in line. I'd pulled myself together by the time I reached Marcus, and he held out his arm for me to take with exaggerated gallantry. Danny turned around and grinned at me, and I smiled back.

"Okay," Linnie said, and I saw Will raise his walkie-talkie. "Let's go."

Will motioned us forward, and Mike and Elizabeth began the procession across the kitchen and out the kitchen door to the backyard. Even though all we were doing was walking through our kitchen, it somehow seemed more than that—everyone in their suits and dresses, filing past the fridge and the coffee maker, a sense of ceremony and reverence, even though we were still just in the kitchen, the place where not that long ago, people had been eating bagels. Even the catering staff seemed to sense this, as most of them stopped working and watched us pass, in a slow line through the kitchen. It looked like most of them were working on the wedding cake, which was gorgeous, on a rolling tray by the island—three tiers, with sugar flowers all around it.

Will held the door open for us, and we all stayed in order, continuing our procession toward the tent. The backyard, in the space of just a few hours, had been transformed. There, right in the center, where we'd played capture the flag last night, stood a beautiful tent. It was cream colored, anchored with posts every few feet, with two pointed peaks on the roof.

As soon as we stepped outside, I drew in a breath—it was cold out there, much colder than it had been the last time I'd been outside. The wind had picked up too, and I saw Jenny K., in front of me, raise a hand to her hair as we walked across the lawn. But it wasn't raining, which I was very grateful for at this particular moment.

Bill was waiting for us at the back of the tent, and he nodded as Mike reached him. He raised his walkie-talkie and said quietly into it, "Go music. Go procession." Then he pulled open the door, and Mike and Elizabeth stepped through, followed a moment later by Danny and Priya.

Marcus and I followed behind them, and as we stepped inside the

　　　　　　　　　　　　　　　　　MORGAN MATSON

tent, I felt my jaw fall open. Because it was beautiful. The back had round tables with numbers in the center, with centerpieces on every table—flowers and unlit candles. On the other side of the tent, there were white chairs separated by an aisle that was strewn with flower petals. There were lights hanging from the ceiling of the tent, in addition to twinkle lights everywhere, making the whole thing feel magical.

And there were rows and rows of people, my relatives and Rodney's, Linnie's friends, my parents' friends, Jesse handsome in a dark suit, everyone dressed up and facing our direction. There was music playing, too, and I was glad to hear it wasn't Journey. But it also wasn't the normal wedding march and I realized after a moment that it was a recording of a doo-wop song, one Linnie had always loved—"Today I Met the Boy I'm Gonna Marry."

I couldn't stop myself from smiling as Marcus and I walked down the aisle. Rodney was standing at the end of it, looking nervous and proud and happy, all mixed into one. He was wearing the dark-gray suit his dad had been wearing, and I could see General Daniels, sitting in the front row next to his wife, wearing his uniform. Ralph was standing next to Rodney, looking official in his judges' robes. But seeing the way his pants seemed much too long for him, spilling over his shoes, I had a feeling he was still wearing Rodney's suit under his robes.

When we got to the front of the aisle, the bridesmaids split off in one direction, to stand on the left side, and the groomsmen went to the right, to stand behind Rodney, all of it going fairly smoothly, even though we hadn't had a real rehearsal. When we were all in place, there was a pause, and then Linnie stepped into the aisle.

Everyone in the tent stood up, people fumbling with their cameras and phones, turning to face my sister, who was walking slowly down the aisle with my mom on one side of her and my dad on the other, looking simultaneously like she was both about to cry and had never been so happy in her life.

I turned and looked at Rodney, who was watching Linnie walk toward him. It was an expression I'd never seen on his face before—it was happiness and wonderment, like he'd just woken up from a dream, only to find out it was real.

Linnie reached Rodney just as the song faded out, and my parents squeezed both of Linnie's hands before going to sit in the front row, across from the Danielses.

"Hey," Linnie said, and even through her veil, I could see that she was smiling at him.

"Hey," Rodney replied, smiling back.

"Good evening," Ralph said, stepping forward, and I noticed some of the guests glancing from him to Max, like they were wondering why he wasn't performing the ceremony. "We are here today to bring Linnea and Rodney together in marriage . . ." Ralph continued with his speech, his voice confident and assured, like he'd done this a lot, despite the fact that he was a death judge. I let myself breathe out a sigh of relief as Ralph went on, talking about how Linnie and Rodney were today, pledging themselves before friends and family and promising to honor each other through good times and bad, in health and in sickness, for better or for worse.

I glanced into the front row and saw that my dad had his handkerchief out and was blinking a lot more than usual, and it looked like Mrs. Daniels was already crying.

Ralph looked out at the assembled guests and raised his voice a little as he said, "If anyone present may show just and legal cause why this couple may not be legally wed, speak now or forever hold your peace." He said this quickly, almost perfunctorily, and had just taken a breath to continue when I heard, from the back of the tent, the sound of a chair scraping back.

"Me. Um, I do. Have something to say." I whipped around to see what was happening, and my stomach dropped when I saw who it was.

There was Olly Gillespie standing up in the back row, holding an oval object in his hand. He was wearing a suit and tie and had a set, determined look on his face. I glanced at Danny, whose expression of horror reflected back what I was feeling.

"Um." Ralph, clearly thrown for a loop, blinked at Olly. "Okay. Well, this is a new one. Usually that question is more of a rhetorical. You, um, have something to—"

"Olly," Linnie interrupted, shaking her head. "What are you *doing*?"

"He asked," Olly said, pointing at Ralph. "He asked if anyone had anything to say, and I do. So can't I talk?"

"No," Mike and Danny said together, both of them turning to face Olly, looking more menacing than I had ever seen them.

"Wedding crasher!" J.J. yelled, pointing at him. He looked around, like he was waiting for the wedding police to show up and take him away.

"I was invited," Olly said, drawing himself up.

"He was?" I asked Linnie.

"It was a gesture of goodwill," Linnie muttered, batting her veil away. "I never thought he'd actually come. He didn't RSVP!"

"I think you'd better sit down," Danny said, his voice low and serious.

"Technically," Ralph said, then cleared his throat. "That's in there just in case someone has evidence that one of you is currently still married, or is wanted by the law . . . things that would invalidate the marriage. So—"

But Ralph didn't get to finish. Olly pressed the button on the oval thing he was carrying, and a song started playing from it, one that sounded vaguely familiar—I was pretty sure I'd heard it coming from Linnie's room a lot when she was in high school, something about someone named Jennifer having her daddy's car.

"What are you doing?" Linnie asked.

"What are you *playing*?" Rodney asked, because Olly had lifted the oval thing—it was a speaker, I saw now—over his head, like he was reenacting *Say Anything* at my sister's wedding.

"It was our song in high school," Linnie muttered, batting her veil away and glaring at Olly.

"Is this yacht rock?" Mike asked, sounding appalled. "Who is this, Air Supply?"

"Eric Carmen," Danny, Olly, and Priya all said at the same time.

"Turn it off," Linnie said, shaking her head. "And J.J., stop dancing." I looked over at J.J., who had started grooving along to the music.

"Sorry," he said, giving Linnie an embarrassed smile. "It just makes me lose control."

"Olly, sit down," Linnie said.

"Not before I've said what I need to say." He turned the music down slightly—though I was pretty sure I could hear the song on it play again, like he'd uploaded a playlist with only one song—and stepped out into the aisle. "Linnea," he said, looking right at Linnie. "You're the love of my life. We found it too early, that's all. And I know that what we had was special. It was more than just a high school thing. And I really think—"

"Oliver," Linnie said, and Olly stopped, looking surprised, like he'd had a lot more prepared. "Turn the music off." Linnie's voice was gentle but firm, and Olly did—the tent seeming much more quiet now that we didn't have any yacht rock playing. "I appreciate that it must have been hard for you to come here and do this," she said, "and it's not that I don't care for you. *As a friend.*"

"But . . . ," Olly said, shaking his head, "Linnie, what we had . . ."

"Was a long time ago," Linnie finished for him. "You meant a lot to me in the past. But that's all it is now. You need to move forward. You can't still be hung up on your high school girlfriend. If you don't move on from the past, you're going to miss out on some really amazing stuff in the future."

Olly just looked at her for a long moment, then nodded. "Okay. I'm—um—really sorry for doing this during your wedding." He looked around, and it was like he was just now seeing himself, standing in the aisle, all the people staring at him, J.J. cracking his knuckles threateningly. "Sorry," he muttered, heading back to his seat again. "Um—do you want me to leave? Or . . . ?"

I saw Rodney roll his eyes, but Linnie nodded. "You can stay," she said, adjusting her veil again. "Just . . . quietly." Olly gave her a thumbs-up, and Linnie turned back to Rodney.

"Um . . . okay," Ralph said, after a moment. "If nobody else has anything to add, we'll continue. . . ." Everyone laughed at that, not because it was all that funny, but because it was like we collectively needed something to break the tension.

The ceremony moved forward, with Linnie and Rodney reciting the vows they'd written to each other. Halfway through Linnie's I had to steal a tissue from Jenny K., and I was beyond thankful that Brooke had put waterproof mascara on me. When they'd finished reciting their vows, Ralph stepped forward again and asked for the rings, which Max produced from his suit pocket. After they'd exchanged rings—and both of them had declared *I do*—Ralph smiled.

"In accordance with the law of Connecticut and by the virtue of the authority vested in me by the law of Connecticut, I do pronounce you husband and wife. You may kiss—" But the rest of Ralph's statement was drowned out as Rodney swept Linnie up in a kiss and everyone else started cheering, the crowd jumping to its feet, applauding—and then wolf whistling as Linnie and Rodney's kiss kept on going.

When they finally broke apart, I smiled at my sister, feeling a lump start to rise in my throat. And just like that—she was married.

CHAPTER 22
Or, When Maple Syrup Goes Bad

---

*H*ELLO, STANWICH!" GLEN YELLED FROM THE
area where the band was setting up on the stage at the
front of the tent—the place where Linnie and Rodney had exchanged
vows had been converted, with remarkable speed, to a dance floor.
There were four other members of Any Way You Want It, all of whom
had Glen's same middle-aged rocker vibe. "How's everyone doing?"
There was some scattered, half-hearted applause, but Glen smiled
like he'd just been given a standing ovation. "Glad everyone's having a
rocking night!"

I winced and caught Danny's eye, and he shook his head and smiled
at me. The cocktail hour had ended, and now people were milling
about, finding their table numbers and starting to wander over to them.
There was a board set up at the back of the tent—complete with pictures of Linnie and Rodney when they were little—that told you where
your table was. These coordinated with the place cards the General had
done, which were set up on the tables, the handwriting maybe a little
less ornate than one might expect, but perfectly legible.

I had positioned myself by the entrance to the tent, hoping to run into Jesse. He'd ducked out right as the cocktail hour had started, and I'd found my attention wandering from my conversations as I looked around, waiting for him to come back. Because aside from him smiling at me as I walked up the aisle, I hadn't had a chance to see him yet. I smoothed my hair down as I sipped my Diet Coke with cherries and tried not to look too obviously toward the door.

All throughout the cocktail hour, during the conversations with my relatives, and Rodney's relatives, and friends of Linnie's I hadn't seen in years, I'd been thinking about what things would be like when Jesse came back. I could get not wanting things to be obvious too soon, but it was a *wedding*. We could dance together without anyone getting suspicious, and maybe I could even switch our place cards around so that we were sitting closer together, and then after the wedding . . .

I took a long sip of my drink just as Jesse came in through the door and headed straight over to his table. "Hi," I said, doing an awkward step-run to put myself in his path. "Hi," I said, then realized a second too late I'd already said that. "It's good to see you—I hadn't seen you here tonight yet."

"Yeah." Jesse smiled at me, then leaned down and gave me a quick kiss on the cheek. "You look great," he said, even though he wasn't look-ing at me, but across the tent, to where Mike was sitting.

"Thanks." I smoothed my curls down, thanking my stars for Brooke. "You do too." He really did—he was wearing a slim-cut black suit with a skinny tie, and his hair was neatly combed.

"Well, I have to do my best as Mike's plus-one," he said. He looked back over at me, then leaned a little closer, the proximity causing my heart to race. "Can I see you later?"

"Yes," I said, not letting myself break eye contact with him.

He gave me a smile and a tiny wink. "Great," he said, giving my hand a squeeze as he started to turn and walk away.

"Or we could also hang out now," I said, and Jesse turned back. "You know . . . at the wedding?"

"Right," Jesse said quickly, giving me another smile as he started to edge away, toward the tables. "We'll totally do that. Save me a dance, okay?"

"Hope you like Journey!" I called after him, then immediately regretted it. But he glanced over his shoulder and gave me a slow smile, and I felt my regret start to ebb away. I would see Jesse tonight. And if Journey had any slow songs, maybe we could dance to one, both of us twirling together in a circle, my hand in his . . .

I watched Jesse pull up a seat at Mike's table, slap him on the back, and sit next to him. Maybe he actually was taking his plus-one duties seriously, not to mention his best friend duties. Not wanting either of them to catch me staring, I headed back to the bar for a refill.

"We're going to get started in just a few minutes," Glen said, then raised an eyebrow as he leaned closer to the mic. "And play some music to serenade you during your dinner. I hope you're all ready . . . to take a *journey*." He'd clearly expected a much bigger reaction to that, and all he got was couple of half-hearted *whoo*s from the back of the room. But if this bothered Glen, he didn't show it, as he dramatically played a chord on his guitar and smiled at the room in general.

"Hey." I looked over and saw Bill had come to stand next to me. "So that was interesting." He nodded toward where Olly was talking to Elizabeth.

"Yeah," I said, shaking my head. "We didn't know we needed to search the guests for speakers."

"Well," Bill said, his voice serious, "this is how you learn things."

I smiled at that. "Exactly." I'd been keeping my eye on Olly in the first few minutes of the cocktail hour, but it seemed like he was keeping his word and behaving—nevertheless, Mike had taken away his speaker and told him he would get it back at the end of the wedding.

"Get you anything?" This was coming from behind us—it was the bartender. I ordered my Diet Coke with cherries, and he rolled his eyes but made me my drink, then turned away to take my aunt Kimberley's order.

"So," Bill said, looking around at the assembled guests, who were either standing around in groups talking or starting to drift over to their tables. "It seems like everything is . . . working out." He practically whispered the last two words, and I smiled, knowing exactly how he felt.

"It does, doesn't it?" I crossed my fingers even as I said it. "I mean, despite the whole ex-boyfriend-trying-to-break-up-the-wedding thing."

"Aside from that."

"I know," I said, looking over at him as I smiled. "It seems like people are having a good time."

"And they haven't even heard the Journey cover band yet."

"Charlotte." I looked over to see Aunt Liz striding up to me, her jaw set and eyes narrowed.

"Um—hi." She was clearly unhappy with me, but at this moment, I couldn't think why. "Are you . . . having a nice time at the reception?"

"I *was*," she said, taking a deep breath and then letting it out, like she was on the verge of screaming at me. "But then I saw where I'd been sat for dinner."

"We changed that." I turned to Bill, who immediately nodded.

"You're Elizabeth?" he asked with a smile. "Don't worry. I moved you. You're nowhere near Jimmy."

"I'm right *next* to Jimmy!" she spat, pointing across the room, then shook her head and stalked away. I looked where she had pointed and saw the man who must be Uncle Jimmy. He looked like he was a little younger than Aunt Liz and looked very dapper in a sport coat, but this was marred slightly by the fact that he was glowering at Liz, his arms folded across his chest.

I turned to Bill, baffled. "What was that about?"

"I don't know," he said. "I moved Elizabeth—I know I did."

"Elizabeth? Or Liz?"

"I—" Bill stopped talking and looked at me, brow furrowing. "Aren't they the same thing?"

I shook my head. "Elizabeth's Rodney's sister—she's in the bridal party. She was named for Liz...."

"Oh," Bill said, and I could see his eyes widening as this sank in. "Oh god."

The seating list that had been assembled from Brooke's picture—the one Rodney's dad had been using to do the place cards—was back in the house. It quickly became clear that we weren't going to be able to get anything done on the board where people were currently picking up their seat assignments. But it also didn't look like anyone would notice if I stepped out for a moment—we were doing dinner first, then the speeches, and if I had to miss the appetizers, it didn't seem to be that big of a sacrifice if we could prevent two people from killing each other. I tried to catch Jesse's eye again, so that he could see that I was leaving and wouldn't wonder where I'd gotten to. But I noticed now that he was talking to Rodney's cousin Kyra, who was a little older than me, smiling easily as he leaned closer to hear what she was saying.

Bill held open the back door of the tent for me, and I stepped outside and winced. Things had gotten worse since we'd done our procession from the house. It was almost totally dark out now, and very cold, and the wind had picked up. But more than that, there was the feeling in the air that a storm was brewing, that sense that it's going to rain, sooner rather than later. I held my skirt down against the wind as we hurried across the lawn to the house.

"The seating chart's in the dining room," Bill said as we both stepped inside. I nodded and headed there, carefully walking around the wedding cake on its rolling cart (presumably to get it out to the tent) in the center of the kitchen. One of the caterers was putting finishing touches on it, and I could see the little bride and groom figurines standing up on the kitchen counter, like they were waiting for the cake to be ready for them.

"It looks great," I said to the man working on the cake, who shot me a quick, hassled smile that disappeared almost instantly. As I looked around, I realized that we'd chosen probably the worst moment to invade the kitchen—the caterers were prepping the plates of appetizers, and there was a buzzing, busy energy that certainly hadn't been there before. I was halfway across the kitchen, nearly to the dining room, when I heard the sound. "What is that?" I asked, stopping short. It was like I could hear the sound of scratching on the wood floors and a faint yowling sound.

Bill stopped too, frowning, just as Max burst into the kitchen, out of breath, looking around a little desperately. "Maple Syrup?" he called. "Where's Maple Syrup?"

"Hey, Max," I said, taking a tentative step toward him, wondering just what kind of munchies he was currently having. "What's up?"

"I have to find Maple Syrup," he cried, looking around the kitchen. "He's gone!"

"*He?*" Bill asked, just as the yowling got louder.

"What are you talking about, Max?"

"Maple Syrup is my cat," Max said, his shoulders slumping. "I've been hiding him in my room."

"There's been a *cat* here this entire time?" I asked. Max nodded. "No wonder Linnie keeps sneezing! She's allergic."

"I'm so sorry, but my cat sitter bailed, so I thought it would be fine, but I went upstairs to . . . um . . ." I nodded, since we all knew what Max had been doing. "And anyway, he got out? So I just need to find him, and—"

With a yowl, a white blur burst into the kitchen, followed closely by a brown-and-white blur that I realized was Waffles. "What—" I started, since I had no idea how the dog had gotten out as well.

The caterers shrieked, and one of them dropped the tray she'd been holding as a cat—and then a dog—ran around her legs. "Hold on," I yelled, though I didn't know if I was talking to the caterers, or the animals, but I jumped into action anyway, and I saw Bill do the same. "Let's just—try—" I yelled, attempting to intercept the dog and cat, who were still racing in circles around the kitchen, zigzagging back and forth as the cat changed direction and Waffles gave chase. He was barking as he ran, a loud, insistent sound, the cat screeching as it tried to get away from him.

"Here, Maple," Max yelled, running for his cat and getting a swipe on the arm as a result.

"Why are there animals in this kitchen?" the caterer who'd dropped her tray yelled as she picked up what looked like sliders off the floor. "We're preparing food here!"

"I'm sorry," I yelled back as I ran around the kitchen island, narrowly missing Waffles's collar, just as the cat shot through Bill's hands. "Max—" But before Max could grab his cat, Maple Syrup jumped up onto the kitchen counter, causing all the catering staff to yell once again.

"I'm so sorry," Max said, grabbing for his cat, who hissed at him while keeping his eyes on Waffles, who was full-on howling now, staring up at the cat in frustration as he ran back and forth.

What happened next seemed to take place in slow motion, like maybe fear of imminent disaster slows things down, just in case you really want to remember it. Waffles jumped for the cat just as the cat leaped for the kitchen island but fell short, and both of them collided with the rolling cart at almost exactly the same time—the cart with the wedding cake on it.

I watched helplessly as the cart tipped over, taking the wedding cake with it. The three tiers seemed to separate as they fell, the top tier sliding off the bottom two as they all landed on the kitchen floor with a muted *splat*.

The animals raced around the destroyed cake and out the kitchen door, while the rest of us just stood, frozen in horror.

"Well," Bill finally said, looking from the cake on the floor to me. "That's not great."

Ten minutes later, I looked across the cab of the Where There's A Will truck. Bill was driving us to the Food Mart—we were en route to try to save the situation, and pick up replacement wedding cakes.

After we'd all just stared at the destroyed cake on the floor for what honestly felt like five minutes, everyone had jumped into action. Max was put in charge of corralling and separating the animals—history had proven that he probably wasn't the best person for this job, but he was all we had at the moment. Bill made sure everything was still on track in the tent, while the caterers had tried to salvage as much of the cake as they could. This wasn't for eating—I had a feeling that the five-second rule *really* didn't count when it came to things like wedding cakes—but so that Rodney and Linnie could at least have something to pose for pictures with. But we still had the issue of the hundred and fifty people in the tent who would be expecting to eat something for dessert. I'd taken over trying to find someone who could provide that, starting to make calls and fire off e-mails.

After a few attempts, I found out pretty quickly that no bakery or catering company could provide a three-tier wedding cake in an hour (which was not, in retrospect, really that surprising). But the bakery department of Food Mart, the local supermarket, was open and they had three sheet cakes with white icing in stock. And that looked like the best we were going to do.

My car had been too blocked in with guests' cars and all the equipment vans, but Bill's truck was parked away from the glut and down the street—"It's WTAW policy," he'd told me—and since AAA had come out that morning to jump his battery, we were good to go.

Even though it was only a ten-minute drive to get into town, I kicked off my heels immediately—they hadn't really started to hurt yet, but I could feel the incipient pain that would be arriving shortly, and I figured any chance to give my feet a break would be a good thing. I tucked my legs up underneath me and looked across the truck's cab at Bill. The two of us were back in a car, driving around like we'd been doing just this morning. Only now we were both in formal wear.

"What?" Bill asked, glancing over at me as he paused at a stop sign.

"Just this," I said, gesturing between the two of us. "I bet we'll be the most dressed-up people in the supermarket."

Bill laughed. "After my senior prom, we stopped at a convenience store, and everyone in there was staring at us—this whole group in dresses and suits, suddenly taking over the snack aisle."

I nodded, smiling. "That's just like—" I stopped myself. I'd been on the verge of telling a story about a prom limo running out of gas, and pumping gas in formal wear. But I'd realized just a second too late this wasn't one of my stories, or even one of my siblings' stories—it had happened in *Grant Central Station*, to Cassie Grant and her ill-fated prom date, and had only ever existed in ink and paper.

We found parking right in front of Food Mart, and even though it wasn't a long walk to the entrance, the second I stepped out of the car, I started to shiver. The wind had picked up and the temperature had dropped, and I was starting to realize that sleeveless silk dresses are not necessarily the best choice of outfit when it was getting colder by the second and clearly about to storm.

We hurried into the supermarket, and I blinked when we got inside, since everything—the white floors, the fluorescent lights overhead—seemed very bright. I was suddenly very aware that we were much too dressed up for the supermarket. There didn't seem to be many people in the Food Mart—maybe not surprising, considering that it was eight o'clock on a Saturday night. Even the piped-in music seemed quieter than normal, right now playing a Muzak version of an old Rush song. I saw a woman pushing a cart past the dairy case and two people in the snack aisle, arguing about popcorn, but that seemed to be it. Even most of the lights on the registers were off, and the one that was on was staffed by a bored-looking guy who was currently leaning over his conveyor belt and flipping through a magazine.

The bakery department was equally deserted—just a woman wearing a white smock and a white Food Mart baseball cap, standing behind the counter and scrolling through her phone.

"Hi," I said as we approached the counter, and I saw her eyebrows rise as she took in me and Bill in our formal wear.

"Hi," she said, setting down her phone. "Can I help you?"

"I called earlier," I said, wishing I'd remembered to write down the name of the person I'd been speaking to. "I'm Charlie Grant. I mentioned that we needed something that could work as a wedding cake? And—"

The woman nodded with recognition. "The three sheet cakes, right?"

I nodded, hugely relieved that in the last half hour, there hadn't been a run on their cakes. "Yes! That's right."

"Just give me a second," she said as she headed toward the door behind the counter, the one marked EMPLOYEES ONLY. "I'll be right back."

I turned to Bill, who looked as relieved as I felt. "Thank god."

I nodded. "Yeah. I was worried at the last moment that something would have gone wrong. . . ."

Bill shook his head. "I feel like we've had enough of that for one wedding." Then he paled and reached out to quickly knock on the wooden paneling on the bakery case. "Hope I didn't just jinx us."

"I'm not even sure what that would look like," I replied honestly. At this point, what else could go wrong? The tent collapsing on everyone? Linnie realizing she'd actually made a huge mistake and running off with Olly? As these possibilities—and more—started to fill my head, I realized Bill might have a point, and I quickly reached out and knocked, in almost the exact same spot as him, and he smiled at me.

"Maybe we ordered too fast," he said, nodding at the pictures displayed on top of the case, which showed all the custom cakes the bakery could make. "Would Linnie and Rodney prefer a themed cake for their wedding? Superheroes or robots or princesses?"

I laughed. "I think the guests might be confused if their piece of wedding cake had a robot on it."

Bill smiled too. "Well, maybe," he said. "But—" He stopped suddenly and tilted his head to the side, like he was listening for something.

"What?"

Bill gave me a smile and pointed up. "Hear that?"

After a moment, I realized the Rush song had ended and the piped-in music was the same song that Olly Gillespie had played when he'd tried to convince Linnie to jilt Rodney at the altar. I shook my head. "Well, that—" But whatever I was about to say got stopped halfway to my lips when I realized Bill was holding out his hand to me, a half smile on his face.

"Want to dance?" he asked. And even though there were lots of reasons to say no—we were in a *supermarket*, we didn't really have time for this, Jesse was waiting for me back at the wedding—but I found that none of these reasons really seemed to matter that much as I looked at Bill, his hand extended toward me.

I didn't reply, just took his hand, his fingers warm against my cool ones. He held my hand lightly in his, and we stood there for just a moment, looking at each other. And then he twirled me around and then away from him. I felt my shoes turn easily on the waxed supermarket floors, and I spun, the produce section and the bread aisle whirling around me for a moment before Bill spun me back. Bill clearly knew how to dance, which, amazingly, seemed to mean that I knew how to dance too. He spun me in and out and then around again as the yacht rock poured through the speakers, singing about turning the radio up for that sweet sound. I didn't care that I was wearing a silk dress in the supermarket, or that we were dancing in a place where, usually, people didn't dance. As we turned in a circle together, there under the fluorescent lights, I had a sense of rightness—of calm—that I hadn't felt all weekend. Maybe even before that.

"Grant!" I looked over and saw that the woman behind the bakery counter was back and that there were three large cakes in boxes on the counter in front of her. "Order's ready."

"Coming," I called. Bill spun me once more, and I just let the world whirl around me for a moment before I came to a stop and smiled at him. He kept his hands where they were for a moment, touching my waist lightly. Then he stepped away and we were back in a supermarket again.

"Okay," the woman behind the counter said, punching some numbers into the register. "That's three sheet cakes. . . . Did you need utensils?" I shook my head, and when she told me the total, I handed her my "in case of emergency" credit card. I had a feeling my parents would more than understand the necessity for it when I told them. "Do you need help out?" she asked as I scrawled my signature on the receipt and looked over at the cakes. They were *big*, in cardboard boxes with clear plastic lids, presumably so you could see what you were getting—so that if you needed a replacement wedding cake, you didn't end up with one covered in robots. I thought I could handle one, but before I could reply, Bill appeared at my side, stacking two of the boxes on top of each other and giving her a smile.

"We've got it covered."

We headed out of the supermarket, neither of us going fast. We were slowed down a little by the fact that we were both carrying very large cakes. But I had a feeling Bill might be walking slowly for the same reason I was—the fact that if these cakes didn't make it home in one piece, we were pretty much out of options. The automatic glass doors slid open, and both of us winced simultaneously as we stepped outside. We couldn't have been in Food Mart very long, but it was as though we'd been gone hours. It was now fully dark out, and the wind was blowing strongly enough that I gripped my cake hard, trying to keep my balance in my heels.

Bill headed over to the truck, and I followed, not even caring that my skirt was blowing every which way—I was just focusing on getting this cake inside. We were halfway across the parking lot when I heard it—a low rumble of thunder, followed immediately by a flash of lightning illuminating the sky for just one moment before disappearing. "Uh-oh," Bill said, and I saw him pick up his pace. He beeped the truck open— the headlights coming to life—just as thunder sounded again and I felt the first drop of rain on my shoulder.

"Oh no," I muttered, moving as fast as I felt I could without dropping my cake. The rain was coming down steadily harder, splashing on my head and arms and leaving faint watermarks on my dress. It was falling in droplets that were bouncing off the plastic top of the cake box, then running down the sides, and I just hoped, as I hurried across the parking lot, that the box was watertight and we weren't going to show up with soggy supermarket cakes to my sister's wedding.

Bill made it to the truck first, and he balanced the cakes under one arm as he opened the back door of the cab. He leaned down to place them inside just as I caught up with him. It was pretty much pouring now, the sky dark except for the occasional lightning bolts that would fork across it, the wind howling. It felt more like October than April, and I could feel myself shivering as I held on even tighter to the cake box.

"Got it," Bill said, reaching for my cake. He placed it on the floor next to the other two, then slammed the door. He ran for the driver's side, and I ran around the hood to the passenger seat, and we both threw ourselves into the car and closed the doors at almost the exact same moment.

It was much warmer, and quieter, inside the cab of the truck, and I looked across at Bill as the rain beat down on the windshield and the roof, all around us.

"Wow," Bill said, looking out through the windshield as he ran a hand through his hair.

"I know," I said, watching the rain run over the glass, then turned to look at Bill. There were still droplets of rain clinging to his tuxedo jacket and on the side of his neck, and I felt the impulse to reach out and brush them off before I caught myself. "Shall we?"

"Let's."

We were almost home when Bill glanced over at me and took a breath. "So," he started, then cleared his throat. "Charlie. I—"

But I never heard what he was about to say, because at that moment a police car, sirens on and lights flashing, zoomed around us to pull into the driveway of my house.

CHAPTER 23
Or, DUUUUUUCK

BILL PARKED ON THE SIDE OF THE STREET, AND as soon as he'd cut the engine, I jumped out. Two officers were already out of the patrol car and heading around to the back of the house. They'd turned the sirens off but left the lights on, a kaleidoscope of red and blue swinging in arcs and flashing against the garage door.

"Hi," I called to them over the sound of the wind as I hurried to catch up. "Um. Officers? Is there a problem here?"

They turned to look at me, and even though I was getting soaked by the rain and holding my skirt down against the wind, I gave them my best responsible, non-lawbreaking smile. This faltered a little, though, when I realized I recognized the older one of the officers—he was the one who'd told me and Mike to move when we'd turned down Grant Avenue.

"We're responding to a call," the older officer—Ramirez—said just as Bill hurried to join me. He looked between the two of us, me in my dress and Bill in his tux, and raised an eyebrow. "Is it prom night already?"

"It's my sister's wedding," I said as I rubbed my hands up and down my arms, trying to get some feeling back in them.

The officers exchanged a look I didn't understand. "Well, that explains it."

"Explains what?" Bill asked, looking between the officers, his hair getting steadily wetter.

"We had a noise complaint," Officer Ramirez said, starting to walk around to the back of the house again. "Wedding this way?"

"In a tent in the backyard," I said, following behind them, still trying to wrap my head around this. "You said a noise complaint? But . . ." All at once I realized, with a flash of white-hot fury, just why I was currently talking to two police officers in the rain. "It was our neighbor, Don Perkins. Wasn't it?"

"We can't disclose that information," Officer Ramirez said as he continued around the house and to the backyard.

"Look," I said, my heels slipping on the slick grass as I struggled to keep up with him. "I think this is all just a big misunderstanding. Our neighbor Don is nursing a personal grudge. There's a whole garden thing involved. I'm sure he called you out here just to wreck my sister's wedding."

"That may be so," Officer Ramirez said as he continued across the backyard to the tent. "But we still have to check out these calls. We don't have the luxury of deciding what is and isn't a problem before we even investigate." The younger officer—I could see now that his name tag read HOPPER—nodded seriously at me as he passed, like he was trying to underscore this point.

"But," I said, talking louder now, and faster, as I tried to keep up with them, brushing my sodden hair out of my face. I didn't know how I was going to do it, but I knew I couldn't let them go into the tent. What would that do to Linnie's wedding, if the police suddenly burst in? Enough had already gone wrong. I couldn't let this happen too. "Look," I called, as Officer Ramirez reached for the handle of the door to the tent. "I promise you it's all fine. And that there's really nothing to see—"

But whatever I was about to say died partway to my lips as Officer Ramirez opened the door to the tent, because I could now see there was a screaming fight going on in the middle of the dance floor.

Everyone was sitting at their tables, and from the plates on them, and the hovering, frozen presence of the catering staff, it looked like dinner was being served. Up by the stage, the members of Any Way You Want It were all standing stock-still, staring at what was happening in front of them.

And what was happening was Jimmy and Liz, and their long feud apparently coming to a head—right now.

"Don't pretend with me," Liz spat at Jimmy, who threw his hands up theatrically. "You *know* what you did. Or have you forgotten what happened in 1982?"

"Why are you bringing that up?" Jimmy yelled back. "Who *cares* what happened in 1982?"

"Well, not *you*, obviously!"

Officer Ramirez took another step inside, with Officer Hopper following behind him. Bill and I came in behind them, but nobody seemed to notice us, let alone the presence of two uniformed officers.

"You always do this," Jimmy yelled, and I noticed that he and Liz were edging closer together, no longer staying in their separate corners. "And I'm sick of it!"

"What, you think *I* like it?" Liz yelled back. The elegant woman I'd gotten used to seeing was now totally gone—her hair was escaping from its chignon, and strands were standing up in the back. But more than that was her expression—like all the steely control I'd seen from her earlier was gone, and she was letting it all out now.

"Yes, I think you do, Elizabeth," Jimmy said, a snide tone in his voice. "You just love playing the victim, don't you?"

"Unlike you, *James*, I'm not too much of a coward to face up to what I've done."

"What did he do?" Bill whispered to me, eyes wide as he followed the unfolding drama.

"Did you just call me a coward?"

"I did," Liz said, raising her voice. "But I should have called you a chicken!"

"I am *not* a chicken!"

"Oh? Is that so?" Liz whirled around to the server who had the unfortunate luck to be standing behind her. She picked up a chicken breast off the plate and hurled it at Jimmy, and it landed right on the lapel of his blazer.

"I cannot believe you did that," Jimmy said, reaching for the nearest plate. "You're—"

"Hey!" Officer Ramirez yelled, his voice carrying across the tent. Both Jimmy and Liz stopped yelling abruptly, and it seemed like every head in the tent swung over to look at the two police officers who'd suddenly appeared. "I'm going to need everyone to just calm down, okay? Sir? Please step away from the steak."

Jimmy looked down at the plate in his hands and immediately set it down.

There was the sound of a chair scraping, then falling over, and I looked across the tent to see Max, his face pale, backing toward the exits as he stared in horror at the cops. "I'm just going to ... check on something ...," he muttered, before turning and fleeing full out toward the door.

"Um," Rodney said, rising from his seat at the head table. "Is there a problem?"

"We received a noise complaint," Officer Ramirez said. "We're here to check it out."

"A noise complaint?" my dad asked, standing up and heading our way. "From who?"

"Whom," J.J. said, also coming to join in the conversation. We all just stared at him, and he shrugged. "What? It's correct."

"We don't disclose the names of citizens who submit noise complaints," Officer Hopper said, like he was reciting something from a textbook. "For their own protection, and ours."

The officers started toward the dance floor, and my dad, Bill, J.J., and I followed Linnie as she also got up from the head table. "What's the trouble here?" Officer Ramirez asked Jimmy and Liz, both of whom had their arms folded and were looking at the ground, like they were trying to pretend they hadn't just been throwing food and yelling at each other a moment earlier.

Jimmy and Liz glared at each other, but neither spoke. I glanced around the tent. The guests were still all sitting at their tables, although it looked like the videographer was filming, as though he thought we'd really want a reminder of this. The catering staff had clustered by the back of the tent, like they weren't sure what the protocol was about serving the entrées now that the police were involved, and the band was still standing onstage like they were watching a particularly interesting TV program.

I looked over and saw that Linnie and Rodney, as well as Danny and my mom and the Danielses, were all coming over.

"Officers, I'm sure all this can't be necessary," my mom said, as she stood next to my dad, looking from the police to Jimmy and Liz.

"When we see a domestic disturbance, we have to investigate," Officer Hopper said, again sounding like he was reading lines he had memorized. "It's procedure."

"Why don't you just tell us how this began?" Officer Ramirez said, pulling a small notepad out of his pocket. "And we can go from there."

Jimmy and Liz just looked at each other again, then away. "Surely something caused the fight that just happened?" he prompted, beginning to sound frustrated, like his patience was finally cracking. "It didn't come out of nowhere."

"It's been going on for a while," General Daniels said, coming to stand next to Rodney. "We usually try to make sure they don't attend events together." Both Jimmy and Liz scoffed in unison at this, then looked uneasy, like they just accidentally agreed on something and didn't like it much.

"Well." Officer Ramirez flipped his notebook closed as he looked between Jimmy and Liz. "I take it that you're not going to continue yelling at each other? The food stays on the plates?" They both nodded. "Good."

"So that's it?" Rodney asked.

"That's it," Officer Ramirez confirmed. "We were called in on a noise complaint, but . . ." He gestured around the tent—now that nobody was speaking, it was almost totally silent. "I think we can say that's no longer an issue here." He looked over at the band, and it was like I could practically see him counting the number of amps. "Maybe just don't play at top volume?" Glen nodded and gave him a salute. "Then in that case, I think our work here is done. And congratulations," he said to Rodney and Linnie, with the first smile I'd yet seen from him.

He gave us a nod, then continued out of the tent, with Officer Hopper following behind. For a second I thought about letting Max know that the coast was clear and he wasn't about to be busted for possession, but then I remembered that we didn't have a real wedding cake thanks to him and decided he could remain in the dark for just a little bit longer.

"Charlie," Linnie said to me as people started to drift back to their tables and Jimmy and Liz walked toward theirs—not speaking to each other, but no longer glaring at each other either—"where have you been?"

"Been?" I echoed vaguely.

"Been," she repeated, taking a sip of her champagne and then raising an eyebrow at me. "You missed the appetizers. I saved you a slider."

"Thanks," I said, feeling now just how hungry I was. "Bill and I needed to sort something out with the cake. But it's all fixed now!"

"The *cake*?" Linnie just looked at me for a moment. "Do I want to know?"

I thought about it, then shook my head. "I don't think you do."

"Then don't tell me," she said with a smile. "I'm having a really good time at my reception and I'd rather not find out anything that would derail that."

"Good call." She squeezed my arm and then headed back to her seat, in the center of the head table next to Rodney.

I started to follow—then realized that there was something I needed to do. I took my phone out of my purse and pressed the contact for my best friend. I felt my heart pound as her phone rang, and just when I was sure she was sending me to voice mail, she picked up.

"Hi," I said, hearing the relief in my voice. "I wasn't sure you were going to answer."

"Hey," she said, her voice a little cooler than normal. "How's the wedding?"

"It's going on now," I said, taking a step farther back, so that I was leaning against the deserted bar.

"Is it fun? Does Linnie look beautiful?" she asked, her voice wistful.

"She does. And it's been kind of crazy. I'll tell you all about it, but . . ." I took a breath and then started speaking quickly, trying to get the words out. "I'm so sorry. I never should have talked to you like that, or stopped calling you back."

"I'm sorry too," she said. "I shouldn't have said those things to you. I just—I don't know. I keep wishing I was there. I should be there."

"It's not your fault your flight was canceled," I said, feeling now just how ridiculous it had been for me to blame Siobhan for this. "And I know I do sometimes forget about you when my siblings are here. And I'm sorry about that."

There was silence on the other end for a moment, and then she said, "Well—thanks, Charlie."

"I don't mean to."

"I know you don't," she said, and I could practically picture the expression on her face as she said it—a half smile and a good-natured eye roll. "And it's not like I don't get it. I mean—not that I would know, but I would imagine that if I had siblings like yours, I'd want to hang out with them too."

"But still."

"Well, thanks for saying it."

"So, what's going on with the roommate?"

Siobhan groaned. "She's the worst," she said. "But I think she hates me too, so hopefully we can get out of it. I'll tell you all about it when I see you. How's the wedding been going?"

"Well," I said, then paused. I wasn't sure I wanted to go into a litany of everything that had happened with this wedding so far. "It's been okay. A few . . . minor disasters."

"Oh my god," Siobhan said, even as she laughed. "I have to hear all about them. Now—what's going on with Jesse?"

I looked across to the dance floor, where he was sitting at his table, next to Kyra and Jenny W., laughing at something they were saying. I suddenly wondered if he'd even noticed that I was gone. And while I could understand not wanting to be so obvious in front of Mike, it wasn't like he couldn't even talk to me. "I'm not sure," I finally said. Unbidden, I suddenly thought about Bill asking me to dance, reaching for my hand underneath the supermarket lights, spinning me out but then always spinning me back to him, not caring how it looked or if anyone was watching. Asking me to dance because he'd wanted to dance with me.

"Well," Siobhan said, letting out a breath, "we can discuss when I'm back? Tomorrow?"

I smiled and nodded, even though she couldn't see me through the phone, already looking forward to laying this out and talking about it for hours with my best friend—the insane weekend we'd had and all the ups and downs. "It's a plan."

"Okay, this one goes out to Linnie and Rodney!" Glen yelled from the stage. The crowd on the dance floor—which included my sister and newly minted brother-in-law, who'd been dancing up a storm—cheered, and Any Way You Want It launched into their take on "Don't Stop Believin'" yet again.

It was the third time, by my count, that they'd played it during the reception, but the group dancing didn't seem to mind very much. The rest of the dinner had gone off without any other major disasters. If people had noticed they were eating supermarket cake when the dessert was served, nobody mentioned it. My dad especially seemed to be a big fan, and had eaten at least three pieces. The speeches had all gone well—my dad's had been lovely, as had Rodney's mom's. And best of all was Rodney's brother, Ellis, who had surprised us all by Skyping in from Japan for his speech. It was very early in the morning there, and he didn't seem entirely awake, but even so, most people in the tent were sniffling by the time he'd finished it.

Danny had stood up and given a toast that had been very moving—about how Linnie and Rodney's love had always been an inspiration to him, and he hoped that he would be lucky enough to find something like it someday. I kept waiting for him to mention Brooke, or their relationship, but then he just continued with his speech. I noticed Brooke getting up and leaving soon after—from what I could tell, she still hadn't returned. And right after that, Any Way You Want It had started playing, and the dancing had begun in earnest.

I'd joined Danny and my siblings on the dance floor and had tried to subtly work my way over to where Jesse was dancing with Mike and Kyra. Because this was it. The wedding was over. The reception was going great, and everyone was having a good time. And now I could finally spend time with Jesse, not having to worry about anything else.

But even though Jesse smiled at me when I joined them and would sometimes take my hand and spin me around, or dip me, he hadn't made any attempt to dance with just me. And it made me trying to dance with just him feel all the more awkward, and after a few minutes I stopped trying. I didn't have a ton of time to dwell on this before the bridesmaids pulled me into a bridesmaid dance-off that had everyone up on their feet, laughing and clapping. Whenever I looked across the room at Jesse, he would smile or wink at me, but he wasn't making any effort to come closer. I was chalking it up to not wanting to be obvious in front of Mike, but the longer it went on, the more it was starting to bother me, and finally I'd gone back to sitting at my table.

"How many times are they going to play this?" J.J. grumbled as he dropped into the seat next to mine. He held up his phone. "DJJJ is all ready to go!"

"Let's give them a few more songs, but then, you should probably take over," I said. I hadn't realized just how *long* a song it was until I'd heard it played, live, three times. "I'm not sure we can handle another one of these."

"Oh, good," J.J. said, brightening, as he started to scroll through his playlists. "Any requests?"

"Just so long as it's not Journey, I'm happy." I leaned back in my seat to look out at the crowd, feeling myself relax.

People were divided between the tables and the dance floor. The ones at the tables were either watching the dancers, or talking in groups, or just lingering over cake and coffee. Olly had shaken off his earlier rejection and had been spending most of the night talking to one of Rodney's cousins, who didn't seem to have much of a problem with the fact that he'd been trying to get the bride to run away with him just a few hours earlier. Ralph had, to my surprise, hung around and was busting serious moves on the dance floor—people had started to give him some room, as his Running Man tended to go wild. Mike was talking to Elizabeth and her husband. Rodney was standing to the side of the dance floor with his parents. My dad and Linnie were dancing, my father doing what we all called the "Jeffrey Grant finger-point dance." Danny was dancing with our mother, twirling her around while she tossed her head back and laughed. I glanced around and still didn't see Brooke anywhere, but I was sure she must have come back—it was just hard to keep track of everyone in the shifting crowd.

"Charlie!" I looked up to see Danny standing in front of me, looking happy and out of breath, his bow tie loosened. "Come on," he said, beckoning me to the dance floor. "No Grant left behind!"

I looked around and realized there was nothing left to do but dance. Things seemed more or less under control. People had enjoyed their supermarket cake, Linnie and Rodney were married, and the band had just launched into "Any Way You Want It." I kicked off my shoes, then ran to join my family on the dance floor.

CHAPTER 24
Or, The Family Grant

WO HOURS LATER, I LEANED BACK AGAINST THE couch in the family room and speared a bite of my supermarket cake. "It was a job well done," I said as I raised a forkful of cake toward my middle brother. "Thanks for saving the music."

J.J. inclined his head. "I just did what was required," he said humbly. He really had done a good job once he took over for Any Way You Want It, curating a surprisingly danceable mix, jumping eras and genres from one song to the next, like he was trying to make sure as many people as possible had at least one song they wanted to dance to.

The rest of the reception had gone great—it had been all of us out on the dance floor, getting down, singing along to the words, and laughing. Danny had snuck me glasses of champagne, the General and Mrs. Daniels had proven that they could *dance*, and my cousin Frannie had, as usual, gotten drunk and started talking too loudly about how she could have been a doctor, if she'd wanted to.

Jesse had left the reception early—he'd said his good-byes and thanked my parents, and then had given me a hug, during which he'd whispered, right in my ear, "Text me when you're done here."

And even though there were plenty of times I could have slipped away, I found that I really wasn't even tempted to. It was Linnie's wedding, I was having a blast with my family, and everything felt like it was finally working out.

Even Jimmy and Liz had appeared to have a good time—albeit from separate sides of the tent—and it was clear that despite their animosity almost shutting down the wedding, they weren't about to bury the hatchet and get over it anytime soon.

The party had gone on, the volume definitely climbing, but maybe Don had given up, or maybe the police weren't responding to him anymore—at any rate, nobody else showed up to tell us to keep it down. At some point, as more and more guests had started to depart, J.J. had set up a playlist and come down to dance with us—dancing close to Jenny W. for the rest of the night. It had been just what I'd wanted—all of us, having a good time together.

The dancing kept going, with people peeling off until it was basically just me, Danny, and J.J. on the dance floor. When J.J.'s playlist came up with three acoustic guitar songs in a row, we decided it was a sign that we should call it a night and head inside.

The caterers had left the kitchen immaculate—much cleaner than it normally was. I was worried that people might have all gone to bed, but when we heard laughter from the other room, we headed out to investigate and found everyone else sitting around the family room, digging into the leftover wedding cake. Linnie and Rodney were there—Linnie had changed into a short white dress halfway through the reception, the better for dancing, and Rodney was still wearing his dad's suit, the tie loosened. My parents were there, sitting on opposite sides of the room, my dad on the couch and my mom in her armchair, my mom having changed into sweats and my dad still in his tux. Seeing that the party was carrying on in here, we'd all headed in and I had wasted no time in grabbing myself a plate and joining them, taking the spot next to Danny on the couch.

"The music really *was* pretty good," Mike agreed from his armchair as he set his empty plate on the coffee table. Mike still being there was a surprise, but one that I was very happy to see. He'd actually participated in the wedding reception—dancing with Linnie, talking to our relatives and family friends, seeming to have a good time. Seeing him in here now, voluntarily spending time with all of us, felt like when a butterfly alights on your hand and you don't want to do anything or make any sudden movements to scare it away.

"Don't encourage him," my mother said quickly.

"You really liked my choices?" J.J. asked, sounding flattered. "You think DJJJ has a future?"

"No," everyone in the room who wasn't J.J. said at the same time. J.J. looked offended as he took a bite of cake, and I laughed as I leaned back against the couch cushions, pulling my legs up underneath me. I looked around the room, feeling really at peace and happy. Despite everything—despite all the mishaps leading up to now—it had turned out okay. Because here we were—my family—together after my sister's wedding, eating cake and laughing.

Everything this weekend had been worth it to get to right now, this moment. I took another bite of cake to stop myself from smiling, and I couldn't help noticing just how *right* everything felt. We were all together, finally. Things were finally going back to how they should be.

"Charlie, don't you think your piece is a little large?" my dad asked, and as I looked down at it, he removed the plate from my hands so skillfully that I didn't even realize it was happening until it was too late. "I'll just help you out with that," he said, taking a bite.

"Hey," I said, laughing as I tried to get it back from him.

"There is so much more cake in the fridge," my mother pointed out, shaking her head. But she didn't sound annoyed—she sounded tired but happy. I looked over at her, curled in her favorite armchair, and smiled at her. She smiled back, giving me a tiny wink. "If any of you would get up, you could easily get some more."

"They've all had enough," my dad said, his mouth full, as he held my plate out of my reach.

"My cake. Dad!"

"Who paid for it?"

"Technically, me," I said, giving up and leaning back against the couch cushions. I'd already told the story of the supermarket cake run— leaving out, of course, the slow dancing by the bread aisle.

"Fine," my dad grumbled, spearing the world's smallest bite on the fork and handing it to me.

"Thanks," I said, shaking my head as I took the bite. I looked around the room—at all of us together—and knew that I had to say something. Mike was sitting on the floor, just a little in front of me, and I nudged him with my toe. "Did you have fun?"

Mike looked back at me and smiled, his expression easy and open for once. "I did," he said, and I was sure I could hear in his voice that he was feeling the same as I was—relaxed and happy to be together with everyone.

"See?" I said, nudging him again. "It's not always so terrible being a Grant, is it?"

The smile slid off Mike's face immediately. "Seriously?" he asked.

"I'm just saying," I said, "that maybe you'd forgotten how much fun we have. I bet you're regretting staying away so long."

"Charlie," Linnie said, looking over at me and widening her eyes. The feeling in the room was starting to shift, like a thermostat had just been adjusted, everything suddenly getting cooler. "Maybe now's not the time."

"I was just thinking," I said quickly, feeling like I had to get this out—I wasn't sure when I'd find a better opportunity. "That we should just all get past this thing with Mike and then things can go back to how they were, right?" I gestured around the room. "Like now."

"Charlie, you don't get it," Mike said, turning around to face me.

"Of course I do," I said, setting my fork down. I noticed J.J. and Danny making eye contact, neither of them looking happy, but I pressed on anyway. "You gave a stupid interview that you shouldn't have and said things you didn't mean. We can all move on now."

Mike shook his head. "You're missing the point," he said. "I gave that interview because she wrecked my relationship with her comic strip. She thought it was all a joke, and she never even apologized. I meant every word I said."

"Michael," my mother said, sitting up in the chair.

"Are we doing this now?" Mike asked, looking from my mom to me. "Are we really going there? Linnie just got married."

"There's a good point," Rodney said, his voice soothing. "Why don't we just finish our cake and head to bed. Everyone's tired—"

"Mom never did that," I interjected, shaking my head at Mike.

"Are you *kidding* me?" he asked, his eyebrows flying up. "Our lives weren't our own. They were just fodder for her. And everything she wanted us to be, she made the Grant kids be. Everything we weren't, she made up for in her comic strip."

"That's not fair," my mother said, her face getting red as she shook her head. "I've never—"

"You know, you never *asked* us if we wanted our lives broadcast every morning to America," Mike said, looking at our mom. "You just went ahead and did it and we never talked about whether it was a good thing—"

"So you decided to humiliate her—all of us?" J.J. asked, jumping into the fray, his arms folded across his chest.

"I'd had enough!" Mike yelled. "Our stories never got to be our own. I told her not to put it in and she did it anyway, and I was just done! I was done with all of it."

Save the Date

339

"Why didn't you say something then?" J.J. asked. "Instead, you just stayed away like a coward."

I heard Linnie draw in a sharp breath, and Danny leaned forward. "Okay, guys," he said, looking from J.J. to Mike, then back to me. "I think we should just take a second—"

"That's really nice, J.J." Mike said, shaking his head. "Nice for you to tell me *now* how you felt about it."

"I would have told you then," J.J. snapped, "but you weren't here to tell, were you?"

"I haven't been here because I can't do this!" Mike yelled, standing up. "She wants us to be this perfect unit, whether that's who we are or not. She doesn't care! She sold us to America like we're this amazing family everyone wants to be a part of."

"But we are!" I yelled, standing up myself now. I saw Linnie and Rodney look at each other apprehensively, but I barreled on anyway. "I love being a Grant and I know how lucky I am. I'm sick of this—sick of begging you to participate in a family anyone else would kill to be a part of. And I'll always love the strip."

"Yeah, well, the strip is over," Mike said, and across the room, I saw my mom flinch. "And the house is sold. So not so wonderful, after all, is it?"

"Well," I said, feeling myself flounder a little. "Yeah, but . . ."

Mike shook his head, rolling his eyes at me. "You're living in a fantasy," he spat. "You're living in a fucking newspaper comic."

"No, I'm not." I was yelling now, feeling tears building up somewhere behind my eyes. "Things are good here. You just haven't been around to see it." I sat down, feeling like I'd gotten a good last word in and wanting to punctuate this with something. I glanced over at Danny, to try and see his reaction, but he seemed to be having some kind of silent conversation with my parents, loaded looks flying between them, my mother shaking her head.

"I think . . . ," Danny started, then let out a long breath. "Is it time?"

"Sheridan," my mother said, her voice low and serious, warning, and I was starting to get a bad feeling in the pit of my stomach.

"Let's not do this now," my dad said, an equally serious note in his voice as he stared hard at Danny. "Okay?"

"What's going on?" Linnie asked. "Don't do what now?"

"I have no idea," J.J. said, and from Rodney's expression, it seemed like he didn't know either.

"It's not the time," my mom said, starting to gather up plates, finality in her tone, like she'd just put a period at the end of a sentence.

"Whatever it is, just tell us," Mike said, sounding disgusted. "Can we please just tell the truth in this family, for *once*?" My parents exchanged a loaded look. I turned to Danny, ready for him to give me a smile, letting me know there was really nothing to worry about—but he was bent forward over his knees, clenching his hands together.

"Mom?" I asked.

"What's going on?" J.J. asked, all his bravado gone, looking somehow younger than he had in years.

"Come on—what's happening here?" Linnie asked, a nervous note in her voice. "Are you—is someone sick?"

"No," my dad said immediately, and my mother shook her head. "God no, nothing like that."

"I'm fine," my mother said emphatically. "Your father's fine."

"Someone needs to tell us what's going on!" J.J. yelled, his voice cracking on the last word.

"They're getting a divorce," Danny said, still hunched over his hands, his voice tired. "That's what's going on."

There was silence in the room, a silence that felt heavy, like it was taking up all the air—you couldn't even hear anyone breathe.

I looked between my mom and dad, feeling my breath caught somewhere in my chest, repeating the words *no please no* over and over in my head like a prayer or a mantra, something you say to keep the bad things at bay. Maybe I had heard wrong. Maybe I'd misunderstood. Maybe Danny had misunderstood because this wasn't—this couldn't—

"We," my dad said, glancing over at my mom, who was staring down at the carpet, her bottom lip trembling. "This wasn't how we wanted to do this. . . ."

Even though I was sitting down, I suddenly understood why people who get bad news in movies are always collapsing to the ground. I knew somehow that if I'd tried to stand up right then, my legs would not have held me. Nor, it seemed, should they—my parents had just pulled my world out from under my feet.

"It's not that we won't always be a family," my mother said, speaking fast, like she was just trying to get this over with. "That won't ever change. We're going to take some time, try a separation. . . ."

"And our priority will always be the happiness of you kids," my dad said now, leaning toward us. Now they were speaking more quickly, and I had a feeling they'd rehearsed this—suddenly, they were actors in a play who'd finally gotten to a section of the lines they knew cold. "And it has nothing to do with any of you. It's just . . ." He made a vague gesture with his hands, spreading them outward for a second, like that would help us see why a thirty-five-year marriage was ending. "One of those things," he finished.

"Why did they tell you?" J.J. was staring at Danny, all his confidence and flash gone, which was as heartbreaking as anything that was happening here. It was like seeing my brother without his protective armor, so much smaller and so much more easily hurt.

"I'm only a year younger than Danny," Linnie said, shaking her head. "And you didn't think I could handle it?"

"Is that really important right now?" Danny asked, shaking his head. "Who knew what?"

"It's important to me," J.J. said, glaring at Danny.

"I handle their finances," Danny said. He sounded exhausted, like he had no more fight left in him. "They needed me to start dividing up assets so that this process could go more smoothly."

"So you're not just 'separating,'" J.J. said, putting half-hearted air quotes around the word. "You guys are getting a divorce. It's been decided."

My parents glanced at each other and then away. Neither spoke, which seemed to be all the confirmation we needed. I turned to my siblings, who all, with the exception of Danny, looked as shell-shocked by this as I was.

"This is why," I said, and I could hear my voice coming out scratchy, like it had been a long time since I'd spoken. It had been another life-time ago. I took a breath and tried again. "This is why you're selling the house." As soon as I'd said it, another, bigger realization hit me. "This is why you're ending the strip."

"Of course she's ending it now," Mike said, shaking his head at me. "You can't write about the perfect family when you're in the process of breaking it up."

"Like you're even one to talk," I said, louder than I knew I was going to, the words coming out of my mouth before I could think them through. "I don't think you can even have an opinion on this when you haven't been home for eighteen months."

"Charlie," Danny said, his voice warning, which only caused me to get madder.

"You don't have a say in this family," I said, ignoring Danny and turn-ing to face Mike more fully, "when you've done all you can for the last year and a half not to be part of it."

"So I don't even get an opinion?"

"I don't think you do," I shot back. "And maybe if you'd been here, maybe if we'd been able to have a real Thanksgiving or Christmas—"

"Oh, so this is my fault now?" Mike asked, two red splotches starting to appear on his cheeks. "I'm the reason they're getting divorced?"

"Of course not," my dad said loudly, clearly trying to stop this. I could tell this wasn't the way he'd expected it to go. "Don't be silly—"

"So, what's going to happen?" I interrupted. I looked at my mom, trying to understand how this could be the same person who, just minutes ago, was getting a second piece of cake and winking at me. How could she have done that when she knew this all along? "You guys are going to sell the house and then—you get two separate places and we split our time?"

"Well," my dad said after a pause in which it became clear my mother wasn't going to jump in, "yes. We have things to sort out, of course. But you'll be headed to college in the fall, so lots of things will be changing regardless."

I felt my stomach clench again. I was having that terrible feeling you have when you know you were right about something but didn't want to be. I thought about all those fights my parents had been having, those months where there had been anger and slammed doors and unsaid things. Even today, with the daybed in my parents' room—I hadn't wanted to see it. I'd just pretended none of it was happening, hoping it would go away on its own. This suddenly seemed like the height of stupidity and childishness.

But was I supposed to stay here in Stanwich, go to school here when I no longer had a home here? When my family wasn't here, together, like they were supposed to be?

"Yeah," I said, shaking my head, my words coming out with a harsh laugh. "Right. No wonder you didn't want me to stay in Stanwich—you knew that everything here was going to change."

"That's not why—" my mother started, but I was already talking over her.

"But you know what? You know what you all had during college?" I looked around at my siblings. "You all had a home to come back to!

You all got to come here, with your bedroom and your stuff on the walls and all of us here waiting for you. What am I going to have? What's that going to look like for me? You guys all have your own places, your own lives. But I'm not going to have that. I'm not going to have anywhere to go. I'm not going to have a home." My voice broke on the last word, and I put my head in my hands—my face felt hot, and there were tears building up behind my eyes, threatening to spill over at any moment.

"And *you*," I said, straightening up, brushing a hand over my face and glaring at Mike, my eyes blurry with tears, "you could have been back here for two years, and you blew it. I bet you're happy, aren't you? You've wanted to be out of this family forever, and now you finally get your wish."

"I'm not," Mike said, and I could see that his eyes looked shiny, "*happy*, Charlie. Of course I'm not, and fuck you for saying that."

"Language," my parents both said, in unison, then looked at each other, like they weren't sure if they should laugh or cry.

Linnie's shoulders were shaking, and Rodney was sitting close to her and rubbing her back. J.J.'s face was very red, and he was blinking hard.

"Guys," my dad said, finally breaking the silence, running his hand across his eyes. He sounded exhausted, and suddenly looked about five years older. "I think we should all get some sleep and maybe in the morning—"

"In the morning, when we're going to be filmed as the perfect family?" J.J. asked , his voice flat. "You know, for national television?"

Linnie let out a short laugh—the kind without any humor in it.

"This will all be for the best," my dad said, his voice quiet. "In the long run."

We just sat there for a moment, and I couldn't help but wonder if it was what people who've just been in an earthquake or a tornado felt. When you're standing among the rubble and wreckage of what just moments earlier had been your life, wondering how you got there and what happened now that everything was destroyed.

"I'm going to bed," my mother finally said, pushing herself to her feet. "We have a big day tomorrow. *Good Morning America's* here at eight, so . . ." Her voice trailed off, and I wondered if what she'd just said had sounded as hollow to her as it had to me. She left the room, and my dad got up a moment later, picking up his tux jacket and folding it over his arm.

"Good night," he said, his voice tired, and this was somehow made all the worse by the fact that he was still in his tux, like a reminder of the fact that only an hour ago, we'd all been dancing. "I just wanted . . ." But his voice trailed off, and what he wanted was left unsaid. He let out a breath, then turned around and left the room, his step heavy on the carpet.

The room was silent for a moment, and I looked around at my siblings, wondering how the family room, which had always been one of the best and most peaceful places in the house, had suddenly been turned into a war zone.

"We should go too," Linnie said, and Rodney nodded and held out a hand to her, helping her to her feet. She was still wearing her white dress and Rodney was in his dad's suit, and I suddenly felt that much worse about everything. This was supposed to be the happiest day of their lives, and this was how it ended? This was what we were sending them off to the honeymoon suite with?

"We'll see you tomorrow," Rodney said, his normally cheerful voice not even trying to be upbeat. His arm was still wrapped around my sister's shoulders, like he was helping to keep her walking upright. "Night."

We all watched them leave in silence, nobody saying good night back to them—and I wondered if none of my brothers had because they felt, like me, that it would be a complete lie, since this had not been, and would never be, a good night.

"You okay, Chuck?" Danny asked, leaning toward me. I just shook my head. It was like *okay* was on another planet entirely.

"I can't believe you didn't tell me," I said, only feeling this betrayal hit me now. How could he—how could *Danny*—have kept this from me?

"They didn't want me to," he said, shaking his head. "If it had been up to me, I would have, Chuck. You know that."

"How could you not have known?" Mike asked, raising an eyebrow at me.

"Mike," Danny said, his voice sharper now, a warning.

"I mean, come on." There was a cruel laugh somewhere in his words. "You *live* here. You're the only one who does! And you had no idea?" He shook his head. "You're so blinded by your Grant worship, always holding this family up like it's something special—"

"It *is*!" I yelled, my voice breaking, another tear hitting my cheek.

"Weren't you listening?" Mike yelled back at me, his own voice cracking now. "There is no more Grant family! It's over!"

I shook my head, but I couldn't make myself say anything. I brushed my hand across my face, wiping away the tears that seemed just to be falling of their own accord now.

"Come on," Danny said, pushing himself up to standing. "I need—I can't be in this house anymore. Let's go. Let's all go."

"Go where?" J.J. asked even as he stood as well.

Danny just shrugged, with a restlessness I recognized. It was the look he'd had when we'd gone for milkshakes when I was nine and ended up at the Canadian border. We would have made it all the way to Montreal, too, if only we'd had our passports with us. "Out," he said with a shrug. He started toward the door, then looked back at me. "Chuck?"

I shook my head. It didn't make sense, but it felt like if I left, if I went outside, this would become real. But if I didn't move from this spot— the same place I'd been sitting before the world had ended—maybe this would turn out to be just a very realistic dream, one I could still wake up from.

"I'll come," Mike said, surprising me, as he joined Danny in the doorway. "I need to get out of here too."

Danny gave me a look from the doorway, and I knew he was trying to see if I was okay. And normally I would have tried, for his sake, to give him a smile, so that he wouldn't worry. But I couldn't seem to manage it right now, and after a moment, Danny turned and left the room, Mike following behind him.

J.J. headed for the door as well, then paused in the doorway and turned back at me. "It'll be all right," he finally said, in a voice that had no conviction in it whatsoever.

"Do you really believe that?" I didn't—but I had no idea what our lives looked like if we weren't all in this house together, if we weren't a family, the seven of us. It was like I couldn't even get myself to imagine it.

"It's what you're supposed to say," J.J. said in a quiet voice after a pause. He stayed there for another moment, then headed out as well. A second later, I heard the kitchen door slam shut, and the sound of a car starting.

I sat alone in the family room, trying not to remember how not that long ago, it had been filled with people eating cake. All this time, I'd been dreaming about everyone coming back—thinking that it meant things were finally going back to how they'd been, not knowing it was the beginning of the end. We'd been on borrowed time, and I hadn't even realized it. An unseen clock had been ticking down, down, down—counting out the time left when the seven of us would be together in the same family, not broken up into pieces. I'd had no idea that we—the Grant family, one family together—had already ended.

I thought about going upstairs, but then remembered, yet again, that Brooke was in there. But I knew that I couldn't stay here—in the room where everything had fallen apart.

Now that they had gone, now that it was too late, I suddenly wished I'd left with my brothers. I understood Danny's impetus to get out, to do something to put all this behind me. I wanted something to go my way tonight, just one thing to work out the way I wanted it to.

Before I even knew I'd made a decision, I was grabbing my bag from where I'd put it beside the couch and pulling up my text chain with Jesse.

Me

Hey—things wrapped up here.

Can I still come over?

CHAPTER 25
Or, Meanwhile, Back in the Basement . . .

I SAT ON THE ARM OF THE COUCH IN JESSE'S basement, twisting my hands together and reminding myself to breathe. Jesse had texted me, letting me know the side door was open and that I should let myself in, and to text him when I got there.

I smoothed my hands over the silk of my dress, flexed my feet in my heels, then pushed myself up to standing and paced around the room. I was feeling restless, like the energy coursing through me was making it impossible to sit still. I ran my fingers through my hair, hoping that some of the curls had stayed and hadn't just turned into frizz. It had been raining steadily, and just getting to my car and then getting to Jesse's had gotten me fairly soaked—I hadn't had the presence of mind, when I'd been fleeing the house, to grab an umbrella.

I stopped pacing and made myself sit back down on the couch, pretzeling my legs so I couldn't go jumping up again. I glanced around the basement—it looked the same as it had over Christmas break. The couch was the same, and the table and chairs in the corner, the dented air-hockey table. The garlands and the Santa hat were gone, of course.

But aside from that, nothing had really changed. So I couldn't figure out why the room felt different now.

Whenever I'd played back the events of that night in my head, Jesse's basement had taken on a grand stature, every detail cataloged in my mind—the feel of the corduroy couch underneath my bare skin, the way Jesse had been framed by the moonlight coming through the windows. It had all seemed perfect and romantic. But now . . .

The longer I was there, taking it in, I realized it was just a basement. There was a stain on the corner of the rug, and I could see where the fabric on the couch arms was worn. There were chip crumbs on the coffee table and a sweating Dr Pepper can slowly leaving a water ring on the wood.

Which was *fine*, I told myself firmly, running a hand through my hair. This was the reality of Jesse's basement, same as it had been in December, and I couldn't be upset because it wasn't matching up to what I'd remembered in my head. And I was here now, back in his house, and this was going to happen. That's what I needed to focus on—not my parents or the fight or how everything with my family was wrecked and in pieces. Just this moment, right now.

I heard steps coming down the stairs and quickly ran a hand through my hair again.

"Hey," Jesse said, taking the last few steps two at a time. He smiled at me. "You made it."

"I made it," I said, trying to keep my voice steady and relaxed, like it was just totally normal for me to be back here, like there was nothing unusual about me being alone with Jesse again.

"How was the rest of the wedding?" Jesse asked, sitting next to me on the couch and throwing one arm over the back of it.

"It was good," I said. This, at least, was true—the wedding had been good. It was just everything that followed that had been awful. All in a rush, I blurted out, "I'm really glad you came home this weekend. It's really—really good to see you."

Jesse smiled at that, leaning back against the couch cushions. He looked totally relaxed, which I supposed made sense, since this was his house, but it made me that much more aware of how jumpy I felt, sitting across from him, my pulse beating hard in my throat. "I was glad to have the chance to hang out with Mike. And you," he added after a pause. "I might actually head out early tomorrow," he added with a shrug. "Some other friends from Stanwich are around, and we're talking about maybe going to Mohegan Sun. . . ." I nodded, even though it felt like something was gripping my stomach. Jesse was going to leave? Tomorrow? I'd just assumed I'd see him tonight, and then we'd somehow work things out, and then we'd be together. I wasn't exactly sure what happened to bridge those two things—I hadn't gotten that far whenever I'd been dreaming about it—but I was pretty sure none of my fantasies about this had included him going off to a resort-slash-casino. "And then back to school," he said with a groan. He turned to me, his brow furrowed, and he tilted his head to the side slightly. "Where are you going again?"

I took a breath, about to say Stanwich—but was I still? If everything that would have kept me here was gone? "I was going to go to Stanwich," I said. "But . . ."

"Staying local," Jesse said with a nod. "Nothing wrong with that. I know you'll have a great time." He gave me a lazy smile. "You'll be breaking hearts all over campus."

I smiled at that, even though it felt like something in my chest had just plunged. Why was he talking about me breaking hearts? Why was he talking about me and other guys at all? Didn't he realize that *he* was the guy? "Um," I started, trying to bring myself back to the moment. Things were still fine. I was here, with Jesse, on his couch, wearing a beautiful dress. Things were *fine*. He was trying to give me a compliment and just going about it in a weird way. "I guess so."

"I know it," he said, giving me another slow-building smile. "I always thought you were cute, Charlie."

All the confusion I'd been feeling a second earlier was immediately swept away. I felt something warm start to spread through me, radiating out from my stomach. "You did?"

"Of course," he said easily. "But now—now you're, like, *super* cute. I know I'm not supposed to think Mike's sister is hot, but . . ." He shook his head. I tried to keep from smiling too wide, and I had a feeling I wasn't doing a great job of it. "What about me?" he asked with a smile that let me know he wasn't worried about my answer to this question. "Did you think I was cute?"

I had to take a moment before answering him—he might have just asked me if the ocean was blue, or made of water. The answer was so clearly, blindingly obvious. I took a deep breath. "Do you remember Mike's fourteenth birthday?" Jesse just raised an eyebrow, and I remembered what he'd said yesterday at the Inn, about how this was kids' stuff. But I needed him to know this. "It was at that laser tag place," I said, talking more quickly now. "And we ended up on the elevator going up to the second level, just the two of us?"

"Oh right," Jesse said, even though I could tell he didn't really remember. "Sure . . ."

"Do you remember when the elevator got stuck? And when I got scared, you reached out and squeezed my hand?" I took a breath and continued, knowing I had to get this out—had to try to tell him how I felt and just how far it went beyond merely thinking he was cute. "Or when you were over senior year doing prom pictures at our house—and you asked me to straighten your bow tie . . ." Even speaking the words brought me back to the moment—standing in the front hall with Jesse, closer than I'd ever been before, reaching up to straighten his black bow tie, breathing in the scent of his cologne as I tried to make the act of straightening a bow tie last absolutely as long as it possibly could, just so I could keep standing next to him.

"Yeah," Jesse said, still looking a little confused, like he didn't understand why I'd just suddenly dragged us down memory lane.

"I more than thought you were cute," I said, feeling my cheeks get hot as I said it but pushing on anyway. "I kind of had this massive crush on you growing up."

Jesse smiled at that. "Had?" He leaned a little closer to me on the couch, reaching up and moving my hair back over my shoulder. "Past tense?" I shook my head, and Jesse's smile widened as he leaned closer still, so that he was right there and we were just a breath away. "That's good," he said, and took my face in his hands as he kissed me.

I kissed him back, sliding my arms over his shoulders as he eased me back onto the couch again, moving his hands over the silk of my dress. "This is nice," he said, breaking away from me for a second as he looked down at it, rubbing the silk between his fingers.

"Thanks," I said a little breathlessly, stretching up to kiss him again, kicking one of my heels to the floor and then trying to kick the other one off, but I felt it get stuck against the couch arm.

"I've got this," Jesse said, pushing himself up slightly and taking off my shoe, then dropping it onto the floor, then sliding his hand up my bare leg, making me shiver as he leaned over and kissed me again.

"Thanks," I said between kisses. Jesse grinned at me, then bent his head down toward me again. Time seemed to lose all its normal properties as we kissed—I only took a tiny time-out to take off my earrings, which were getting caught in my hair—so I wasn't sure how long it had been when his hands slid around my back and he fumbled with the zip on my dress. I paused in kissing him and pushed myself to sit up a little more, and Jesse drew back slightly.

"Everything okay?"

"Yes," I said immediately. "I just . . ." I looked at him, trying to take

MORGAN MATSON

in this moment, hold on to it, freeze the picture somehow. "I just still kind of can't believe that this—that you and me . . ." I shook my head, failing to find the exact words I needed. "That this is really happening." I smiled at him then and kissed him, and he kissed me back, but it was like I could feel he was hesitating. And a second later, he broke away, propping himself up on the couch arm and letting his head hang down over my shoulder. "Jesse?" I asked after a moment, not sure what was happening.

"Yeah," he said, lifting his head and rolling slightly off me, to my side, so that I could see him a little more clearly. "I just wanted to make sure we were on the same page here. Because I think you're great." He ran his finger down my cheek and then played with a lock of my hair. "But . . ." He gave me a slightly confused smile. "I just don't want you to think this is something it's not. We're just having fun, right? It's not like this is *serious*." He said this in a tone of voice that made it seem like the only response would be to agree with him.

"No," I said, smiling, trying to act like he hadn't just hit the dimmer switch on my happiness, like it was slowly starting to fade out, tiny bit by tiny bit. "Not serious like right this minute," I said with a laugh that was a little more high-pitched than mine normally were. "But—that doesn't mean that someday . . ." I traced my fingers up his arm as my voice trailed off, giving him a hopeful smile he didn't return.

"I just . . ." Jesse let out a short breath. "I mean, I'm at school. . . . You're going to be starting school next year. . . . Let's not turn this into something it doesn't need to be, okay? Why put pressure on it, you know what I mean?" He smiled at me like I'd answered him, or agreed, and bent down to kiss me again.

I kissed him back even as my thoughts were swirling. It was almost like I couldn't get myself to understand what I'd just heard. Because Jesse Foster wasn't supposed to say things like that—he just wasn't.

A second later, I realized what was wrong with that logic. Jesse *was* saying this. He'd just said it. Jesse, the real person in front of me. Not the version of him I'd had in my head all these years, until he'd become this separate thing entirely.

He was a nice guy. He was cute, and he was a great kisser. But that was actually all I really knew about him, Jesse the actual person. I couldn't have told you his favorite movie, or his roommate's name, or his greatest fear. He wasn't who I thought he was all those years, because that person didn't exist. That Jesse was just a compilation of everything I'd projected onto him, coupled with a handful of real-life interactions that I'd given far too much value to.

And as the realization of this hit me full force, I broke away from him, pushing myself up on my elbows. "Jesse . . ."

"What?" Jesse asked, looking confused. Then he smiled at me, raising one eyebrow. "You want to head up to the guesthouse?"

"No," I said, maybe a little too quickly, because Jesse's face fell. "It's just . . ." I tucked my hair behind my ears and looked over at him. And for the first time in maybe ever, I didn't see Jesse Foster—the person I'd thought about for years and made far too many birthday wishes about. The guy who had seemed to loom so large in the halls of Stanwich High but now just seemed like . . . a guy. I didn't see the boy I'd thought about for hours and hours on end, imagining just what it could be like to have him see me, choose me. It was like something had fallen away, some of the aura that had always surrounded him, the one that I was beginning to understand was all my doing. It was like I'd turned him into a character in my mother's comic strip, a little too polished and perfect—and utterly two-dimensional. I didn't know the guy sitting on the couch next to me. And he didn't know me.

"I think . . . maybe I should go," I said, realizing as I spoke the words that it was what I wanted.

"Oh," Jesse said, sitting up even more, looking at me. "Is . . . ? Did I do something?"

"No," I said quickly, because this was the truth. It wasn't anything Jesse had or hadn't done. It's that he wasn't the person I'd talked myself into believing he was all these years. And that wasn't his fault. But it did mean that as fun as kissing him had been, I probably needed to go. "I just . . ." I took a breath, then gestured between us. "I'm thinking this might not be the best idea."

"Oh." Jesse blinked at me, and I had a feeling he was having trouble understanding what had changed in the last few minutes.

"I'm sorry," I said, pushing myself off the couch and picking up my bag, knowing that if I looked at him lying on the couch, his shirt slightly rumpled where I'd been running my hands over it, I'd find myself back on the couch, kissing him again. I stopped by the side door, already extracting my keys so that I wouldn't be tempted to return to the couch. "Um . . . I'll see you around?"

"Yeah," Jesse said, giving me a smile that was still slightly confused but was amiable enough. I saw that he was already reaching for the remote—like he was just going to transition his night, so easily, to watching TV. And seeing that was maybe all the proof I needed that I was doing the right thing. "Take care, Charlie."

"You too." I gave him a smile, but he was leaning back against the couch, not looking at me. And after a moment, I turned and left the basement, stepping outside into the cool night air and taking a deep breath. Since I'd been in there, it had stopped raining.

I had just gotten into my car when my phone rang. I pulled it out of my bag and saw that it was J.J. calling. I hesitated for only a second before sliding my finger across the screen. "J.J.?"

"Hey, Charlie," J.J. said, speaking fast. "So. Um. We kind of got arrested?"

CHAPTER 26
Or, Give Me a Sign

$\mathcal{I}$ BARRELED DOWN THE ROAD, HOLDING MY PHONE with one hand and gripping the steering wheel with the other. J.J. hadn't been very forthcoming with where he was. I'd assumed the police station on Stanwich Avenue, but when he tried to tell me where they were, he started using J.J.-style directions, which never used street names and always involved way too many descriptions of trees that resembled celebrities in profile. Finally, Mike had wrested the phone away from him, sent me a dropped pin, and after that, the line had gone dead.

If it had been J.J. alone, I might have been doubtful of what was actually happening—after years of exaggerations, I'd learned not to take him at his word. But the fact that Mike and Danny were with him—and that Danny hadn't gotten on the phone to reassure me that everything was okay—was making me more nervous than I wanted to admit. And there was also the expression on Danny's face when he'd left the family room—like he'd been looking for trouble. It certainly seemed like they'd found it.

I put the dropped pin into my map and followed the directions to it, my brights on against the pitch-black night. I'd been driving for only a few minutes when I realized I should not be the only person coming to help and that I probably shouldn't have headed straight for my brothers, but should have let someone else know what was happening—like my parents.

Even as the thought entered my head, though, I dismissed it. That just wasn't how the five of us did things—even when I was three and still getting the hang of complex sentences and running without falling over, I knew not to tattle if one of my siblings was tormenting me. We settled things on our own and only brought in a higher authority when it was absolutely necessary.

But even so, it seemed like I should not be the only cavalry who was coming. When I reached a stop sign, I paused for a little longer than usual—not that it mattered, there was nobody behind me—and called Rodney. I figured it couldn't hurt to call the one lawyer whose number was saved in my phone. As I waited for the call to connect, I just hoped it wouldn't matter that he hadn't passed the bar yet. His phone went straight to voice mail—not surprising, considering that I'd called him on his wedding night. So I left him a message, conveying the little I knew about the situation, then texted him the dropped pin J.J. had sent me.

I was following the directions, making the turns that the automated voice on my map app (I'd changed it to an Australian guy I always called Hugh) told me to make, and it wasn't until I was nearly there that I realized, my stomach sinking, where I was actually heading.

This was certainly not the police station. It was, of all places, Grant Avenue. There, on the side of the road, was Danny's rental SUV, parked at an angle. There was a Stanwich Police car up the street from it, the sirens off but the lights on, the whirling blue and red lights against the darkness looking somehow out of place and cheerful—like they belonged at a carnival and not at the site of someone's arrest.

My brothers were all standing by the curb, in a line, and there was a police officer in front of them, a flashlight in his hand that was pointing down at the ground, a small circle of light shining on the pavement. I pulled up behind the police car, then killed my engine and got out of the car, my heart beating fast. This looked serious, and it did *not* look good.

"Hold up there," the police officer's voice said sharply, and I stopped in my tracks immediately. He raised his flashlight toward me, and I squinted against it, but the whole world had just become washed out.

"That's my sister" I heard J.J. say. "So if you could stop blinding her with a flashlight?" There was a tiny pause, maybe in which J.J. realized he was speaking to someone with a firearm and the ability to put him in jail. "Please?"

The flashlight beam was lowered, and I blinked quickly, trying to get rid of all the floating white lights that were now impairing my vision. "Can I—" I gestured toward my brothers, not sure if I was allowed to move or not yet. The walkie on the officer's shoulder crackled, and he bent his head toward it, motioning me forward as he did with an annoyed wave.

I hurried up to my brothers before he could change his mind. They were still standing in a line—Danny, then J.J., then Mike. "What's going on?" I hissed at them.

"Thanks for coming," Danny said, giving me a quick smile as he ran his hand over his face. He looked exhausted, and somehow older than I had ever seen him. I was happy to see that none of them were handcuffed—that would take this into a whole new level of seriousness. And it was serious enough, what with the cop car and its flashing lights and my brothers standing shivering in a line on the side of the road.

"Why are you guys getting arrested?" Even though I was still trying to speak as quietly as possible, I could hear my voice getting high-pitched and squeaky with worry.

"We're not," Mike said quickly. "We're just being, what—detained?"

"No charges have been made," J.J. agreed, nodding. "We haven't been Miranda-ized or anything."

"But why are you—" I started, just as my brothers all exchanged simultaneous guilty looks. Danny glanced toward the Grant Avenue sign, and I realized why I was standing here. "You guys tried to steal the sign," I said, not exactly phrasing it like a question.

"It seemed like a good idea at the time," J.J. said in a small voice. "We were just driving around. We needed to blow off some steam, and then we saw the street, so . . ."

"I don't know why there was even a cop there," Danny said, shaking his head. "It was like he was *waiting* for us or something. All the other times we took the sign, it was totally deserted, not—"

"The governor of Connecticut lives in Stanwich Woods," I said, pointing to where we could see the entrance from here. "There's always a police officer there when he's in town."

"Oh." This information seemed to deflate Danny somehow, and his shoulders slumped.

"Well, the good news is that we didn't actually *do* anything," J.J. said, in a voice that was straining to be upbeat. "We'd only just started to climb the sign when the five-oh showed up."

"I don't think that's good news," Mike said, shaking his head.

"Well, it's better news than if he caught us red-handed, like, removing the sign," J.J. pointed out. "All he has us on right now is suspicion. And a grudge."

I just blinked at my brother. "Why would he have a grudge?"

J.J. shrugged. "We've just taken up a lot of his time tonight, that's all."

"What—" I started, just as the police officer lowered his walkie and turned back around toward us. Now that there wasn't a flashlight beam or the aftereffects of a flashlight beam shining in my eyes, I could see that I recognized the police officer—it was Officer Ramirez, who we'd all seen just a few hours before.

Officer Ramirez frowned at me, and I gave him a small wave, but he just shook his head and turned back to my brothers. "I need to ask you again why you're here," he said, his voice low and serious.

They exchanged a glance and realized at once what the problem was—they couldn't admit that they were attempting to steal town property. But that might be the only thing that would clear them of being suspected of having ill intent toward the governor of Connecticut. "Um," I said, jumping in as the silence stretched on. "I'm sure that—" But I was saved from having to spin some kind of explanation, because at that moment a hybrid rolled silently down the street, then swung into place behind my car, which was behind Danny's—making this suddenly look like the world's strangest and most poorly planned tailgate.

The doors opened, and Rodney and Linnie got out, both of them squinting in the flashlight beam. "J.J.?" Linnie called, trying to shield her eyes.

"Is that the bride and groom?" Officer Ramirez asked.

"Why are Rodney and Linnie here?" Mike asked.

"I called Rodney," I said, feeling simultaneously relieved and massively guilty that they'd had to leave the honeymoon suite to come and stand outside in the cold with us. "I thought it might not be a bad idea to have a lawyer around."

"Hey," Rodney said as he approached us, eyes widening as he took in the police car and my brothers all in a line. "What's—what's going on?"

"Oh, hi again, Officer," Linnie said, waving at Officer Ramirez, who just shook his head as he looked at the six of us—I had a feeling the addition of more Grants hadn't improved his mood any.

"That's our lawyer," J.J. interrupted, nodding at Rodney. "Um, Rodney Daniels, esquire at law."

A muscle twitched in Rodney's jaw, and I knew just by looking at him how hard it was for him not to correct J.J. in this situation, tell him that he wasn't actually a lawyer yet. "Right," Rodney said after a moment. "That's me." He looked around at all of us and sighed. "Thanks for this, guys. This really was how I wanted to spend my wedding night."

"What's the problem here?" Linnie asked.

"Well, we're here on *Grant Avenue*," I said, looking at my sister and widening my eyes. "But I think the problem is that they got too close to the governor's mansion."

I saw understanding dawn in my sister's expression. "Seriously?" she asked our brothers, shaking her head. "Tonight?"

"When the governor is in residence, no non-local cars are permitted to be parked on this road," Officer Ramirez said as he pointed to Danny's SUV. "I saw this vehicle parked on the side of the road, empty, and then soon saw the three individuals attempting to climb that sign." He pointed to it. "They refused to tell me what they were doing here, and I detained them on suspected suspicious behavior."

"Um," Rodney said, then cleared his throat as he pulled on the hem of his sweatshirt. I knew Rodney well enough to tell that he was wishing he was in his suit and tie, not in jeans and an ancient Dartmouth hoodie. "What is the behavior you suspected?"

"They were clearly trying to vandalize town property," Officer Ramirez said, shaking his head. "It's not like they were climbing that sign for the view."

My brothers all exchanged a glance. I had been hoping Officer Ramirez hadn't picked up on that part of things—but then I realized it was probably good to have a police force that was capable of putting things like this together.

"But they didn't, right?" Rodney asked carefully, taking a step forward. "They didn't actually do any property damage?" The second he asked this, he quickly looked at my brothers, like he was worried they might actually have damaged the sign. But Mike gave him a quick, subtle head shake.

"No," Officer Ramirez said after a small pause. "But the fact of the matter is, they're not permitted to be here at all. The governor's safety—"

"The governor wouldn't mind if we were here," J.J. said blithely. "He's a fan."

"A *fan?*" It looked like Officer Ramirez was getting to the end of his patience, and I silently tried to communicate to J.J. to dial it back.

"Our mother draws a comic strip," I hurried to explain. "The governor, um, likes it. But I'm sure he wouldn't care—"

"This is about protocol!" Officer Ramirez exploded. "It isn't up to you to decide what the governor would or wouldn't want—"

"Well, we could ask him," J.J. said.

"Oh, *great* idea," Officer Ramirez said sarcastically, his voice rising. He'd clearly had more than enough of all of us tonight. "Why don't we just wake up the *governor* and ask him—"

"We don't have to," J.J. said with a shrug, pointing toward the entrance to Stanwich Woods. "He's right there."

We all turned to look. Sure enough, there was Governor Walker, in a windbreaker and jeans, coming toward us, being half pulled by a large dog who was straining against a reflective orange leash. The dog looked like five different dogs had all been tossed in a blender and this was the result—a yellowish body, a shaggy coat, stand-up ears, and a slightly smushed face. When it caught sight of us, its tail wagged frantically and it strained against the leash even more.

"Evening, Governor," Officer Ramirez said, his tone very *nothing to see here* despite overwhelming evidence to the contrary.

"Evening," Governor Walker responded, heading in our direction. "What's going on?" He stopped a few feet away from where my brothers were still standing in a line.

"Just . . . a minor incident," Officer Ramirez said. "It's fine."

"Are those the Grants?" the governor asked, taking a step closer to us all.

"Hi," Linnie said, giving him a bright smile and a wave.

"Oh," Governor Walker said, blinking a few times, clearly at a loss to understand what was happening here. "Well, it's nice to see you all again so soon. But . . . um . . . what are you doing here?"

"I caught these three," Officer Ramirez said, indicating my brothers, "attempting to deface town property." His voice had already snapped into an official-sounding cadence, like he was polishing up what he was going to say at the press conference, which didn't make me feel any more relaxed about the whole thing.

"Town property?" the governor echoed, still sounding baffled. "But what . . . ?" He looked around, and his eyes landed on the Grant Avenue sign. "You don't mean the sign?" he asked, shaking his head even as he started to smile. "But that's just like in the comic! Too funny."

Officer Ramirez cleared his throat loudly, and the governor seemed to remember himself. "Not that it's a good thing," he said, shaking his head firmly, like he was trying to force himself to be serious. "Not at all. It's . . . bad."

"But there was no actual property damage," Rodney jumped in, speaking to the governor while keeping his eyes on the police officer. "The sign wasn't removed or damaged in any way. Right, Officer?"

"Correct," Officer Ramirez said after a pause. "But the intention—"

"But you can't charge people on an intention," Rodney said, his eyes now on the governor. "Not in an incident this minor." The governor nodded, and I suddenly remembered reading, in one of the articles about him, that he'd been a lawyer before he was a congressman.

"It's true," he said. "If they weren't doing anything, the most they could be charged with is—what, trespassing? And since this is public property, well . . ."

"But they were far too close to your house," Officer Ramirez said, with the air of someone clearly grasping at straws. I couldn't help but wonder if he would have just let my brothers go if the governor of the state hadn't come along. Now that he was there, it was almost like he needed to justify himself. "As you know, if they aren't residents, they're not permitted to be here. And . . ."

"Oh, they aren't a danger to me," the governor said, waving this away, sounding incredulous. "They're the Grants. They're an institution around here."

"So they're all free to go?" Rodney asked, enunciating each of the words he spoke, like he was trying to make sure there was no misunderstanding.

Officer Ramirez just looked at my brothers for a long moment, then nodded. "I would recommend not trying this again."

"Absolutely," Danny chimed in immediately.

"Wouldn't think of it," J.J. added.

"Never," Mike added.

"Then you're free to go," Officer Ramirez said, then looked down at his watch. "And as it's now three a.m., I'd recommend you all go home."

"Sounds like a plan," Danny said, nodding. "Thank you, Officer. Sorry to bother you. . . ." Officer Ramirez nodded and walked back to his car, looking annoyed at all of us. It wasn't until he was nearly back to the patrol car that I finally let myself breathe out again.

"Thank you so much," Rodney said fervently to the governor. "We really appreciate it."

"Oh, it was nothing," Governor Walker said, being pulled a few steps away by his dog, who clearly had had enough with all this standing around and talking we were doing. "He just gets a little overzealous sometimes. It's not personal."

I nodded, keeping my face impassive, feeling that the governor probably didn't need to know that he'd also been called to our house earlier tonight and forced to mediate a family feud.

"Well, he's getting impatient," he said as the dog strained against the leash again. "I'd better go."

"Have a good night," Linnie called to him, and he raised his non-leash-holding hand in a wave.

"Looking forward to reading the last strip tomorrow!" he called, and then a second later, he'd vanished around the corner, the dog pulling him out of sight.

Nobody spoke for another moment, like we were all waiting to make sure things were really okay, that the coast was clear. "Oh my god," Linnie said, when a few seconds more had passed. "You guys almost got in so much trouble." She started to laugh, then clapped her hand over her mouth, her shoulders shaking.

"Stop," Danny said, looking at her with an overly serious face, but he wasn't able to hold it—the sides of his mouth were trembling with the effort of keeping it in a straight line, and I could see he was on the verge of cracking up as well.

"I mean, what would the headline on this even look like?" Linnie asked, turning to me, not even trying to stop from laughing now.

"Sign of Foul Play," I started, and Linnie shook her head. *"No Laughing Matter? Guv to Rescue."*

"I'm sorry I asked," Linnie said, laughing.

"It *would* be attention grabbing," J.J. said. "I mean, I'd read that."

"Were you a part of this whole thing?" Rodney asked me. "I noticed you didn't seem to be lined up with the rest of the perps."

"God no," Danny said, shaking his head. "Charlie's much too sensible for that."

"Oh," Rodney said, tilting his head to the side, like he was trying to figure something out. "When you called me, I wasn't sure . . ."

"I called Charlie to come and help," J.J. explained.

"But why did you call me?" I asked, turning to J.J. Of course I had come when he'd called, but it was just now hitting me that I probably shouldn't have been the first call. My parents, or Rodney, or one of Danny's crazy-expensive Wall Street lawyers would have made a lot more sense.

"Well—because we knew you'd come," Danny said, like this was obvious, and Rodney and Linnie both nodded. "Because—" He looked around, a little helplessly, like he was being asked to explain something basic and obvious, like the presence of gravity or why the sky was blue. "Because you're the person we call."

I looked at my brothers, and Linnie, and Rodney, and felt something within me that had been clenched tight start to loosen a little. So maybe I wasn't just the youngest, the one who didn't get told things. I was also the one who came to help, who tried to make things work, who they called when they were in trouble.

But it also hit me as I looked around at them that this was my family. That even though my parents might be splitting up and it wouldn't be the seven of us together, the five of us would still have each other. That we were still here for each other and that—just maybe—things might be okay. Certainly not right away. But if I had my siblings with me, the fact that we wouldn't all be the same unit as before didn't seem quite so painful as it had. I wouldn't be going through it alone, after all—we'd all be in it together.

Mike glanced back at the patrol car, where the lights were still on. "We should go before we get arrested for loitering or something."

"Good call," Linnie said, glancing over her shoulder as well. She headed toward the Prius. "You guys should get some sleep. *Good Morning America* tomorrow."

"God," Mike, shaking his head. "That'll be fun."

"See you in the morning," Rodney said, heading around to the driver's side.

Linnie hung back a second and looked at me, then pulled me into a quick hug. "Thanks for the call," she said to me. "You okay?" I knew she meant everything that had happened in the family room, and while I wasn't sure *okay* was the word I would use, it was like I could see *okay*, somewhere in the distance, a shore I could hopefully get to someday in the future. I nodded and she smiled. "See you in the morning."

She got into the hybrid, which, a moment later, pulled forward, made a quick U-turn, then headed down the road and disappeared.

"I'll drive with Charlie," Danny said, tossing his keys to J.J., who caught them with one hand. "Seems like since she came all the way out here, it's the least we can do."

"See you at home," I called to them. Mike was already ducking into the passenger seat, and J.J. gave me a nod. "And maybe just go straight home. Don't knock over a liquor store on your way, or anything."

I walked back to my car, Danny falling into step next to me. "Thanks for coming, Chuck," he said, dropping an arm around my shoulders. "And for calling Rodney too. That was great."

"I can't believe you guys almost got arrested," I said, lowering my voice to a near whisper on the last word.

Danny grinned at me. "Wouldn't have been the first time."

"What?"

"A story for another day." He got into the passenger side, and I climbed into the driver's seat and started the car, cranking the heat up—it wasn't until I was back inside that I really felt just how cold it had been while we'd all been standing around, trying to keep the Grant brothers out of jail.

I pulled the car around and made sure to signal, then pause, when I reached the main street—I was all too aware that there was a police officer who could, presumably, see everything I was doing, and one who was probably a little annoyed with all of us at the moment. When I was sure I'd paused long enough, I pulled out onto the empty road and headed toward home.

"So, let's not mention that to Mom and Dad," Danny said, sprawling out in the passenger seat, turning to lean against the door so he could face me.

"If we told Mom, she'd probably just be mad she could no longer use it for the strip."

Save the Date

Danny let out a short laugh. "Well, that's certainly true."

"Was it—" I started, then hesitated. Asking Danny why he'd done something foolish and ill conceived was something I had very little practice in; I was much more used to it with J.J. "Was it just because of what's happening with Mom and Dad?"

Danny let out a breath and gave me a half shrug. "Mostly," he said after a moment. "It's also . . ." He hesitated, and I glanced over at him. "Brooke and I broke up."

"Oh," I said, blinking at him for a moment but then turning back to the road, trying to get my head around this. It had seemed like something had been going on with Brooke and Danny all weekend—but I hadn't realized they'd gotten to that level. Only yesterday, I would have been secretly thrilled about this, but that was yesterday. "I'm sorry."

He shrugged again. "It's for the best. She's a great girl, but I just don't think we were really in the same place."

"When did this happen?" I suddenly remembered Brooke leaning over me, concentrating hard as she applied mascara to my lashes, talking about how coming here, with Danny, hadn't been what she'd expected.

"Middle of the reception," Danny said, with a grimace. "Obviously not when I would have chosen . . . but I don't think Linnie noticed, did she? You didn't, right?"

"No," I said, glancing over at him, but then back at the road. "I mean, I saw Brooke leave, but I think there were enough people around that it wasn't obvious."

"Good."

"Did you guys have a fight?"

"No," he said automatically. "Well . . . kind of. She didn't like the toast I gave." He shook his head.

I remembered Danny's toast with sudden clarity—when he'd said he hoped someday to find something like what Linnie and Rodney had.

What must it have been like for Brooke to sit there and listen to that, knowing it wasn't about her?

"Anyway," Danny said with a yawn, "I guess that started the conversation, but it wasn't like it was a total surprise—things hadn't been working with us for a while, actually."

"But . . ." I shook my head, trying to understand this. "If things weren't working out, why did you bring her to Linnie's wedding?"

"Because she wanted to go," Danny said, like it was the most obvious thing in the world. "She was always bringing up how she wanted to meet everyone, see the house where we grew up. . . . She started talking about it all the time, and I didn't want her to be disappointed. So I told her she could come, and she practically freaked out, she was so happy."

I gripped the steering wheel. I was used to being on Danny's side whenever he talked about his breakups, when he sketched them out in the most general of terms. And I never had any trouble believing that the fault lay with the other people, all of these girlfriends of Danny's who came and went. But now . . . I couldn't stop myself from feeling that it was Danny who was utterly in the wrong here. That if you ask someone to come home with you, to a family wedding, it means something.

"But ultimately, it's for the best," Danny said around a yawn as he looked out the window. "I think we'll be able to stay friends, which is good."

I nodded, fighting not to let what I was feeling show on my face. Because this was *Danny*. But right now, he kind of sounded like an asshole.

"Anyway," Danny said after another huge yawn, "I think we got lucky back there. Good thing the governor showed up when he did."

"I bet that's the first time you've ever said that sentence." It felt like a relief, to go back to talking about something else—something that would let me stop thinking about this other version of my favorite brother, the one I didn't like very much.

Danny laughed. "You're right about that."

I took a breath to say something—what, I wasn't sure—and looked over at my brother to see that he'd closed his eyes and was resting his head against the window. I glanced over at him for just a moment longer, then looked back at the road.

Even though almost no time had passed—it had been ten minutes, maximum, that we'd been in the car—my brother looked different to me now. It was like some of the glow that had always surrounded him had dimmed, like his gloss had rubbed off. He had always been my big brother, who knew everything and could do anything. He was the one who found fortunes under soda bottle caps, the one who had all the answers, the one who wasn't afraid of anything.

But now, in this moment, he no longer seemed perfect, the one who knew everything, the one who was always right. Because he wasn't. He was in the wrong with Brooke—and what's more, I could see it and he couldn't. It was the latest revelation in a night that had been chock-full of them. But it felt like it had tilted the world on its axis a little. Because who was Danny if he wasn't my big brother, the one who could fix anything and do everything? Who was I if I wasn't looking to him for answers?

As I drove in silence, my headlights cutting through the darkness, I realized that maybe it meant we could be closer to equals. Maybe I could actually find out who he was, now that I wasn't blinded by the vision of him that I had been holding on to, the one left over from when I was six and he was the best person in the world.

I pulled into the driveway, and Danny stirred. "We here?" he asked, yawning again, covering his mouth with his hand.

"Yeah," I said, shifting the car into park and glancing over at him, feeling in that moment just how tired I was. "We're home."

SUNDAY

GRANT CENTRAL STATION

CHAPTER 27
Or, About Last Night

---

*I*T WAS VERY EARLY WHEN I CREPT DOWNSTAIRS into the kitchen, dog at my heels. It was barely light outside, but I'd been lying awake for the last hour, so finally I'd just given up and headed downstairs. I'd been sleeping in Linnie and Rodney's room. When Danny and I arrived home, I headed to J.J.'s room just in time to see Jenny slipping inside and closing the door behind her. I wasn't really mad at him about this—given the night we'd all had, if any one of us could have turned it around a little bit, that seemed good to me.

I'd thought about going back down and sleeping on the couch again, but somehow, the thought of sleeping in the room where, not very long ago, everything had fallen apart was more than I could handle at the moment. As I stood on the landing, I turned and saw Linnie and Rodney's room, the door ajar, and realized that since they'd gone back to the Inn, there was a room free for the night. I'd just gotten settled in and turned out the light when the door had creaked open, and I looked over to see Waffles nudging it with his nose. I was about to motion him over, but he was already crossing the room and hopping up onto the foot of the bed, turning around twice, and then curling into a ball, all with an air of detachment, like he would have done this whether or not I happened to be sleeping there. When I'd woken up, though, I'd found he'd moved a lot closer to me during the night, his head resting in the crook of my leg.

I stepped into the darkened kitchen, yawning, and opened the door to let Waffles out, noticing how only after a day, we already had our routine.

"Hey there."

I jumped, startled, and whirled around to see my mother sitting at the kitchen table, in her robe, a mug of coffee in front of her. "Jeez," I said, putting a hand to my racing heart. "You scared me."

"Sorry about that." She nodded toward the coffeepot. "There's coffee if you want it."

Considering I'd gotten three hours of sleep, maximum, I nodded and took down one of the mugs that still remained in the cupboard. I turned it in my hands once. It was a red Stanwich College mug—my dad thought it was the one that he'd gotten thirty years ago, when he went to interview for his assistant professor position, but J.J. had actually broken that one a decade ago and replaced it, and none of us had told him. As this thought flashed through my head, the weight of everything that had happened the night before came crashing down on me again. What was going to happen to this mug when my parents moved into separate houses? What was going to happen to the story behind it?

Halfway through filling up my mug, the dog scratched once at the back door, and I let him in—it looked like his paws were, thankfully, staying clean—and headed to the fridge for milk. It was packed with leftovers from the caterers, plastic wrapped neatly and fit into our fridge almost mathematically, like catering Tetris. I had just finished adding the milk to my mug when my mother said, "I think we should talk."

I looked over at her and realized for the first time that she probably wasn't up before anyone else, just sitting and enjoying her coffee. She was lying in wait for whichever one of us woke up first. "Yeah," I said, coming over to sit across from her. She just looked at me, and suddenly I wondered if she'd found out about the near arrest outside the governor's house. "About last night?" I asked, then realized this could be referring to many things.

"About what happened in the family room," she said. I nodded, but my relief only lasted for a moment as I remembered everything I'd said to her—I'd talked to my parents the way I *never* talked to them, and the memory of it was making my cheeks burn.

She didn't seem mad, though—mostly, in the cool morning light, she just looked tired. I took a breath. "Sorry for yelling like that."

"It's okay," she said, then took a long drink of her coffee. "I'm so sorry you had to find out that way. Your dad and I had a whole plan . . . how we were going to tell you kids."

"The rest of us, you mean."

My mom winced. "Right." She looked at me for a long moment, then gave me a smile. "I'm not surprised, actually. That you took it the hardest. You, my youngest, have always hated change."

"No, I haven't," I said automatically.

"It's not a bad thing," she said, taking another sip of coffee, and I took one of my own as the dog started sniffing around my feet, clearly looking for some crumbs that had gone unnoticed. "Remember when you could no longer fit into your kindergarten dress? And how you cried and cried when you couldn't wear it anymore?"

I nodded, even though I was mostly remembering the stories I'd been told about it, the pictures I'd seen, and the way it had made its way into Cassie Grant's biography—how I wanted to wear the same dress, blue with sailboats on the collar, to basically every day of kindergarten, and how my mother had secretly bought three and rotated them. "Maybe," I finally allowed.

"You don't like to see things end," my mother said, looking at me with a sad smile. "But if you don't . . ." She trailed off.

"What?" I asked, in a voice that came out cracked.

"You miss so much," she said simply. "And sometimes the harder you try to hang on to something, the less you can see that." She tilted her head slightly to the side. "Did I ever tell you I almost kept the strip frozen in time?"

"What?" I just stared at her. I had thought I had known everything about *Grant Central Station*—but I'd never heard this before, not in a single interview or note in one of her collections.

She nodded. "It's what my syndicate wanted me to do. They didn't like the idea of everyone aging, kids eventually moving out of the house, going to college, Waffles dying. . . ." The real Waffles looked up at her when she said this, then plopped down at my feet, resting his head against my arch. It seemed like he was actually learning his name.

"So why didn't you?" I couldn't even get my head around the idea that we wouldn't have grown up in the strip, parallel to life.

"Because," she said, setting down her mug and looking at me, "it would have been cheating, in a way. You don't get to freeze the picture when you want it. It would have been living in the past, and eventually, you just start doing the same jokes over and over again."

I nodded slowly, clearing my throat around the lump that had suddenly formed in it. "So, what are you saying?"

"I'm saying," she said, giving me a smile, "that you may not believe me—or like me—very much right now. But that eventually it is all going to be okay." She reached into her pocket and slid two twenties across to me. "And that you should go pick up some donuts."

Even though I'd drunk most of my coffee before changing into clothes I borrowed from Linnie's side of the closet, I was still not feeling totally awake yet—which was maybe the reason that as I pulled out of the cul-de-sac and onto the main road, it took me a little longer than it should have to recognize the figure who was standing on the side of the road, shivering next to a suitcase and a leather duffel. It was Brooke. I unrolled the passenger-side window and leaned across the car's console to talk to her.

"Hey," I called. She looked up from her phone and blinked at me.

"Charlie? What are you doing out so early?"

"Breakfast run," I said. "Um—what's going on?" I asked, when she just glanced down at her phone again, apparently not in a hurry to explain what she was doing standing in the road with monogrammed luggage.

"I booked an early flight back to California," she said, crossing her arms over her chest. "And I called a car, but apparently the driver's lost. He's about half an hour late at this point. I was just about to cancel it and see if I can get another. I have a flight to catch."

"Are you going out of JFK?" I asked, thinking I could get her the number for the airport shuttle everyone in Stanwich used.

Brooke shook her head, folding her arms. "That little airport had the soonest flight," she said, looking down at her phone again. "But at this point, I'm getting close to missing it."

I hesitated for just a second longer before I leaned over and pushed the passenger-side door open. "I can give you a ride," I said. "Hop in."

Brooke just looked at me for a moment, like she was trying to decide if she should. Then she looked down at her phone, and maybe it was the time—or the utter lostness of her driver—that decided her. But either way, she nodded, and I shifted my car into park, and she loaded her bags into the back.

We drove in silence, and it was like I could feel it like a physical presence between us—the reason she was riding next to me in my car, the reason she'd been on the street with her luggage at all. I wasn't sure if I should ask—pretend not to know—or if I should wait for her to tell me, but the longer we went without speaking, it was like the elephant in the car with us just seemed to get bigger.

Save the Date

Brooke seemed as put together as ever, in dark jeans and a blue and white striped top, her hair hanging sleek and straight. But underneath all that, I could see how tired she looked, how her face looked drawn in the early-morning light. I had just taken a breath when Brooke, still looking out the window, and not at me, finally spoke.

"Danny and I broke up."

I glanced over at her, then back at the road, deciding that this early, with my coffee not fully kicking in, I didn't have it in me to act surprised. "He told me."

Brooke let out a short laugh and looked out the window. "I guess I should have figured."

"I'm really sorry."

"Are you?" she asked, giving me a direct, questioning look that felt like it was going right through me.

"Yeah, I am."

Brooke nodded as she looked out the window, at the scenery flying past. It was early enough that there weren't many people on the street—just the occasional dog walker or stroller-pushing parent. "I think," she finally said, like she was choosing her words carefully, "I knew it wasn't working out. But when he invited me to come this weekend, not only to meet his family, but to his sister's wedding . . . I thought it meant more than it did. Like we were finally going to take the next steps. And I just wanted everything to be perfect. . . ."

I nodded, feeling like I understood this all too well. "Right," I said softly.

"I hope it didn't ruin Linnie's wedding weekend."

"Of course not." The anger toward Danny I'd first felt last night reared up again. "And he shouldn't have done it. He shouldn't have asked you here if he really didn't mean it. It's just not fair to you and he shouldn't . . ." I stopped and took a shaky breath.

"But it was probably easier," Brooke said quietly, and I glanced over at her as I slowed for a yellow. "It was easier just to ask me than to have the hard conversation."

"Still," I said, shaking my head, feeling this new, unfamiliar anger toward my brother filling my chest. "He shouldn't have—"

"He's not a bad person," Brooke interrupted, surprising me. "He's not. He's just a guy," she said with a sad smile. "He's just . . . human."

I nodded, since this was the same revelation I'd come to last night—the one that really shouldn't have been a revelation at all. But in the cold light of the morning, it was becoming clear to me just how wrong I'd been about so much. Danny, Jesse, my parents' marriage, all of these were more complicated than I had believed—or wanted—them to be. Danny was his own, flawed person, as much as I might have wanted to keep him in one box and keep everything simple and neat. He was just more complicated than that. *Life* was more complicated than that.

"You know, when Danny told me that he was one of the Grants from the comic strip, I couldn't believe it."

"But—" I slowed for a stop sign, then sped up again. "I didn't think you read it." Brooke hadn't said anything about the strip the whole weekend, not even when we were at the exhibit at the Pearce.

Brooke let out a soft laugh, then looked back at me. "Are you kidding?" she asked. She shook her head. "I read it all throughout my childhood, and even in college, I'd spend hours online, catching up on strips I'd missed. Reading all about this family who were always there for each other, all together in their perfect house. . . ." Her voice trailed off. "And then to get to meet you all this weekend—not only Danny's family, but the *Grants*."

"Sorry we didn't live up to expectations."

"It's not that," Brooke said, raising her eyebrows at me. "It was better, in a way. I got to see the real thing."

"Are you going to make it?" I asked, as I pulled in front of the tiny stretch of terminals.

She glanced at the dashboard clock. "I think it'll be okay." I shifted the car into park and started to get out and help her, but Brooke waved me off. "I'm fine." She got her bags out, closed the back door, and walked back over to the passenger-side window.

I lowered it, and she leaned forward slightly. "Thank you for the lift," she said. She turned to walk away, but then came back again. "And whatever you decide about college—you need to actually *make* a decision. You'll feel better when you do."

"Hey," I called, just as she was starting to turn away again. I knew I hadn't asked her anything about herself this weekend, or bothered to find out the most basic things, which was now seeming like a huge missed opportunity, since I would probably never see her again. But there was one thing I wanted to know. "Brooke. What kind of doctor are you?"

She just looked at me, then smiled. "I'm a psychologist." She held my eye for a moment longer, then gave me a nod. "Good luck to you, Charlie." She turned and walked through the automatic doors into the airport, not once looking back.

I watched her until she disappeared into the terminal. Then I shifted the car into gear and headed to the donut shop.

CHAPTER 28
Or, If It Weren't for You Meddling Kids . . .

---

*W*HEN I ARRIVED HOME, I TRIED TO PARK in the driveway, but there was a truck parked at the very end, preventing this. So I'd looped around the cul-de-sac and come back around to park on the street—and as I did, I saw a hatchback stopped in front of the house. I got out of the car just as the hatchback pulled away—and Mike was standing there.

"Hey," I called.

Mike looked over at me. "Hey." I looked where the hatchback had gone and realized that it was Jesse who had dropped him off—and for the first time ever, I was happy I hadn't seen him. "Why are you out and about?"

"Donut run," I said, reaching into the backseat and pulling out the four pink bakery boxes.

"I can help," Mike said, reaching for the top two.

"Do you just want first dibs on the tiger tails?"

Mike smiled. "You got me a tiger tail?"

"I got six of them. Whether or not you get one is up to you. So you stayed at Jesse's again last night?"

"Yeah." He reached into his pocket and held his hand out to me. "I think you left these there."

I looked over and saw that he had my earrings in his palm—the ones, I now realized, I'd left on Jesse's coffee table. "Oh," I said, taking them with my free hand. "Right." Mike was looking at me levelly, and I figured there was no point in even pretending anymore. "Was that when you found out? I wasn't sure if you heard Siobhan on the phone. . . ."

Mike just rolled his eyes. "Um, I didn't need to hear Siobhan on the phone. Or to see you guys the night of the rehearsal dinner. I've known forever that you liked Jesse."

I glanced over at him, surprised, and my feet tangled. I quickly steadied the donut boxes. "You—have?"

He shook his head. "I know you, Charlie. I didn't just get here."

"Well, there's nothing going on. Not anymore."

"Good."

"I had a feeling you'd be happy."

"No, it's not that—it's just, I've seen how Jesse is with girls. And you deserve someone who'll treat you better than that."

I blinked, trying to hold back a sudden tide of emotions. "Oh. Um . . . thanks, Mike." I glanced over at him. "And just for the record, you deserve someone *way* better than Corrine."

Mike groaned, even though he was smiling. "Oh, that's long over. Don't worry."

"Good."

We were halfway up to the house when I heard the familiar sound of a bike coming down the street and the *whoosh* then *thwack* of a paper flying through the air and landing on a lawn. I turned around, and sure enough, there was Sarah Stephens on her pink bike, throwing papers as she rode down the street.

"What?" Mike asked, clearly wondering why I'd stopped.

"It's the papergirl," I said, walking a few steps back to the end of the driveway. "We're finally early enough to catch her in the act."

"Of what?"

"She's been refusing to deliver our paper for months now."

"That story line was *real*?"

I turned to Mike, surprised that he'd kept reading it this whole time—that he hadn't really turned his back on us after all.

Mike nodded to the street. "Here she comes."

I turned around, ready to catch Sarah skipping our house. I only wished that my hands weren't full of donuts so that I could record it on my phone and my dad could finally have proof for the *Sentinel*.

But Sarah rode up to our house, reached into her bag, and a newspaper, tucked inside its plastic sleeve, arced over and landed perfectly, faceup, almost directly at my feet. I stood there, feeling beyond confused, and Sarah rolled to a stop, eyebrows raised beneath her pink helmet. "See?" she said, sounding vindicated as she dropped a foot to the ground and pointed at the paper, like I somehow might have missed it. "I told you I've been delivering it."

"But . . ." I just looked at Mike, then at her. I realized Sarah wouldn't have seen me until after she'd thrown the paper, so it wasn't like it was for my benefit. But then what was going on? "You've really been delivering them the whole time?"

Sarah threw her arms up in exasperation. "What have I been telling you?"

"So then what's happening to the paper?" Mike asked.

"I don't know," she said, rolling her eyes. "I don't, like, track its progress. I'm just supposed to drop it off. That's literally my whole job."

"But somehow we're not getting it. So . . ." I suddenly had a thought about what might be happening, but dismissed it immediately. Surely nobody was that petty. Right?

We must have heard the sound at the same time—footsteps approaching, twigs and leaves crunching. It was really loud in the quiet of our early-morning street, and it sounded like someone was coming our way fast. And because I wanted to see if it bore out my theory, I hustled, still carrying the donuts, around to hide behind the Where There's A Will truck that was parked at the end of the driveway, and motioned for Mike and Sarah to come too.

"Come here. Quick!" I hissed.

"What?" Mike asked, even as he ran with the donuts. Sarah hopped off her bike and started to run, and I whisper-yelled, "Take the bike!"

She crouch-ran, holding the bike by the handlebars, then dropped it onto our driveway and knelt down next to us. "What?" she whispered.

"Maybe nothing," I said, straightening up just enough so that I could see above the bed of the truck. "But maybe something."

Sarah rolled her eyes hugely. "You know I have other papers to deliver, right? And they're heavier on Sunday, so they take longer."

I took a breath to reply when we all saw it, and the three of us simultaneously ducked down again. There, hurrying up the street in his robe and slippers, looking like he was trying very hard—and failing—to seem nonchalant, was Don.

"Who's that?" Sarah asked, her voice barely a whisper now as we watched him get closer and closer to our driveway.

"Is that *Don*?"

"Yeah. It's our neighbor," I muttered, keeping my eyes on him, not really able to believe this was what had been happening the whole time. "He's mad about Dad's garden."

"*What?*"

"Shh!" I was fighting every impulse to jump out and yell at Don, but I knew I had to actually see him doing it for it to count or I had no doubt he would just endlessly deny and stonewall later. I held my breath as Don looked around, then bent down, pretending to brush some dirt off his leather slipper before he grabbed our paper, then straightened up and started hustling away with it.

I popped up from behind the truck, and Mike and Sarah did too. "Hey, Don?" He froze, our paper in his hand, looking at me, his eyes wide. "Whatcha got there?"

"Oh." He looked down at our *Stanwich Sentinel*, then up at me, and I could practically hear the gears of his mind frantically working as he tried to come up with an explanation. "Um . . ."

"Better think fast," Mike said.

"You were stealing the Grants' paper," Sarah said, stalking out from behind the truck, arms folded across her chest. "I saw it. And as a paper carrier, it *offends* me."

Don blinked at her. "Who are you?"

"She's our papergirl," I said, coming out to join her. "And we've been blaming her this whole time for not delivering it—but you've been stealing our paper every day? Since *February*?"

Don glanced back at our house, then at me. "You don't have any proof of that," he said weakly.

Sarah and I scoffed in unison, and Mike let out a short laugh. "Come off it, Don," I said. I pointed to the paper. "Are you really going to deny it?"

Don looked at me for another second, then dropped our paper on the ground. "You *don't* have any proof," he said, brushing his hands off. "Perhaps I was just coming to deliver it to you in person. But I will just say that I did not appreciate being in your mother's comic strip."

"You weren't in the—" Mike and I started automatically, but he talked over us.

"And I for one am thrilled you all are finally leaving. Your father's a mediocre gardener at best and didn't deserve half the praise that was heaped on him."

It was Mike who spoke, surprising me. "My father is twice the gardener you'll ever be," he said.

"Yeah, well," Don muttered, turning around and starting to walk away.

Save the Date

"I will be contacting the *Sentinel* about you!" Sarah yelled after him. "Don't think you're getting away with this!"

Don hunched his shoulders, but he didn't turn around as he continued walking back toward his house, and I waited until he was gone before I let out a breath. "Jeez," I said, shaking my head.

"Your lives are really interesting," Sarah said, picking up her bike and wheeling it down to the end of the driveway. "My parents don't have feuds with *anyone*."

"I'm sorry we doubted you," I said to Sarah, thinking of all the times she'd insisted she was delivering our paper and I'd basically called her a liar to her face.

"It's okay," she said stoically, straightening her helmet. She reached down and picked up our Sunday paper—the one that, I realized with a start, contained the very last *Grant Central Station* ever—and held it out to me. "Here."

I took it from her. "Thanks."

She nodded and got back on her bike, already reaching into her bag for the next paper as she started to pick up speed. "See you tomorrow!" she called as she headed down the street, the paper for the house across from ours already sailing through the air.

Mike turned to me. "Can you believe that?"

I smiled. "Never a dull moment." I watched Sarah bike up the street, papers arcing out and landing on stoops and driveways. "Thanks for sticking up for Dad."

"You mess with one Grant, you mess with us all." I smiled at him, and after a second, he gave me a tiny smile in return. We started walking up the driveway together, just as Bill came out of the house.

He was heading to the truck, with two huge canvas bags—WHERE THERE'S A WILL was printed on them—over each shoulder. He was back in his jeans and his fleece, and despite that it was just a little after seven, he looked as cheerful as ever. Halfway down the driveway, he must have seen me, and he smiled.

"Hey," he called to me.

"Hi," I said, walking a few steps closer, trying to balance the donut boxes and the paper. "Morning."

"I'll take these," Mike said, reaching for the donut boxes. He raised an eyebrow at me. "Hungry people are waiting."

"Save me a strawberry frosted!" I yelled after him as he walked up to the house.

"You're up early," Bill said as Mike passed him with a nod. He reached the truck and dropped the canvas bags into the truck bed.

"Donut run."

He smiled. "Got it. Worth getting up for."

"Are you leaving?" I asked. A second later, I realized this was a stupid question—of course he was leaving. The wedding was over, so there wasn't much of a job for the wedding coordinator's assistant. After all, it wasn't like he was going to just keep hanging around our house.

"Afraid so," he said. "My uncle's organizing an anniversary brunch this morning in Hartfield. So he needs me there."

"Oh," I said, nodding. "Right."

"He's going to send some people to take down the tent later," he said. "I told him you have that TV thing this morning, so to maybe wait until after it's done."

"Thanks," I said, giving him a quick smile. "That's great."

"Well," he said, leaning back against the truck, "I know you're staying around here, but if you're ever in Chicago, you should look me up. Or Mystic. Or Albuquerque."

"I actually don't know where I'm going," I said slowly, thinking about what Brooke had said. "I guess I haven't made a final decision." I

Save the Date

391

thought about the folders on my desk again and shook my head. "I don't know. I'm not really that excited about it."

Bill just blinked at me. "Not excited about *college?*" he asked, sounding stunned. "But why not?"

I shrugged. "I don't know," I finally said, since it seemed easier than going into everything that had come out last night—including the revelation that I'd been holding on as tight as I could to something that actually didn't exist any longer.

"I really love it," he said. "But that's me. I only think that you shouldn't discount it before you even get there. I mean, who knows? Maybe college will be the most amazing time of your life. Maybe it'll surprise you by how great it is. Maybe there will be a Journey cover band and all the supermarket cake you can eat."

I laughed. "You think?"

Bill smiled wide. "I have no idea. And that's the really exciting thing."

I nodded, feeling these words hit me somewhere deep inside. He was more right than he knew—after all, Cassie Grant's story had already ended. And starting tomorrow, I'd be moving forward without a shadow version of my life trailing after me. "Thanks," I said quietly, meaning it and hoping he knew that. I looked at the packed truck and realized that he probably didn't have all morning to be standing on our driveway, giving me life advice. "Well, I don't want to keep you too long."

Bill glanced at his watch, then nodded. "I probably should head out."

We just looked at each other for a moment, and I found myself taking him in, all his details—his dark hair, his snub nose, the way even when he wasn't smiling he seemed like he was about to, like it was just waiting in the wings. It was like I was trying to memorize him—in case this was the last time I would ever see him.

"Well," Bill said, after a moment, "it was nice to meet you, Charlie."

I smiled back at him. "You too. Thanks so much for everything."

Bill waved this away. "I was just doing my job." He grinned at me.

MORGAN MATSON

"Though I have a feeling if I do another wedding, it's going to seem tame by comparison."

"I should hope so."

I took a breath to say something—what, I didn't know yet—when he leaned down and kissed me on my cheek, such a soft and sweet gesture that I closed my eyes for just a moment, taking it in, before he straightened up again, a sad smile on his face.

"If you end up in Chicago, let me know," he said, taking a step backward. "We can hang out."

I smiled at him, even though I was feeling with every step he took away from me that I would miss him, this person I hadn't even known three days ago. "I will."

Bill smiled wide and nodded. "It's a plan, then."

I nodded as well. And then, not wanting to watch him drive away, not wanting to see his taillights disappearing down the road, I started toward the house. I looked back at the top of the driveway and saw that he hadn't moved yet, that he was still standing there, a sad smile on his face. I raised one hand in a wave, and he waved back.

And then, feeling like I needed to make myself go, I turned around and headed inside the house.

O KAY!" JILL, THE SEGMENT PRODUCER, CLAPPED her hands together and frowned at the group that had gathered to stand behind the cameramen. "I'm just going to say this once more. If you are going to be here during the filming—and, again, I'd love it if you would just watch it on TV, possibly in another room, or maybe even in your own homes. But if you are going to be here, I'm going to need quiet. All right? Are we understanding each other?"

She looked at the group in the back, some of whom nodded, but most of whom didn't really seem to be paying attention, and I could understand the look of consternation on Jill's face as she turned back around again.

Standing around, in various stages of hungoverness, were the assorted wedding guests who'd wandered down looking for breakfast and decided it might be fun to observe us all being filmed on national television. The Jennys were in robes and slippers and had broken out some champagne in the kitchen, having decided that the best remedy for the wedding guests' hangovers was plentiful mimosas. They were sipping them now, while Priya, who'd gotten dressed in workout clothes but had not, so far as I could tell, actually worked out, was drinking coffee from a *Grant Central Station* mug with a picture of Waffles on it.

General and Mrs. Daniels were among the few who had gotten dressed, and they were standing in the doorway with Liz, who looked more dressed up this morning than she had at the wedding, and was craning her neck, trying to get the first glimpse of Jackson—apparently, she was a *big* fan—who was still in the trailer that was parked on our driveway.

Max was sprawled on one of the armchairs that had been dragged out of the shot, eating a glazed donut and wearing shorts and a hoodie. He seemed much less stressed, now that the secret about his cat was out—he was no longer staring up at the ceiling, worried, and running out of the room every five seconds. He had assured us that Maple Syrup was locked inside my dad's study and wasn't going anywhere, but he'd agreed to stay up in his room with him when the segment was being filmed, just to make sure. And adding to the chaos was my uncle Stu wandering around in his stolen hotel robe, talking to the cameramen and giving unsolicited advice.

I'd been sending as many texts to Siobhan as I could—she was heartbroken her rescheduled flight wouldn't get her here in time—but since Jackson hadn't emerged yet, these were mostly just pictures of his trailer in our driveway.

The last hour had been a blur of the *Good Morning America* crew taking over our house. I hadn't realized that the crew who had come to set up on Friday were just the advance team—there had to be twenty people here now, everyone bustling around at speeds that seemed to get faster the closer we got to airtime. The last twenty minutes or so had been Jill trying in vain to get rid of the spectators and then getting us camera ready, which meant three makeup artists were basically working in a line, going remarkably fast. And considering that none of us had gotten much sleep, I was very grateful for their presence.

We'd all gone through makeup, even my dad, who protested this very loudly and sneezed whenever the powder brush came near him. It seemed like maybe it was good that things had been so busy and frenetic. It had meant that we didn't have the time—or the privacy—to discuss what had happened the night before.

Waffles was sitting on my lap—we'd discovered the hard way that he had a tendency to growl at either the boom mic or the boom mic operator; we still weren't sure which, and as the time of the interview got closer and closer, I found myself smoothing down his ears nervously, which he thankfully didn't seem to mind.

"Okay," Jill said, clapping her hands together as she looked at us. Waffles jumped at the sound, and I ran my hand over his back, trying to calm him down. "Are we set, Grant family? We're going to be live in"—she glanced at her tablet—"four minutes, so I need to make sure we're prepped."

"Where's Jackson?" Liz called from the doorway.

"He's getting ready," Jill called back, her voice tight with tension. "So, like I mentioned, this isn't a super-long segment—we're going to go through the questions and answers we talked about. And don't worry," she added, glancing down at her tablet again, then speaking much faster. "Jackson's a pro, so he'll be guiding this whole thing. Okay? Great." She turned and left the room without waiting for a response, speaking into her walkie as she went.

"So, this will be fun," J.J. said after a pause in which the enormity of what we were about to do seemed to hit us all simultaneously.

"You guys will be great!" Jenny W. called from the doorway, holding up her mimosa glass and winking at J.J.

"Totally," Jenny K. echoed.

"Okay, then, here we go!" Jill said, returning, her voice bright and cheerful, even though she was speaking twice as fast as she had been before. She gestured behind her, and Jackson Goodman came into the room. He was taller than he looked on TV—but he had the same close-cropped black hair and the same blindingly white teeth. For some reason, there were two tissues tucked into either side of his shirt. The Jennys waved at him and Liz pulled out her phone and started snapping pictures. "Jackson's here, and we're just about ready to roll, so is everyone set? Great," Jill said without waiting for an answer. The crew was moving a lot faster now that Jackson had arrived—there seemed to be more of them than there had been just a moment before, everyone hustling around, and a chair was produced from somewhere and placed in the center of the room.

"Hi," Jackson said, giving us all a bright smile. "I'm Jackson Goodman."

We all nodded at him, just staring mutely, and Rodney was the one who recovered fastest. "Right," he said, nodding a few too many times. "Hi."

"It's such an honor to be here in your lovely home," Jackson said, looking around at all of us and holding eye contact with everyone. He seemed to blink less than normal people. I figured maybe it was an anchorperson thing.

"Thanks," I murmured back, now looking a little nervously at the cameras that were pointing our way and getting closer, the camera crew pushing them into place. I didn't watch *Good Morning America* all that often, but I knew who Jackson Goodman was, and he was sitting in our family room, only a few feet away from me. I glanced up at the lights and the boom guy standing just out of frame and felt my palms start to sweat. I quickly wiped them on the dog.

"Jackson, we're going in two," Jill said, glancing at her tablet. She gestured to one of the PAs, who handed her nine copies of the *Stanwich Sentinel*, which she fanned out on the coffee table. "Prompter is ready for you, and these are for the final shot, where we'll film the family reading the paper. Then we'll cut from you to a slide of the strip itself. Sound good?"

"Sounds great," Jackson said. He had the same peppy demeanor that he had on TV, and I wasn't sure if it was just the way he was, or if this would drop the minute he went outside to his temporary trailer.

I'd thought everyone was moving fast before, but it was like things went into hyperspeed, as crew members were practically running as they moved plants, adjusted lights, and hair and makeup people descended on Jackson, calling for "last looks."

"Don't worry," Jackson said, his eyes closed as his face got powdered. "I promise this isn't going to be painful." The makeup artist stepped back, pulled the tissues from his shirt, and hustled away just as Jill shushed the group standing out of the shot.

"And if we could have quiet," Jill said, eyes fixed on her tablet. "We're being patched in live in five . . . four . . ."

I smoothed my hair down quickly, then the dog's ears, and then Jill was pointing at us, and the red light on the center camera flashed on.

"Welcome to 'The Family Behind *Grant Central Station*,'" Jackson said smoothly, straight to camera, and I felt myself staring into the lens, not blinking, thinking of all the people on the other side of it staring back at me. The lines Kevin had read were now scrolling on a little screen next to the center camera. I noticed my mouth suddenly felt very dry. "I'm Jackson Goodman. I'm here in the Connecticut home of the cartoonist Eleanor Grant, where she and her family have lived for more than two decades. We're here to talk about the wildly popular comic strip *Grant Central Station*, which came to an end this morning—and to meet the people behind your favorite cartoon family."

He looked at my mother expectantly, and a moment later, she seemed to realize this. The screen was flashing the line my mother had practiced saying—*Welcome to our home. We're so happy to have you here.* But from the way my mother was squinting, I realized, much too late, that she didn't have her glasses on. "Welcome?" she said, leaning forward to look at the screen, sounding incredibly unsure. "It's . . . happy you're here. Eleanor." She frowned for a moment, then shook her head, and I realized she must have just read her name on the prompter like it was part of what she was supposed to say. "I'm so sorry about that," she said, and I noticed her cheeks were bright pink. "*I'm* Eleanor. You're Jackson."

I heard a muffled, kind of squeaking sound and looked down, thinking it was the dog, only to realize that it was Linnie, pressing her lips together very hard, and I recognized the unmistakable signs of my sister getting the giggles. Rodney had clearly noticed too, as his smile had gotten a little frozen and he was patting Linnie's hand while shooting her looks that clearly said, *Keep it together.*

"Eleanor," Jackson went on, smiling like nothing was amiss, "you've been drawing a version of your family for twenty-five years. What has been your favorite part of the journey?"

Linnie burst into laughter, then clamped her hand over her mouth. "I'm sorry," she said, looking stricken, but not like she was going to stop herself from laughing. "So sorry." She put on a very serious face, one that cracked immediately. "It's just . . . ," she said, then took a big breath, clearly trying to get herself under control. "You said *journey.*"

"I . . . did," Jackson said, still smiling, glancing toward the teleprompter like it might help him.

"It's just that we had a band last night," my dad jumped in.

"So to speak," J.J. said, shaking his head.

"And they were a Journey cover band," my dad went on, which seemed to set Linnie off again. "You know, like the band? Journey?"

"Right," Jackson said, his tone getting a little more steely, even though his expression remained as smiley as ever. I glanced away briefly to see it looked like Jill had dropped her tablet and had both hands in her hair, like she was contemplating tearing it out. "So. Eleanor. You famously based the characters in your comic on your real family. What are the biggest differences between you and the characters in the strip?"

We all turned to Danny, who was supposed to answer here with an anecdote about how Donny was a slob but he wasn't. But Danny was looking down, his shoulders shaking, and I realized that Linnie had just passed on her giggles to him. "Hrm," he said, like he was trying to clear his throat and pull himself together. "I'm different," he said, clearly trying to get a grip, which was manifesting in Danny talking more slowly and about an octave lower than he normally did. It was like he was suddenly imitating Darth Vader, and I could feel laughter start to build somewhere in the back of my throat. "I mean . . ." He cleared his throat again, and I could see that he was fighting against cracking up. "Not—I'm not messy."

"We're all different," Rodney jumped in, looking like he was one of the few people holding it together. I was glad he'd spoken up, but also concerned that the camera had now focused on him, and he was sitting next to Linnie, who currently had a throw pillow pressed against her face, her shoulders shaking.

"Yes," Mike jumped in, and I could see that the corners of his mouth were twitching. "Like, in the strip, my name is Mark. But my name is actually Mike." J.J. burst out laughing, then coughed several times to try to disguise it, which didn't work, even a little bit.

"Moving on," Jackson said, his smile faltering a little as he looked around at us, clearly wondering just where he'd ended up. "*Grant Central Station* did such a wonderful job of showing this family that everyone wanted to be a part of."

"Not everyone," I said, without even thinking about it. I was still on the verge of bursting out laughing on national television, but it was like we were all strapped into a roller coaster that was only going one way. It was like the punchy energy that was currently coming from every member of my family except Rodney was taking me there. I pointed to Mike. "Not him."

"Right," Mike said, raising an eyebrow at me. "Not so much with me. In fact, this weekend is the first time I've been home in over a year."

"Ah," Jackson said, squinting at the monitor like it would have some answers for him. "Yes, there was some . . . controversy."

"I shouldn't have done that interview," Mike said, his smile fading as he looked across to my mom. "I'm sorry I did."

"Well . . ." My mom paused, then smiled at him. "You made some good points. I'm sorry I reacted the way I did." I looked between them, and it was like in this disastrous interview, live on national television, I could see them both lowering their guard, agreeing on détente.

"But what a great family," Jackson said, his smile more like a grimace. "All their adventures . . . Waffles the dog . . ." On my lap, Waffles started growling as he looked at the boom mic operator, and Jackson drew back, alarmed.

"It's always interesting," J.J. said, grinning. "But really not perfect."

"Nope," my mother said, shaking her head, as Linnie, finally pulling herself together, raised her head from the pillow and smoothed her hair back.

"I mean, they're getting a divorce," I said, pointing to my parents, who looked at me with alarm, which set Linnie off again, and she pressed her face back into the pillow, her shoulders shaking.

"And just last night," J.J. went on, "we almost got arrested!"

"You *what?*" my parents asked in unison, sounding horrified, which was enough to make me burst out laughing.

"Not me," I said, trying to control myself and failing. "Just the guys."

"Well, that's not going to make the funny pages," Jackson said, clearly grasping at straws. Jill, looking like she was on the verge of an aneurysm, was making the *wrap it up* motion with her hand.

"Could you imagine?" Linnie asked, still giggling. "It would be like *Grant Central Station* goes dark. Like, Cassie joins a biker gang and Waffles attacks the mailman."

"A.J. gets in too deep on the ponies," J.J. added, laughing, "and Donny starts insider trading."

I covered my mouth, but I knew I wasn't going to be able to stop laughing, and I couldn't help but notice how nice it felt—not trying to make everything perfect. Not trying to fit into some preconceived image. All the members of the Grant family were finally—in front of the entire country—being real.

"Well, I think that's all the time we have here," Jackson said, his tone now very annoyed and no longer trying to hide it. "So—"

"Wait," I said, looking down at Waffles. "The dog! Someone adopt him!"

"Yes!" J.J. yelled, picking him up from my lap and holding him up, like this was the beginning of *The Lion King*. "This isn't even our dog! We don't have a dog! It's all a lie!"

Just then the kitchen door slammed. "Whoops," I heard my uncle Stu say. A second later, the alarm started going off.

"Gah!" The sound guys ripped off their headphones, and the boom operator fumbled the boom mic, which swung down into the shot. Waffles, maybe seeing his chance, leaped straight up in the air after it and landed on Jackson, who shrieked.

We were all laughing hysterically at this point, the alarm was wailing, and Waffles was barking ferociously at the boom mic. "*The final strip of Grant Central Station is in newspapers today,*" Jackson screamed to be heard over the alarm, as the crew ran around frantically behind the cameras, clearly trying to get it to shut off. "*Bob?*" he yelled, throwing it back to the anchor in New York.

"And we're out," Jill yelled, sounding disgusted. But I didn't care about that—or about the fact that Jackson Goodman was storming out of our family room, or that the alarm was still going off. I was still laughing, with little hiccups punctuating each one, and Rodney was wiping tears from the corners of his eyes. I met Mike's eye, which set us off again, and like he wanted to join in, Waffles threw back his head and started to howl.

* * *

"So, how soon do you think we'll be asked back?" my mother said, raising her eyebrows over her mug of coffee. We'd all pulled ourselves together, somewhat. Our performance had caused a *lot* of commentary from the people who'd been watching it—and in the middle of Liz lecturing us about how we'd disrespected Jackson Goodman, my phone had buzzed with a text.

Siobhan

OH MY GOD CHARLIE
WHAT THE FORK WAS THAT?
FORK
What the duck
DUCK!!
Anyway—what happened?
It was the best/worst/best thing I've ever seen
Did you get Jackson's autograph for me??

We'd all ended up in the kitchen. The wedding guests were spread out in the dining room and family room, drinking coffee and eating donuts and offering theories as to why the Grant family had suddenly decided to collectively go off the rails on national television. Occasionally, someone would wander into the kitchen for more coffee—or mimosas, in the Jennys' case—but for the moment, it was just the seven of us and Rodney.

"I bet not anytime soon," Mike said, raising his eyebrows. "Though I hope we can get a copy of it for posterity."

"No need," J.J. said, shaking his head. "You know that's going to be all over the Internet."

"Oh, good," Rodney said with a sigh. "Just what I wanted."

"Wait," Linnie said, looking around. "Did they take the papers with them? We never got to see the last strip."

Save the Date

403

"I can show it to you," my mother said, gesturing out toward the office. "I have the original, you know."

"I kind of want to see it in the actual paper," Mike said, and Danny nodded too. I felt the same way—we'd waited so long for this, it didn't seem right to see the print my mom would have in her office, uninked, with penciled-in numbers for the colorist. I wanted to see out the Grants' story properly—in the comic section of our paper, the way I'd been reading it my whole life.

"We got the paper," I said, and Mike nodded.

"We finally got one?" my dad asked, eyebrows flying up.

I nodded. "We were falsely accusing Sarah Stephens." I looked around, finally spotting it on the kitchen counter under an empty donut box and shaking it out of its plastic wrapper. "Don's been stealing it this whole time."

"Don?"

"Don," Mike confirmed.

"Really?" my mother asked, not sounding upset by this, but intrigued.

I gave her a look. "You're upset you can't write about this, aren't you?"

"Well . . . ," my mother said and then laughed. "I mean . . . it just would have been such a nice ending to the Sophie plotline." She shrugged. "Ah well."

Silence fell, and we all looked at the paper sitting on the counter. There, folded inside, was the way my mom had chosen to end the Grants' story.

"What do you think?" my mom asked as she picked up the paper, unfolded it, and turned to the comic section. "Should we do this?" She looked at each of us in turn, and I nodded.

My mom held it, and the seven of us crowded around her. I knew we could have taken turns, or passed it around, but nobody did. Without having to talk about it, I could tell that we all wanted to experience this moment together.

My dad was on one side, next to Mike. J.J. was next to him, with Danny on his other side, and I was in between Danny and Linnie, with Rodney holding down the other end and my mom in the center. I looked around at all of them for a moment. I wasn't sure when we would be here like this again—all of us, together, in the same house. But maybe to be here with them, in this moment, was enough.

"Ready?" my mom asked. We all nodded. And then she took a breath and opened the comics to the place that *Grant Central Station* had always occupied, the top left-hand corner. She held the paper open so we could all see.

And then we leaned forward to read it, together.

GRANT CENTRAL STATION

ONCE UPON A TIME IN CONNECTICUT...

THERE WAS A FAMILY.

AND OVER THE YEARS, THEY HAD THEIR UPS AND DOWNS. DISASTERS...

TRIUMPHS...

FIGHTS...

RECONCILIATIONS ...

I'M SO SORRY.

BUT ALTHOUGH BIG CHANGES WERE AHEAD,

COLLEGE

FOR SALE

THEY ALL KNEW THAT WHEREVER LIFE TOOK THEM—AND WHATEVER HAPPENED...

THEY WOULD ALWAYS BE A FAMILY.

SEPTEMBER

CHAPTER 30
Or, Once Upon a Time
in Connecticut

———————————

*A*RE YOU SURE YOU HAVE EVERYTHING?" MY
dad asked for what had to be the millionth time. "You didn't
forget anything?"

"I'm sure," I said, but even so, I glanced into the back of the car just
to double-check, though all I could see were suitcases and boxes. It was
absolutely packed to the gills—which made sense, since the car was
packed with all the stuff that not one but two people would need for a
year at college.

"I don't like the idea of you driving halfway across the country all by
yourself," my mother said, shaking her head, and Mike straightened up
from where he'd been arranging boxes in the backseat.

"Hey," he said, raising an eyebrow. "What about me?"

I looked over at Mike and smiled. We were standing in the driveway
of my dad's new town house. He'd found it at the very beginning of
May and was totally moved in by the first week in June, the weekend
before the new owners took over.

It had been really hard saying good-bye to our house—seeing all the
furniture vanish from the rooms, the pictures from the walls. But we'd all

been there to clear it out together, which had helped a lot. Even Danny had come back from California, as opposed to just sending someone to do it for him, like J.J. and Rodney had been betting he would. But it had been all of us saying good-bye to the house, sitting on the floor of the empty family room, eating pizza off paper plates, since we no longer had furniture or dishes. Linnie and Rodney had even brought Waffles with them. They'd adopted him after the *GMA* interview—they both felt guilty that our interview had damaged his chances of anyone else taking him. And though they'd tried to change his name, he steadfastly refused to answer to anything other than Waffles.

My dad's place was much smaller than our house had been, but there were still enough bedrooms for all of us to be there together, if you counted the pullout couch he'd gotten for the basement. He'd already gotten started on his new garden and had shown me the plans for it. I didn't mind being there, not the way I'd thought I would. It didn't feel like home—at all—but there was a piece of me that figured maybe it shouldn't. We were all still figuring out what this new family arrangement of ours looked like, so maybe nothing would feel like home until we got used to the fact that things had changed, that they were different now.

"He has a point, El," my dad said, smiling at my mom. "She's not actually going to be driving alone. Our capable youngest son will be with her."

"Oh, you know what I mean," my mom said, shaking her head at him.

"And I drove myself last year," Mike said, sounding exasperated—but not actually exasperated, more like he was enjoying being fake exasperated around my mom.

"But you're a much better driver than Charlie," my mom said to him in a fake whisper.

"Hey!" I said, and my mom and Mike both laughed. I still wasn't quite used to it—Mike and my mom, getting along. They weren't back to where they'd been before, but the incremental progress they'd been making nonetheless felt major.

I dropped my purse onto the driver's seat and straightened up. It was a gorgeous morning—the sun shining down onto the driveway, the sound of birdsong in the trees, the leaves not even beginning to think about turning yet. "You sure you don't miss this?" I asked my mom as I gestured around. "I mean, trees . . . birds . . . nature?"

"I have nature," my mom said, shaking her head at me. "In case you've forgotten, I live near a gigantic park. And we have all three of those things."

I caught my dad's eye, and he shook his head. *Doesn't count,* he mouthed to me, and I smiled.

My mom, to our collective surprise, had moved to New York City and had gotten an apartment that absolutely did not have enough bedrooms for all of us. But Danny was already looking into hotels and apartment-sharing sites so that when we were all in town again, we could stay there, in the city, together. She hadn't let herself enjoy retirement very long—when I was staying with her the week before, she'd told me one morning, at what was quickly becoming my favorite diner on the Upper West Side, that she was playing around with a new comic strip, about a woman starting over after a divorce. But she'd promised me—and then all of us—that the protagonist of her new strip would be fictional. And that she would have no children.

My things that weren't coming with me to college had been split between my parents' places—but due to her lack of space, more of it had ended up at my dad's, and that's why Mike and I were both leaving from here. Well, that and the fact that we could park a car here, and it was the car we'd be sharing at school.

I'd decided, after everything, to go to Northwestern, where I would get to study journalism in one of the best schools in the country. It was a three-hour plane ride from the East Coast, which seemed like the right amount of time and distance. And with my parents in two different places and my siblings all over the country, I liked the idea of being closer to at least one brother. And since it was the brother I actually knew the least, I figured we could use some time to fix that. Siobhan was thrilled, since we'd only be four hours away from each other. She'd already mapped out the route from Ann Arbor to Evanston and was planning a road trip to come to me in just a few weeks.

Mike and I didn't have to be on campus until next week, so we were using the drive to Chicago to go on what J.J. had dubbed the Sibling Tour. We weren't taking the direct path there—tonight we were heading up to visit Linnie and Rodney (and Waffles) in Boston, and then we were meeting J.J. in Pittsburgh. We were going to a Pirates game, and just this morning, he'd e-mailed to tell me that he'd paid off the scoreboard programmer so that at the game, it would read GOOD LUCK AT COLLEGE, CHARLIE. Then, a few minutes later, he wrote me again and told me to delete all our correspondence about this so he could disavow any knowledge of it when people started asking questions.

And then Danny was going to meet us in Chicago, which Mike and I were both relieved about, since we didn't have time to drive to California and then back again. Danny seemed basically the same—he was dating someone new, and he assured us all that she was great. But things had shifted between us, subtly, over the summer. I would call him out on things, more often than not, when I disagreed with him or what he was doing. And to my surprise, he handled it well, even occasionally taking my advice. It felt as though we were more like equals now and, in a weird way, getting to know each other for the first time.

But I hadn't seen him in a month and was looking forward to seeing him in Chicago, as the best way to cap off the sibling tour. I was a little bit sad that we were doing it this way, as opposed to all of us being in the same house, together. But this was what life looked like now, and maybe that was okay.

I did miss us—I missed all seven (eight with Rodney) of us in the same house, with all our systems and traditions and jokes firmly in place. But I was trying to accept that this was just a new thing. Just like Linnie and Rodney had formed their own family, we were all learning what this new version of us would look like. And I knew it was going to be hard—especially at Thanksgiving and Christmas. But I had a feeling—at least, I hoped—that we would find our way through it. It wouldn't be *Grant Central Station* anymore, with four panels and reassuring humor, things always working out for the best in a tidy way. But maybe that was actually a good thing.

My phone buzzed in my back pocket, and I pulled it out and looked at it.

Bill
How's the trip going? Hit the road yet?

I smiled at that, then put my phone back in my pocket, planning to respond when my family wouldn't be watching. It hadn't played a part in my decision making, but the fact that Bill would only be twenty minutes away was definitely an added bonus. To my surprise, we'd stayed in contact after the wedding, and even though I hadn't seen him, we'd been talking—either texting or e-mailing or having hours-long phone calls—all summer. I wasn't sure what, if anything, was going to happen with us. I was hoping something might. But at the very least, I was glad to have a friend in the Chicago area.

"So," Mike said, looking down at his phone, then back at me. "We should probably hit the road. We told Linnie and Rodney we'd be there before dinner."

I nodded, realizing that he was right. The car was packed and I had the directions programmed into my phone—now the only thing to do was go.

"We'll see you at homecoming?" Mike asked my dad as they hugged, and my dad patted him on the shoulder. "And you said you were coming at the end of October?" he asked my mom.

I tried to smile as my mom nodded, but this—the fact that there wasn't just one plan anymore, one way where I would get to see both my parents at the same time—I definitely wasn't used to yet. Bill had told me that it would just take time, and I was trying to believe him.

"Call me when you guys get to Linnie's," my mom said, hugging Mike. "And drive safe," she called after him. He nodded as he headed for the passenger seat, and I realized that he was giving me a moment to do my good-byes with my parents alone.

I turned to them and immediately felt a lump rise in my throat. I tried to tell myself I was being ridiculous, that people left for college all the time, and I'd be seeing my dad in a few weeks.

"Learn lots of stuff," my dad said, and I noticed his voice sounded a little hoarse. "But also remember to have a good time."

"But not too good a time," my mother cautioned. "Don't stop going to classes like that semester J.J. decided he was on strike."

"I don't think you have to worry about that," I assured them. My dad gave me a smile that didn't quite meet his eyes, then pulled me into a hug.

"Proud of you, kiddo," he whispered to me, and I brushed away a tear that had fallen as I stepped away.

"Call me at least once a week," my mother said as I hugged her, trying for stern but not really pulling it off. "Have fun," she said to me as she stepped away, giving my hand a squeeze. "Have the most amazing adventure."

I nodded, brushing my hand over my face as I tried to pull myself together. "I'll do my best," I said, and my dad smiled. "And . . ." I took a breath, not even knowing how to put this into words. How was it that you only fully realized what you had when it was gone? And I knew there would be new friends, new experiences, maybe even amazing adventures ahead of me. But I felt like I needed, for just a moment, to appreciate what I was—what we all were—leaving behind. "Thank you, guys. For everything. For . . ." I shook my head, not able to find the words for what we'd all had together. "Thanks," I finally finished, and my parents both nodded—and it looked like they understood what I'd been trying to say.

I smiled at them both, then made myself turn and walk toward the car. I got into the driver's seat, and Mike looked over at me. "You okay?"

I nodded, taking a deep breath. "I am." I started the car and was about to drive forward, when I turned around and looked through the back window to see my parents standing there, closer than I would have expected, watching us go. I lifted my hand and waved, and they waved back.

Then I turned around and looked at what was in front of me. I took a deep breath, shifted the car out of park, and drove forward.

It's bonus content time!

When my editor and I talked about doing a special edition, I jumped at the chance (startling my dog, Murphy, in the process). And since *Save the Date* is set during a wedding, I thought it might be fun to have four pieces of bonus content—Something Old, Something New, Something Borrowed, and Something Blue(s). I had a blast putting these together, and I hope you enjoy them!

Xoxo,
Morgan

Something Old

This is a prequel of sorts—to get a peek into the Grant family two years before *Save the Date*. And since all the events of *Save the Date* revolve around Linnie and Rodney's wedding . . . why not look at how this whole story started? (Also, this was basically an excuse to write a Thanksgiving story. I've always wanted to write a Thanksgiving book but could never figure out what the plot would be. So this might be as close as I get!☺)

TURKEY & ANARCHY

WHEN RODNEY'S CAR PULLED INTO THE driveway, I hurried down to meet him. I'd been watching from the front window, and as soon as he'd signaled, I'd grabbed my coat and run out. But I'd only gotten a few feet before I started shivering—it was thirty degrees out and blustery, and the forecast had been calling for snow all day, despite the fact it had been almost a decade since we'd had snow on Thanksgiving.

"You're here," I said, hurrying up to his hybrid, which was covered with bumper stickers—*Nature Can't Be Restocked*; *Save the Whales*; *Save the Spotted Owl*; *Massachusetts Nature Society*. Rodney had endured one internship in a corporate law firm, and that had been enough for him to switch his focus to environmental law and never look back. "Finally!"

"Sorry," Rodney said as he got out of his car, adjusting his glasses.

"I didn't factor in all the holiday traffic." Linnie hadn't had classes this week at all—leading my dad to ask her if she was actually getting a master's in vacation—so she'd been here since Monday. Rodney, though, had had his constitutional law class Wednesday night and couldn't drive down from Boston until today.

Rodney pulled his duffel out of the back of the car and I looked at him closely, wondering if we were still on track. "Did you bring it?"

Rodney smiled and reached into his jacket pocket, and pulled out a small velvet-covered box. I held my breath as he flipped the top up and I found myself staring at an absolutely beautiful ring—a small diamond with two opals on either side of it. "Rodney," I said, and somehow just looking at the ring was enough to make me feel like I was going to cry. "It's so beautiful."

"I hope she likes it," he said, closing the ring box and carefully putting it into his jacket, then immediately patting that pocket, like he was worried something might have happened to it in the last three seconds. "I hope she says yes," he said, his eyes growing wide. "What if she doesn't? Charlie, what if I propose in front of everyone at dinner and she says *no?*"

"She's not going to say no," I said as we both started up the driveway together toward the house. "And you know Thanksgiving is her favorite holiday. Proposing to her today was *your* idea."

"I know," Rodney said, and even though the wind had started to pick up again, it looked like he had started to sweat. "But . . . I just want everything to go perfectly. You only have one chance to propose to the love of your life, you know."

"It'll go great," I assured him.

Rodney reached for the kitchen door, then took a step back and turned to me. "You didn't tell anyone, did you?"

I shook my head and held up my hand. "Grant family honor." Rodney had told only me that he was planning on proposing to Linnie, since he'd needed to enlist my help. I'd been the one to sneakily figure out Linnie's ring size for him, and try to get out of her what kind of ring she might want by pretending to take online quizzes over the phone with her that I made up on the spot—things like *What Kind of Precious Metal Are You?* and *Choose Your Favorite* Friends *Character and We'll Tell You Your Favorite Gemstone!* He'd made me promise not to tell anyone—and he wasn't telling anyone else because, as a group, we were terrible at keeping secrets.

"Great," Rodney said as he pulled the kitchen door open, then stopped short in the doorway, his jaw falling open.

"Yeah," I said, maneuvering around him. "Things have gotten a little crazy around here."

There were pots bubbling on all four of the burners, and a delicious turkey smell was already starting to fill the kitchen. We weren't going to be eating until three, but things were already in high gear, and the kitchen was full of people. My mom was manning the stove, while J.J. was next to the oven, peering through the closed door. Mike was standing by the sink, peeling potatoes at a glacial pace, like he was trying to set a record for just how slowly it could be done. Linnie and my dad were at the island, kneading the dough for the rolls, and Danny was sitting on the kitchen counter, talking on the phone.

"Oh, also," I said quickly, remembering as I turned back to Rodney, "J.J. brought Anarchy home with him."

"What else is new?"

"No, *actually*—"

"Rodney!" My dad spotted us in the kitchen, and Linnie looked up, smiling wide when she saw her boyfriend. "Happy Thanksgiving! Come give us some help. It's all hands on deck."

"Then what is J.J. doing?" Mike asked as he peeled his potato a millimeter at a time.

"I'm the turkey checker," J.J. said, drawing himself up to his full height. "Hey, Rodney. How was the drive?"

"Hey," Linnie said, hurrying around from behind the kitchen island and hugging him. "Sorry about my hands—they're all sticky."

"You're perfect," Rodney said, giving her a quick kiss.

"Was the traffic bad, Rodney?" my mother asked as she stirred the cranberry sauce. I wandered over, hoping for a taste, and she turned me around and pushed me toward the sink. "Wash your hands first." But before I could do this, a petite girl around J.J.'s age, with long blond hair and blunt bangs, swept into the kitchen.

"I'm back," she said, smiling, as she headed over to J.J. "I had to try and talk to my parents before their ridiculous football game started." She put "football" in air quotes for some reason.

"Rodney, this is Anarchy," J.J. said, gesturing to her as Rodney's eyes widened.

"*Oh,*" he said, glancing over at me, like he finally got what I'd been trying to tell him. "Hi. Are you . . ." He looked on, confused, as J.J. put his arm around her waist. "I thought J.J. was dating someone named Alyssa."

"That's my given name," Anarchy said scornfully as she ran her fingers through J.J.'s hair. "Anarchy is my chosen name. Which makes it that much more significant." I caught Danny's eye and then looked away fast, since I had a feeling I was about to burst out laughing.

"What have you got against football?" Danny asked, setting his phone down and raising an eyebrow.

"Um, just that it goes against my entire belief system? Like I'm going to support a violent game in which the corpse of a beautiful pig is manhandled."

"Anarchy is a vegan," J.J. said proudly.

"We both are," she said, running her hands through his hair again. Everyone else in the kitchen burst out laughing. Of all of us, J.J. loved meat the most. For a while in college, he'd worn a sweatshirt that just said BACON! on it with a drawing of two strips sizzling in a pan. There wasn't even a clever pun—J.J. just wanted to wear it to express his love for it.

"I *am*," J.J. said, widening his eyes at us.

"Oh," I said, stopping laughing. "Is this . . . recent?"

"No," Anarchy said, smiling at him. "It was one of the first things we connected over. How we love and respect all living things."

I raised an eyebrow at my brother, trying to square this with last month, when he'd come home and we'd immediately all gone out for barbecue.

"In fact," she said, frowning at the oven. "If there is going to be bird murder going on in here, I don't think I can be a part of it."

"The turkey's already dead," Linnie pointed out.

"Why don't you go into the family room," J.J. suggested, "and I'll be there in just a moment." Anarchy glared at the oven, then stalked out, and J.J. turned to us. "Guys!" he said, keeping his voice low. "Be cool. Anarchy thinks I'm vegan too."

"Yeah, we picked up on that," Danny said.

"But you're not," Mike said. "Right?"

"Scoff," said J.J. "Are you kidding? I go directly from our dates to Arby's. But she doesn't know that, okay?" Without waiting for a response, he pulled open the oven door, took a big sniff of the turkey aroma, then hurried into the family room. A second later, he reappeared. "Oh, mom," he said. "Anarchy doesn't approve of any industry that conducts itself by murdering innocent trees."

"Meaning?" Linnie asked.

"Meaning the comic strip. So if you wouldn't mind just saying that you transitioned to an all-digital format? Thanks!" J.J. hurried out of the room again, and I shot my mother a look.

"You're totally putting this in the strip, aren't you?"

"That's what you get for pretending to be a vegan," my mom said, and my dad laughed. "Lin," she said, as a timer started beeping, "would you bring in the pies from the garage? I'm worried it's getting too cold for them out there."

"Sure," Linnie said. She turned to Rodney. "Can I borrow your coat, sweetheart? It's chilly out there."

Rodney started to take it off, then froze. "No," he said, pulling the jacket around him more tightly. "I'm . . . cold."

"But you're inside," Linnie pointed out.

"But I need it," Rodney said. "I don't . . . want to give it to you. Or anyone." He was looking at me a little desperately, and a moment later, I remembered the ring in the jacket pocket.

"Here," I said, picking up my jacket that I'd hung on the mudroom hook. "Use mine."

"Thanks," Linnie said. She shot Rodney a questioning look, then headed out the kitchen door.

The second she was gone, Rodney peeled off his jacket. "I'm just going to go put this away," he said, holding his coat tightly with both hands. "Somewhere . . . safe." He hurried out of the kitchen, and Danny turned to me.

"He okay?"

"He's fine," I said quickly. "Just . . . tired from his drive." I looked around the kitchen. "So what can I do?"

Three hours later, the turkey was done, the potatoes were mashed (Danny had finally gotten fed up with Mike and taken over peeling them himself, which I would bet had secretly been Mike's plan all along), the rolls were cooked, and we were just about ready to sit down to dinner.

"Charlie, put this on the table, would you?" my mom asked as she handed me the cranberry sauce. I was en route to the table in the dining room—where we almost never ate except for holidays—when I heard my name shout-whispered from the front hall.

I headed out and saw Rodney pacing in front of the door. He was wearing a perfectly pressed dress shirt, complete with the cuff links his parents gave him as a graduation gift. "You look nice."

"Thanks," Rodney said, adjusting his cuffs. "Linnie gave me this shirt for my birthday. She always likes when I wear it." He took a shaky breath. "So, I think that I'm going to do it when we all go around and say what we're thankful for. I'm going to say I'm thankful for her, and for all the years we've had together, and then I'll tell her that I want to spend the rest of my life with her."

"Sounds perfect."

"Charlie?" my mom called, just as Linnie yelled, "Rodney?"

"Coming!" we both yelled simultaneously. I turned away from Rodney, toward the door, just as Rodney took a step in my direction— and we crashed into each other, the cranberry sauce sloshing out of the bowl I was carrying and across the front of Rodney's white shirt.

"Oh no," I gasped. "Oh no!"

"Aaagh," Rodney said, looking down at himself in horror, as the stain spread across the front of his shirt.

"Guys, come on," J.J. said, coming around the corner. "What's the hold up?" He stopped in his tracks when he saw Rodney and looked between the two of us. "Did you two have a duel or something?"

"I just . . . have to change," Rodney said. "I only have one ironed shirt, but . . ."

"I can lend you a shirt," J.J. said, heading toward the front stairs and gesturing for Rodney to follow him. "I have the perfect thing for you."

"Something nice," I called after them. "It's . . . really important to Rodney that he look good today."

"Why?" J.J. asked.

"Um . . . ," Rodney said after a very long pause in which we both looked at each other, neither one of us coming up with an answer. "I'm . . . really vain these days."

"At least you're owning it," J.J. said, clapping him on the shoulder, then lifting up his hand and, seeing there was cranberry sauce on it, wiping the sauce back onto Rodney's shirt, then heading up the stairs.

"Charlie?" my mom called again, sounding annoyed this time. "We're waiting!"

"Coming!" I called back as I hustled—but carefully this time—into the dining room with what was left of the cranberry sauce.

"Who needs more sweet potatoes?" Linnie asked from across the table. She was sitting next to Rodney, who had barely spoken for most of the meal, or eaten much either—every time I looked over at him, he was either looking down at his plate, lips moving like he was rehearsing what he was going to say, or glaring at J.J. But that might have been because of what he was wearing.

Rodney had finally come back downstairs, wearing J.J.'s BACON! sweatshirt and looking miserable. "I just . . . ," he said as he came into the dining room. "I can't believe you didn't have anything else you could lend me."

"Sorry, bud," J.J. said with a shrug as he shook his head. "That's all there was."

I looked at J.J., who was sitting next to me, and he shook his head. "That was not all there was," he whispered. "But Alyssa—I mean, Anarchy—saw it in my closet and started asking questions, and I thought it would be best to get rid of it ASAP."

"I think maybe . . . ," I said as I glanced at Rodney, who looked deeply unhappy in his illustrated bacon shirt, "Rodney wanted to be a little more . . . dressed up today?"

"Why?" J.J. asked with a shrug. "It's just Thanksgiving."

"Sweet potatoes?" Linnie asked now, and I reached out for them.

"Me," I said, moving some turkey over on my plate to make room.

"Me too," J.J. said as he watched them come around the table.

"Jameison," Anarchy said, shaking her head. "They have milk in them. Remember?"

"Oh. Right." I looked down at J.J.'s plate, which looked like Anarchy's plate—some salad and a few green beans and a little of the cranberry sauce. It was the saddest Thanksgiving plate I'd ever seen, and that included the year Siobhan and her dads came over and every single thing they brought was maize or blue colored.

I served myself some sweet potatoes and J.J. grumbled. "This is the worst," he hissed at me. "I look forward to Thanksgiving all year! Do you know how long it's been since I've had meat?"

"I don't know, like an hour?" I asked. "You're not actually a vegan," I reminded him in a whisper.

"How's the turkey?" he whispered, looking longingly at my plate.

"Okay," my mom said, tapping her wineglass with her knife, "I think we should go around and say what we're all thankful for. Who wants to start?"

"Me," Rodney said, immediately leaping to his feet. He cleared his throat. "I just wanted to say, this year, what I'm most thankful for. And it's—"

"Jameison!" Anarchy gasped, and I looked over to see that my brother's mouth was full and the turkey had vanished off my plate. "Did you just—eat—that turkey?"

J.J. swallowed hard, then nodded. "I did," he said, and Anarchy's jaw dropped. "And in the spirit of Thanksgiving, I need to confess something to you. I'm not actually a vegan."

"*What?*"

"Guys," Rodney said, a pained look on his face. "I'm kind of . . . trying to do something here."

"Meat is delicious!" J.J. said, starting to pull dishes toward him and fill up his plate. "Why would you deny yourself that?"

"This is over," she said, throwing down her napkin. "We're through! You clearly don't care about the same things I do."

"Guys!" I said, and both of them turned to me. "I think Rodney's trying to speak."

"Exactly," Danny said, widening his eyes at me.

"Just one more thing," J.J. said, and Danny shot me a *What did you expect?* look. "I can't believe you're breaking up with me, just like that, on Thanksgiving, in front of my whole family!"

"I was in the middle of what I'm thankful for!" Rodney said, raising his voice. "Okay," he said, taking a big breath. "I want to say that I'm grateful for Linnea. Lin, ever since we met, you've been—"

"You know what? I want to say some things I'm *not* thankful for," Anarchy said, talking over Rodney. "Like . . . liars. And people who lie. And phonies, and carnivores."

"Yeah? Well, I'm not thankful for lots of stuff too," J.J. snapped. "Like people who are self-righteous. And judgmental. And—"

"Hey!" Rodney yelled. "Can you keep it down? I'm trying to propose here!" The words just seemed to hang in the air for a moment, like we were looking at the panels in one of my mother's comic strips.

"You—are?" Linnie asked, her voice trembling. The whole room was suddenly very quiet.

"I am," Rodney said, and pulled the ring box out of his pocket, and lifted the top. "I love you so much. Will you—"

"Yes!" Linnie yelled as she threw herself into Rodney's arms.

And then everyone was standing up and running over to Linnie and Rodney, to congratulate them and hug them and look at the ring and ooh and ahh over it. My dad went in search of a bottle of champagne, and my mom—who'd burst into tears when she saw Linnie wearing the ring—went in search of more tissues.

"Sorry about that," I said to Rodney, who hadn't stopped smiling ever since Linnie had said yes. "I know that wasn't the way you'd planned it."

"It was wonderful," Rodney said, then his glance drifted over to

Anarchy, who was still glowering at the other side of the table. "You know, for the most part."

"I'm so happy for you guys," I said, letting my sister pull me into a hug. "And don't worry," I said, giving Linnie's hand a squeeze and smiling confidently up at Rodney. "The wedding is going to go absolutely perfectly."

Something New

I thought it might be fun to include a scene that made it through all first four drafts, before it was cut in draft five. I loved this scene, but it slowed things down too much. But I always had a soft spot for it, so I'm happy to be able to share with you!

A CHICKEN, A FOX,
AND A BAG OF CORN

*T*WENTY MINUTES LATER, I DROVE THROUGH THE
entrance of the Hartfield-Putnam Airport and stopped in
front of baggage claim. There was no sign of Mike, so I put my car
into park, got out, and had just taken out my phone to text him when
a hybrid pulled up in front of me. I realized after a second that I knew
it—this was my future brother-in-law's car.

"Hey," I called, and Rodney turned to look at me, his eyes widening.

"Charlie?" He reached into the backseat and pulled out a cellophane-
wrapped bunch of flowers, the kind you can get at a convenience store.
"What are you doing here?"

"I'm here to pick up Mike." Rodney's eyebrows flew up, and I
nodded. "He came for the wedding after all."

"Really?"

"Really."

"Wow," Rodney said, smiling. "I didn't think he—but I hoped, because I knew how much it meant to Lin, but I didn't . . ." His voice trailed off, and he looked at me, tilting his head to the side. "So why'd he call *you*?"

"Ha." The truth was, though, it wasn't that strange a question. Of the list of our family members Mike would normally call for a ride, I was at the very bottom. "Well, we know what happens when you ask J.J. to pick you up from an airport."

"This is true. We did get that guy back to his family eventually, though."

"I think *eventually* is the operative word there." Four years ago, J.J. had been tasked with picking up my grandmother's new man friend (boyfriend seemed a weird word for someone who was pushing eighty) and bringing him to our family reunion. He picked up the wrong old guy at baggage claim—the gentleman thought J.J. was just his driver, and things didn't get cleared up until hours later, when the guy J.J. was driving woke up from his nap and groggily demanded to know why he wasn't in Delaware, and my grandmother's man friend finally called from baggage claim where he'd been standing around for two hours, getting increasingly concerned. "Why are you here?"

"I'm here to take my aunt Liz to the house," he said, looking down at his bunch of flowers and smoothing out the cellophane.

A sports car, top down, careened around the idling taxis and pulled to a jerky stop in front of me, brakes squealing. Rodney shook his head. "That person's driving like an idiot."

"That person *is* an idiot," I said. He gave me a disapproving look, and I pointed to the driver that I knew all too well. "It's J.J."

"Hey," J.J. called to us as he struggled to get out of my dad's car by vaulting over the side, and not actually opening the door. Our dad had a bit of a sports-car fixation. He traded in for a new one every few years and my mother had given up telling him that, since we lived in

Connecticut, there was no point in having a car that you could only drive for three months of the year. My dad's love of them had been a part of the strip for years, starting with the collection *Midwife Crisis*, which chronicled both my birth and my dad's first sports car purchase.

"Use the door," I called.

"Never," J.J. said, finally getting himself over and falling on the pavement. He stood up and brushed off his jeans, then leaned against the car in what he must have thought, mistakenly, was a suave pose. "What's up?"

"What are you doing here?" Rodney asked.

"I was about to ask Charlie the same question," J.J. said. "It's like we're having a family reunion at the airport."

"You really want to talk about family reunions and airports?"

J.J. waved this away. "That was one time."

I could hear the sound of muffled yelling, and looked around for the source of it. "It sounds like your pants are mad at you."

"Whoops!" he pulled his phone out of his pocket, and I could now hear more clearly the sound of my sister's voice.

"Are you there? *Jameison?*" Linnie was yelling through the speaker.

"Here!" J.J. said, taking a step closer to me and Rodney. "And Charlie and Rodney are here too. So come on down, it's a party."

"What's Charlie doing there?" Linnie asked.

"Yeah," J.J. said, looking at me. "What are you doing here?"

"I'm picking up Mike," I said, and J.J. and Linnie both drew in a shocked breath.

"Mike?" J.J. echoed.

"Mike's coming?" Linnie asked.

"Seriously?"

"Are you sure?"

"He texted me and asked me to pick him up," I said.

"Oh, so *him* you'll pick up," J.J. huffed.

"You didn't call anyone," Rodney reminded him.

"Technicality."

"I just can't believe . . . ," Linnie said, and her voice trailed off. "He actually came home." There was a small pause in which we looked at one another, like the impact of this was hitting us all—and Linnie, over the phone.

"Mom doesn't know, does she?" I asked.

"Maybe," Rodney started, then cleared his throat. "Maybe you should tell her? So it doesn't come as a total shock?"

"Me?" Linnie asked.

I glanced at J.J. and Rodney and all of us simultaneously grabbed our right earlobes. "Not it," we all said in unison.

"I'm the bride," Linnie sputtered. "I shouldn't have to do things like this. Why do you think I sent J.J. to the airport?"

"Wait, why *did* you send J.J. to the airport?" I asked.

"That's what I needed to talk to Rodney about. Take me off speaker?"

"No," J.J. and I said at the same time.

"Fine," she said, maybe realizing that since she wasn't physically present, there wasn't much she could do about this. "Bad news, honey. Your uncle Jimmy just called. He took an earlier flight."

"Meaning what?"

"Meaning that he's coming in now. I thought it might be best to have J.J. drive him so they didn't have to be in the same car."

"Good thinking," Rodney said. "Thanks for the heads-up."

"See you soon."

"What's going on?" J.J. asked his phone, but Linnie had hung up, and he turned to Rodney.

"It's my aunt Liz and uncle Jimmy," Rodney said with a grimace as he glanced toward baggage claim. "They can't be around each other at all. They've been in a fight for the last twenty years."

I felt my jaw drop. "Twenty *years?*"

"What was the fight about?" J.J. asked.

"I've never been able to get my mom to tell me," Rodney said. "It's like omertà in our family, we just don't talk about it. But whatever it was, it's bad. Whenever we have family functions, we always have to make sure they're separated."

"I get then why you need two cars for them," I said.

"And it would be great if they could not see each other right now," Rodney said, glancing at his watch, then looking toward the baggage claim again. "If they go into this weekend already mad at each other . . ." He shuddered.

"Sure," J.J. said, nodding. "Heard and understood. So let's divide and conquer. Charlie, why don't you take Mike and Liz to the house and Rodney can take his uncle?"

"Why aren't you taking anyone?"

"Well, since I have dad's car, and I'm still looking for the lucky lady to be my date, I was thinking that if I showed up in a sweet ride . . ."

"No," Rodney and I said simultaneously.

"What?" J.J. asked, looking offended. "Don't you *want* me to get a date? Am I not allowed to find happiness?"

"How about you take Mike," I said, thinking that I would actually prefer not to be in a car with him. "I'll go back to the Inn to help Bill. Rodney takes Jimmy and Liz—"

"They can't be in the same car," Rodney reminded me.

"That's why we're all here," J.J. pointed out.

"This is like that riddle," I said, turning to my brother. "Remember? About the fox and the chicken and the corn."

"The what?" Rodney asked, looking baffled.

"You haven't heard that?" J.J. asked, exchanging an incredulous look with me. It was one of the many shibboleths of our family, things you knew before you could even remember learning them. "There's this farmer, and he has a rowboat . . ."

"I didn't think he was a farmer," I interjected. "I thought he was just a dude with a boat."

"Why would a dude with a boat have a chicken and bag of corn?"

"Why would a farmer have a fox?"

J.J. considered this. "Okay, good point. So there's this guy with a boat."

"He may or may not be a farmer," I added.

"And he has a chicken and a fox and a bag of corn," J.J. said.

"And he has to get to the other side," a voice said. I whipped around and saw my brother Mike standing on the curb behind us.

"Michael!" J.J. cried, crossing over to him and giving him a bear hug that picked him up off his feet.

"Good to see you," Rodney said, giving him a hug after J.J. set him back down.

Mike stepped away from Rodney and we looked at each other for a moment. "Hey," he finally said.

"Hey." After another second of awkward silence, we gave each other the kind of hug we always did—fast, a pat on the back, barely touching.

"Uh—why are there so many of you?" Mike asked as he glanced between our cars. "How much luggage did you think I had?"

"We're all here because Rodney's relatives are in a blood feud," J.J. said. "And they can't see each other."

"They're *what*?" Mike asked just as the glass doors slid open, and people started streaming out, carrying duffel bags and rollerboards.

"Okay, here they come," Rodney said, keeping his eyes on the doors. "So really quickly, figure out who's taking who."

"Whom," Mike and I said at the same time. J.J. shook his head.

"I don't think that's right," he said. "It *sounds* right but I think it's wrong."

"*Grants!*" Rodney said, and we all turned to face him. "Come on. Stay with me. There's my aunt," he said, pointing at a fifty-something woman stepping through the doors, pulling a suitcase behind her. She looked a lot like Rodney's mom, her dark hair streaked with gray. "And there's my uncle," he said, pointing to a tall, sharply dressed man who was holding a duffel bag and looking around. "Aunt Liz," Rodney called, and his aunt turned toward him, smiling.

"Roddy!" She walked over, and Rodney bent down so that she could kiss his cheek. "So good to see you, dear."

"Same," Rodney said, steering his aunt toward his car. "So let's get going . . ."

"Jimmy!" J.J. yelled, and several men—in addition to Rodney's uncle—turned around. J.J. waved. "Hey! I'm Rodney Daniels's future brother-in-law. Here to take you to your destination."

"So the car's right here," Rodney said, turning his back on his uncle. He hustled his aunt over to his car, opened the passenger door for her, and then tossed her suitcase unceremoniously into the backseat.

Jimmy walked over, just as Rodney and his aunt closed their car doors. He frowned at Rodney's car, then turned to J.J. "Hello there." He set his bag down and held out his hand. "Dr. James Wilson."

"J.J. Grant," J.J. said. "Pleasure. My car's this way . . ." He picked up Jimmy's bag and dropped it into the trunk of the sports car—it had always unnerved me that it was in the front. J.J. vaulted into the car by going over the door again, then pushed the passenger-side door open for Jimmy.

Rodney's car pulled out, and a second later, J.J. sped away with a screech of tires, waving at me and Mike through the open roof.

In the silence that followed, Mike and I looked at each other. "I guess you're with me."

"Don't sound so excited," Mike said under his breath.

I rolled my eyes as I got into the driver's seat, slamming the door probably harder than I needed to, not offering to help Mike with his bags. A moment later, Mike got into the passenger seat, and I put the car in gear and headed toward the exit.

Something Borrowed

For this one, I wanted to borrow another character's point of view—and see some of the events through the eyes of characters other than Charlie, characters who would just be observing the pre-wedding chaos from the outside.

JENNY & JENNY ON
THE THIRD-FLOOR BENCH

So," JENNY K. SAID, TURNING TO JENNY W. "TALK."
They were sitting on the bench on the third-floor landing,
mostly out of necessity, because it was getting harder and harder to find
a place to gossip privately in this house. Priya had kicked them out of
their room so that she could talk to her fiancé, and this seemed to be the
one spot they could talk without being overheard.

It was the morning of the wedding, and still early—too early, both
Jennys thought—but once everyone had started running around, it
had been impossible to stay asleep. But at least there was coffee, and
someone had gotten bagels. When they'd been kicked out of the room,
they'd retreated here, with a cinnamon raisin for Jenny W., a poppyseed
for Jenny K., and a cup of coffee each.

Jenny W. took a long sip of her coffee to hide her smile. "Talk about
what?"

Jenny K. whacked her on the arm. "Um, about J.J.! I saw you sneaking
in from his room at five o'clock this morning!"

"Oh, right, that." Jenny W. grinned. "So what do you want to know?"

"Well, for starters, everything. How did this happen, how was it, was it weird at all? Since we've known him since he was fifteen? Do you feel kind of like a creepster?"

"First of all, no," Jenny W. said, rolling her eyes. "That stuff doesn't matter when we're twenty-eight and he's twenty-five. And before I tell you anything, you have to promise not to tell anyone."

"What about Priya?"

"Of course you can tell Priya. And Elizabeth, too, I don't want her to feel left out, especially since all the rest of us have known each other for so long. You don't think we've been excluding her, do you?"

"I don't, but I certainly think we can do better. So basically, what you're saying is that I can tell everyone but Linnie."

"Pretty much."

"That makes sense."

"Okay." Jenny W. took a long drink of coffee. "So—" before she could continue, there was a groaning sound coming from the stairwell.

"What's that?" Jenny K. asked.

"No idea. You okay?" Jenny W. called in the direction of the stairs.

"Yeah," a voice said faintly. A moment later, a head appeared as Mike dragged himself up the stairs, keeping a death grip on the banister.

"Morning, Mike," Jenny K. said, and Mike winced. "He doesn't look great," she whispered to Jenny W.

"Mike!" Jenny W. yelled. *"You okay?"*

"Gah!" Mike lifted his hands to cover his ears, but then—having let go of the banister—wobbled and fell out of view, and they heard him thump down the stairs. "Ouch."

"You don't look so great," Jenny K. said as he dragged himself back to the top of the staircase again.

"I had . . . kind of a rough morning," he said, blinking at them. "I'm just . . . going to lie down for a while."

"Drink some water!" Jenny K. called after him. Mike winced and moved, very slowly, over to J.J.'s room and disappeared inside. "Yeesh," she said, turning to Jenny.

"You have to learn how to handle yourself," Jenny W. said with a shrug. "That's the whole point of college."

"The *whole* point?"

"You know what I mean."

"Anyway, back to the story. So at some point last night, you randomly decided to hook up with Linnie's younger brother. . . ."

Jenny W. grinned. "It's not *that* random. You know I always thought he was cute. Okay. So—"

Rodney came up the kitchen stairs, taking them two at a time. "Morning, ladies," he said with a nod. "I see you got some breakfast?"

"Jenny got more than breakfast," Jenny K. said, waggling her eyebrows.

"Do I want to know?" Rodney asked, laughing, as he headed for Linnie's room.

"What are you doing?" Jenny W. asked, jumping to her feet. "Stop that this minute!"

Rodney looked around, like he wasn't sure what she was talking about. "What am I doing?"

"You can't go in there," Jenny K. said, sounding scandalized. "Are you crazy?"

"Into . . . my room? Is there something wrong with it?"

"Um, yeah," Jenny W. said, rolling her eyes at Jenny K., who shook her head in agreement. "Because Linnie's wedding dress is in there. And you're not supposed to see it before the wedding. It's really bad luck."

"I think I'm not supposed to see the *bride* before the wedding," Rodney said, reaching for the doorknob again. "And I've been seeing her all morning, so . . ."

"Stop it!" Both Jennys said together as Rodney started to turn the knob. "Do you really want to curse your union forever?" Jenny W. asked, glaring at him.

"Well . . . no," Rodney said slowly. "Of course not. But I do have to get some stuff out of there. . . ."

"Not with the dress in there you don't," Jenny K. said firmly, turning him around and pointing him back down the stairs. "We're doing this for your own good!"

"You'll thank us someday," Jenny W. called after him as he started heading down the stairs again, looking thoroughly baffled.

"Good thing we were here," Jenny K. said as she and Jenny W. took their seats on the bench again.

"Seriously."

"Okay! So. Spill."

"Maple!" they both turned to see Max hurrying up the other staircase, crouched low to the ground, looking around wildly. "Kitty, kitty, kitty! Here, boy!"

"Max?" Jenny K. asked. He jumped, and turned around to face them.

"Hey," he said, tugging at his beard, his eyes wide and panicked. "Morning."

"What happened to your arm?" Jenny W. asked, pointing at the long gash peeking out from under his hoodie sleeve.

"Nothing," he said quickly as he looked around. "Um . . . have you guys seen . . . anything out of the ordinary? Like did something maybe come up here and you were like, wait, *that* shouldn't be here? What's that doing here? Maybe something white with black spots?"

The Jennys exchanged a look. "Buddy," Jenny W. said, getting up and crossing over to him, her voice soothing. "We've been friends for a long time now. And I think we need to have a talk about your habits. Maybe it's time to take a break, hmm?"

"Or share the wealth with your friends?" Jenny K. suggested. "That's an idea too."

"Just let me know if you see anything, okay?" Max said as he turned and ran back down the stairs, still looking around.

"I can't believe you dated him sophomore year," Jenny W. said, shaking her head.

"You really want to talk about people we dated sophomore year?"

"I really do not. So where was I?"

"Does anyone have a sewing kit?" this was shouted ahead of the sound of someone taking the stairs two at a time, and a moment later, J.J. appeared at the top of the staircase. When he saw the Jennys, he immediately dropped an elbow down onto the banister and struck a suave pose. "Ladies."

"Hey," Jenny W. said with a casual indifference.

"I was just wondering," J.J. said, "if either of you had a sewing kit?" They shook their heads. "Too bad. Well—I should go try and find one. Maybe I'll see you after the wedding?" he asked Jenny W.

She smiled. "Maybe you will."

"I just think," J.J. said, smiling as he started to back down the stairs, "that we were having such a great talk last night and we should continue it."

"I wouldn't be opposed to that," Jenny W. said, her cheeks starting to turn pink.

"Okay, I'll see you later."

"Okay."

"Bye."

"Bye."

J.J. headed down the stairs, and Jenny K. turned to Jenny W. "Oh my god," she said, shaking her head. "You've got it bad. You are such a smitten kitten."

Jenny W. opened her mouth to respond just as the alarm started going off at full volume. They both covered their ears, and Jenny K. winced. When the alarm finally went quiet few moments later, the third floor was totally silent, except for the sound of Mike groaning behind J.J.'s bedroom door. "Why so loud?" they heard him whimper.

"That had better not happen during the wedding," Jenny W. said, finishing the last of her coffee.

"It won't. I'm sure they'll get it sorted, and—"

"Rodney, what are you *doing*?" Jenny W. asked, standing up and striding over to where he was standing outside Linnie's room again.

"I have to get inside," he said, starting to sound a little desperate. "I don't want to make you mad, or 'curse my union,'" he said, using air quotes. Jenny W. batted his hand away.

"Don't make ironic air quotes," she said, shaking her head. "That's how, like, all curses begin!"

"That really cannot be correct."

"Tell you what," Jenny K. said, joining them. "We'll take the dress somewhere else, and then you can go into your room. Sound okay?"

"Sure," Rodney said, looking relieved. "That sounds good."

"Who should we give it to?" Jenny K. asked.

"Let's give it to Charlie," Jenny W. said, opening the door to Linnie's room. "I feel like the other bridesmaids have been doing all this work, and she's just been hanging out."

"Good call." Jenny K. nodded. "It's the least she can do to help out."

"Totally."

"Totally."

Something Blue(s)

Instead of doing a regular playlist, I've included what has always felt to me like the soundtrack to *Save the Date*—the songs I was listening to while I was writing, the songs that just seemed to capture the feeling of the story, and one or two songs that I had a feeling would have been on heavy rotation on Charlie's playlists. Even DJJJ would approve! (But Glen might not. Sorry, Glen.)

SAVE THE DATE—THE SOUNDTRACK

Jessie's Girl	Rick Springfield
Cut to the Feeling	Carly Rae Jepsen
Our House	Madness
Big Weekend	Tom Petty
Take the Money and Run	Steve Miller Band
Wedding Bell Blues	Fifth Dimension
Danny's Song	Loggins & Messina
Guest Room	National
Down Under	Men at Work
The Puppy Song	Harry Nilsson
Jenny & the Ess-Dog	Stephen Malkmus
Sleep on the Floor	Lumineers
Australia	Shins
Let It Be Me	Everly Brothers
Superman	Taylor Swift

Can't Keep Checking My Phone	Unknown Mortal Orchestra
Capture the Flag	Henry Gales
Two Sleepy People	Dean Martin
Things Happen	Dawes
Any Way You Want It	Journey
Cigarettes, Wedding Bands	Band of Horses
Lights Out	Santogold
(Today I Met) The Boy I'm Gonna Marry	Darlene Love
Make Me Lose Control	Eric Carmen
Don't Stop Believin'	Journey
The Beginning After the End	Stars
Get Me Away from Here, I'm Dying	Belle and Sebastian
5-1-5-0	Dierks Bentley
Long Ride Home	Patty Griffin
He Ain't Heavy, He's My Brother	Hollies
Always on Sunday	Tammany Hall NYC
Thank You	Francis and the Lights